The Translator and Editor

STANLEY CORNGOLD has been Professor of German and Comparative Literature at Princeton University since 1981. He is past President of the Kafka Society of America and the author of many books and articles on Franz Kafka. Among his major publications are *The Commentators' Despair: The Interpretation of Kafka's "Metamorphosis"*; *The Fate of the Self: German Writers and French Theory*; *Borrowed Lives* (with Irene Giersing), a novel; *Franz Kafka: The Necessity of Form*; *Complex Pleasure: Forms of Feeling in German Literature*; and, most recently, *Lambent Traces: Franz Kafka*. He has also edited and translated Kafka's *The Metamorphosis* in a Norton Critical Edition.

A NORTON CRITICAL EDITION

KAFKA'S SELECTED STORIES

NEW TRANSLATIONS
BACKGROUNDS AND CONTEXTS
CRITICISM

Translated and Edited by

STANLEY CORNGOLD

PRINCETON UNIVERSITY

W. W. NORTON & COMPANY

New York • London

W. W. Norton & Company has been independent since its founding in 1923, when William Warder Norton and Mary D. Herter Norton first published lectures delivered at the People's Institute, the adult education division of New York City's Cooper Union. The Nortons soon expanded their program beyond the Institute, publishing books by celebrated academics from America and abroad. By midcentury, the two major pillars of Norton's publishing program—trade books and college texts—were firmly established. In the 1950s, the Norton family transferred control of the company to its employees, and today—with a staff of four hundred and a comparable number of trade, college, and professional titles published each year—W. W. Norton & Company stands as the largest and oldest publishing house owned wholly by its employees.

This volume is dedicated to Noel Corngold.

The text of this book is composed in Fairfield Medium
with the display set in Bernhard Modern.
Composition by PennSet, Inc.
Manufacturing by the Maple-Vail Book Group, Binghamton.
Production manager: Benjamin Reynolds.

Library of Congress Cataloging-in-Publication Data
Kafka, Franz, 1883–1924.
   [Short stories. English. Selections.]
   Kafka's selected stories: new translations, backgrounds and
contexts, criticism / Kafka; translated and edited by Stanley Corngold.
      p. cm. — (A Norton critical edition)
   Includes bibliographical references.

ISBN 0-393-92479-3 (pbk.)

1. Kafka, Franz, 1883–1924—Translations into English.   2. Kafka,
Franz, 1883–1924—Criticism and interpretation.   I. Corngold, Stanley.
II. Title.   III. Series.

PT2621.A26A226 2005
833'.912—dc22

2005053927

W. W. Norton & Company, Inc., 500 Fifth Avenue, New York, NY 10110-0017
www.wwnorton.com

W. W. Norton & Company Ltd., Castle House,
75/76 Wells Street, London W1T 3QT

2   3   4   5   6   7   8   9   0

Contents

1. The second of these four stories, "A Little Woman," is not included in this edition.

Preface

The fascination of Kafka's stories borders on the miraculous. In 1945 the poet W. H. Auden remarked that Kafka stands in the same relation to his century as Shakespeare stood to his—he is its representative, the poet who gives it shape and form. It seemed a somewhat extravagant claim to make, but how perceptive it was. Today we might measure the intensity of Kafka's vision by the sheer quantity of hours that men and women devote to the reading and study of his work. There is a bookshop in the center of Prague, just yards away from the Kinsky "palace" where Kafka went to high school and his father had his business in ladies' finery; here, readers from all over the world can be seen poring over the copious new editions and translations of Kafka's work. And to read a story of Kafka's appears to require from the reader that he or she *interpret* it. In a famous image by the critic Theodor Adorno, Kafka's sentences come at the reader with the force of an onrushing locomotive: "Each sentence of Kafka's says 'interpret me'. * * * Through the power with which Kafka commands interpretation, he collapses aesthetic distance. He demands a desperate effort from the allegedly 'disinterested' observer of an earlier time, overwhelms you, suggesting that far more than your intellectual equilibrium depends on whether you truly understand; life and death are at stake."

What propels this fascination? Two qualities can be felt immediately: on the one hand, an extraordinary intelligence, subtle and rational—driven by tireless intellectual energy—as alert to its subject matter as to the condition of *being a writer*. Kafka inscribes his hyperconsciousness in the hero of the great story *The Burrow*, who imagines "the joy of sleeping deeply and at the same time of being able to keep a close watch on myself." On this question of Kafka's intellectual energy, one anecdote speaks volumes. According to Dora Diamant, the woman with whom Kafka spent almost the last year of his life, Kafka wrote all fifteen thousand words of this witty, haunting late masterpiece in a single sitting: he sat down at his desk in the early evening and very nearly finished in the hours before daybreak.

On the other hand, on the side of passion, there is Kafka's acute sensitivity to the irrational currents that move all living beings, ranging from the badger-narrator's perpetual worry in *The Burrow* about noise, a frightening modulation of the still, sad music of humanity that implies his death, to the murderous lunacy of the figure named Schmar in "A Fratricide" and including, along the way, what the philosopher Nietzsche calls "the milder, more middling and indeed the lower levels of psyche in perpetual play that weave the texture of our character and our fate." The first set of intellectual qualities Kafka terms "the clarity of the gaze"; this, together with the second—a full imagination of the bodily passions—join forces in his writing, so that the net effect is of great energy restrained in small, perfectly turned vessels. One of his translators, Michael Hofmann, speaks of Kafka's "astonishing gift of expression, a compound of imagination, drama, economy, and balance." These qualities are present even in the syntax of individual sentences.

Such features have not gone unnoticed by Kafka's readers and commentators. What is new—a discovery that is foregrounded in this Norton Critical Edition—is Kafka's sensitivity to the deeper political issues of his day, as they were embedded (and concealed) in real, daily events. In the words of Benno Wagner, who has written an essay on this topic especially for this volume, Kafka is a gifted political analyst, whose "writings are intricately connected to the vibrancy of political issues and events of his day" (p. 302). In addition to profiling this new current of thought in freshly translated critical essays by several German scholars, this volume contains the first American translations of many of Kafka's greatest stories, works unpublished in his lifetime but salvaged in manuscript by his friend and editor Max Brod. This volume is also the first American edition of such a wide range of Kafka's stories to include notes and a critical apparatus. And, finally, the German text from which these translations are made is new and reliable—the Fischer "manuscript version" (*Kritische Ausgabe in der Fassung der Handschrift, KKA*)—an edition that has been appearing over the last twenty years under the editorship of Hans-Gerd Koch, Michael Müller, and the late Malcolm Pasley.

A Word about the Translation

"God employs several translators"
—John Donne

I have translated each story "cold" and then, after many revisions, profited from consulting other published translations. For it is my firm belief that translators should stand on the shoulders of their predecessors. We are, after all, a collective—translators and readers alike; we are one community in our devotion to the most truthful possible understanding of the works of this master writer, an understanding that in every case involves a personal "rewriting" of the text. If one were writing an essay on Kafka, would one make a point of never consulting any previous writer who had written on Kafka? Of course not. And should one, as a translator, fail to consult any or all previous translations of Kafka? Of course not. But then the question of the originality of one's reading or writing about the author could arise. There are well-documented practices in the matter of attributing phrases and formulations cited from the works of previous writers: you footnote them. And what is the right thing to do as a translator if you encounter in a previous translation a rendering that is simply, straightforwardly better than your own? Ignore this knowledge for the sake of a putative absolute original-ity? No. But how can you indicate your debt now and again to your inspired predecessor? You cannot footnote this or that phrase. And so here I wish to compose a blanket dedication to the predecessors whose work has, in Kafka's words, "refreshed me, satisfied, liber-ated, exalted me" (p. 206) and I hope you too, reader. Chief among them are Stanley Applebaum, Edwin and Willa Muir, Malcolm Pasley, and J. A. Underwood. I have also profited from consulting the work of Kevin Blahut, Michael Hofmann, Siegfried Mort-kowitz, Joachim Neugroschel, and Richard Stokes.

In saying that I have not hesitated on occasion to employ the lo-cutions of other translators when they seemed better than my own, I should note, in this vexed matter of "originality," that all too often, with both delight and despair, I found I had hit upon exactly the same formulations as my predecessors. That is inevitably the case, because Kafka's syntax is exquisitely clear, his word choice is rela-tively limited, and key words are prone to recur. In many instances there are simply no two ways about it.

One further point about my translation practice: I have avoided translating Kafka's plain phrases with colloquial expressions more vivid than his own. You can understand the temptation to give a colorful, colloquial bounce to a certain luminous plainness in Kafka's prose. For example, Kafka writes of the hero of *The Burrow*, a most articulate badger, vole, or mole, that he nurtured the wild hope, which he now considers flimsy, that his vast and intricate burrow would make him "superior to anyone who might come." One excellent translator expresses this idea as granting him "the upper hand of anyone who came." This is vivid but not quite Kafka's tone and somewhat odd, too, considering that we are deal-ing here with an animal with paws and claws. Again, the hero's an-tagonist, in my translation, is given "an opportunity for a moment's rest"; he does not "snatch a moment's rest." The Muirs write that the jackals in "Jackals and Arabs" suddenly "turn tail and flee." That is wonderfully vivid, but Kafka wrote simply that they "run away." I have chosen to keep his fluent evenness of tone; I have rarely sought out or adopted vivid colloquialisms.

At the same time, the level, the major tone, contains fine modulations. In the great late stories, especially *The Burrow* and *Researches of a Dog*, monologues are spoken by narrators who are very smart and very articulate. They love swift, elegant language as much as they love to think, although this elegance is nonetheless at war, once again, with all-too-colorful colloquialisms, with fancy words, archaic words, word coinages. Yet their reports are far less monotonous than the legalistic protocols often claimed to be Kafka's natural tone (the embodied narrator of "Josefine, the Singer or The Mouse People," for one, no doubt loves puns; the compulsive– obsessive genius who narrates *The Burrow* sings arias to his burrow while at other times he analyzes its acoustics and its fortifications). I will highlight a general observation on Kafka's style by the linguist Marek Nekula, which emphasizes in Kafka's prose its "*range* of regional, phonic, morphological and syntactical as well as lexical characteristics," the outcome of a series of choices driven by "Kafka's conscious will to self-stylization."

A Word about the Critical Apparatus

The amount of critical literature on Kafka's stories is huge and ever growing. After the fall of the Iron Curtain, Kafka, who had been regarded as an enemy of socialist progress and whose works were therefore kept in the dark, has now been duly translated into the light of the public world. Scholars and laypeople in Czechoslovakia, Russia, Poland, Hungary, and other former Eastern bloc countries have not failed to add their voices to that "chorus of voices" that Kafka saw as promising the only true commentary on the text of the world—and, we will add, on his works. This production of voices adds to the secondary literature on Kafka that has continually been produced in the West and in Japan as well. It is said that more criticism of Kafka's relatively slim body of works is published each year than of the work of any imaginative writer except Shakespeare. One can now read more than two hundred critical essays on *The Judgment* alone; imagine the size of the bibliography of such essays on all of the thirty stories included in this volume.

Since it is impossible to print essays on each of these stories without bursting the bounds of this edition, I have been forced to make drastic cuts. This critical apparatus at least mentions almost all the major stories, meaning the longer stories; but a moment's reflection will suggest that even Kafka's shorter stories, which barely occupy a page—stories like "Before the Law" and "On Parables"—are by any account also major stories, to judge from the amount of commentary they have produced. Yet, with few exceptions, the essays included here focus on the longer stories, such as the essay on *In the Penal Colony* by Danielle Allen and on *The Burrow* by Gerhard Kurz. One outstanding exception is the article by Benno Wagner that I have already mentioned, which refers to a considerable number of different, shorter works. In another instance, in the essay by Vivian Liska, we have an exposé of a single very short story, "Poseidon," which will illuminate that work, of course, but which is also meant to illustrate how closely—and profitably—Kafka can be read. Hence it will supply a model of reading that can be used with other stories by Kafka as well. The essays by Danielle Allen, Nicola Gess, and Benno Wagner, meanwhile, are models of how the new Cultural Studies approach can be used without losing sight of the special primacy for Kafka of the experience of writing. Finally, the essay by Walter Sokel has the capacious intellectual-historical character that marks the work of one of the greatest of Kafka scholars. As to the apparatus, the notes to *Kafka's Selected Stories* are the editor's unless otherwise indicated.

This volume is graced by the vitality and dedication of my wife, Regine Corngold, who got up at five a.m. in the stillness of an Easter morning in Prague to photograph the detail of the Charles Bridge that appears on the cover—*sine qua non*. I wish to thank Carol Bemis for the warmth and spirited intelligence that she brought to the production of this book; my good friends Peter Musolf, Eric Patton, and Benno Wagner, who read through all the translations and made wonderful, incisive suggestions; Jean Yin, for her practical help in reading proofs and constructing the critical apparatus; and the Directorate of the Internationales Forschungszentrum, Geisteswissenschaften, in Vienna, especially Professor Gotthard Wunberg, for allowing me, while in residence there, to spend my nights on this adventure of bringing Kafka's stories to the American language. My greatest debt of gratitude, however, is owed to my editor, Ruth Hein, indispensable collaborator and friend, who has once again brought to a translation of Kafka's work her perfect sureness of touch, leaving only me to blame for any faults that still remain. I hope that we shall continue to work together on many such projects in the future.

The Texts of
KAFKA'S SELECTED
STORIES

THE JUDGMENT[1]

A Story

FOR F.

It was a Sunday morning when spring was at its most beautiful. Georg Bendemann, a young businessman, sat in his private room on the second floor of one of the low, jerrybuilt houses that stretched along the river in a long row, hardly distinguishable from one another except for their height and color. He had just finished a letter to a boyhood friend who was living abroad, toying with it as he slowly put it in the envelope, and then, his elbow propped on the desk, looked out the window at the river, the bridge, and the rising ground on the opposite shore covered in a pale green.

He was thinking about how this friend, dissatisfied with his prospects at home, had practically fled to Russia several years before. Now he was running a business in St. Petersburg, which having gotten off to a very good start, for a long time now seemed to be stagnating, as his friend[2] complained during his increasingly less frequent visits home. So there he was, uselessly working himself to the bone in a foreign country, his foreign-looking full beard imperfectly concealing the face well known to Georg from childhood, its yellow complexion appearing to indicate some incipient illness. As he had told Georg, he had no real contact with the colony of his countrymen there, but he also had almost no social intercourse with local families either, and so was settling into a terminal bachelorhood.

What could one write to such a man, who had obviously become stuck and whom one could pity but not help? Should one perhaps advise him to come home again, to re-establish himself here, take up all the old connections—there was nothing to prevent this—and

---

1. Kafka wrote this story on the night of September 22–23, 1912 (for the diary entry that tells the story of its composition, see p. 197). "F" on the title page alludes to Felice Bauer, the woman whom Kafka had met at the house of his friend and eventual editor Max Brod on the evening of August 13, 1912. Felice made a strong impression on Kafka; and although they were thereafter engaged (twice!), they never married. On September 20, 1912, Kafka had written the first letter to her in their long correspondence; now, two days later, he sat down to write—indeed he exploded into—*The Judgment.*

2. Literally, "the friend." As Ruth Hein observes, "Kafka made a deliberate choice between 'der Freund' ('the friend') and 'sein Freund' ('his friend'); he had that luxury in German. But in American English, 'the friend' seems just not possible. The change to 'his friend' or 'Georg's friend' is at odds, in its implication of intimacy, with Kafka's alienating formulation; but it reads normally, whereas the reader is startled and distracted by 'the friend.'" At various times, though, when the implication was unmistakable and normal English diction allowed it, I have underlined this alienation effect by translating "der Freund" (literally, "the friend") as "this friend of his" or "this friend of yours."

3

for the rest rely on the help of his friends? But that meant nothing less than telling him at the same time—and the more one spared his feelings, the more hurtful it was—that so far his efforts had failed, that he should give them up once and for all, that he would have to come back and be gaped at by everybody as a man who had come back for good, that only his friends knew the score, and he was an overgrown baby who would simply have to do as he was told by his successful friends who had stayed at home. Besides, was it even certain that all the anguish that would have to be inflicted on him would serve any purpose? Perhaps it would not even succeed in bringing him back—after all, he himself had said that he no longer understood how things worked at home—and so, despite everything, he would remain abroad, embittered by the suggestions and alienated even further from his friends. But if he really did take their advice and then became depressed—of course, not from any-one's doing but because of the situation—if he could not make a go of it either with his friends or without them, felt disgraced, and now no longer had either a real home or friends, would it not be much better for him to have stayed abroad, just where he was? Un-der such circumstances, was it possible to believe that he could ac-tually make any headway here?

For these reasons, if one still wanted to keep up this connection by way of correspondence, one could not communicate freely, the way one could with even the most casual acquaintances. His friend had not been home for over three years now, attributing this, rather lamely, to the unstable political situation in Russia, which would not permit even the briefest absence of a small businessman while a hundred thousand Russians went calmly traveling all over the world. In the course of these three years, however, a great many things had changed, especially for Georg. News of the death of Georg's mother, which had occurred about two years earlier, since which time Georg had been sharing a household with his old fa-ther, had obviously reached Georg's friend, and in a letter this friend of his had expressed his condolences with a dryness whose only cause could be that the grief provoked by such an event was simply unimaginable for someone living in a foreign country. Since that time, however, Georg had taken hold of his business, as with everything else, with greater determination. Perhaps while his mother was alive, his father's insistence that only his own opinions counted in running the business had kept Georg from taking a truly active part in the company. Perhaps, since his mother's death, his father, although continuing to work at the office, had become more withdrawn; or perhaps—something that was very likely—lucky co-incidences had played a far more important role; in any case, in these two years the business had grown in completely unexpected ways. The number of employees had had to be doubled, the sales volume grew fivefold, and further growth was no doubt just around the corner.

Georg's friend, however, had no idea of this change. In the past, the last time being perhaps in that letter of condolence, he had tried to persuade Georg to emigrate to Russia while expounding on the prospects that St. Petersburg offered to Georg's particular line of business. The figures were infinitesimal next to the volume of business that Georg was now doing. But Georg had had no desire to write to this friend of his about his business successes, and to do so now, after the fact, would have seemed truly odd.

So Georg always confined himself to writing his friend about insignificant events in the way they accumulate pell-mell in one's memory when one reflects on a quiet Sunday. He wanted nothing more than to keep intact the picture of his hometown that his friend had probably formed and come to terms with during the long interval. And so it happened that three times, in letters written fairly far apart, Georg announced to his friend the engagement of some inconsequential fellow to an equally inconsequential young woman, until his friend, completely contrary to Georg's intentions, actually began to take an interest in this curious fact.

But Georg was much happier writing such things to him than having to admit that a month before, he had himself become engaged to a Miss Frieda Brandenfeld, a young woman from a well-to-do family. He often spoke to his fiancée about this friend and the special relationship of correspondence between them. "So, he won't be coming to our wedding," she said; "but don't I have a right to meet all your friends?" "I don't want to bother him," Georg replied; "don't misunderstand, he would probably come, at least I think so, but he would feel constrained and at a disadvantage, perhaps envious of me and certainly dissatisfied and incapable of ever shaking off his dissatisfaction, and then he'd go back alone. Alone—do you know what that means?" "Well, but can't he find out about our marriage in some other way?" "I can't prevent it, of course, but it's unlikely, given his way of life." "Georg, if you have such friends, you should never have become engaged." "Well, that is both our fault; but now I wouldn't want it any other way." And when, breathing rapidly under his kisses, she still exclaimed, "Really, I am hurt," he considered it harmless after all to write to the friend and tell him everything. "That's the way I am, and that's the way he'll have to accept me," he said to himself; "I can't cut myself into the shape of someone who might be better suited to a friendship with him than I am."

And in fact, in the long letter that he had written this late Sunday morning, he informed his friend of the engagement that had taken place, in the following words, "The best news I've saved for last. I'm engaged to a Miss Frieda Brandenfeld, a young woman from a well-to-do family that did not move here until long after you left, so it is hardly likely that you know them. There will certainly be opportunities for me to share with you further details about my fiancée, but for today just let me say that I am truly happy and that our relationship has changed only to the extent that now, instead of a perfectly ordinary friend, you will have in me a happy friend. Furthermore, you will have in my fiancée, who sends you her warmest regards and will soon write to you herself, a true friend of the opposite sex, something not entirely insignificant for a bachelor. I know that there are many things keeping you from paying us a visit, but wouldn't my wedding be just the occasion to sweep all obstacles aside for once? But be that as it may, act without concern for us and do only what you think best."

With this letter in his hand Georg had sat at his desk for a long time, his face turned to the window. He had barely responded with an absentminded smile to an acquaintance passing by who had greeted him from the street.

Finally he put the letter in his pocket and went out of his room across a small corridor into his father's room, where he had not been for months. There hadn't been any particular need, since he and his father continually interacted at work. They both had lunch at the same time in a restaurant; and although evenings each fended for himself as he saw fit, they usually sat for a little while, for the most part each with his newspaper, in the shared living room, when Georg was not seeing friends as he usually did or, these days, visiting his fiancée.

Georg was amazed at how dark his father's room was, even on this sunny morning. So, the high wall that rose up on the far side of the narrow courtyard cast so much shadow! His father was sitting by the window, in a corner adorned with various mementos of Georg's late mother, reading the newspaper, which he held off at an angle in front of his eyes so as to compensate for some weakness of sight. On the table were the leftovers of breakfast, which seemed hardly to have been touched.

"Ah, Georg," his father said and immediately went toward him. His heavy robe fell open as he walked, the sides flapping around him— "My father is still a giant," thought Georg to himself.

"It's unbearably dark in here," he then said.

"Yes, it certainly is dark," replied his father.

"You've closed the window, too?"

"I like it better that way."

"It's really very warm outside," said Georg, as if in afterthought to what he had just said, and sat down.

His father cleared away the breakfast dishes and put them on a cabinet.

"I just wanted to tell you," Georg continued, who absent-mindedly followed the old man's movements, "that I've sent news of my engagement to St. Petersburg after all." He pulled out the letter from his pocket a little, then let it fall back in.

"To St. Petersburg?" his father asked.

"To my friend, of course," said Georg, attempting to meet his father's eyes. "At work he's a totally different person," he thought; "look how he sits here all spread out, with his arms crossed over his chest."

"Yes. Your friend," said his father, with emphasis.

"You remember, Father, at first I wanted to keep my engagement a secret from him. Out of consideration for his feelings, for no other reason. You know yourself that he's a difficult person. I said to myself, true, he might hear about my engagement from some other source, even if it's unlikely given his solitary way of life—that's something I can't prevent—but he's definitely not going to hear it from me."

"And now you've changed your mind?" his father asked, putting down the big newspaper on the window sill and then, on top of the newspaper, his glasses, which he covered with his hand.

"Yes, now I've changed my mind. If he is a good friend, I said to myself, then my being happily engaged will make him happy too. And that's why I haven't hesitated any longer to tell him. Still, before I mailed the letter, I wanted to tell you."

"Georg," his father said, stretching wide his toothless mouth, "listen to me! You've come to me about this matter in order to ask my advice. That does you credit, no doubt. But it's nothing, it's worse than nothing, if you don't tell me the whole truth now. I don't want to stir things up that don't pertain. Since the death of our dear mother, certain unpleasant things have taken place. Perhaps the time is coming for them too, and perhaps it's coming sooner than we think. At work there's a lot that escapes me, maybe it's not being hidden from me—I don't want to start assuming that it's being hidden from me—but I don't have the strength anymore, my memory is going. I can no longer keep track of all the different things. That is, first of all, the course of nature, and secondly our dearest mother's death has taken a lot more out of me than of you. But since we're now on this subject, this letter, I'm pleading with you, Georg, don't fool me. It's just a trifle, it's not even worth mentioning, so don't fool me. Do you really have this friend in St. Petersburg?"

Georg stood up, embarrassed. "Let's leave my friends out of it. A thousand friends cannot replace my father for me. Do you know what I think? You're not taking good enough care of yourself. But age demands its due. You're indispensable to me in the office, that's something you know very well; but if the business is going to jeopardize your health, I will shut it down tomorrow, for good. That won't do. We are going to have to introduce a whole new way of life for you. And I mean from the ground up. You sit here in the dark, and in the living room you'd have a nice light. You just pick at your breakfast instead of properly fortifying yourself. You sit with the window closed when fresh air would do you so much good. No, Father! I will call the doctor, and we will follow his orders. We'll exchange rooms, you'll move into the front room and I'll move in here. It won't be a disruption for you; we'll move all your things over with you. But there's time for all that: now just lie down in bed for a while, you definitely need rest. Come, I'll help you get undressed, you'll see, I can do it. Or do you want to go into the front room right away, in which case you can lie down on my bed for the time being. That would actually make a lot of sense."

Georg was standing right next to his father, who had let his head of disheveled white hair sink to his chest.

"Georg," said his father, softly, without stirring.

Georg immediately kneeled down beside his father; he saw the pupils in his father's weary face peering at him from the corners of his eyes, larger than life.

"You have no friend in St. Petersburg. You have always been a joker, and you've never drawn the line even at me. How could you have a friend there, of all places! I can't believe that for a minute."

"Just try to remember, Father," said Georg, lifting his father out of the armchair and, while he stood very feebly there, taking off his robe, "it's been almost three years since my friend visited us here. I still recall that you did not especially like him. At least twice I denied to you[3] that he was in the house when he was actually sitting with me in my room. I could certainly understand your dislike of him, my friend does have his peculiarities. But then, later on, you also enjoyed being with him. I was so proud when you listened to him, nodding and asking questions. If you think back, you're bound to remember. That was the time he told us incredible stories about the Russian Revolution. How, for example, on a business trip in Kiev, during a riot he had seen a priest on a balcony cut a broad, bloody cross into the palm of his hand, raise this hand, and appeal to the crowd. Why, you even repeated this story to others from time to time."

Meanwhile, Georg had managed to get his father to sit back

3. St. Petersburg (German: *Petersburg*, "the city of Peter"), while commemorating the Russian czar who founded the city, also connotes the biblical Peter, who three times denied Christ and who, for his sinful hour, suffered thirty years of remorse and thereafter a monstrous upside-down crucifixion. Now we read that Georg denied the presence of his perishing exiled friend "at least twice."

down and carefully take off the long stockinet drawers he wore over his linen underpants, as well as his socks. At the sight of the not especially clean underwear, he blamed himself for having neglected his father. It would certainly have been his duty to supervise his father's change of underwear. He had not yet expressly spoken to his fiancée about how they proposed to arrange for his father's future, for they had assumed without further discussion that his father would live by himself in the old apartment. Yet now in an instant he resolutely made up his mind to take his father along into his future household. On closer inspection, it looked almost as if the care his father would receive there might come too late.

He picked up his father and carried him to his bed. He had a ghastly feeling on noticing, during the few steps to the bed, that his father was playing with the watch chain at Georg's chest. He could not put him in the bed right away because his father was holding on to this watch chain so tightly.

He was no sooner in bed, however, than everything seemed to be in order. He covered himself on his own and then pulled up the blanket especially high over his shoulders. He looked up at Georg in a not unfriendly way.

"You've already begun to remember him, right?" asked Georg and nodded encouragingly to him.

"Am I completely covered up now?" his father asked, as if he were unable to see whether his feet were covered well enough.

"So, you already like being in bed," Georg said and tucked the blanket in tighter around him.

"Am I completely covered up?" asked his father once again, seeming to pay particular attention to the answer.

"Don't worry, you're completely covered up."

"No!" his father shouted, sending his answer banging into the question, throwing the blanket off with such force that for one minute it completely unfolded while flying through the air, and standing upright in the bed. He just held one hand lightly on the ceiling. "You wanted to cover me up, I know that, you scamp,[4] but I'm not covered up yet. And even if it is my last ounce of strength, it's enough for you, too much for you. I know your friend all right. He would have been a son after my own heart. That's why you've been deceiving him all these years. Why else? Do you think I haven't cried over him? Yes, that's why you lock yourself up in your office, do not disturb, the boss is busy—just so you can write your lying little letters to Russia. But fortunately no one has to teach your father to see through his son. And now, when you thought you'd got him on his back, so flat on his back that you could plant

4. In German, *Früchtchen*, literally, "little fruit," which suggests, positively, "fruit of my loins" but, negatively and much more commonly, "scoundrel, rascal, scapegrace."

your behind on him and he wouldn't budge, then my lord and master son decided to up and get married!"

Georg looked up at this bogeyman of a father. The St. Petersburg friend, whom his father suddenly knew so well, gripped his imagination as never before. He saw him lost in far-off Russia. He saw him at the door of his empty, plundered establishment. He was just barely able to stand among the wreckage of his shelves, the ransacked goods, the collapsing gas brackets. Why had he had to go so far away?

"Look at me, will you!" shouted his father, and Georg ran almost distractedly to the bed in order to grasp everything but halfway there stopped short.[5]

"Because she hiked up her skirts," his father began to warble, "because she hiked up her skirts like this, the disgusting ninny," and to illustrate, he hiked his nightshirt up so high that the scar from his army days could be seen on his upper thigh; "because she hiked up her skirts like this and like this and like this, you went after her, and so that you could satisfy your lust with her undisturbed, you disgraced your mother's memory, betrayed this friend of yours, and tucked your father in bed so he couldn't move. But can he move or can't he?"

And he stood up completely unsupported and kicked out his legs. He beamed with his insight.

Georg stood in a corner as far from his father as possible. A long time ago he had firmly decided to observe everything very exactly so as to avoid being taken by surprise in some devious way, from behind or from above. Now he remembered that long-forgotten decision once again and forgot it, the way one draws a short thread through the eye of a needle.

"But now the friend hasn't been betrayed at all," his father shouted, and his index finger, waving back and forth, corroborated it. "I was his local representative."

"Play actor!" Georg could not help shouting, immediately saw the harm he had done, and bit his tongue so hard, except too late—his eyes gaped—that he staggered from the pain.

"Yes, of course I've been play acting! Play acting! A great word! What other consolation was left your old widowed father? Tell me—and for the little while it takes you to tell me, may you still be my living son—what was left for me in my back room, persecuted by disloyal employees, old deep down to my bones! And my son went triumphantly through the world, closing deals that I had set

5. Literally, "in the middle of the way." Compare the first words of Dante's *Inferno*, the first part of *The Divine Comedy*, which also unfolds from a moment of spiritual crisis: "Midway on this way of life we're hard upon/I found myself in a dark wood, where the right way was wholly lost and gone."

up, turning somersaults for joy, and marching off in front of his father with the composure of a man of honor! Do you think I didn't
love you, I, from whom you sprang?"

"Now he's going to lean forward," thought Georg; "if only he
would fall and smash to pieces!" These words went hissing through
his brain.

His father leaned forward but did not fall. Since Georg did not
approach him, as he had expected, he straightened up again.

"Stay where you are, I don't need you! You think you're still
strong enough to come over here, and you're holding back only because you want to. Just don't make any mistake about that. I am
still much stronger than you. If I were on my own, I might have to
retreat, but Mother gave me her strength, I've got a splendid ally in
your friend, and I've got your clientele here in my pocket!"

"He's got pockets even in his nightshirt,"[6] Georg said to himself,
thinking that with this remark he could make his father look ridiculous in front of the whole world. He thought so for only a second
because he kept forgetting everything.

"Just take your fiancée's arm and start coming toward me! I'll
swat her away from you, you have no idea how!"

Georg grimaced to indicate that he wasn't persuaded. His father
merely nodded toward Georg's corner to confirm the truth of what
he had said.

"Oh, how you amused me today when you came to ask me
whether you ought to write to your friend about your engagement.
He knows everything, you foolish boy, he knows absolutely everything! I've been writing him, because you forgot to take my writing
things away from me. That's why he hasn't come for years now, he
knows everything a hundred times better than you. He crumples up
your letters in his left hand without reading them, while in his right
he holds up my letters to read!"

He swung his arm enthusiastically over his head. "He knows
everything a thousand times better," he shouted.

"Ten thousand times!" said Georg, to make fun of his father, but
while still in his mouth, the words took on a deadly serious note.

"For years I've been watching and waiting for you to come with
this question! Do you imagine I care about anything else? Do you
think I read newspapers? There!" and he threw at Georg a sheet of
newspaper that had somehow been carried into the bed along with
him. An old newspaper, with a name completely unknown to
Georg.

6. The first part of this sentence reads in German, "*Sogar im Hemd hat er Taschen*" (Even
in his shirt he has pockets). A familiar German proverb says: "*Das letzte Hemd hat keine
Taschen*" (The last shirt you wear—i.e., a funeral shroud—has no pockets). Georg's remark produces such extravagant thoughts in him because his words resemble the cruel
proverb and, hence, conjure his father's death.

"How long you waited for your time to ripen! Mother had to die, she could not live to see this joyous day, this friend of yours is going to the dogs in his Russia, three years ago he was already yellowed enough to be tossed out, and I, well, you see how I am faring. That you have eyes for!"

"And so you've been lying in ambush for me!" shouted Georg.

Pityingly, his father casually said, "You probably meant to say that before. Now it doesn't even pertain."

And louder: "So now you know what else there was in the world beside you, until now you knew only about yourself! True, you were an innocent child, but truer still, you were a devilish man!—And therefore know this: I now sentence you to death by drowning!"

Georg felt himself driven from the room; the crash with which his father collapsed behind him onto the bed went on ringing in his ears. On the staircase, down whose steps he raced as if down a ramp, he nearly bowled over his cleaning woman, who was just coming upstairs to tidy the apartment after the night. "Jesus!" she shouted, covering her face with her apron, but he was already gone. He leaped out of the gate, across the avenue, driven on toward the water. He was already clutching the railing the way a starving man clutches food. He swung himself over, like the excellent gymnast he had been in his youth, the pride of his parents. Even as his grip weakened, he continued holding on, between the bars of the railing he caught sight of a bus[7] that would easily muffle the sound of his fall, and crying out softly, "Dear parents, I really always loved you," he let himself drop.

At that moment, the traffic going over the bridge was nothing short of infinite.

THE STOKER

A Fragment

As Karl Rossmann, a sixteen-year-old who had been sent to America by his stricken parents because a maid had seduced him and had had a child by him, sailed on the now slowing ship into New York harbor, he glimpsed the Statue of Liberty, which he had

---

7. The German word here translated as "bus" is *Autoomnibus*, a capacious word if ever there was one, for it contains both the Greek root *auto*, meaning "self-empowered," and the Latin root *omni*, meaning "containing all." Though much qualified by its alliance with motor exhaust and traffic (*Verkehr*)—the latter word also connotes sexual intercourse—*Autoomnibus* continues to suggest divinity, and it is this complex image that Georg glimpses now.

long been observing, as if in a sudden burst of sunlight. Her arm with the sword towered above as if raised for the first time, and around her form the free breezes blew.

"So high," he said to himself, and since he had given no thought to leaving the ship, he was gradually pushed to the railing by the continually swelling crowd of porters shoving past.

A young man whom he had come to know slightly during the voyage said as he passed, "So, aren't you ready to get off yet?" "Oh yes, I'm all set now," Karl said, laughing, and from high spirits, being a strapping young fellow, lifted his trunk onto his shoulder. But as he was glancing past his acquaintance, who with a casual swing of his walking stick was now leaving with the others, he realized to his consternation that he had forgotten his own umbrella below. He quickly asked the fellow, who did not seem particularly pleased, to do him a favor and watch his trunk for a minute; then, taking note of his whereabouts to be sure of finding his way back, he rushed off. Below decks he was disheartened to discover that a gangway that could have been a shortcut was barred for the first time, probably because all the passengers were leaving; and so he had to find his way effortfully through countless little rooms, short flights of stairs—one continually following the other—through corridors that kept branching off, and through an empty room with an abandoned writing desk, until, in actual fact, since he had taken this route only once or twice before and always in a group, he was completely lost. In his confusion, meeting no one and continually hearing above him only the scrabbling of a thousand feet and sensing in the distance, like a gasp, the last workings of the stopping machines, he began to bang impulsively on the first small door he happened to come upon in his wanderings.

"Hey, it's open," shouted a voice from inside, and Karl opened the door with genuine relief. "Why do you bang on the door like a madman?" asked a huge man, hardly looking at him. Through some sort of hatch or skylight, a dim light, long since used up on the top decks, fell into the wretched cabin, where, ranged alongside one another, as if stowed there, were a bunk, a locker, a chair, and the man. "I'm lost," said Karl, "I never realized it during the voyage, but this is an awfully big ship." "You're right there," said the man with some pride, without stopping fiddling with the lock of a small trunk and pressing the lid down with both hands so as to listen to the bolt snapping shut. "But come on in," the man continued. "What are you standing outside for?" "I'm not disturbing you?" Karl asked. "How would you be disturbing me?" "Are you German?" Karl asked, seeking further reassurance, since he had heard a lot about the dangers threatening new arrivals to America, particularly from the Irish. "That I am, that I am," the man said. Karl still hesitated.

Then the man unexpectedly grabbed the door handle and rapidly shutting the door, swept Karl inside. "I can't stand to have anyone looking in from the gangway," the man said, beginning once again to fiddle with his trunk. "Everyone runs past, and everyone looks in; there isn't one man in ten who could put up with it." "But the gangway's completely deserted," said Karl, who stood there, uncomfortably squashed against the corner of the bunk. "Sure," said the man, "now." "But we're talking about now," thought Karl; "it's not easy to get through to this guy." "Lie down on the bunk; you'll have more room there," said the man. Karl crawled in as best he could, laughing out loud at his first futile attempt to swing himself over. But he was hardly settled in when he cried, "Oh my God, I've completely forgotten about my trunk!" "Well, where is it?" "On the top deck; someone I know is watching it. What's his name again?" And he took a visiting card out of a secret pocket that his mother had sewn into his jacket lining especially for the voyage. "Butterbaum, Franz Butterbaum." "Do you really need the trunk?" "Of course I do." "Then why did you leave it with a total stranger?" "I forgot my umbrella below and went running off to get it, but I didn't want to lug the trunk down with me. Then, on top of everything, I got lost." "Are you all by yourself? You're traveling alone?" "All by myself." "Maybe I should stick with this man"—the thought went through Karl's head; "where would I find a better friend this easily?" "And now you've lost your trunk as well. Not to mention the umbrella"; and the man sat down on the chair, as if Karl's predicament had finally begun to be interesting to him. "But I don't believe my trunk is lost yet." "He that believeth shall be saved," the man said and vigorously scratched his short, thick, dark hair; "on shipboard, morals change along with ports of call. In Hamburg, your Butterbaum might have watched your trunk, but here most probably there's no trace of either of them anymore." "Then I really have to go up right away and see," said Karl, looking around for the best way to get out. "Stay here," said the man, with one hand against Karl's chest to push him quite roughly back into the bunk. "Why should I?" Karl asked, with annoyance. "Because there's no use," said the man. "I'm going up in a minute myself; we can go together. Either the trunk has been stolen and there's nothing you can do about it, or the fellow has left the trunk standing, in which case it'll be that much easier to find when the ship empties. The same with your umbrella." "Do you know your way around the ship?" Karl asked suspiciously, and it seemed to him that the otherwise convincing idea that it would be easiest to find his things when the ship was empty had a hidden catch to it somewhere. "I am, after all, a stoker," said the man. "You're a stoker!" Karl cried, overjoyed, as if the news surpassed all expectations, and, propped up on his elbow, he looked at the man more closely. "Right in front of the cabin, where I slept with the Slovaks, there was a porthole through which you could look into the engine room." "Yes," said the stoker, "that's where I worked." "I've always been interested in machinery," said Karl, following his own particular train of thought, "and I would certainly have become an engineer if I hadn't had to go to America." "Why did you have to go?" "Oh, nothing in particular," said Karl, dismissing the whole story with a wave of his hand. At the same time he smiled at the stoker, as if to beg his pardon even for what he had been unable to admit. "I expect there was a reason," the stoker said, and it was hard to tell whether his remark was intended to produce or forestall an account of the reason. "I could become a stoker, too," said Karl, "now that my parents no longer care what becomes of me." "My job will be available," said the stoker, who, on growing fully aware of the fact, stuck his hands in his trouser pockets and kicked his legs, which were garbed in creased, leathery, iron gray trousers, onto the bunk to stretch them. Karl had to shift closer to the wall. "You're leaving the ship?" "Sure, we're clearing out today." "Why? Don't you like it?" "It's the way things are. It isn't always a matter of liking something or not. Anyway you're right, I don't like it. You're probably not serious about becoming a stoker, though that's just when it's easiest to become one. I for one strongly advise you against it. If you wanted to go to a university in Europe, why don't you go to one here? American universities are much better than the European ones: there's no comparison." "Maybe," said Karl, "but I hardly have the money to go to a university. Actually, I did read about someone who worked in a store during the day and went to school nights until he got his doctor's degree and then I think became a mayor. But for that you need plenty of stamina, right? I'm afraid I don't have it. Anyway, I was never a particularly good student; it was no sacrifice for me to leave school. And I think the schools here are even harder. I can hardly speak English. Besides, I think people here are generally prejudiced against foreigners." "Oh, so you've already had a taste of that? Well, then, that's just fine. You're my man. Look, we're on a German ship, right? It belongs to the Hamburg-America Line, so why aren't we all Germans here? Why is the chief engineer a Romanian? His name is Schubal.[1] It's unbelievable. And this dirty dog slave-drives us Germans on a German ship! Don't think"—he ran out of breath, his hands went flying

---

1. Şubă is Romanian for fur coat. The *l* ending in Austrian German adds the diminutive; hence *Schubal* means "little fur coat." In Kafka's story *The Metamorphosis* (Norton Critical Edition), the hero Gregor Samsa is sexually attracted, by means of a picture, to a person wearing a fur muff; meanwhile, the country doctor in "A Country Doctor" (n. 4, p. 64) is sexually attracted in a roundabout way to the sleeve of a fur coat. Here in *The Stoker*, Karl aims a sexually tinged affection at the stoker, who is under the sway of Schubal, the "little fur coat."

in the air—"that I'm complaining just for the sake of complaining.
I know that you have no influence, and that you're only a poor kid
yourself. But it's really too much!" And he pounded on the table repeatedly with his fist, never taking his eye off his fist as he
pounded. "I've served on so many ships in my time"—he reeled off
twenty names one after the other as if they were all one word, and
Karl's head began to spin—"and distinguished myself, been praised,
I'm the kind of worker my captains appreciated, was even on the
same merchant clipper for a number of years"—he stood up as if
that were the high point of his life—" and here on this tub, where
everything's done according to regulations, where you don't need
any brains at all—here I'm worthless, always in Schubal's way, I'm a
shirker who deserves to be thrown out and gets paid as a big favor.
Do you understand any of this? I don't." "You mustn't put up with
it," said Karl excitedly. He had almost lost the sense of being on the
unsteady bottom of a ship off the coast of an unknown continent,
he felt so much at home on the stoker's bunk. "Have you gone to
see the captain yet? Have you pleaded with him for your rights?"
"Oh, go away, get out of here. I don't want you around. You don't
listen to what I'm saying, and then you give me advice. How could
I go to the captain?" And wearily the stoker sat down again and put
his face in his hands.

"There's no better advice I can give him," said Karl to himself.
And he concluded that in general he would have been better off
getting his trunk instead of staying here giving advice that was only
considered stupid. When his father had handed over the trunk for
good, he had asked as a joke: "How long will you hold on to it?" and
now this expensive trunk might already really be lost. The one remaining consolation was that even if his father were to investigate,
he could not find out anything about Karl's present situation. The
most the shipping company could say was that he had arrived safely
in New York. But Karl was sorry to think that he had hardly made
use of the things in his trunk, even though, for example, he should
have changed his shirt a long time ago. That had been the wrong
place to economize; now, just at the beginning of his career, when
he needed to be well dressed, he would have to show up in a soiled
shirt. Otherwise, the loss of his trunk would not have been so bad,
since the suit he was wearing was even better than the one in the
trunk, which was actually only a suit for emergencies, which his
mother had had to mend just before his departure. Now he also remembered that a piece of Verona salami was still in the trunk; his
mother had packed it as something special for him, but he had
been able to eat only the smallest part of it, since during the voyage
he had completely lost his appetite and the soup that was passed
out in steerage had been plenty for him. Now, though, he would

gladly have had the salami at hand so as to make the stoker a present of it. For such people are easily won over when one slips them a little something: Karl had learned that from his father, who passed out cigars and so won over all the low-level workers with whom he dealt in his business. Now in the way of gifts Karl had only his money left; and in case he had already lost the trunk, for the time being he did not want to touch the money. Again his thoughts returned to the trunk, and now he really could not understand why he had watched the trunk so attentively during the voyage that it had almost cost him sleep, if now he could let this very trunk be taken away from him so easily. He remembered the five nights during which he had unrelentingly suspected a short Slovak, who had slept two berths to the left of Karl, of having his eye on the trunk. This Slovak had just been waiting for Karl, finally overcome by weariness, to nod off for an instant so he could drag the trunk to his side by using a long rod that he spent the day playing or practicing with. By day this Slovak looked innocent enough, but as soon as night had fallen, he would raise himself from his berth from time to time to look mournfully over at Karl's trunk. Karl could see this quite distinctly, for there was always someone in one spot or another who, with an emigrant's restlessness, had lit a small lamp, although this was prohibited by ship's regulations, trying to decipher the unintelligible prospectuses of the emigration agencies. If such a lamp was nearby, then Karl could doze a little; but if it was off at a distance or all was dark, then he had to keep his eyes open. The strain had completely exhausted him, and now it seemed as if it might have been utterly in vain. This Butterbaum, if he might just run into him, somewhere!

At this moment, from a long way away, little pattering sounds as if from the feet of children broke into what had been the perfect silence outside the cabin: they came closer, growing steadily louder, and now it was the steady tread of marching men. They were evidently moving in single file, as was natural in the narrow gangway, and you could hear a clatter as if of weapons. Karl, who had been on the verge of stretching out on the bunk for a nap, free of all worries about trunks and Slovaks, was startled, and he poked the stoker to make him aware at long last, for the head of the column seemed to have just reached the door. "That's the ship's band," said the stoker; "they were playing up on deck, and now they're going to pack. Everything is over now, and we can go. Come on!" He took Karl's hand, removed at the last minute a framed picture of the Virgin Mary from the wall over the bunk, crammed it into his breast pocket, grabbed his suitcase, and, with Karl, rapidly left the cabin.

"Now I'm going to the office to give these gentlemen a piece of my mind. There are no passengers left, so I won't have to mince my words." The stoker repeated this in various forms, and, as he walked, he tried with a sideways kick to stomp on a rat that crossed their path but succeeded only in pushing it more quickly into its hole, which it had reached just in time. The stoker's movements were generally slow, for even if he did have long legs, they were still too heavy.

They passed through a section of the kitchen, where several girls in dirty aprons—they were deliberately splashing them—were washing dishes in great vats. The stoker called a girl named Line over, put his arm around her waist, and, as she continued to press herself coquettishly against his arm, briefly led her along with them. "It's payday—do you want to come?" he asked. "Why bother, just bring me the money here," she replied, slipping out from under his arm and running off. "Where did you pick up that pretty boy?" she called out without waiting for an answer. One heard the laughter of all the girls, who had stopped their work to listen.

They, however, continued on their way and came to a door with a small protruding gable overhead, borne by little gilded caryatids. For a ship's fitting, it did seem rather wasteful. Karl realized that he had never been in this part of the ship; during the voyage it had probably been reserved for first- and second-class passengers, while now the dividing doors had been removed for the ship's great scrubbing down. In fact they had already encountered a number of men carrying brooms on their shoulders who had greeted the stoker. Karl marveled at the amount of activity; in steerage he had, of course, experienced very little of this. Along the gangways the wires of the electric cables were strung up, and a small bell could be heard without cease.

The stoker knocked respectfully on the door, and when a voice called out, "Come in," he motioned to Karl with a wave of his hand to go in and not be afraid. Karl did go in but remained standing inside the door. Through the three windows of the room he could see the waves of the ocean; and at the sight of their cheerful movement his heart beat faster, as though he had not been looking at the ocean uninterruptedly for five long days. Great ships coursed across each other's paths, yielding to the breaking waves only so far as their bulk allowed. If you half-closed your eyes, the ships seemed to be staggering under their own weight. On their masts hung narrow but long flags, and though they grew taut from the ships' motion, they still flapped back and forth. Saluting salvos sounded, probably from the warships; the cannon barrels of one such battleship sailing by not too far away, gleaming from the reflection of their steel casing, seemed to be fondled by its sure, sleek, yet not altogether level passage through the water. The smaller ships and boats could be seen, at least from the doorway, only in the distance, darting in

droves into the gaps between the great ships. But behind all this
stood New York, looking at Karl with the hundred thousand windows of its skyscrapers. Yes, in this room you realized where you
were.

Three men were seated at a round table—one, a ship's officer in
a blue naval uniform; the other two, officials of the port authority,
in black American uniforms. On the table lay high piles of various
documents, which the officer first scanned, pen in hand, before
handing them over to the other two, who now read them, now
made excerpts, now put them in their briefcases, whenever one of
the others, whose teeth made an almost constant little noise, was
not dictating something to his colleague into the record.

At a desk by one window sat a smaller man, his back to the door,
fiddling with the massive ledgers that were lined up on a sturdy
bookshelf at eye level in front of him. Next to him stood an open
cashbox that at least looked empty at first glance.

The second window was vacant and had the best view. But near
the third stood two gentlemen, conversing in an undertone. One of
them, also in a ship's uniform, leaned against the window, toying
with the hilt of his sword. The man he was speaking to stood facing
the window, and now and again one of his movements exposed a
portion of the row of ribbons on the other man's chest. He was
dressed in civilian clothes and carried a thin bamboo cane that, because both his hands were pressed against his hips, also stuck out
like a sword.

Karl did not have much time to take everything in, since an orderly soon came up to them and giving the stoker a look as if he did
not belong here, asked him what he wanted. The stoker replied, as
softly as he had been asked, that he wanted to speak to the head
cashier. For his part, the orderly rejected this request with a wave
of his hand but, nonetheless, giving the round table a wide berth,
went up on tiptoe to the man with the heavy ledgers. This man—
one could see this clearly—practically went rigid on hearing the
words of the orderly but finally turned to face the man who wanted
to speak to him and began waving his hands at the stoker in a gesture of strict refusal and, to be on the safe side, at the orderly too.
Whereupon the orderly turned back to the stoker and said in the
tone of someone passing on a confidential message, "Clear out at
once!"

At this reply the stoker looked down at Karl as if he were his own
heart to whom he was mutely lamenting his sorrows. Without further thought Karl broke loose and ran straight across the room,
even lightly brushing the officer's chair; the orderly ran after him as
well, bent over, arms outstretched, to catch him as if he were chasing some vermin, but Karl was the first to reach the head cashier's

table, which he gripped firmly in case the orderly should try to drag him away.

Naturally, the entire room immediately came alive. The ship's officer at the table sprang up; the men from the port authority watched calmly but intently; the two men at the window moved close to one another; the orderly, who thought he was now out of his element where such lofty personages were showing an interest, retreated. The stoker waited tensely at the door for the moment when his help might be needed. The head cashier, in his easy chair, finally made a great turn to the right.

Karl rummaged in his secret pocket, which he had no hesitation in betraying to these people, took out his passport, and in lieu of further introduction laid it open on the table. The head cashier seemed to consider the passport beside the point, for he flicked it to one side with two fingers, whereupon Karl, as if this formality had now been satisfactorily concluded, put his passport back in his pocket.

"May I take the liberty of saying," he began, "that in my opinion the stoker has been done an injustice. We have here a certain Schubal, who has been harassing him. The stoker has already served to everyone's complete satisfaction on many ships, all of which he can name for you; he is a hard worker, devoted to the job; and it is really hard to understand why, on this of all ships, where the work is not so exceedingly difficult, unlike, for example, on clipper ships,[2] he is supposed to be inadequate. And so it can only be slander that prevents him from moving up and deprives him of the recognition that he would most certainly otherwise have had. I have stated the matter in only the most general terms: he will present his specific complaints to you himself." Karl had addressed this speech to all the men in the office because all of them were actually listening; and it seemed much more likely that among them all a just man would be found, than that this just man should happen to be the head cashier. Karl had also shrewdly concealed the fact that he had known the stoker for such a short time. Furthermore, he would have spoken far better had he not been distracted by the red face of the man with the bamboo cane, which, from his present vantage point, he now saw for the first time.

"Every word of it is true," said the stoker before anyone had even asked him—indeed, before anyone had even looked in his direction. The stoker's overhastiness would have been a great mistake had not the gentleman with the ribbons who, it now dawned on Karl, was definitely the captain, had not evidently already made up his mind to hear the stoker's complaint. For he stretched out his

2. It is hard to imagine what role a stoker might play on a clipper ship with sails. With this word choice Kafka would appear to be underscoring Karl's enthusiastic credulity.

hand and called to the stoker, "Come here," in a voice so firm you could hit it with a hammer. Now everything depended on the behavior of the stoker, since when it came to the justness of his case, Karl had no doubts.

Fortunately, it now became clear that the stoker had a good deal of experience of the world. With exemplary calm he thrust his hand directly into his little suitcase and took out a small bundle of papers and a notebook, brought them, as if this went without saying, over to the captain while completely ignoring the head cashier, and laid them on the windowsill as documentary evidence. The head cashier had no option except to make the effort of joining them. "The man is a well-known troublemaker," he said, by way of explanation; "he spends more time in the pay room than in the engine room. He has driven Schubal, this peaceful fellow, to complete despair. Listen, you!" he said, turning to the stoker, "this time you and your pushiness have really gone too far. How many times have you been thrown out of the pay room for your completely, totally, and unfailingly unjustified demands, just as you deserve! How many times have you then come running here to the head office! How often have you been told nicely that Schubal is your immediate superior and that it is with him and with him alone that you, his subordinate, must come to terms! And now you even barge in here when the captain is present: aren't you ashamed of pestering him, of all people, and what's more, of having the effrontery to bring along this young fellow, whom you've trained to be the spokesman of your vapid accusations, someone whom I am effectively seeing on the ship for the first time!"

Karl had to restrain himself forcibly from leaping forward. But the captain himself was already there, saying, "Give this man a chance to speak. Besides, this Schubal is gradually becoming much too independent for my taste, though that doesn't mean I am saying anything in your favor." This last remark was intended for the stoker; it was only natural that the captain could not take his side immediately, but everything seemed to be moving in the right direction. The stoker began his explanations, exercising self-control from the outset by giving Schubal the title of "Mister." How delighted Karl was, standing at the head cashier's vacated desk, where, in all his pleasure, he kept pressing down a letter scale.— Mr. Schubal is unfair! Mr. Schubal is prejudiced in favor of foreigners! Mr. Schubal ordered the stoker out of the engine room and made him clean toilets, which is certainly not part of a stoker's job description!—Once, Mr. Schubal's very work ethic was put into question as something more apparent than real. At this point Karl fixed his gaze on the captain with great concentration, confidingly, as if he were his colleague, just so that the captain would not be influenced by the stoker's somewhat clumsy way of expressing himself. Still, there was nothing substantial to be learned from his speeches; and even though the captain still looked straight ahead—his eyes expressing his determination to hear the stoker out this one time—the other men were growing impatient; and soon the stoker's voice no longer reigned uncontested in the room, which was a cause for worry. First, the gentleman in civilian clothes set his little bamboo cane in motion, tapping it, though gently, on the parquet floor. The other men naturally looked over at him from time to time; the men from the port authority, who were evidently pressed for time, reached for their files again and began, even if still somewhat absentmindedly, to examine them; the ship's officer moved closer to his table again; and the head cashier, who believed that he had victory in his sights, heaved a deep, ironic sigh. Only the orderly seemed exempt from the air of distraction that had generally set in, and sympathizing a little with the sufferings of a poor man placed among the great ones, he nodded gravely to Karl, as if trying to explain something.

In the meantime the life of the harbor continued outside the windows; a flat barge went by with a mountain of barrels, which must have been wonderfully stowed for them not to start rolling, and filled the room with near darkness; little motorboats, which Karl could have observed more carefully had he had more time, rushed past straight as arrows, responsive to the fluctuating hands of a man standing erect at the steering wheel; here and there peculiar floating objects, bobbing up out of the restless waves on their own, were immediately swamped and sank back before his astonished gaze; boats from the ocean liners, propelled ashore by fiercely rowing sailors, were filled with passengers sitting quietly and expectantly in the places they had been squeezed into, although many of them could not help twisting their heads to look at the changing scenery. Movement without end, a restlessness communicated from the restless element to these helpless men and their works!

But everything urged speed, precision, clarity of presentation; and what did the stoker do? He was certainly talking himself into a sweat; for a long time now his trembling hands could no longer hold the papers at the windowsill; complaints about Schubal rushed at him from all directions, every single one of which, in his opinion, would have been enough to bury this Schubal completely; but all he could offer the captain was only a sad, whirling hodgepodge of them all. For a long time now the gentleman with the little bamboo cane had been softly whistling at the ceiling; the men from the port authority detained the officer at their table again, showing no sign of ever letting him go; the head cashier was visibly prevented from forcibly interfering only by the captain's calm; the orderly stood at attention waiting for a command from his captain regarding the stoker that might be issued at any second.

At this point Karl could no longer stand idly by. And so he slowly walked over to the group, considering all the more quickly while proceeding how he could handle the matter in the most skillful way possible. It was really high time; a little while longer, and both of them might well be tossed out of the office. The captain might be a good man and, in addition, or so it seemed to Karl, might have had some special reason just then to show himself to be a fair superior, but he was not, in the last analysis, an instrument that you could keep playing until it fell apart; yet this was just how the stoker was treating him—the result, of course, of his uncontainable feeling of outrage.

And so Karl said to the stoker, "You have to explain things more simply, more clearly; the captain can't do it justice the way you tell it. Does he know all the machinists and messengers by name, let alone by their first names, so that all you have to do is say one of these names and he'll know right away whom you mean? Put your complaints in order, state the most important one first and the others in descending order of importance, and then it may not even be necessary to mention most of them. You always explained it to me so clearly!" If you could steal trunks in America, he thought, absolving himself, you could also tell the occasional lie.

If only this had helped! Was it perhaps already too late? The stoker did immediately interrupt himself on hearing the familiar voice; but, with eyes blurred by tears of injured masculine honor, of terrible memories and agonizing immediate distress, he could barely recognize Karl. How could he now—Karl, silent before him, understood this very clearly as the stoker himself fell silent—how could he now suddenly change his whole way of speaking, when it seemed to him that he had already said everything there was to say without receiving the slightest acknowledgment and, on the other hand, that he hadn't said a thing yet and could not now expect the gentlemen to listen to it all. And at such a moment Karl, his only supporter, steps in, meaning to give him good advice but instead showing him that everything was utterly, utterly lost.

"If I'd only stepped in sooner, instead of looking out the window," Karl said to himself, lowering his eyes before the stoker and clapping his hands against his trouser seams as a sign that all hope was lost.

But the stoker misunderstood, probably detecting in Karl's gesture some sort of veiled reproach aimed at him, and with the worthy intention of talking him out of it, he capped his actions by starting to quarrel with Karl. Just now: when the gentlemen at the round table had long since been outraged by the senseless racket that was disturbing them in their important work; when the head cashier was gradually finding the captain's patience incomprehensible and was about to explode; when the orderly, who was once again wholly within the circle of his masters, was measuring the stoker with wild looks; and finally, when the gentleman with the little bamboo cane, at whom even the captain now and again sent a friendly glance and who by now was totally inured to the stoker, indeed disgusted by him, took out a little notebook and, evidently occupied with entirely different matters, let his eyes wander back and forth between the notebook and Karl.

"I know, I know," said Karl, who was having trouble defending himself against the tirade the stoker was now directing at him, although he still managed a friendly smile for the man throughout all their quarreling. "You're right, you're right, I never doubted it for a minute." Karl would have liked to hold the stoker's flailing hands for fear of being hit; even better, to force him into a corner and whisper a few gently calming words that none of the others would have to hear. But the stoker was completely out of control. Karl now even began to find a sort of consolation in the thought that if it came to that, the stoker could crush all seven men present with the strength of his despair. On the desk, however, as a glance in that direction revealed, sat a fixture with altogether too many push buttons connected to the electricity; and a hand, simply laid upon them, could have the entire ship up in arms and all its gangways full of hostile men.

Whereupon the gentleman with the little bamboo cane, who had showed so little interest, came up to Karl and asked, not loudly but distinctly through all the stoker's ranting, "What is your name, actually?" At this very moment there was a knock at the door, as if someone on the other side had been waiting for the gentleman to say just these words. The orderly looked over at the captain, who nodded. The orderly therefore went to the door and opened it. Outside, wearing an old imperial coat,[3] stood a man of middling stature who, to judge from his appearance, was really not suited to working with engines, and yet this man was—Schubal. If Karl had not been able to see this in everyone's eyes, which expressed a certain satisfaction from which not even the captain was exempt, he would, to his horror, have had to see it in the stoker, who clenched his fists at the end of his rigid arms so tightly that this clenching seemed to be the most important element in him, something for which he was ready to sacrifice all the life he possessed. All his force was concentrated in them now, even the force that kept him upright.

So here, then, was the enemy, all fresh and easy, in his holiday

---

3. The kind of formal jacket that civilians were required to wear on official occasions at the Imperial Court in Vienna.

best, a ledger under his arm—probably the stoker's payment list and his work record—looking into the eyes of all those present, one after the other, not afraid to admit that he intended above all to gauge the mood of every single one of them. All seven men were already his friends, for even if earlier the captain had had or perhaps had only pretended to have had certain reservations about him, it seemed likely that after the pain the stoker had caused him, he could no longer find even the slightest fault with Schubal. In dealing with someone like the stoker, no measure was too harsh; and if there was anything to reproach Schubal for, it was for his not having been able to tame the recalcitrance of the stoker over time enough to keep the latter from daring to show up today before the captain.

Now, there might be a chance that the confrontation of the stoker and Schubal would not fail to have the same effect on the human order that it would have on a higher tribunal; for even if Schubal were to succeed in acting a part, he might still not be able to keep it up to the end. A single flash of his vileness would be enough to make it evident to the gentlemen, something that Karl intended to see to. He already had a rough idea of the sharp-sightedness, the weaknesses, the moods of the individual gentlemen; and in this respect the time he had spent here up to now had not been wasted. If only the stoker had been better on the playing field, but he seemed totally unable to keep up the fight. If someone had held Schubal in his reach, he could probably have bashed open his hated skull with his fists. But now just taking the few steps over to him seemed more than he could manage. Why, then, had Karl not foreseen something that could so easily have been foreseen—namely, that Schubal was bound to appear sooner or later, if not under his own steam, then summoned by the captain? Why had he not discussed a definite plan of attack with the stoker on the way here, instead of doing what they had in fact done: simply walked in, disastrously unprepared, at the first door they happened on? Was the stoker even able to speak, to say yes and no, for that would be necessary at his cross-examination, though, admittedly, that eventuality would occur only in the most favorable circumstances? He stood there, his legs spread apart, his knees unsteady, his head raised somewhat, and air flowed through his open mouth as if there were no longer any lungs inside him that could process it.

Karl, on the other hand, felt more powerful and alert than he had perhaps ever felt at home. If only his parents could see him now, fighting for the good cause in a foreign land in front of prestigious persons, and even if not yet triumphant, holding himself in complete readiness for the final victory! Would his parents change their opinion of him? Sit him down between them and praise him? Just for once, just for once, look into his eyes—eyes so devoted to them? Doubtful questions, posed at the most inappropriate moment!

"I've come because I believe that the stoker is accusing me of some sort of dishonesty. A girl in the kitchen told me that she had seen him on his way here. Captain, sir, and all you gentlemen, I am ready to refute every one of these accusations with the documents I have here and, if necessary, with the depositions of unprejudiced and impartial witnesses who at this moment are standing outside the door." Thus spake Schubal.[4] It was certainly a lucid, manly speech; and to judge from the changed expressions of the listeners, one might have thought that these were the first human sounds they had heard in a long time. Of course they did not notice that even this beautiful speech had holes in it. Why was the first relevant word that occurred to Schubal "dishonesty"? Should the accusation perhaps have begun with this, instead of with his national prejudices? A girl in the kitchen had seen the stoker on his way to the office, and Schubal had understood at once? Wasn't it his guilty conscience that had sharpened his understanding? And he had immediately brought along witnesses whom, additionally, he called "unprejudiced" and "impartial"? Trickery, nothing but trickery! And these gentlemen tolerated it, even acknowledging it to be correct behavior? Why had Schubal indisputably let so much time pass between the maid's report and his arrival? Surely to no other purpose than to have the stoker so exhaust the gentlemen that they would gradually lose their powers of clear judgment—the thing Schubal had to fear most. And, after surely having stood for a long time outside the door, hadn't he waited to knock at the precise moment when, as a result of one of the gentlemen's casual questions, he could hope that the stoker had been dealt a lethal blow?

Everything was clear, had even unwittingly been presented as such by Schubal, but it had to be offered in a different way, made absolutely obvious to the gentlemen. They needed to be shaken up. And so, Karl—hurry, at least make good use of the time before the witnesses appear and swamp the whole thing!

But just then the captain waved Schubal away, and—as his case seemed to have been postponed for a time—he immediately stepped to one side and struck up a quiet conversation with the orderly, who had immediately attached himself to him—a conversation that did not fail to include side glances at the stoker and Karl, as well as the most emphatic hand gestures. With this, Schubal seemed to be rehearsing his next great speech.

"Didn't you want to ask the young man a question, Mr. Jakob?"

4. The sentence "Thus spake Schubal" appears to mimic the refrain "Thus spake Zarathustra," in the great work of that name by the philosopher Friedrich Nietzsche (1844–1900). Kafka began reading this book in the summer of 1900.

said the captain to the man with the bamboo cane amid the general silence.

"Indeed," the man said, with a slight bow of gratitude for the captain's attentiveness. And once again he asked Karl, "Exactly what is your name?"

Karl, who thought that in the interest of the overriding central issue this intrusion by the stubborn questioner ought to be dealt with quickly, answered briefly, without, as was his habit, introducing himself by producing his passport, which he would have had to search for: "Karl Rossmann."

"Well!" said the gentleman who had been addressed as Mr. Jakob, taking a step back with a smile almost of disbelief. Now the captain, the head cashier, the ship's officer, indeed, even the orderly clearly displayed inordinate astonishment on hearing Karl's name. Only the gentlemen from the port authority and Schubal remained indifferent.

"Well," Mr. Jakob repeated, walking up to Karl somewhat stiffly, "then I am your Uncle Jakob and you are my dear nephew. I suspected as much the whole time!" he said to the captain before hugging and kissing Karl, who let everything unfold without comment.

"What is your name?" asked Karl once he felt that he had been released, certainly very politely but totally unmoved, straining to visualize the consequences that this new turn of events might have for the stoker. For the moment nothing pointed to the possibility that Schubal could profit from the situation.

"Don't you realize how lucky you are, young man?" said the captain, who felt that Karl's question injured the personal dignity of Mr. Jakob, who had placed himself at the window, evidently in order to keep the others from seeing the agitation on his face, which he kept dabbing with a handkerchief. "The gentleman who has identified himself to you as your uncle is Senator Edward Jakob. You now have a brilliant career awaiting you, certainly altogether contrary to your earlier expectations. Try to realize this as well as you can in the first shock of the moment and pull yourself together."

"It is true that I have an Uncle Jakob in America," Karl said, turning to the captain, "but if I understood you correctly, Jakob is only the Senator's second name."

"That's true," said the captain expectantly.

"But Jakob is my Uncle Jakob's first name, and he is my mother's brother, so his second name, of course, is the same as my mother's maiden name, Bendelmayer."

"Gentlemen!" cried the senator, in reaction to Karl's explanation, as he returned in high spirits from his restorative station at the window. Everyone except the port officials broke out laughing, a number of them as if moved, others for impenetrable reasons.

"What I said wasn't that funny," thought Karl.

"Gentlemen!" repeated the senator. "You are taking part, against my wishes and yours, in a little family drama, and so I cannot help but provide you with an explanation, since I believe that only the captain"—this mention produced an exchange of bows—"is thoroughly informed of the matter."

"Now I really must pay attention to every word," Karl said to himself and was delighted to notice from a sideways glance that life was beginning to return to the figure of the stoker.

"During all the long years of my American sojourn—the word 'sojourn' is certainly not the right word to apply to the American citizen that I wholeheartedly am—during all these long years, I have lived completely cut off from my European relatives for reasons that, first of all, are not important here, and second, would really take too much out of me to tell. I even dread the moment when I may be forced to explain them to my dear nephew, where certain home truths about his parents and their progeny unfortunately cannot be avoided."

"It's my uncle, all right," Karl said to himself, listening intently; "he probably changed his name."

"My dear nephew has been—let us use the word that truly describes the matter at hand—simply tossed aside by his parents, the way you kick out a cat that has begun to make a nuisance of itself. I do not intend by any means to prettify what my nephew has done to deserve such punishment, but his fault is such that the mere statement of it contains an adequate excuse."

"I like the sound of that," Karl thought, "but I don't want him to tell the whole story to everyone. And he can't possibly know what happened. Who could have told him?"

"In a word," his uncle continued, supporting himself by rocking slightly forward from time to time on the bamboo cane propped up before him, allowing him in fact to rob the affair of an unnecessary solemnity that it would otherwise have been bound to have, "he was, in a word, seduced by a housemaid, one Johanna Brummer,[5] a person of about thirty-five. I use the word 'seduce,' not to hurt my nephew's feelings, but it is truly hard to find another word that is equally befitting."

---

5. The family name of the housemaid, "Brummer," means "horsefly" whereas the family name of our hero Karl—Rossmann—means "steed man." Although "Rossmann" permits of various readings, it is probable evidence of Kafka's subliminal sense of the low animal character of sexual intercourse; in his diaries for August 14, 1913, he wrote, "Coitus is the punishment for the happiness of being together." Peter Musolf suggests other implications of the name "Rossmann": "as something or someone to ride upon, it is a Pegasus for Kafka's imagination. As something or someone that is ridden, it becomes a reflective image of Kafka ridden by his story; further, of Karl being ridden by his aspirations. When Kafka wrote, at the time of writing this story, 'I carried my own weight on my back' (p. 197), he had become a 'Ross-mann.' Meanwhile, the 'horse' in 'horsefly' and the 'steed' in 'Rossmann' are a fortuitous harmony: in German, 'Brummer' does not imply anything equine."

Karl, who had already stepped quite close to his uncle, turned around at this point in order to read the faces of the others for the impression that the story had made on them. No one was laughing; all of them were listening patiently and seriously. After all, one does not laugh at the nephew of a senator at the first opportunity that presents itself. It might, rather, be said that the stoker smiled, if only very faintly, at Karl, an expression that was, first of all, gratifying in that it was a new sign of life and, second, excusable, since back in the cabin Karl had tried to make a particular secret of this affair, which was now so completely out in the open.

"Now this Brummer woman," his uncle continued, "has had a child by my nephew, a healthy boy, who was christened Jakob, no doubt with my humble self in mind, because even my nephew's surely quite casual references to me must have made a considerable impression on the girl. Fortunately, I might add. For since his parents, to avoid the costs of child support or further scandals coming back at them—I must emphasize that I am not acquainted either with the laws there or anything else about the parents' situation—since they, so as to avoid the costs of child support and the scandal, had their son, my dear nephew, shipped off to America, irresponsibly ill-provided for, as you see, so that the boy, without the signs and wonders that continue to happen, at least in America, being dependent only on himself, would probably by now have come to grief in some back alley in New York at the harbor, if it were not for the maid who, in a letter addressed to me, which after lengthy detours was delivered the day before yesterday, informed me of the whole story, including a description of the person of my nephew and, very sensibly, the name of his ship. If, gentlemen, it had been my intention to entertain you, I could indeed read several passages from that letter"—he took two huge, closely written sheets of letter paper from his pocket and waved them about— "aloud to you here. The letter would no doubt have an effect, since it is written with a certain simple, though consistently well-meaning cleverness and with much love for the father of the child. But I will neither entertain you longer than is necessary for the purpose of enlightening you nor perhaps, at this first moment of my nephew's reception, damage the feelings that may still be alive in him, who, if he likes, can read the letter for his own edification in the quiet of the room that already awaits him."

But Karl had no feelings for the housemaid. In the crush of images from a past that was growing ever remoter, she sat in the kitchen next to the cupboard, her elbows propped on its shelf. She would look at him whenever he occasionally came into the kitchen to get a glass of water for his father or to tell her something his mother wanted done. Sometimes she would be writing a letter, sitting in a convoluted posture to one side of the cupboard and would draw her inspiration for it from Karl's face. Sometimes she covered her eyes with her hand, and then it was impossible to get through to her. Sometimes she would be kneeling in her narrow little room next to the kitchen, praying to a wooden crucifix. At those times Karl, walking past, would watch her shyly through the crack in the narrowly opened door. Sometimes she would race around in the kitchen and shrink back, laughing like a witch, if Karl got in her way. Sometimes she shut the kitchen doors after Karl had come in and kept holding on to the door handle until he demanded to be let out. Sometimes she brought him things that he did not even want and pressed them silently into his hand. But once she called him "Karl" and, while he was still amazed at the unexpected form of address, she led him grimacing and sighing into her little room and then locked it. She twined her arms around his neck, nearly choking him; and while she begged him to undress her, she actually undressed him and laid him in her bed, as if from now on she would never let anyone else have him and would caress him and care for him until the end of the world. "Karl, oh you, my Karl!" she cried, as if she were looking at him and confirming that he was hers, while he could not see anything at all and felt uncomfortable in the warm bedding that she appeared to have heaped up especially for him. Then she lay down beside him and asked him to tell her some secrets, but he had none to tell, and she became angry, in jest or in earnest, shook him, listened to the beating of his heart, offered her breast for him to listen to hers too, though she was unable to get Karl to do it, pressed her naked belly against his body, her hand fumbling between his legs so disgustingly that Karl's head and neck shot up from the pillows, then thrust her belly several times against him—it seemed to him as if she were a part of him, and this may have been why he was overcome by a terrible feeling of helplessness. In tears, and after she had begged again and again for future meetings, he finally reached his own bed. That was all there had been to it, and yet his uncle was able to turn it into an epic. And so the cook[6] had also thought about him and informed his uncle of his arrival. She had done well, and he hoped to pay her back someday.

"And now," cried the senator, "I want you to state very clearly whether I am your uncle or not."

"You are my uncle," said Karl, kissing the senator's hand and receiving a kiss on the forehead in return. "I am very glad to have met you, but you are mistaken if you think that my parents have only bad things to say about you. But apart from that, there were a few other mistakes in your account, that is to say, I mean, not every-

---

6. From this point on, Kafka refers to the seductive serving maid as "the cook." Cooking was evidently one of her duties.

thing actually happened the way you said it did. But you cannot really judge things so well from here; and anyway, I don't think it will do a great deal of harm if the gentlemen are given some slightly inaccurate details in a matter that cannot be of great concern to them."

"Well put," said the senator, leading Karl to the visibly sympathetic captain and asking, "Don't I have a splendid nephew?"

"I am happy, Senator," said the captain, bowing in the way that only someone with military training can, "to have made the acquaintance of your nephew. It is a special honor for my ship to have been able to provide the occasion for such a meeting. But the voyage in steerage was no doubt very disagreeable; after all, you can never know who is traveling with you. Now, we do everything we can to make the voyage for steerage passengers less of an ordeal, much more, for example, than the American shipping companies, but turning such a voyage into a pleasure cruise is admittedly something that we have still not succeeding in doing."

"It didn't do me any harm," said Karl.

"It didn't do him any harm!" the senator repeated, laughing out loud.

"Except I'm afraid I've lost my trunk—" and with this Karl remembered everything that had happened and still remained to be done, and he looked around and saw all the men still in their places, silent with respect and astonishment, their eyes fixed on him. Only the port officials showed—to the extent that one could read anything at all into their stern, self-satisfied faces—their regret at having come at so inopportune a time; and the pocket watch that lay on the table before them was probably more important to them than anything that had happened or might still happen in the room.

The first person after the captain to express his enthusiasm was, oddly enough, the stoker. "Heartfelt congratulations," he said and shook Karl's hand, by which gesture he also intended to express something like respectful regard. But as he was about to turn to the senator and address him in the same way, the latter stepped back, as if now the stoker were overstepping his bounds, whereupon the stoker stopped at once.

But the others now understood what needed to be done and promptly formed a milling crowd around Karl and the senator. And so it happened that Karl received congratulations even from Schubal, which he accepted with thanks. The last to come up to them, once things had calmed down again, were the port officials, who spoke two words in English, making a ridiculous impression.

The senator was thoroughly in a mood to enjoy this pleasurable occasion to the full, reminding himself and the others of some of the less momentous details of the affair, and naturally they not only tolerated this but even took it in with keen interest. And so he drew their attention to the fact that he had jotted down into his note-book Karl's most prominent and easily recognizable features as mentioned in the cook's letter, in case it might become necessary for him to make use of them at short notice. During the stoker's in-tolerable blather, he had taken out his notebook trying, merely to distract himself, to connect Karl's appearance with the cook's ob-servations, which did not, of course, have quite the accuracy that a detective would require. "And that's how a man finds his nephew!" he concluded, in a tone inviting another round of congratulations.

"What will happen to the stoker now?" Karl asked, talking past his uncle's last story. In his new status, he thought, he could say whatever occurred to him.

"The stoker will get what he deserves," the senator said, "and what the captain considers proper. I think we've had enough and more than enough of the stoker, as everyone of the gentlemen pres-ent will surely agree."

"But that is not what's at stake when it's a matter of justice," Karl said. He was standing between his uncle and the captain and felt, perhaps influenced by this position, that he had the outcome in his hand.

And yet the stoker appeared to have given up all hope. He kept his hands stuck halfway into his waistband, which, along with a strip of his checkered shirt, had been exposed by his excited ges-tures. That did not worry him in the least; he had poured out his heart, now they might as well see the few rags he still had on his back and then cart him away. He had planned that Schubal and the orderly, as the two lowest-ranking persons here, would show him this last kindness. Schubal would then be left in peace and no longer be driven to despair, as the head cashier had put it. The cap-tain could now hire nothing but Romanians; everyone would speak Romanian; and perhaps things would then really be better. There would be no more stoker to blather away in the head cashier's of-fice; his last bit of blather would be held in rather fond remem-brance, since, as the senator had expressly said, it had led indirectly to his nephew's recognition. And this nephew had often sought to be of use to him before, and so he had now already repaid him more than adequately for his services in this recognition scene; it did not occur to the stoker to demand anything more from Karl now. Add to this that even if he was the senator's nephew, he was far from being a captain, and it was, finally, from the lips of the captain that the harsh verdict would fall.—And in accordance with his view, the stoker tried not to look over at Karl, but in this room full of enemies there was, unfortunately, nowhere else his eyes could rest.

"Do not misunderstand the situation," said the senator to Karl; "it may be a question of justice, but at the same time it is a matter of discipline. Both matters, and especially the second, are subject to the captain's judgment."

"That's true," murmured the stoker. Whoever heard this and understood, smiled though somewhat taken aback.

"In any case, we have already hindered the captain in his official duties, which must increase to an unbelievable extent, particularly on arrival in New York, so it is high time for us to disembark, for it would be the crowning touch if, through some kind of totally unnecessary interference, we were to turn this trivial squabble between two engineers into a major incident as well. Actually, my dear nephew, I understand your behavior perfectly, but that is precisely what gives me the right to take you away from here in a hurry."

"I will have a boat lowered for you at once," said the captain without, to Karl's amazement, raising the slightest objection to his uncle's remarks, which could doubtlessly be seen as an act of self-abasement on the part of his uncle. The head cashier rushed headlong to his desk and telephoned the captain's order to the bosun.

"Time is flying," Karl said to himself, "but without insulting everyone there is nothing I can do. I can't abandon my uncle now that he has just found me again. The captain is certainly polite, but that is all he is. His politeness ends where discipline begins, and my uncle has surely expressed the captain's innermost thoughts. I don't want to speak to Schubal; I am even sorry I shook hands with him. And all the other people here are just chaff."

And with such thoughts in mind, he slowly went up to the stoker, pulled his right hand from his belt, and took it playfully into his own. "Why don't you[7] say something?" he asked. "Why do you put up with everything?"

The stoker just furrowed his brow, as if searching for the right expression for what he had to say. For the rest, he looked down at Karl's hand and his.

"You've been the victim of injustice more than anyone else on board this ship; I know that for a fact." And Karl slipped his fingers back and forth between the fingers of the stoker, who looked around him with shining eyes, as if overcome by a bliss that no one could begrudge him.

"But you have to defend yourself, say yes and no, otherwise people will never have an inkling of the truth. You must promise that you will do as I say, because I'm afraid, for many good reasons, that I will not be able to help you at all anymore." And now Karl wept as he kissed the stoker's hand and took that almost lifeless hand with

7. Here, in this intimate moment, Karl addresses the stoker as *du* for the first time.

its cracked skin and pressed it to his cheek, like a treasure that one must forego.—But there was his uncle the senator, already at his side and drawing him away, though with only the slightest pressure.

"The stoker seems to have bewitched you," he said and glanced knowingly over Karl's head at the captain. "You felt abandoned, whereupon you found the stoker, and now you are grateful to him: that is entirely praiseworthy. But don't go to extremes, if only to do me a favor, and do begin to realize your position."

Outside the door a tumult of voices arose, people were shouting; it even seemed as if someone were being brutally shoved against the door. A sailor entered with a girl's apron tied around his middle, looking as if he had run wild: "There's a bunch of people outside," he cried and suddenly thrust around with his elbows, as if he were still being jostled by the crowd. Finally he came to his senses and was about to salute the captain when he caught sight of the apron, tore it off, and threw it on the ground, crying: "It's disgusting, they tied a girl's apron on me." But then he clicked his heels and saluted. Someone began to laugh, but the captain said sternly, "I see that someone's in a good mood. Who are these people outside?"

"They're my witnesses," said Schubal, stepping forward, "I humbly beg your pardon for their unseemly conduct. When these people have a voyage behind them, they sometimes go pretty crazy."

"Call them in immediately!" the captain ordered; and turning at once to the senator, he said politely but quickly: "Please be good enough, Senator, to take your nephew and follow this sailor, who will escort you to the boat. I need hardly tell you, Senator, what a pleasure and an honor it has been for me to make your personal acquaintance. I can only hope, Senator, that at the earliest opportunity we might resume our interrupted conversation about the state of the American fleet and then, perhaps, be interrupted once again in as pleasant a fashion as today."

"For the time being this one nephew will be enough," said his uncle, laughing. "And now accept my deepest thanks for your kindness, and good-bye. It may not be altogether impossible"—here he drew Karl warmly to his side—"that on our next trip to Europe we may perhaps be able to spend a longer period of time together in your company."

"That would be my great pleasure," the captain said. The two gentlemen shook hands. Karl could only remain silent and swiftly give his hand to the captain, for the latter's attention was already taken up by the fifteen people or so who had marched in under Schubal's command, somewhat awestruck but nevertheless with a great deal of noise. The sailor asked the senator's permission to lead the way and then cleared a path through the crowd for the senator and Karl, who passed easily along the bowing rows. It looked as if these basically good-natured people considered the quarrel between Schubal and the stoker a joke, and the ridiculousness of it did not end even in front of the captain. Karl noticed in the crowd the kitchen maid Line, who winked gaily at him while tying on the apron that the sailor had tossed away, for it was hers.

Continuing to follow the sailor, they left the office and turned into a narrow passage that, after a few steps, brought them to a small door from which a short flight of stairs led down into the boat that had been readied for them. The sailors in the boat, into which their escort sprang with a single jump, rose and saluted. The senator was just warning Karl to climb down carefully when, still on the top step, Karl broke into deep sobs. The senator put his right hand under Karl's chin, hugged him tight, and caressed him with his left. In this way they went down slowly, step by step, in a close embrace, and got into the boat, where the senator picked out a good seat for Karl directly facing him. At a signal from the senator the sailors shoved off and in no time were rowing at full strength. Hardly had they gone a few yards from the ship when Karl unexpectedly discovered that they were precisely on the side of the ship where the windows of the head cashier's office were located. All three windows were filled with Schubal's witnesses, who were shouting goodbye and waving in the friendliest manner; even Karl's uncle acknowledged their greetings, and one sailor accomplished the feat of blowing them a kiss without actually breaking the even dipping of the oars. It was really as if there were no longer a stoker. Karl looked more intently at his uncle, whose knees were almost touching his, and doubts rose in him as to whether this man would ever be able to take the place of the stoker. And his uncle avoided his gaze and looked out at the waves on which their boat was tossing.

IN THE PENAL COLONY

"It is a peculiar piece of machinery," said the officer to the traveler[1] and with a look that contained some admiration surveyed the

---

1. The phrase "piece of machinery" translates Kafka's German word *Apparat*. The German word is difficult to translate consistently because to write the phrase "piece of machinery" wherever Kafka uses the word *Apparat* would be awkward. But since at other times Kafka refers to this *Apparat* as a *Maschine* (machine) with no apparent change of meaning, we will translate both *Apparat* and *Maschine* by "machine."

   The German word translated here as "traveler" is *Forschungsreisender*. A complete translation of the word would be "one who travels (*Reisender*) in the wake of explorers with the goal of doing research (*Forschung*) and returning home with his findings." This translation is too elaborate to use each time the word is mentioned, so I will call him a "traveler." At a later place in the story, however, the officer refers to the traveler—for rhetorical effect—as a *Forscher* (someone who does research); with this term the officer means to heighten his witness's prestige. Kafka wants both meanings—traveler and ex-machine that was after all so familiar to him. It was apparently only from politeness that the traveler had accepted the invitation of the commandant, who had requested his presence at the execution of a soldier condemned to death for disobeying and insulting his superior officer. The interest in this execution, even in the penal colony, did not seem to be very great. At any rate, apart from the officer and the traveler, here in the deep, sandy little valley enclosed on all sides by bare slopes there were only the condemned man—a stupid fellow with a big mouth and unkempt hair and face—and a soldier who held the heavy chain into which the small chains ran with which the condemned man was bound at the wrists, ankles, and throat and which were further linked together by connecting chains. In fact, the condemned man looked so doggishly submissive that it seemed you could let him run around freely on the slopes and would only have to whistle at the start of the execution for him to come.

The traveler had little feeling for the machine and walked back and forth behind the condemned man with an almost visible lack of interest while the officer occupied himself with the final preparations, now crawling under the machine, which was sunk deep into the ground, now climbing a ladder to inspect the upper sections. These were tasks that might well have been left to a mechanic, but the officer carried them out with great enthusiasm, either because he was a special devotee of this machine or because, for other reasons, the work could not be entrusted to anyone else. "Now everything is ready!" he finally called and climbed down the ladder. He was extraordinarily exhausted, breathing through his wide-open mouth, and had stuffed two delicate ladies' handkerchiefs under his uniform collar. "These uniforms are surely too heavy for the tropics," said the traveler instead of asking about the machine, as the officer had expected. "True," the officer said, washing his oil- and grease-smeared hands in a pail that stood by, "but they represent our homeland, and we don't want to lose touch with our homeland.—But now look at this machine," he added at once, drying his hands with a cloth and gesturing at the same time at the machine. "Until now we still had to do some things by hand, but from now on the machine works entirely on its own." The traveler nodded and followed the officer. The latter sought to safeguard himself against all contingencies by saying: "Of course malfunctions do occur; I certainly hope there won't be any today, but you still have to be prepared for them. After all, the machine is meant to function for twelve hours without interruption. But if malfunctions do occur, they will only be very minor ones, and they will be fixed immediately."

---

plorer—to be held in play. This visitor to the island is a traveler with a purpose: he is more than a tourist and less than an explorer.

"Won't you sit down?" he finally asked, pulling a cane chair out from a stack of them and offering it to the traveler; the latter could not refuse. He was now sitting at the edge of a pit, into which he cast a fleeting glance. It was not very deep. On one side of the pit the excavated earth was heaped up into a rampart; on the other side stood the machine. "I don't know," said the officer, "whether the commandant has already explained the machine to you." The traveler made a vague gesture with his hand; the officer desired nothing better, for now he could explain the machine himself. "This machine," he said and grabbed a cranking rod, against which he leaned, "is an invention of our former commandant. I participated in the very first experiments and was involved at every stage of the work right up to its completion. The credit for the invention, of course, goes exclusively to him. Have you heard about our former commandant? No? Well, I'm not saying too much when I tell you that the organization of the entire penal colony is his work. We, his friends, already knew at the time of his death that the organization of the colony was so self-contained that his successor, even if he had a thousand new plans in his head, would not be able to alter a thing in the old order, for many years at least. Our prediction has indeed come true; the new commandant has had to acknowledge it. A pity that you never knew the former commandant!—But," the officer interrupted himself, "I'm babbling, and his machine is here before us. It consists, as you see, of three parts. Over the years people have developed various nicknames, so to speak, for each of these parts. The lower one is called the bed, the upper one is called the scriber,[2] and, here, the middle part, the free-hanging one, is called the harrow. "The harrow?" asked the traveler. He had not been listening with his full attention; the sun was much too strongly concentrated in the shadowless valley; it was hard to collect your thoughts. And so the officer seemed all the more admirable as, in his tight parade dress coat, laden with epaulets and covered with braid, he explained his subject with such enthusiasm and even as he spoke, still busied himself with his screwdriver, turning screws here and there. The soldier's attitude, it seemed, was much like the traveler's. He had wrapped the condemned man's chain around both wrists, propped himself up with one hand on his rifle, dropped his head on his chest, and couldn't care less about anything. The traveler showed no surprise at this, since the officer was speaking French, and certainly neither the soldier nor the condemned man understood French. Hence, it was all the

2. The German word that indicates the designing part of the mechanism of punishment is *Zeichner*. Following the practice of J. A. Underwood I have called it the "scriber," literally a tool for marking off the parts of material to be cut away. The same German word also means "draftsman," which is used below (see p. 39) to designate one of the former commandant's skills.

more remarkable that the condemned man still made an effort to follow the officer's explanations. With a sort of drowsy persistence he continued to direct his gaze at the spot the officer indicated; and when the officer was now interrupted by a question from the traveler, he too, like the officer, looked at the traveler.

"Yes, the harrow," said the officer. "The name fits. The needles are arranged in harrow fashion, and the whole works like a harrow, even if in only one place and with much more artistic skill. Anyway, you'll soon understand. The condemned man is laid here on the bed.—What I want to do first is describe the machine and then let it run through the procedure by itself. You'll be able to follow it better this way. Besides, one cogwheel in the scriber is very worn; it screeches badly when it's in operation, and then you can hardly hear yourself speak. Unfortunately, spare parts are very hard to come by here.—All right, so here is the bed, as I was saying. It's completely covered by a layer of absorbent cotton; you'll see what it's used for later. The condemned man is laid on his stomach on this cotton—naked, of course; to hold him, here are straps for his hands; here, for his feet; and here, for his neck. Here, at the head of the bed, where, as I've said, the man first lies face down, is this little felt plug, which can easily be regulated, as you see, so that it practically pops into the man's mouth. Its purpose is to prevent him from screaming and biting his tongue. Naturally, the man has to take the felt into his mouth, since otherwise his neck would be broken by the neck strap." "This is absorbent cotton?" asked the traveler, bending forward. "Yes, of course," said the officer with a smile; "feel for yourself." He took the traveler's hand and drew it over the bed. "It's specially treated absorbent cotton, that's why it looks so unusual. I will get to its purpose in due course." The traveler was already a little taken by the machine; shading his eyes from the sun with his hand, he looked up at the top of the machine. It was a large construction. The bed and the scriber were of equal size and looked like two dark chests. The scriber was installed about six feet over the bed; the two were connected at the corners by four brass poles, which were close to flashing in the sunlight. Between the chests the harrow swayed on a steel band.

The officer had hardly noticed the traveler's earlier indifference, but now he became fully aware of his dawning interest; and so he interrupted his explanations to allow the traveler time for undisturbed contemplation. The condemned man imitated the traveler; and since he could not put his hand over his eyes, he blinked upward with unprotected eyes.

"So now the man is lying down," said the traveler, leaning back in his chair and crossing his legs.

"Yes," said the officer, shoving his cap back a little and wiping his hand over his hot face. "Now listen. Both the bed and the scriber have their own electric battery; the bed needs one for itself, the scriber, for the harrow. As soon as the man is strapped down, the bed is set in motion. It quivers with very rapid, tiny vibrations, both from side to side and up and down. You will have seen similar machines in sanatoriums, but all the movements of our bed are precisely calibrated; that is, they have to be painstakingly attuned to the movements of the harrow. The actual execution of the judgment,[3] however, is reserved for the harrow."

"So what is the judgment?" asked the traveler. "You don't know that either?" said the officer in astonishment, biting his lips. "Excuse me if my explanations might have seemed incoherent; I do very much beg your pardon. In times past, you see, the commandant used to give the explanation; the new commandant, however, has shirked his bounden duty; but that so distinguished a visitor"— the traveler attempted to ward off the honor with both hands, but the officer insisted on the expression—"that so distinguished a visitor is not even apprised by him of the form of our judgment is yet another innovation, which"—he had an oath on his lips but controlled himself and merely said: "I was not informed of this; it's not my fault. Anyway, I am certainly the person best qualified to explain our kind of judgment, since I carry here"—he smacked his breast pocket—"the former commandant's designs, which he drew with his own hand."

"The hand-drawn designs of the commandant himself?" asked the traveler. "So, was he a combination of everything? Was he soldier, judge, engineer, chemist, draftsman?"

"Yes, indeed," said the officer, nodding, with a fixed, thoughtful stare. Then he looked critically at his hands; they did not seem to him clean enough to touch the drawings, and so he went to the pail and washed them again. Then he took out a small leather folder and said, "Our judgment does not sound severe. The harrow will write the commandment he has violated on the condemned man's body. For example, on the body of this man"—the officer pointed to the man—"the harrow will write the words: Honor thy superiors!"

The traveler looked briefly at the man; when the officer had

---

3. Note that Kafka's German word for "judgment," *Urteil,* is also the title of his breakthrough story *The Judgment* (*Das Urteil*), written in one go on the night of September 22–23, 1912 (n. 1, p. 3). Here Kafka is suggesting that the person who does not know his own judgment deserves punishment—which, in Kafka's own case would point back to his ignorance or neglect of his own story *The Judgment.* Kafka would have forgotten the promise of literary productivity contained in that night of ecstasy; he would have failed to fulfill this promise. Can Kafka himself now expect to be punished on his own body for this omission, deserving, so to speak, to die from a stabbing consciousness of what he has failed to do? See also Corngold's essay on p. 221. Other translators have preferred to translate Kafka's word *Urteil* as "sentence," which is also correct, but to do so is to erase Kafka's reference to his first great story.

pointed to him, he was standing with his head lowered, appearing to strain all his powers of hearing so as to learn something. But the movements of his bulging lips, tightly pressed together, clearly showed that he could not understand a thing. The traveler had wanted to ask various questions, but at the sight of the man he merely asked, "Does he know the judgment?" "No," said the officer, intending to continue his explanations at once, but the traveler interrupted him, "He doesn't know his own judgment?" "No," said the officer again, then paused for a moment, as if demanding from the traveler a more cogent reason for his question; then he said, "It would be pointless to tell him. After all, he is going to learn it on his own body." The traveler now wanted to remain silent, but he felt the eyes of the condemned man on him; he seemed to be asking whether the traveler could approve the procedure that had just been described. And so the traveler, who had already leaned back, once again bent forward and asked: "But at least he knows that he has been condemned?" "Not that, either," said the officer, and smiled at the traveler, as if he now expected to have a few strange revelations from him. "You mean," the traveler said, rubbing his brow, "that even now the man still does not know how his defense was received?" "He did not have the opportunity to defend himself," said the officer and looked to one side, as if he were talking to himself and did not want to embarrass the traveler by telling him things that were so obvious to him. "But he must have had the opportunity to defend himself," said the traveler, getting up from his chair.

The officer saw that he was in danger of being held up for a long time in his explanation of the machine; he therefore went up to the traveler, put his arm through his, pointed at the condemned man, who, now that attention was so openly directed at him, straightened up smartly—the soldier tugged on the chain as well—and said, "The matter is as follows. Here, in the penal colony, I have been appointed judge. Despite my youth. For I assisted the former commandant in all penal cases, and I also know the machine best. The principle according to which I decide is: 'Guilt is always beyond all doubt.' Other courts cannot follow this principle, since they comprise various authorities and have even higher courts above them. That is not the case here, or at least it wasn't so under the former commandant. It is true that the new commandant has already shown an inclination to meddle in my court, but so far I have managed to ward him off, and I will continue to do so.—You wanted to have this case explained: it's as simple as all the others. This morning a captain reported that this man, who is assigned to him as his orderly and sleeps outside his door, was found sleeping while on duty.[4] You see, it is his duty to get up whenever the clock strikes the hour and salute the captain's door. Certainly not a very difficult duty, but a necessary one, since he needs to stay fresh in order both to keep watch and be on call. Last night the captain wanted to check whether his orderly was doing his duty. As the clock was striking two, he opened the door and found the man curled up asleep. The captain went for his riding crop and hit the man in the face. Now, instead of getting up and begging forgiveness, the man seized his master by the legs, shook him, and cried, 'Throw the whip away, or I'll eat you alive.'[5]—Those are the facts of the matter. The captain came to me an hour ago; I took down his statement and immediately added the judgment. Then I had the man put in chains. That was all very simple. If I had first summoned the man and interrogated him, it would only have led to confusion. He would have lied; if I had succeeded in refuting these lies, he would have substituted new lies for them, and so forth. Now, however, I've got him and will not let him go.—Does that explain everything? But time flies; the execution is already supposed to begin, and I still haven't finished explaining the machine." He urged the traveler to take his seat, went up to the machine again, and began: "As you see, the harrow corresponds to the form of a man's body; here is the harrow for the upper part of the body, here are the harrows for the legs. For the head there is only this little graver. Is that clear to you?" He leaned over to the traveler in a friendly fashion, prepared for the most comprehensive explanations.

The traveler looked at the harrow with his brow creased. The account of the legal procedure had not satisfied him. Nevertheless, he had to remind himself that this was a penal colony, that special disciplinary measures were necessary here, and that military procedures had to prevail throughout. Besides, he had some hope for the new commandant, who apparently intended introducing, however slowly, a new procedure, one that could not penetrate the narrow-

4. This moment alludes to a similar moment in "Before the Law" (p. 68). Like the wretched orderly in *In the Penal Colony*, the man from the country is also found in front of a door—the Gates of the Law. Since this petitioner passes the rest of his days there, he too can occasionally be found asleep. But whereas the man from the country is shown questing for a higher authority—the Law—the poor wretch in *In the Penal Colony* encounters an authority no higher than a penal battalion commander who wants him killed. Here we have an expression of Kafka's impulse to parody his higher concerns. Tragic moments in his work tend to have a comic or dispiriting counterpart: the attempt to escape ordinary life in the pursuit of (outlandishly) high values is revealed to be futile or blind, a mere invitation to death. But both the higher quest and its mockery are essential aspects of his vision.
5. The German word for what human beings normally do when they eat is *essen*; the word for what animals do when they eat is *fressen*. Here Kafka uses the word *fressen*: the orderly, who has been treated like a dog, threatens to eat his tormentor like a dog.

mindedness of this officer. Following this line of thought, the traveler asked: "Will the commandant attend the execution?" "It is not certain," said the officer, pained by the direct question, and his amiable expression grew contorted: "That's precisely why we have to hurry. And as sorry as I am, I will have to curtail my explanations. But tomorrow, certainly, when the machine has been cleaned—the only thing wrong with it is that it gets so filthy—I can fill in more detailed explanations. So for now, only the essentials.—When the man is lying on the bed and the bed begins to vibrate, the harrow is lowered onto his body. It adjusts automatically so that it just barely touches the body with the tips of its needles; once it has settled into position, this steel cable immediately stiffens into a rod. And now the play begins. The uninitiated observer notices no outward difference between punishments. The harrow appears to operate uniformly. Quivering, it sticks its needles into the body, which is itself quivering from the vibration of the bed. In order to make it possible for everyone to examine the execution of the judgment, the harrow is made of glass. Various technical difficulties were involved in inserting the needles, but after a number of trials we succeeded. That's right, we spared no effort. And now anyone can watch through the glass as the inscription takes shape on the body. Won't you come closer and have a look at the needles?"

The traveler rose slowly, walked toward the machine, and bent over the harrow. "Here you see," said the officer, "two sorts of needles in multiple arrangements. Each long one has a short one next to it. The long ones do the writing, and the short ones squirt water to wash away the blood and keep the inscription clear at all times.[6] The bloody water is then channeled into little runnels and finally flows into this main runnel and down the drainpipe into the pit." With his finger the officer indicated the exact route the bloody water was forced to take. When, to make it as vivid as possible, he acted out actually catching the water at the mouth of the drainpipe with both hands, the traveler raised his head and, groping backward with his hand, tried to return to his chair. Then he saw to his horror that, like him, the condemned man had also accepted the officer's invitation to have a look at the harrow up close. He had dragged the sleepy soldier forward a little by the chain and was also bending over the glass. One could see how, with shifting eyes, he was searching for what the two gentlemen had just observed, but since he had not grasped the explanation, he could not succeed. He bent over this way and that. Again and again he ran his eyes over

6. The German word that is translated throughout as "inscription" or "writing" is *Schrift*, which has the overtone of a sacred text: in German the Bible is *Die Heilige Schrift* (literally, "Holy Scripture," "holy writ"). Furthermore, the word *Schrift* in its meaning of "what has been written" can direct our attention to the meaning of the words or signs on the page and the shape of the letters or graphic elements forming these words or signs.

the glass. The traveler wanted to drive him back, since he was probably committing a punishable offense. But the officer restrained the traveler firmly with one hand and with the other took a lump of dirt from the rampart and threw it at the soldier. The latter opened his eyes with a jerk, saw what the condemned man had dared to do, dropped his rifle, planted his heels into the ground, yanked the condemned man back so hard that he immediately fell down, and then stood looking down at him as he writhed and rattled his chains. "Get him up!" shouted the officer, for he noticed that the traveler was becoming much too distracted by the condemned man. The traveler was even leaning all the way over the harrow, oblivious of it, only trying to determine what was happening with the condemned man. "Handle him carefully," shouted the officer again. He ran around the machine, grabbed the condemned man under the arm himself, and, as the man's feet were continually sliding out from under him, got him up with the help of the soldier.

"I know everything now," said the traveler when the officer returned. "Except the most important part," the officer said, taking the traveler by the arm and pointing upward: "There, in the scriber, is the mechanism that regulates the movement of the harrow, and this mechanism is calibrated to the design that corresponds to the text of the judgment. I am still using the designs of the former commandant. Here they are,"—he pulled several sheets from the leather folder— "but unfortunately I cannot let you hold them; they are the most valuable things I own. Sit down, I'll show them to you from this distance, then you'll be able to see everything clearly." He showed the first sheet. The traveler would gladly have said something in the way of acknowledgment, but he saw only labyrinthine lines intersecting at various points, covering the paper so thickly that it was an effort to detect the white spaces between them. "Read it," said the officer. "I can't," said the traveler. "But it's clear," said the officer. "It is very artistic," said the traveler evasively, "but I cannot decipher it." "Yes," said the officer, laughed, and stuck the sheet back into the folder, "it's not a primer of beautiful lettering for schoolchildren. You've got to study it for a long time. I'm sure that even you would recognize it in the end. Of course it can't be just a simple script; after all, it's not supposed to kill right away but only over twelve hours, on average; the turning point is calculated for the sixth hour. So the genuine script has to be surrounded by many, many ornaments; the real script encircles the body only in a narrow belt; the rest of the body is meant for adornments. Now can you appreciate the work of the harrow and of the whole machine?—Watch this!" He jumped on the ladder, turned a wheel, and called down: "Careful, step to one side," and the whole apparatus was set in motion. If the wheel had not squeaked, it would have been magnificent. As if the officer had been surprised at this irritating wheel, he threatened it with his fist, then, excusing himself, held out his arms to the traveler and hurriedly clambered down in order to observe the movement of the machine from below. Something that only he noticed was still not right; he clambered up again, thrust both hands into the bowels of the scriber, then, so as to get down more quickly, instead of using the ladder, slid down one of the rods and in order to be heard over the din, shouted as loudly as he could into the traveler's ear, "Do you understand the process? The harrow begins to write; when it has finished writing the first draft on the man's back, the cotton layer rolls and slowly heaves the body to one side in order to make more room for the harrow. In the meantime the places where the wounds have been inscribed[7] settle against the cotton, which, because of its special preparation, immediately stops the bleeding and clears the way for the script to sink in more deeply. Here, as the body continues to turn, the serrated edge of the harrow tears the cotton from the wounds, flings it into the pit, and the harrow gets back to work. And so it goes on writing, more and more deeply, for twelve hours. During the first six hours the condemned man lives almost as he did before, except that he is in pain. After two hours the felt plug is removed, since the man no longer has the strength to scream. Here, in this electrically heated bowl at the head of the bed, we put warm congee, from which the man, if he so desires, can have whatever he can lap up with his tongue.[8] Not one of them passes up the opportunity. I know of no one, and my experience is vast. It is only around the sixth hour that he loses all pleasure in eating. At that point I usually kneel down here and observe this phenomenon. The man rarely swallows the last mouthful, he just rolls it around in his mouth and spits it out into the pit. Then I have to duck; otherwise it flies into my face. But how quiet the man becomes around the sixth hour! Understanding dawns even on the dumbest. It begins around the eyes.

7. To convey this idea, Kafka has invented a German phrase, *wundbeschriebene Stellen*. German has a similar-sounding phrase, the familiar expression *wundgeriebene Stellen*, which means, literally, "places [on the body]" (*Stellen*) that have been "rubbed" (*gerieben*) "sore" (*wund*). Kafka uses the phonic resemblance between *gerieben* (rubbed) and *beschrieben* (described, "be-written") to indicate the wounds that the writing inflicts. A parallel to such a conception is found in the biblical phrase, "I will put my law in their inward parts, and write it in their hearts" (Jeremiah 31:33).

8. Note the strange luxury of the electrically heated bowl—the word *Napf* (bowl) is used particularly for an animal's food bowl. The tortured man is both treated as an animal and pampered; we have here a visualization of the logic of carrot and stick, which is even more vivid in the original, for the German expression of this logic is *Zuckerbrot und Peitsche*—sweet cakes and the whip!

   The German word for what the prisoner eats is *Reisbrei*, literally "rice porridge." I have chosen "congee," the term in general use in Asian communities for this sort of porridge, since the setting of this penal colony is Asian, as we can deduce both from internal clues and from the fact that this story at times mirrors Octave Mirbeau's 1899 novel *Torture Garden*, which is set on an Asian island.

From there it spreads. A sight that could seduce one to lie down alongside him under the harrow. Nothing more actually happens, the man merely begins to decipher the script, he purses his lips as if he were listening hard. You've seen that it is not easy to decipher the script with your eyes, but our man deciphers it with his wounds. Certainly it's a lot of work; it takes six hours before it's done. But then the harrow skewers him through and tosses him into the pit, where he splashes down on the bloody water and the cotton. With that, the judgment has been accomplished, and we—the soldier and I—put him in the ground.

The traveler had inclined his ear to the officer and with his hands in his jacket pockets was watching the machine do its work. The condemned man was watching it too, though understanding nothing. He bent down a little and was following the wavering needles when the soldier, at a signal from the officer, took his knife and cut through the back of the condemned man's shirt and trousers so that they dropped off him; he tried to snatch at the falling garments to hide his nakedness, but the soldier lifted him into the air and shook the last shreds from his body. The officer turned off the machine, and in the silence that followed, the condemned man was laid under the harrow. His chains were removed and the straps were fastened instead; in the first moment it seemed almost to be a relief to the condemned man. And now the harrow dropped down a little farther, for he was a skinny man. As the points of the needles touched him, a shudder ran over his skin; while the soldier was busy with his right hand, he stretched out his left, without knowing where, but it was pointing toward the place where the traveler was standing. From the side the officer looked uninterruptedly at the traveler, as if he were trying to read his face for the impression the execution—which he had, after all explained, at least superficially—was making on him.[9]

The strap meant for the wrist tore; the soldier must have pulled it too tight. The officer's help was needed; the soldier showed him the piece of torn-off strap. So the officer went over to him and said, his face turned to the traveler: "The machine is a complex of so many parts that at one point or another something must tear or break, but that is no reason to be shaken in one's basic judgment. Besides, a substitute for the strap is immediately procured; I'll use a chain; true, the delicacy of the oscillations meant for the right arm will be impaired." And while he put on the chains, he added: "At present the means for maintaining the machine are very limited. Under the former commandant I always had access to an ac-

---

9. The officer is reading an impression on the surface of the flesh of the traveler—as though the judgment had been inscribed on him as well and could be read on his skin as a literal "impression."

count designated just for this purpose. There was a warehouse here in which every conceivable spare part was stored. I admit that I made rather excessive use of it, I mean formerly, not now, as alleged by the new commandant, for whom everything serves as a pretext for attacking the old institutions. Now he has personally taken charge of the machine account; and if I send for a new strap, the torn one is demanded as proof, and it takes ten days for the new one to get here, and then it's of an inferior make and of almost no use. But how I'm supposed to operate the machine in the meantime without a strap—that's something no one is concerned about."

The traveler reflected: It is always a sensitive matter to interfere decisively in other people's affairs. He was neither a citizen of the penal colony nor a citizen of the country to which it belonged. If he wanted to condemn or even block this execution, they could say to him: You're a foreigner, keep quiet. To this there was no response except to add that in this case he did not even understand himself, since he was traveling with the sole purpose of observing and by no means altering other people's legal institutions. Here, however, the situation was certainly very tempting. The injustice of the procedure and the inhumanity of the execution were beyond all doubt. No one could attribute any sort of self-interest to the traveler, since the condemned man was a stranger to him, he was not a compatriot, and he certainly did not arouse pity. The traveler himself came with recommendations from high authorities, had been received here with great politeness, and the very fact that he had been invited to this execution appeared to indicate that his judgment on this court was desired. This last was all the more likely since the commandant, as had by now been made more than clear to him, was no friend of this procedure and had an almost hostile attitude to the officer.

At this point the traveler heard a scream of rage coming from the officer. Not without difficulty, he had just managed to shove the felt plug into the condemned man's mouth when the man, in an irresistible fit of nausea, shut his eyes and vomited. The officer hurriedly pulled him off the plug, trying to turn his head toward the pit, but it was too late, the filth[1] was already running down the machine. "It's all the fault of the commandant!" cried the officer, beside himself, rattling the brass rods in front; "my machine is being soiled like a pigsty." With trembling hands he showed the traveler what had happened. "Haven't I spent hours and hours trying to make the commandant understand that you are not supposed to

---

1. Kafka uses an elevated word for "filth" (*Unrat*), which contains the idea of helplessness, of literally being without *Rat* or "counsel." The man has had no counsel. The choice of words again shows Kafka's tendency to elevate things that are disgusting and to make a mockery of higher things (see n. 4, p. 41).

serve the condemned man any food for one whole day before the execution? But the new lenient thinking is of a different opinion. Before the man is led off to execution, the commandant's ladies stuff his face full of sweets.[2] All his life he's lived on stinking fish, and now he has to eat sweets! But I could accept that, I would have no objection, but why haven't I been given a new felt plug, something I've been pleading for for the past three months. How could anyone not be disgusted by putting into his mouth a piece of felt[3] that more than a hundred men have sucked and bitten on as they lay dying?"

The condemned man had laid his head down and looked peaceful; the soldier was busy cleaning the machine with the condemned man's shirt. The officer went up to the traveler, who having some sort of presentiment, had taken a step backward, but the officer took him by the hand and led him to one side. "I want to tell you something in confidence," he said; "may I?" "Certainly," said the traveler and listened with lowered eyes.

"This procedure and this execution, which you now have the opportunity of admiring, have no open advocates in our colony any longer. I am their only defender and at the same time the only one who defends the old commandant's legacy. I can no longer plan a further expansion of the procedure, it takes all my energy just to hold on to what we have. When the old commandant was alive, the colony was full of his followers; I have something of the old commandant's power of persuasion but none of his authority; as a consequence his followers have gone into hiding; there are still plenty of them, but no one admits to it. If today, look, an execution day, you go to the teahouse and eavesdrop, you'll probably hear only ambiguous utterances. All of them are loyal followers, but under the present commandant and given his present views, they are totally useless for me. And now I ask you: on account of this commandant and the women who influence him, is such a lifework"—he pointed to the machine—"to be ruined? Can we let that happen? Even if one is only a foreigner visiting our island for a few days? But there's no time to lose, preparations are being made to move against my jurisdiction; deliberations have already begun in the office of the commandant, from which I am excluded; even your visit today seems to me characteristic of the whole situation; they are cowards and send you, a foreigner, out in advance.—How different executions were in former times! As early as the day before the execution

2. The German word here translated as "face" is actually the German word for "throat"; recall that the back of the officer's own "throat"—his neck—is stuffed full of ladies' handkerchiefs.
3. This felt (*Filz*) is the ultimate proof of the new commandant's stinginess regarding replacement parts; *filzen* in German means "to be mean or stingy." Again, we see Kafka playing with the literal meaning of a figure of speech.

the whole valley already overflowed with people, everyone came just to watch; early in the morning the commandant would appear with his ladies; fanfares roused the entire camp; I gave the report that everything was in readiness; the audience—no high-ranking official was allowed to be absent—took their places around the machine; this stack of cane chairs is a paltry remnant from that time. The machine would gleam, freshly polished; for almost every execution I installed new spare parts. Before hundreds of eyes—all the spectators, all the way up there, to the heights, stood on tiptoe—the condemned man was laid under the harrow by the commandant himself. What today a common soldier is allowed to do used to be my task, the task of the presiding judge, and it honored me. And so the execution would begin! No discordant note disturbed the work of the machine. Many people had stopped watching and lay in the sand, their eyes closed; everyone knew: Now justice is being done. In the silence you heard only the condemned man's moans, muted by the felt plug. Today the machine no longer manages to squeeze a moan out of the condemned man louder than the felt can stifle, but in those days the writing needles dripped an acid fluid that we are no longer allowed to use. Well, and then the sixth hour would come around! It was impossible to grant everyone's request to watch from up close. In his wisdom the commandant ordered that children should be given priority; I, of course, by virtue of my office, was always allowed to stay. I would often be squatting there, with two little children in my arms, right and left. How we all took in the expression of transfiguration from his martyred face, how we bathed our cheeks in the radiance of this justice finally achieved and already vanishing![4] What times these were, my comrade!" The officer had evidently forgotten who was standing before him; he had embraced the traveler and laid his head on his shoulder. The traveler was completely at a loss;[5] he looked impatiently past the officer. The soldier had finished cleaning up and was now pouring congee from a can into the bowl. The condemned man, who seemed to have recovered completely, had hardly noticed this than he began to snap at the porridge with his tongue. Again and again

4. The word here translated as "radiance" is the German word *Schein*, which means "shining" but also "semblance, seeming." The word produces an ambiguity impossible to capture in a single English word, suggesting that this moment of alleged illumination is also a mere illusion. The sentence contains another moment of exquisite ambiguity. The German word *endlich* usually means "finally," but it can also mean "finitely" or "earthly," so that the alleged radiance occurs in a merely finite, earthly manner, expressive of what is called "finitude" and hence without transcendental significance. Thus, running through the passage is the subtle countersense that what we are dealing with is a mere semblance of higher illumination, an event that takes place in a finite, limited, world barren of truth.

5. The German words are *in grosser Verlegenheit*, the same words that begin the story "A Country Doctor" and reappear in "A Dream," where, for reasons of context, they are translated as "deeply embarrassed"—a primordially Kafkan situation.

the soldier shoved him away, since the porridge was meant for later, but it was certainly highly irregular, too, that the soldier should stick his filthy hands into the basin and eat out of it in front of the ravenous condemned man.

The officer quickly recovered his composure. "I wasn't trying to play on your emotions," he said. "I know, it's impossible to make those times comprehensible today. In any case, the machine still works and is effective in its own way. It is effective even when it stands by itself in this valley. And at the end the corpse still drops into the pit in an incomprehensibly gentle glide even if hundreds of people no longer congregate as they did then, like flies around the pit. In those days we had to install a strong railing around the pit; it was torn down long ago."

The traveler wanted to avert his face from the officer and looked around aimlessly. The officer thought that he was contemplating the barrenness of the valley; he therefore seized his hands, spun around him in order to catch his eye, and asked: "Do you see the disgrace?"

But the traveler kept silent. For a while the officer let him be; with legs spread apart, his hands on his hips, he stood still and looked at the ground. Then he smiled encouragingly at the traveler and said, "Yesterday I was standing nearby when the commandant invited you. I heard the invitation. I know the commandant. I understood the purpose of his invitation at once. Although he has enough power to proceed against me, he does not yet dare to do so; instead he will subject me to your judgment, the judgment of a distinguished foreigner. He has calculated carefully: this is your second day on the island; you did not know the old commandant and the range of his ideas. You are conditioned by European points of view, maybe you are fundamentally opposed to the death penalty in general and this sort of execution by a machine in particular. You notice, furthermore, how the execution proceeds without the participation of the public, in a sorry state, on a machine that is already somewhat damaged—now, all things considered (so the commandant thinks), would it not be easily possible that you would not consider my procedure correct? And if you do not consider it correct, you will not keep quiet (I am still speaking from the commandant's point of view), since you are sure to rely on your own tried-and-true convictions. Admittedly, you have seen and learned to respect many peculiar customs of many peoples. And so you will probably not speak out against the procedure with all the force at your command, as perhaps you might do at home. But the commandant doesn't need that at all. A passing remark, merely an unconsidered word is enough. It does not even have to represent your true opinion as long as it seems to serve his purpose. He will ask you one shrewd question after another, I'm certain of that. And his ladies will sit around in a circle and prick up their ears. You might say something like, 'In our country the legal procedure is different,' or 'In our country the defendant is interrogated before the judgment,' or 'In our country the condemned man is informed of his judgment,' or 'In our country not all penalties are death penalties,' or 'In our country we used torture only in the Middle Ages.' All these remarks are just as correct as they seem self-evident to you, innocent remarks that do not invalidate my procedure. But how will the commandant react to them? I can see him, our good commandant, immediately shoving his chair to one side and hurrying onto the balcony; I can see his ladies streaming after him; now I can hear his voice—his ladies call it a thunderous voice—and he speaks: 'A great researcher[6] from the West, with the mission of examining the legal procedures in all the countries of the world, has just declared that our old traditional procedure is inhumane. Given this judgment by so distinguished a personage, it is naturally no longer possible for me to tolerate this procedure. And so, from today on, I decree'—and so forth. You are on the point of interjecting that you never said what he proclaims, you did not call my procedure inhumane; on the contrary, in accordance with your deep insight, you consider it the most humane of procedures, most worthy of a human being; you also admire this machinery—but it is too late; you never get on the balcony, which is already full of ladies; you want to draw attention to yourself; you want to shout; but a lady's hand covers your mouth—and both I and the work of the old commandant are done for."

The traveler had to suppress a smile; so the task he had imagined to be so difficult was that easy. He said evasively: "You overestimate my influence; the commandant read my letter of introduction, he knows that I am not an expert on legal procedure. If I were to offer an opinion, it would be the opinion of a private person,[7] no more significant than that of any other person and in any case a lot less significant than the opinion of the commandant, who, if I'm right in my belief, exercises very extensive authority in this penal colony. If he has made up his mind about this procedure as definitely as you think, then, I'm afraid, the end of this procedure has certainly come and doesn't require my modest assistance."

Had the officer finally grasped this? No, he still had not grasped it. He shook his head vigorously, looked back briefly at the condemned man and the soldier, both of whom flinched and stopped eating the congee, stepped close to the traveler, looked not at his

6. Here the man who has previously and most often been described as a *Reisender* (literally, "traveler") is described by the officer as a *Forscher* ("research scientist").
7. Compare *der Private Pallas* (a person of private means) in "A Fratricide" (p. 73).

face but somewhere at his jacket, and said more softly than before: "You do not know the commandant; your relation to him and to all of us—forgive the expression—is, so to speak, without guile; your influence, believe me, cannot be estimated too highly. In fact, I was overjoyed to hear that you were to attend the execution by yourself. This order of the commandant was aimed at me; now, however, I shall turn it to my advantage. Undistracted by biased whispers and contemptuous glances—something that could not have been avoided if more people were participating in the execution—you have heard my explanations, seen the machine, and are now about to view the execution. Your judgment no doubt already stands firm; should some small uncertainties still remain, the sight of the execution will do away with them. And now I ask of you: Help me against the commandant!"

The traveler did not let him speak further. "How could I do that?" he cried out, "That is quite impossible. I can no more help you than I can harm you."

"You can," said the officer. With some apprehension the traveler saw that the officer was clenching his fists. "You can," the officer repeated even more urgently. "I have a plan that can't help but succeed. You think that your influence would not be enough. I know that it is enough. But even granted that you're right, isn't it still necessary to leave nothing untried to keep this procedure alive, even measures that might not be adequate? So listen to my plan. To carry it out, it will be necessary first of all for you to keep all judgment about the procedure to yourself as much as possible in the colony today. Under no circumstances must you say anything unless you are specifically asked; if you must speak, your remarks must be brief and noncommittal; let people notice that it is difficult for you to discuss the matter, that you are embittered, that if you were to speak openly, you'd be tempted to break out in curses. I'm not asking you to lie, not at all; you should just answer briefly, for example, 'Yes, I saw the execution,' or 'Yes, I've heard all the explanations.' That's all, nothing more. There are certainly grounds enough for the bitterness that they are supposed to notice—even if not in the way the commandant thinks. Naturally he will completely misunderstand and interpret matters to suit himself. That is the basis of my plan. Tomorrow an important meeting, chaired by the commandant himself, will take place at the commandant's headquarters, attended by all the high-ranking administrative officials. Naturally, the commandant has managed to turn these meetings into public spectacles. They have built a gallery that is always packed with spectators. I am forced to be present at the councils, but I shake with revulsion. In any case, you will certainly be invited to the session; if today you act according to my plan, the invitation will turn into an urgent request. But if for some obscure reason you are not invited, you must certainly ask for an invitation; there's no doubt then that you'll receive it. So, tomorrow you are sitting with the ladies in the commandant's box. He'll glance upward again and again to make sure you're there. After various trivial, ridiculous items on the agenda intended only for the audience—mostly harbor construction, always harbor construction!—the legal proceedings are submitted for discussion. In case the topic should not be raised, or not raised soon enough, by the commandant, I will make sure to bring it up. I will stand and deliver my report of today's execution. Very briefly, just the report. Admittedly, such a report is not usually delivered there, but I will do it anyway. The commandant thanks me, as always, with a friendly smile, and now, unable to contain himself, he seizes this propitious opportunity. 'Just now,' he'll say, or words to that effect, 'the report of the execution has been delivered. I should like to add to this report only that this very execution was attended by the great researcher whose visit you are all aware of and which brings such extraordinary honor to our colony. His presence here also increases the importance of our meeting today. Shall we not now ask this great researcher for his judgment on our traditional mode of execution and on the procedure that leads up to it?' Of course, there is general applause, everyone is in favor, and I am the loudest. The commandant bows to you and says, 'Then, in the name of all those assembled here, I submit the question.' And now you step up to the railing. Place your hands for everyone to see, otherwise the ladies will grab them and play with your fingers.—And now, finally, you are about to speak. I don't know how I can bear the tension, the hours to that moment. Don't hold back in your speech, raise a big ruckus with the truth, lean over the railing, roar, yes, roar your judgment, your unshakable opinion, at the commandant. Or perhaps you don't want to do that, it's not in your nature, perhaps in your home country people behave differently in such situations; that, too, is all right, that, too, is perfectly satisfactory; don't even stand up, just say a few words, whisper them so that the officials below you can barely hear them, that will be enough; you don't even have to mention the lack of attendance at the execution, the squeaking wheel, the torn strap, the disgusting piece of felt; no, I'll take over and do all the rest, and believe me, if my speech doesn't drive him out of the conference hall, it will force him to his knees, so that he must confess: Old commandant, I bow down before you.—That is my plan, are you willing to help me carry it out? But of course you're willing, and more than that, you must." And the officer took hold of both the traveler's arms and looked into his face, breathing heavily. He had shouted the final sentences so loudly that even the soldier and the condemned man had begun to take notice; despite the fact that they understood nothing, they stopped eating and, chewing, looked at the traveler.

From the outset the traveler had no doubt about the answer he had to give; he had experienced too much in his lifetime to waver here; he was basically honorable, and he was not afraid. Even so, he hesitated for a heartbeat now at the sight of the soldier and the condemned man. Finally, however, he said, as he had to: "No." The officer blinked once, and then again, but never took his eyes from the traveler. "Do you want an explanation?" the traveler asked. The officer nodded silently. "I am opposed to this procedure," the traveler said; "even before you took me into your confidence—I will, of course, under no circumstances betray your confidence—I had already considered whether I would be within my rights to take steps against this procedure and whether my intervention would have the smallest chance of success. It was clear to me to whom I had to turn first in this matter: naturally, to the commandant. You have made that even clearer to me—without, however, having strengthened my decision. On the contrary, your honest conviction affects me deeply, even if it cannot sway me from my purpose."

The officer remained silent, turned toward the machine, took hold of one of the brass rods, and then, leaning back a little, looked up at the scriber, as if to check that everything was in order. The soldier and the condemned man appeared to have made friends; the condemned man made signs to the soldier, as difficult as this was to do while he was strapped down tightly; the soldier bent down to him; the condemned man whispered something, and the soldier nodded.

The traveler followed the officer and said, "You still don't know what I intend to do. I will tell the commandant my views on the procedure, true, but privately, not during the meeting; I am also not going to stay here long enough to be called in to any sort of meeting. I shall leave early tomorrow, or at least I'll go aboard my ship."

It did not seem that the officer had been listening. "So the procedure has not convinced you," he said to himself and smiled, the way an old man smiles at the nonsense of a child and keeps his own true thoughts to himself behind the smile.

"Then, the time has come," he said finally and suddenly looked at the traveler with shining eyes that held a kind of summons, some call to participate.

"The time for what?" asked the traveler uneasily, but he did not receive an answer.

"You are free," said the officer to the condemned man in the man's language. At first the latter did not believe it. "I said you're free," said the officer. For the first time the face of the condemned man showed real signs of life. Was it the truth? Was it just a whim on the part of the officer, one that might pass? Had the foreign traveler obtained a pardon for him? What was it? This was what his face seemed to ask. But not for long. Whatever the case might be, he wanted to be really free, if possible, and he began to shake himself to the extent that the harrow allowed it.

"You're tearing my straps," shouted the officer; "hold still. We're opening them." And together with the soldier, to whom he signaled, he set to work. The condemned man laughed softly to himself without speaking, turning his face now to the left, to the officer, and now to the right, to the soldier; nor did he forget the traveler.

"Pull him out," the officer ordered the soldier. Some precautions had to be taken here because of the harrow. By dint of his impatience, the condemned man's back had already suffered some minor lacerations.

From now on, however, the officer hardly concerned himself with him. He went up to the traveler, again produced the little leather folder, leafed through it, and finally found the sheet he was looking for, which he showed to the traveler. "Read it," he said. "I can't," said the traveler; "I already told you I cannot read these sheets." "But look closely at the sheet," said the officer and came up next to the traveler in order to read it along with him. When that did not help either, he waved his little finger high over it, as if in no case must the sheet be touched, in order to make it easier for the traveler to read. The traveler made an effort, so that he could oblige the officer at least in this respect, but it was impossible. Now the officer began to spell out the inscription letter for letter and then read it again in context. "It says, 'Be just!'" he said once more; "now you can surely read it." The traveler bent so low over the paper that the officer moved it farther away, fearing that it would be touched; the traveler said nothing more, true, but it was clear that he still had not been able to read it. "It says, 'Be just!'" the officer repeated. "Maybe," said the traveler, "I believe that that's what it says." "Well, good," said the officer, at least partly satisfied, and page in hand, climbed up the ladder; with great care he embedded the sheet in the scriber and appeared to rearrange the machinery completely; it was very arduous work; it must have involved very small gears as well; sometimes the officer's head disappeared into the scriber altogether, since he had to examine the mechanism so minutely.

From below, the traveler followed the work without respite; his neck grew stiff and his eyes hurt from the sky drenched in sunlight. The soldier and the condemned man were occupied only with each other. The condemned man's shirt and trousers, which already lay in the pit, were fished out by the soldier with the point of his bayonet. The shirt was horribly filthy, and the condemned man rinsed it in the water pail. When he put on his shirt and trousers, the soldier, like the condemned man, had to laugh out loud, for the garments were, of course, slit in two in the back. Perhaps the condemned man felt it his duty to entertain the soldier; in his tattered clothing he whirled around in a circle before the soldier, who squatted on the ground and slapped his knees with laughter. Still, they restrained themselves out of consideration for the gentlemen's presence.

When the officer was finally finished up above, he gazed, smiling, once again at the whole and all its parts; now he clapped shut the lid of the scriber, which until now had been open, climbed down, looked into the pit and then at the condemned man, noted with satisfaction that he had pulled out his clothing, then went to the pail to wash his hands, saw too late the disgusting filth, was sad that he could not wash his hands now, finally dipped them in the sand—he was not satisfied with this substitute but had to make do—then stood and began to unbutton his uniform jacket. On doing so, the two lady's handkerchiefs that he had squeezed under the back of his collar immediately fell into his hands. "Here are your handkerchiefs," he said, throwing them to the condemned man. And to the traveler he said by way of explanation, "A gift from the ladies."

Despite the obvious haste with which he took off his uniform jacket and then fully undressed, he still treated each garment very carefully, deliberately stroking the silver laces on his tunic and shaking a tassel into place. But it hardly fitted in with the care he was taking that as soon as he had finished handling a piece of clothing, he immediately threw it into the pit with an indignant jerk. The last thing left to him was his short sword with its belt. He drew the sword from the sheath, broke it, then collected everything—the pieces of sword, the sheath, and the belt—and threw these things away with such a violent gesture that they clanged down in the pit below.

Now he stood there naked. The traveler bit his lips and said nothing. He knew what would happen, true, but he had no right to stop the officer in any way. If the legal procedure to which the officer was devoted was really so near to being eliminated—possibly as a consequence of the traveler's intervention, to which the latter, for his part, felt committed—then the officer was now acting quite correctly; the traveler would not have acted any differently in his place.

The soldier and the condemned man understood nothing at first; at the beginning they were not even watching. The condemned man was very glad to get the handkerchiefs back, but he was not permitted to enjoy them for long, for the soldier took them from him with a rapid grab that was impossible to anticipate. Now the condemned man tried once again to pull the handkerchiefs from the back of the soldier's belt, where the soldier had stowed them, but the soldier was watchful. And so they fought, half-jokingly. It was only after the officer was completely naked that they diverted their attention. The condemned man, especially, appeared to have been struck by the intimation of some great reversal. What had happened to him was now happening to the officer. Perhaps the process would play out to the bitter end. The foreign traveler had probably given the order for it. So this was revenge. Without himself having suffered all the way, he was avenged all the way. A broad, noiseless laugh appeared on his face and never left it again.

The officer, however, had turned to the machine. If it had been clear before that he understood the machine well, it was now almost staggering to see the intimacy he enjoyed with it and how it responded to him. He had merely brought his hand near to the harrow when it raised and lowered itself several times until it achieved the correct position to receive him; he merely clutched the edge of the bed when it began to vibrate; the felt plug met his mouth halfway, you could see that the officer did not really want it, but his hesitation lasted only a moment, he immediately acquiesced and took it in. Everything was ready except that the straps still hung down at the sides, but they were evidently unnecessary, there was no need to strap the officer down. Then the condemned man noticed the loose straps; in his opinion the execution was not perfect as long as the straps were not buckled tight; he zealously waved to the soldier, and the two of them ran to strap in the officer. The latter had already stretched out one foot to kick the crank that would set the scriber in motion when he saw that the men had arrived; he pulled back his foot and let himself be strapped down. Now, of course, he could no longer reach the crank; neither the soldier nor the condemned man would be able to find it, and the traveler was determined not to budge from the spot. It wasn't necessary; the straps had hardly been fastened when the machine began to run; the bed vibrated, the needles danced over his skin, the harrow swayed up and down. The traveler had already been staring at this for some time before he remembered that one of the scriber's wheels was supposed to be squeaking; but everything was still, not the softest humming could be heard.

As a result of this quiet operation, the machine literally escaped notice. The traveler looked over at the soldier and the condemned man. The condemned man was the livelier of the two; everything about the machine interested him; now he was bending down, now he was stretching up; his index finger was continually pointed to show the soldier something. The traveler was painfully embarrassed. He was determined to stay here to the end, but he could not have endured the sight of these two for long. "Go home," he said. The soldier might have been ready to do so, but the condemned man felt the order like a punishment. He pleaded with clasped hands to be allowed to stay; and when the traveler, shaking his head, would not agree, he even went down on his knees. The traveler saw that commands were useless here and was about to go over to the men and drive them away. Then he heard a noise in the scriber overhead. He looked up. Was that one cogwheel going to cause trouble after all? No, this was something else. Slowly the lid of the scriber lifted and then flew wide open. The teeth of a cogwheel became visible and rose up farther, and soon the whole wheel appeared; it was as if some great force were compressing the scriber so that there was no longer any room for this wheel; the wheel rotated to the edge of the scriber, fell to the ground, rolled upright for a ways in the sand, and then lay on its side. But above, another wheel was already rising, followed by many others, big ones and small ones and others hardly distinguishable from one another; the same thing was happening with all of them; you kept thinking that by now the scriber would have to be empty when a new, especially numerous group appeared, rose, fell down below, rolled in the sand, and came to a stop. With such goings on, the condemned man completely forgot the traveler's order; he was totally delighted by the wheels; he kept trying to grab one, at the same time urging the soldier to help him, but then he pulled back his hand in fright, for the wheel was immediately followed by another, which terrified him, at least as it started to roll.

The traveler, on the other hand, was deeply uneasy; the machine was obviously falling apart; its quiet motion was deceptive; he felt that now he had to look out for the officer, since the latter could no longer take care of himself. But while the falling of the cogwheels was demanding all his attention, he had forgotten to observe the rest of the machine; now, however, after the last wheel had left the scriber and he bent over the harrow, he had a new, even worse surprise. The harrow was not writing, it was merely stabbing, and the bed was not turning the body but merely lifting it, quivering, into the needles. The traveler wanted to intervene, possibly bring the whole thing to a stop: this was not the torture that the officer had wanted to achieve, this was plain murder. He stretched out his hands. But the harrow where the body was impaled was already tilting to one side, as it usually did only in the twelfth hour. Blood flowed in a hundred streams, not mixed with water: this time the water pipes had also failed. And now the final stage also failed: the body did not become detached from the long needles; it poured out its blood but hung over the pit without dropping. The harrow was attempting a return to its old position but, as if it had noticed that it had not yet been freed of its burden, stayed motionless over the pit. "Come and help!" shouted the traveler to the soldier and the condemned man, and he grabbed the officer's feet. He meant to push against the feet on his side while on the other side the two men would grab the officer's head so that he might slowly be lifted clear of the needles. But now the two of them could not make up their minds to come; the condemned man practically turned the other way; the traveler had to go to them and forcibly shove them toward the officer's head. While doing so, he saw, almost against his will, the face of the corpse. It was as it had been in life; no sign of the promised deliverance could be detected; what all the others had found in the machine the officer did not find; his lips were firmly pressed together; his eyes were open, had an expression of life, their look was full of calm and conviction, the forehead was pierced by the point of the great metal thorn.[8]

* * *

When the traveler, with the soldier and the condemned man behind him, came to the most outlying houses of the colony, the soldier pointed to one and said, "Here is the teahouse."

On the ground floor of the house was a deep, low, cavelike room, its walls and ceiling blackened with smoke. On the street side it was open along the whole of its width. Although the teahouse was hardly different from the other houses of the colony—which, except for the palatial buildings of the commandant's headquarters, were all badly run down—it still gave the traveler the impression of a historical memory, and he felt the power of the past. He came closer, accompanied by the two men, walked between the empty tables that stood on the street outside the teahouse, and breathed in the cool, musty air coming from the interior. "The Old Man is buried here," said the soldier; "the priest refused to give him a plot in the cemetery. For a while they couldn't decide where to bury him, finally they buried him here. The officer certainly never told you anything about that; of course, that was the thing he was ashamed of the most. A few times he even tried to dig up the Old Man at night, but they always chased him away." "Where is the grave?" asked the traveler, who could not believe the soldier. Immediately both of them, the soldier as well as the condemned man, ran ahead of him and pointed with

8. Here the German word for the sharp metal piece that enters the head of the victim is *der Stachel* (thorn or spike); Kafka calls it the "great metal or iron" thorn or spike. Earlier on, the officer described this piece differently, calling it *dieser kleine Stichel* (this little graver, chisel, or gouging tool).

outstretched hands to the place where the grave was to be. They led the traveler all the way to the back wall, where customers were sitting at a few of the tables. They were probably dockworkers, strong men with short, full, shiny, black beards. None of them had jackets, their shirts were torn, they were poor, abused people. As the traveler approached, some of them rose, backed against the wall, and stared at him. "It's a foreigner," the whisper went around the table; "he wants to see the grave." They shoved one of the tables to one side, and underneath it there actually was a gravestone. It was a simple stone, low enough to be hidden under a table. It bore an inscription in very small letters; the traveler had to kneel to read it. It ran, "Here lies the old commandant. His followers, who must now be nameless, dug this grave for him and laid the stone. A prophecy exists that after a certain number of years the commandant will rise again and lead his followers from this house to reconquer the colony. Have faith and wait!" When the traveler had read this inscription and risen, he saw the men standing around him smiling, as if they had read the inscription along with him, found it ridiculous, and were inviting him to share their opinion. The traveler acted as if he had not noticed, distributed a couple of coins among them, waited until the table had been pushed back over the grave, left the teahouse, and went down to the harbor.

In the teahouse the soldier and the condemned man had run into acquaintances who delayed them. But they must have quickly torn themselves away, for the traveler was only halfway down the long flight of steps that led to the boats when he saw that they were running after him. They probably wanted to force the traveler at the last minute to take them with him. While the traveler was arranging down below with a boatman about his transfer to the steamer, the two men raced down the stairway, keeping quiet, since they did not dare to shout. But when they arrived below, the traveler was already in the boat, and the boatman was just casting off from shore. They might still have been able to jump into the boat, but the traveler picked up a heavy, knotted tow rope from the floorboards, threatened them with it, and thus warded off their leap.

The New Lawyer

We have a new lawyer, Dr. Bucephalus. In his outward appearance there is little to recall the time when he was the warhorse of

Alexander of Macedonia. Admittedly, whoever is acquainted with these circumstances does notice a thing or two. In fact, on the main staircase I recently saw a quite simple court usher with the knowing eye of a little racetrack regular marveling at the lawyer as the latter, lifting his thighs high, mounted step by step with a stride that made the marble clang.

In general the bar approves the admission of Bucephalus. With remarkable insight people tell themselves that in the modern social order Bucephalus is in a difficult position and that in any case, for this reason as well as on account of his world-historical significance, he deserves our eagerness to oblige. Nowadays, as no one can deny, there is no great Alexander. To be sure, many know how to commit murder; nor is there any absence of skill in striking one's friend with a lance across the banquet table; and many feel that Macedonia is too narrow, so that they curse Philip the father—but no one, no one, can lead the way to India. Even in those days India's gates were beyond reach, but their direction was indicated by the royal sword. Today the gates have been carried off to another place entirely, farther away and higher up; no one shows the way; many carry swords but only wave them in the air, and the gaze that tries to follow them grows confused.

Perhaps, therefore, it is really best, as Bucephalus has done, to immerse oneself in law books. Free, his flanks unburdened by the loins of the rider, by quiet lamplight, far from the tumult of Alexander's battle,[1] he reads and turns the pages of our old books.

A Country Doctor

I was completely at a loss: I had an urgent trip to make; a patient, seriously ill, was waiting for me in a village ten miles away; a heavy snowstorm covered the wide expanse between him and me; I had a carriage, light, with large wheels, perfectly suited to our country roads; bundled up in my fur coat, my medical bag in my hand, I was standing in the yard, ready to leave; but the horse was missing, the horse. My own horse had expired the previous night from overexertion during this icy winter; my maid was now running through the village looking for a horse to borrow; but it was hopeless, I knew it, and I stood there aimlessly, with more and more snow piling on top of me, growing more and more motionless. The

---

1. The *Alexanderschlacht* or Battle of Issus, fought in 333 B.C.E., resulted in a decisive victory for the Macedonian Army of Alexander the Great over the Grand Army of the Persian king Darius. The battle was stunningly commemorated in 1529 by Albrecht Altdorfer (1480–1538) in a painting of the same name, a painting thereafter praised by Friedrich Schlegel (1772–1829), the great German Romantic writer, as conveying the soul of chivalric culture.

girl appeared at the gate alone, swinging the lantern; of course—
who would lend a horse for such a trip now? I walked across the
courtyard once again; I saw no further possibility; distracted, worried, I kicked at the rotted door of the pigsty, which had not been
used for years. The door opened and clattered back and forth on its
hinges. Warmth came through it, and a smell like that of horses. A
dim stable lantern was swinging on a rope inside. A man, huddling
in the low shed, showed his open, blue-eyed face. "Shall I harness
up?" he asked, crawling out on all fours. I could think of nothing to
say and merely bent down to see what else was in the sty. The maid
stood next to me. "You never know what things you have in your
own house," she said, and we both laughed. "Hey there, Brother,
hey there, Sister!" shouted the groom; and two horses, powerful animals with strong flanks, their legs tucked in beneath them, lowering their well-formed heads like camels, one after the other simply
by the force of their twisting rumps pushed their way out the low
doorway, which they crammed full to bursting. But in a moment
they rose up high on their long legs, their bodies thickly steaming.
"Help him," I said, and the willing maid hurried to hand the carriage harness to the groom. But she had hardly reached him than
the servant wraps[1] his arms around her and slams his face into
hers. She screams and comes fleeing to me: imprinted on the
maid's cheek are the red marks of two rows of teeth. "You beast," I
shout furiously, "do you want a whipping?" but immediately remember that he is a stranger; that I don't know where he comes
from; and that he is helping me of his own free will when all the
others have failed. As if he knew my thoughts, he does not react
badly to my threat but, still busy with the horses, just turns toward
me. "Climb in," he says, and in fact everything is ready. I note that
I have never before ridden with so beautiful a team and cheerfully
get in. "But I'll do the driving; you don't know the way," I say.
"Sure," he says, "I'm not coming anyway, I'm staying with Rosa."
"No," Rosa screams, and with a correct premonition of the in-
evitability of her fate she runs into the house; I hear the chain clatter as she fastens it in the door; I hear the lock click shut; I even
see her in the corridor and then racing through the rooms turning
off all the lights so she won't be found. "You're coming with me," I
say to the groom, "or I'll forget about the trip, no matter how urgent it is. I'm not about to give you the maid as payment for the
trip." "Giddy up!" he says; claps his hands; the carriage is swept
along like a piece of wood in a current; I still hear the door of my
house bursting and splintering under the groom's assault, then my
eyes and ears fill with a rushing that penetrates all my senses

1. This surprising passage into the present tense is part of Kafka's narrative strategy aiming
   at expressionist intensity.

equally. But that, too, only for a minute, because, as if my patient's yard opened up right in front of my own gate, I have already arrived; the horses stand quietly; the snowfall has stopped; moonlight all around; the patient's parents come rushing out of the house, his sister behind them; they all but lift me out of the carriage; I understand nothing of their confused talk; in the sickroom the air is hardly breathable; smoke billows from the neglected stove; I will thrust open the window, but first I need to see the patient. Gaunt, without any fever, not cold, not warm, with vacant eyes, shirtless, the boy raises himself up under the stuffed quilt, clings to my neck, whispers into my ear: "Doctor, let me die." I look around; no one has heard him; the parents bend forward, silently awaiting the verdict; the sister has brought a chair for my bag. I open the bag and look through my instruments; the boy continues to grope toward me from the bed to remind me of his request; I take up a pair of forceps, examine them in the candlelight, and put them down again. "Yes," I think, blasphemously, "in such cases, the gods help, they send the missing horse, add a second one for the sake of speed, and for good measure donate the groom as well—." Only now do I think of Rosa again; what will I do, how can I save her, how can I drag her out from under this groom, ten miles away, with unruly horses before my carriage? These horses, which have somehow loosened the reins by now, have thrust open the windows, I don't know how, from the outside; each sticks his head in through a window and, undeterred by the family's screams, observes the sick boy. "I am going to go back, right away," I think, as if the horses were inviting me to begin the trip, but I let the sister, who thinks I am dazed by the heat, take off my fur coat. A glass of rum is set before me, the old man slaps me on the shoulder, the surrender of his treasure justifies the familiarity. I shake my head; the narrow confines of the old man's thoughts would make me sick; for this reason alone I decline the drink. The mother stands at the bed and lures me over; I obey, and while one horse neighs loudly at the ceiling, I lay my head on the boy's chest, who shivers under my wet beard. What I know is confirmed: the boy is healthy, his circulation somewhat weak, saturated with coffee by his worried mother, but healthy and best driven out of bed with a good kick. I am not one to reform the world, and I let him lie. I am employed by the district and do my duty to the utmost, to the point where it becomes almost too much. Badly paid, I am nevertheless generous and ready to help the poor. I still have to take care of Rosa, and then the boy may be right, and I too will want to die. What am I doing here in this endless winter? My horse has expired, and no one in the village will lend me his. I must haul my team out of a pigsty; if they did not happen to be horses, I would have had to ride with sows. That's the

way it is. And I nod at the family. They know nothing about it, and
if they knew, they wouldn't believe it. Writing prescriptions is easy,
but all other communications with people are difficult. Well, this
seems to be the end of my visit here; once again I've been called
out unnecessarily. I'm used to that, with the help of my night bell I
am tormented by the entire district; but that this time I also have to
give up Rosa, this pretty young maid who has lived in my house for
years almost without my noticing her—this sacrifice is too great,
and I must somehow sort things out, subtly and cleverly, for the
time being, so as to keep from letting loose at this family, which
even with the best will in the world cannot bring Rosa back to me.
But when I close my bag and signal for my fur coat, and the family
stands there together, the father sniffing at the glass of rum in his
hand, the mother, probably disappointed by me—look, what do
these people expect?—tearfully biting her lips, and the sister waving a blood-soaked towel, I am somehow ready to admit that, under
certain conditions, the boy might really be sick. I go over to him, he
smiles at me as if I were bringing him, say, the most powerful
soup—oh, now both horses are neighing; the racket, ordered by a
higher authority, is probably supposed to make the examination
easier—and now I discover: yes, the boy is sick. On his right side,
near the hip, there is an open wound the size of a palmprint. Many
shades of pink,[2] dark in its depths and growing lighter at the edges,
tender and grainy, with unevenly pooling blood, open at the surface
like a mine. Thus from a distance. Close up, further complications
are apparent. Who can look at that without giving a low whistle?
Worms, as thick and as long as my little finger, rose-pink themselves and also blood-spattered, firmly attached to the inside of the
wound, with little white heads, with many little legs, writhe up toward the light. Poor boy, no one can help you. I have discovered
your great wound; this blossom in your side will destroy you. The
family is happy, they see me in action; the sister tells the mother,
the mother tells the father, and the father tells the several guests
who are tiptoeing in, arms outstretched for balance, through the
moonlight of the open door. "Will you[3] save me?" whispers the boy,
sobbing, blinded by the life in his wound. That's how people are
where I live. Always asking the doctor to do the impossible. They
have lost their old faith; the pastor sits at home, plucking his vest-
ments into shreds, one after the other; but the doctor is supposed
to accomplish everything with his tender, surgical hand. Well, just
as you please: I never foisted my services on you; if you use me up

2. The German word for pink is *rosa*, which, coming at the beginning of the sentence, is
capitalized. Hence the word is indistinguishable from the name of the maid, Rosa.
3. Somewhat surprisingly, the boy uses the intimate pronoun *du* in addressing the doctor
(see n. 7, p. 33 and n. 1, p. 110).

for holy purposes, I will put up with that, too; what more can I ask for, an old country doctor, robbed of my maid! And they come, the family and the village elders, and undress me; a choir of school-children with their teacher at the head stands outside the house and sings an extremely simple melody with these lines:

> "Undress him, then he'll cure us,
> And if he doesn't cure us, kill him!
> It's only a doctor, it's only a doctor."

Then I am undressed, and with my fingers in my beard and my head bowed, I look calmly at these people. I am fully composed and superior to them all and remain so as well, even though it in no way helps me, for now they take me by the head and feet and carry me into the bed. They place me against the wall, beside the wound. Then all leave the room; the door is closed; the singing stops; clouds drift in front of the moon; the bedclothes lie warm around me; the horses' heads in the window openings sway like shadows. "Do you know," a voice says in my ear, "I have very little confidence in you. You too were just cast off somewhere, you haven't come on your own two feet. Instead of helping, you're crowding my deathbed. I'd really love to scratch your eyes out." "Right," I say, "it is a disgrace. But then, I am a doctor: What should I do? Believe me, it's not easy for me, either." "Am I supposed to be satisfied with this excuse? Oh, I guess I have to be. I always have to be satisfied. I came into the world with a beautiful wound; that was my whole endowment." "My young friend," I say, "your mistake is: you lack perspective. I, who have already been in all the sickrooms near and far, tell you: your wound is not so bad. Made with two blows of the ax at an acute angle. Many offer their sides and hardly hear the ax in the forest, let alone that it is coming closer to them." "Is it really so, or are you deluding me in my fevered state?" "It is really so, take a government doctor's word of honor with you as you pass over to the other side." And he took it and became quiet. But now it was time to think of saving myself. The horses still stood faithfully in their places. Clothes, fur coat, and bag were quickly bundled together; I did not want to delay by getting dressed; if the horses hurried as they had on the trip here, I would, so to speak, spring from this bed into my own. Obediently a horse drew back from the window; I threw the bundle into the carriage; the fur coat flew too far, it clung to a hook[4] by only one sleeve. Good enough. I swung my-

---

4. The German word for "hook" is *Haken*; the German word for the ax that allegedly caused the boy's wound is *Hacke*. This family resemblance of words is more than sound based: as the fur coat clings to the *Haken with one arm*, the boy "clings" to the wound of the *Hacke in one side*. By association Kafka now conjures a near-identity of wound and sleeve, so that we will read the doctor as taking the feminine sexual wound along with him in the form of the fur sleeve; see also n. 1, p. 15.

self onto the horse. The reins loosely dragging, one horse barely attached to the other, the carriage swerving behind, the fur coat the last item in the snow. "Giddy up!" I said, but things did not go briskly; as slowly as old men we rode through the snowy waste; for a long time there sounded behind us the new but mistaken song of the children:

> "Be glad, you patients,
> The doctor's laid in bed beside you!"

I shall never arrive home this way; my blossoming practice is lost; a successor is stealing from me, but to no avail, because he cannot replace me; in my house the disgusting groom is raging; Rosa is his victim; I do not want to think matters through to the end. Naked, exposed to the frost of this unhappiest of ages, with an earthly carriage, unearthly horses, I, an old man, wander aimlessly around. My fur coat is hanging at the back of the carriage, but I cannot reach it, and not one of this agile rabble of patients lifts a finger. Betrayed! Betrayed! A false ringing of the night bell once answered—it can never again be made good.

Up in the Gallery

If some frail, consumptive lady trick rider on a staggering horse were to be driven in circles around the ring before a tireless audience by a merciless, whip-cracking ringmaster for months without pause, whirling on the horse, blowing kisses, swaying back and forth at the waist, and if this performance were to continue on and on into the ever-unfolding gray future to the incessant blare of the orchestra and ventilators, accompanied by the fading and freshly swelling applause of clapping hands that are really steam hammers—then perhaps some young spectator in the gallery would come running down the long flight of stairs past all the tiers and bursting into the ring would shout: "Stop!" through the fanfares of the continually modulating orchestra.

But since matters are not like this; a beautiful lady, white and red, comes flying in between the curtains that the proud, liveried attendants open before her; the ringmaster, submissively trying to catch her eye, approaches, breathing heavily and bent over in the posture of an animal; solicitously lifts her onto the dappled gray as if she were his adored granddaughter about to leave on a dangerous trip; cannot decide to give the signal with his whip; finally, overcoming his reluctance, cracks it like a shot; runs open-mouthed alongside the horse; follows with keen glances the rider's leaps; can hardly comprehend her artistry; attempts to alert her with exclamations in English; furiously warns the grooms who hold the hoops to be most scrupulously attentive; raises his hands before the death-defying somersault to beseech the orchestra to be silent; finally lifts the little one down from the trembling horse, kisses her on both cheeks, considering no ovation from the audience good enough; while she herself, supported by him, standing high on tiptoe, dust blowing around her, her arms outstretched and her little head thrown back, is intent on sharing her happiness with the entire circus—since matters are like this, the spectator in the gallery lays his face on the railing, and sinking into the final march as in a deep dream, he weeps without being aware of it.

A Page from an Old Document

It looks as if a great deal had been neglected in the defense of our fatherland. Until now we have not been concerned about it and have gone about our work; but recent events are causing us concern.

I have a shoemaker's shop on the square outside the Imperial Palace. No sooner have I opened my shop at dawn than I see armed men occupying the openings to all the streets that run into the square. But they are not our soldiers, they are evidently nomads from the north. In a manner incomprehensible to me they have penetrated to the capital, although it lies a long way from the border. In any case, they are here; it seems that every morning there are more of them.

True to their nature they camp under the open sky, for they detest houses. They busy themselves with whetting their swords, sharpening their arrows, with maneuvers on horseback. They have turned this quiet square, which we have always kept compulsively clean, into a real stable.[1] We do sometimes try to run out of our shops and clean up at least the worst of the filth, but this happens less and less often, since the effort is useless and, furthermore, puts us in danger of being trampled by the wild horses or injured by the whips.

You cannot talk to the nomads. They do not know our language; indeed, they hardly have one of their own. They communicate with each other like jackdaws.[2] Again and again we hear this screech

---

1. A moment of Kafka's (serious) word play: "a real stable" is normally used only figuratively, which is to say, not to mean a real stable at all but only a "mess," "a pigsty," so to speak. A parent might complain that a child has turned his or her tidy bedroom into "a real stable." In Kafka's story the metaphor regains its primordial meaning.
2. The Czech word for jackdaw is *kafka*. It is a small black crow normally seen in larger groups. Acrobatic fliers, in flocks the birds will often chase each other and tumble together in flight. On the ground, they both walk and hop.

of jackdaws. They are indifferent to our way of life, our institutions, and find them incomprehensible. As a result they are also ill-disposed to any sort of sign language. You can dislocate your jaw and twist your hands out of joint, but they have not understood you, and they will never understand you. They often grimace: then their eyes roll up in their heads and foam flows out of their mouths, but these are not meant either to convey anything or to frighten people; they do it because that is how they are. What they need, they take. You cannot say that they use force. When they make a grab at something, you step aside and let them have it.

From my stock, too, they have taken more than one choice item. But I cannot complain when I see, for example, what is happening to the butcher across the street. No sooner has he brought in his goods than everything is snatched from him and devoured by the nomads. Even their horses are meat eaters; often a rider lies next to his horse while both feed off the same piece of meat, one at each end. The butcher is frightened and does not dare to stop the meat deliveries. We understand this, however, pool our money, and support him. If the nomads were not to get meat, who knows what would occur to them to do; who knows, for that matter, what will occur to them even if they do get their daily meat.

Recently the butcher thought that he could at least save himself the trouble of slaughtering, and in the morning he brought in a live ox. That is something he had better not repeat. For about an hour I lay flat on the floor far back in my workshop, with all my clothes, blankets, and pillows piled on top of me just so as not to hear the ox's bellowing as the nomads sprang on it from all sides to tear pieces from its warm flesh with their teeth. It had been quiet for a long time before I dared to go out; like drunks around a wine barrel, they lay exhausted around the remains of the ox.

It was just at that time that I thought I saw the emperor himself in a palace window; as a rule he never comes into these outer rooms and always keeps to the innermost garden; but this time he was standing, or so at least it seemed to me, at one of the windows, looking down, with his head lowered, at the goings-on outside his palace.

"What is to come of this?" we all ask ourselves. "How long will we put up with this burden, this torment? The Imperial Palace has attracted the nomads but does not know how to drive them away again. The gate remains shut; the watch that used to march ceremoniously in and out remains behind barred windows. To us craftsmen and businessmen the salvation of the fatherland is entrusted; but we are not up to such a task; certainly we have never boasted of being capable of it. It is a misunderstanding, and it means our destruction."

Before the Law

Before the law stands a doorkeeper. A man from the country comes to the doorkeeper and asks for admittance to the law. But the doorkeeper says that he cannot grant him admittance now. The man reflects and then asks whether he will be allowed to enter later. "It is possible," says the doorkeeper, "but not now." Since the door to the law stands open, as always, and the doorkeeper steps aside, the man bends down to look through the doorway into the interior. When the doorkeeper notices, he laughs and says, "If you find it so tempting, just try to go in despite my prohibition. But note: I am powerful. And I am only the lowliest doorkeeper. But outside each hall stands a doorkeeper, each more powerful than the last. The mere sight of the third one is more than even I can stand." The man from the country has not expected such difficulties; after all, he thinks, the law ought to be accessible to everyone at all times, but when he now looks more closely at the doorkeeper in his fur coat, his large, pointy nose, his long, thin, black Tatar beard, he decides that it would be better, after all, to wait until he has permission to enter. The doorkeeper gives him a stool and lets him sit to one side of the door. There he sits for days and years. He makes many attempts to be admitted and tires out the doorkeeper with his requests. The doorkeeper often begins little interrogations with him, asks him one question after another about his homeland and many other things, but these are uninterested questions, such as higher-ups ask, and in the end he always tells him that he still cannot be admitted. The man, who has come plentifully equipped for his journey, uses up everything, even his most valuable items, to bribe the doorkeeper. The latter accepts everything but says each time: "I am accepting this only so that you won't think that you've neglected anything." During the long years, the man watches the doorkeeper almost continuously. He forgets the other doorkeepers, and this first one seems to him the sole obstacle to his admittance to the law. During the first few years he curses his miserable luck loudly and carelessly; later, as he grows old, he merely mutters to himself. He becomes childish, and since during his long years of studying the doorkeeper he has also come to know the fleas in his fur collar, he begs the fleas to help him change the doorkeeper's mind. Eventually his eyesight grows dim, and he does not know whether the darkness is really deepening around him or whether his eyes are deceiving him. But in the darkness he perceives a radiance that breaks out inextinguishably from the doorway of the law. Now he does not have much longer to live. Before his death all the experiences of the entire time gather in his head to form one question that he has not yet asked the door-keeper. He beckons to him, since he can no longer raise his stiffening body. The doorkeeper must bend down very low, for the difference in height has changed very much to the man's disadvantage. "What can you still want to know now?" asks the doorkeeper. "You are insatiable." "Everyone strives for the law," says the man; "so how is it that in all these years no one except me has ever asked for admittance?" The doorkeeper perceives that the man has reached his end, and so as to be heard even as the man's hearing is failing, he shouts at him, "No one else could gain admittance here, because this entrance was intended only for you. Now I will go and shut it."

Jackals and Arabs

We made camp in the oasis. My companions were asleep. An Arab, tall and white, walked past me; he had been tending to the camels and was going to his sleeping place.

I threw myself on my back in the grass; I wanted to sleep; I could not; the howling lament of a jackal in the distance; I sat upright again. And what had been so far away was suddenly near. A writhing mass of jackals all around me; eyes of dull gold gleaming and fading; lean bodies, as if under the whip, moving nimbly, compliant with some law.

One came up from behind, pushed through under my arm, close to me as if it needed my warmth, then came up to me and said, almost eye to eye to me:

"I am the oldest jackal far and wide. I am glad to still be able to welcome you here. I had almost given up hope, since we have been waiting for you for time without end; my mother waited, and her mother and, farther back, all her mothers up to the mother of all jackals. Believe me!"

"That comes as a surprise to me," I said, forgetting to set fire to the stack of wood that lay ready to keep the jackals away with its smoke; "I am very surprised to hear it. It is pure chance that I have come from the far north, and I am on a brief trip. What is it, then, that you jackals want?"

And as if encouraged by this perhaps overly friendly reception, they tightened their circle around me; all of them were panting and hissing.

"We know," the eldest began, "that you have come from the north, that is exactly what our hope is based on. There is a rationality there that cannot be found here among the Arabs. From their cold arrogance, you know, not a spark of reason can be struck.

They kill animals to eat them like animals,[1] and they despise carrion."

"Don't speak so loudly," I said, "there are Arabs sleeping nearby."

"You really are a stranger," said the jackal, "or else you would know that never in the history of the world has a jackal been afraid of an Arab. We're supposed to be afraid of them? Isn't it enough of a misfortune to have been banished among such people?"

"Maybe, maybe," I said, "I do not presume to judge matters so remote from me; it seems to be a very old quarrel; hence it probably runs in the blood; and so it will probably end only in blood."

"You are very clever," said the old jackal; and all the jackals began panting even more quickly; with racing lungs, although they were standing still; an acrid smell, bearable only intermittently with gritted teeth, streamed from their open muzzles, "you are very clever; what you say corresponds to our ancient lore. And so we will draw their blood, and the quarrel is ended."

"Oh!" I said, more fiercely than I intended, "they will defend themselves; they will shoot down packs of you with their muskets."

"You misunderstand us," he said, "in the manner of humans, which, I see, is not lost even in the far north. We are certainly not going to kill them. All the waters of the Nile would not wash us clean. The mere sight of their living bodies is enough to make us run away, into purer air, into the desert, where we make our home for this very reason."

And all the jackals in the circle, who in the meantime had been joined by many others coming from afar, lowered their heads between their front legs and polished them with their paws; it was as if they wished to conceal a revulsion so terrible that I would have been happiest fleeing from their circle with one great leap.

"What is it you intend to do?" I asked, trying to stand; but I could not; two young animals had fastened their teeth on the back of my jacket and shirt; I had to remain seated. "They are holding your train," said the old jackal gravely, in explanation, "a mark of respect." "Make them let go!" I shouted, turning first to the old one, then to the young ones. "They will let go, of course," said the old one, "if that is what you wish. But it will take a little while, for, as is customary, they have sunk their teeth in deep, and they must first slowly pry their jaws open. In the meantime hear our request." "Your behavior has not made me very receptive to it," I said. "Do not hold our clumsiness against us," he said, for the first time calling to his aid the wailing tone of his natural voice, "we are poor creatures, we have only our teeth; for everything we want to do,

---

1. The phrase "to eat them like animals" translates the verb *fressen*, which means "to eat the way that animals eat" (see n. 5, p. 41). *Fressen* is an important word in Kafka's poetic lexicon.

good and bad, all we have is our teeth." "So what is it you want?" I asked, only a little mollified.

"Master," he cried, and all the jackals began howling; in the most distant distance it came to my ears like a melody. "Master, we want you to put an end to the quarrel that divides the world in two. You are precisely the man whom our ancestors described as the one who would accomplish this. We must have peace from the Arabs; air we can breathe; a view of the horizon cleansed of them; no bleated lament from a ram slaughtered by the Arab; all creatures must perish quietly; undisturbed, they must be drunk dry by us and purified right down to the bone. Purity, nothing but purity, is what we want"—and now all the jackals were weeping and sobbing— "how can you bear to live in this world, you with a noble heart and bowels of tenderness? Filth is their white; filth is their black; their beard is a horror; one has to spit at the sight of the corner of their eye; and when they lift their arm, all hell breaks loose in their armpits. Therefore, oh Master, therefore, oh dear Master, with the help of your all-powerful hands, with the help of your all-powerful hands, cut their throats with these scissors!" And in response to a jerk of his head, a jackal came up, a small pair of sewing scissors covered with old rust dangling from one of his eye teeth.

"Well, finally, the scissors, and that's enough of that!" shouted the Arab leader of our caravan, who had crept up against the wind and now cracked his giant whip.

All the jackals scattered hurriedly but remained at a distance, crouching closely together, the many animals so packed together and rigid that it looked like a narrow pen with will-of-the-wisps flickering around it.

"So, Master, you too have seen and heard this spectacle," said the Arab, laughing as gaily as the reserved nature of his tribe permitted. "And so you know what these animals want?" I asked. "Of course, Master," he said, "it is common knowledge; for as long as there are Arabs, this pair of scissors will go wandering through the desert, and it will wander with us until the end of time. It is offered to every European so he will execute this great work; every European is just the man who seems to them to have been chosen. These creatures possess an absurd hope; fools, true fools they are. That is why we love them; they are our dogs; more beautiful than yours. Just look, a camel expired in the night, I have had it brought here."

Four bearers came and threw the heavy carcass down in front of us. Hardly had it hit the ground when the jackals lifted up their voices. As if irresistibly drawn on cords, every one of them, they came up, haltingly, their bodies scraping the ground. They had forgotten the Arabs, forgotten their hatred: the all-obliterating presence of the powerfully reeking corpse bewitched them. One was already at the throat, and its first bite found the jugular. Like a small, rushing pump, which struggles both wholeheartedly and hopelessly to extinguish an overwhelming fire, every muscle of his body tugged and twitched in place. And already, hard at the same work, all lay piled high up on the carcass.

Then the leader whipped his sharp lash back powerfully and forth across their backs. They raised their heads; half in ecstasy, half in a stupor; saw the Arabs standing in front of them; now were made to feel the whip on their muzzles; retreated with a jump and ran backward a ways. But the camel's blood already lay in steaming puddles; the body was torn wide open in several places. They could not resist; they were back again; the leader raised the whip again; I took him by the arm.

"You are right, Master," he said, "we will leave them to their vocation; besides, it is time to break camp. Now you have seen them. Wonderful animals, aren't they? And how they hate us!"

The Worry of the Father of the Family

Some say that the word *Odradek* has roots in the Slavic languages, and they attempt to demonstrate the formation of the word on that basis. Still others maintain that its roots are German and that it is merely influenced by the Slavic. The uncertainty of both interpretations, however, makes it reasonable to conclude that neither pertains, especially since neither of them enables you to find a meaning for the word.

No one, of course, would occupy himself with such studies if there were not really a creature called Odradek. At first it looks like a flat, star-shaped spool for thread, and in fact, it does seem to be wound with thread; although these appear to be only old, torn-off pieces of thread of the most varied kinds and colors knotted together but tangled up in one another. But it is not just a spool, for a little crossbar sticks out from the middle of the star, and another little strut is joined to it at a right angle. With the help of this second little strut on the one side and one of the points of the star on the other, the whole thing can stand upright, as if on two legs.

It is tempting to think that this figure once had some sort of functional shape and is now merely broken. But this does not seem to be the case; at least there is no evidence for such a speculation; nowhere can you see any other beginnings or fractures that would point to anything of the kind; true, the whole thing seems meaningless yet in its own way complete. In any case, it is impossible to say anything more definite about it, since Odradek is extraordinarily mobile and impossible to catch.

He stays alternately in the attic, on the staircase, in the corridors, in the hallway. Sometimes he disappears for months at a time; he has probably moved into other houses; but then he inevitably returns to our house. Sometimes, when you step out of the door and he is at that very minute leaning against the banisters downstairs, you feel like speaking to him. Naturally you do not ask him hard questions but treat him—his diminutive size alone inclines you to do so—like a child. "So, what's your name?" you ask. "Odradek," he says. "And where do you live?" "No permanent residence," he says and laughs; but it is a kind of laughter that can only be produced without lungs. It sounds more or less like the rustling of fallen leaves. At this point the conversation is usually over. Furthermore, you do not always get even these answers; he is often mute for a long time, like the wooden thing he seems to be.

I ask myself in vain what will become of him. Can he die? Everything that dies has previously had some sort of goal, some kind of activity, and that activity is what has worn it down; this does not apply to Odradek. And so, can I expect that one day, with his bits of thread trailing behind him, he will come clattering down the stairs, say, at the feet of my children and my grandchildren? True, he clearly harms no one; but the idea that, on top of everything else, he might outlive me, that idea I find almost painful.

A Fratricide

The evidence shows that the murder happened as follows:

Around nine o'clock in the evening on a moonlit night Schmar, the murderer, positioned himself at the corner where Wese, the victim, was expected to turn from the street where his office was into the street where he lived.

Cold night air, sending a shudder through everyone. But Schmar wore only a thin blue suit; furthermore, his jacket was unbuttoned. He did not feel the cold; besides, he was continually in motion. He kept a tight grip on his murder weapon, half bayonet, half kitchen knife, fully exposed to view. Held the knife up to the moonlight; the blade flashed; not enough for Schmar; he struck it against the bricks of the pavement until it gave off sparks; regretted that move, perhaps; and to repair the damage, he drew it like a violin bow over the sole of his boot while, standing on one leg, bending forward, he listened to the sound of the knife on his shoe and for any sound from the fateful side street.

Why was all this tolerated by Pallas, a person of private means, who, close by, was watching everything from his second-story window? Go and fathom human nature! With his collar turned up, his dressing gown belted around his ample body, he looked down, shaking his head.

And five houses farther down, diagonally across the street from him, her fox fur over her nightgown, Frau Wese was keeping an eye out for her husband, who was unusually delayed today.

Finally, the doorbell of Wese's office rings, too loudly for a doorbell, across the city, up to the heavens, and Wese, the diligent night worker, emerges from the building, still invisible in this street, announced only by the sound of the bell; the pavement immediately counts his quiet steps.

Pallas leans far out; he must not miss a thing. Frau Wese, reassured by the bell, shuts her window with a clatter. But Schmar kneels; since for the moment no other parts of him are exposed, he presses his face and hands against the pavement. Where everything is freezing, Schmar is on fire.

Exactly at the line dividing the two streets, Wese remains standing, only propping himself up on his walking stick in the farther street. A whim. The night sky has enticed him, the dark blue and the gold. Unsuspecting, he glances at the sky, unsuspecting, he smooths his hair under his raised hat; up above, nothing shifts into a pattern to indicate to him his immediate future; everything stays in its senseless, inscrutable place. In principle it is very sensible for Wese to walk on, but he walks into Schmar's knife.

"Wese!" screams Schmar, standing on tiptoe, his arm thrust upward, his knife sharply lowered, "Wese! Julia waits in vain!" And into the throat from the right, and into the throat from the left, and a third thrust deep into the belly, Schmar sticks his knife. Water rats, slit open, produce a sound like Wese's.

"Done," says Schmar and throws the knife, the superfluous bloody ballast, against the nearest house front. "The bliss of murder! Relief, a lightening, won through the flow of another's blood! Wese, old phantom of the night, friend, beer-hall companion, you seep away in the dark earth beneath the pavement. Why aren't you just a bubble of blood, so that I could sit on you and make you disappear for good? Not everything will be fulfilled, not every blossoming dream will flower, your heavy remains lie here, already unresponsive to any kick. What sense is there to the mute question you pose in this way?"

Pallas, all the poison in his body chaotically choking him, stands in the doorway of his house, the two sides of the door flying open. "Schmar! Schmar! Everything noted, nothing overlooked." Pallas and Schmar scrutinize each other. Pallas is satisfied, Schmar does not come to a conclusion.

Frau Wese, a crowd of people on either side, comes hurrying up, her face heavily aged by terror. Her fur coat falls open, she topples onto Wese; this nightgowned body belongs to him, the fur coat that closes over the couple like the grass of a grave belongs to the crowd.

Schmar, struggling to stifle the last wave of his nausea, his mouth pressed against the shoulder of the policeman who, stepping lightly, takes him away.

A Dream

Josef K. was dreaming:

It was a beautiful day, and K. wanted to go for a walk. But he had only taken a step or two when he was already in the cemetery. Its paths were highly artful and impractically serpentine, but he glided over one such path in an imperturbably floating posture, as if over torrentially rushing water. Even at a distance he caught sight of the mound of a freshly dug grave, where he wanted to stop. This burial mound exerted an almost seductive lure, and he felt that he would not be able to reach it quickly enough. But at times he could barely see the burial mound, it was hidden from view by flags twisting and turning and flapping against one another with great force; no flag bearers were to be seen, but the scene had an air of triumphant joy.

While he was still gazing into the distance, he abruptly saw the same burial mound at his side on the path; indeed, it was already almost behind him. He quickly jumped onto the grass. Because the path raced on under his foot as he jumped, he staggered and fell to his knees right in front of the grave mound. Two men stood behind the grave, holding a tombstone in the air between them; no sooner had K. appeared than they thrust the stone into the ground, and it stood as if cemented. Immediately a third man stepped out from behind some bushes, a man whom K. recognized at once as an artist. He wore only trousers and a badly buttoned shirt; a velvet cap sat on his head; in his hand he held an ordinary pencil with which he had begun to draw figures in the air as K. approached.

He now set his pencil to work on the top part of the stone; the stone was very tall, the man did not have to bend down, but he did have to lean forward because the burial mound, which he did not want to trample, came between him and the stone. And so he stood on tiptoe and braced himself with his left hand against the flat face of the stone. Through an especially adroit piece of manipulation he managed to produce golden letters with an ordinary pencil; he wrote, "Here lies—." Each letter emerged clear and beautiful, deeply engraved with perfect gilding. After he had written the two words, he looked back at K.; K., who was very eager to see how the inscription would continue, paid little attention to the man but instead looked only at the stone. In fact, the man did get ready to write further, but he could not go on, there was some obstacle, he let his pencil sink and again turned toward K. Now K. also looked at the artist and noticed that the latter was deeply embarrassed[1] but could not say why. All his former vigor had disappeared. As a result K. also grew embarrassed; they exchanged helpless looks; there was a terrible misunderstanding, which neither of them could clear up. At just the wrong time a little bell in the cemetery chapel began to peal, but the artist gestured with his raised hand, and the bell stopped. After a little while it began again; this time quite softly and without anyone's special request, immediately stopping; it was as if it had only wanted to test its sound. K. was disconsolate at the artist's predicament, he began to weep and for a long time sobbed into his hands held to his face. The artist waited until K. had calmed down and then, since he saw no other way out, decided to continue writing. The first little stroke he made was a vast relief for K., but the artist evidently produced it only with the greatest reluctance; the script was also no longer so beautiful, above all it seemed to be lacking in gold; the line dragged on, pale and uncertain: the letter merely became very large. It was a "J"; when it was almost finished, the artist stamped his foot furiously into the burial mound so that the earth flew into the air all around. Finally K. understood what the artist meant; there was no more time to apologize; he dug all his fingers into the ground, which offered practically no resistance; everything seemed prepared; for mere appearance's sake a thin crust of dirt had been set up; below it a deep hole with steep sides opened up, and into this, turned onto his back by a gentle current, K. sank. But while down below, his head still raised, he was already being received by the impenetrable depths, up above his name raced with mighty embellishments across the stone.

Enchanted by this sight, he awoke.

A Report to an Academy

Exalted Gentleman of the Academy!

You have granted me the honor of summoning me to submit to the Academy a report on my previous life as an ape.

Unfortunately I am unable to comply with the intent of your request. Almost five years separate me from apedom, a span of time that is short, perhaps, when measured on the calendar, but infi-

---

1. *In grosser Verlegenheit*: clearly a privileged expression for Kafka. The phrase appears in *In the Penal Colony* (p. 48) as well as at the outset of "A Country Doctor" (p. 60).

nitely long when galloped through in the way I have done, accompanied for stretches by excellent persons, advice, applause, and orchestral music but basically alone, since all my accompaniment kept its distance, to continue the metaphor, from the railing. This achievement would have been impossible had I wanted to cling obstinately to my origin, to the memories of my youth. In fact, to give up all such obstinacy was the supreme commandment that I had imposed on myself; I, a free ape, accepted this yoke. But as a result, for their part my memories have become more and more closed off from me. If at first my return—had the world of humans wanted it—was open to me through the entire gateway that the sky forms over the earth, at the same time it became ever lower and narrower under the lash that drove my evolution forward; I felt more comfortable and more fully enclosed in the human world; the storm that blew at my back from my past subsided; today it is only a draft that cools my heels; and the far-away gap, through which it comes and through which I once came, has grown so small that, if ever my strength and will were even adequate to run back to that point, I would have to scrape the hide from my body in order to pass through. To speak frankly, as much as I like to employ figurative images for these things, to speak frankly: Your apedom, gentlemen, to the extent that you have something of the sort behind you, cannot be more remote from you than mine is from me. But everyone who walks about here on earth feels a tickling in his heels: from the tiny chimpanzee to the great Achilles.

In the most limited sense, however, I may indeed be able to respond to your inquiry, and I do so with great pleasure. The first thing that I learned was to shake hands; the handshake signifies openness. Now, today, at the high point of my career, let frank speech be coupled with that first handshake. It will not contribute anything essentially new to the Academy and will fall far short of what you have asked of me and which, with the best will in the world, I cannot tell you—nonetheless, it should reveal the guideline a former ape has followed in penetrating the human world and establishing himself in it. Yet I certainly would not have been able to tell you even the trivial things that follow were I not entirely sure of myself and were my position on all the great vaudeville stages of the civilized world secure to the point of being impregnable.

I come from the Gold Coast. In describing how I was caught, I am dependent on the reports of others. A hunting expedition of the Hagenbeck company[1]—by the way, since that time I have emptied more than one good bottle of red wine with its leader—lay in wait

1. Carl Hagenbeck (1844–1923), a German animal dealer, was world famous in Kafka's time for his benevolent manner of encouraging the intelligence of the animals he caught and then trained. He pioneered the creation of open-air zoos.

in the bushes along the shore when, one evening, running with the pack, I went to drink. There was a shot; I was the only one hit; I was hit twice.

One shot in the cheek; it was slight; but it left a great hairless, red scar that has won me the name—coined, as it were, by a monkey—the repulsive, utterly inappropriate name of Red Peter, as if the only difference between me and that trained animal ape Peter, who had a minor reputation and who recently croaked, was a red mark on the cheek.[2] This by the by.

The second shot struck me below the hip. It was serious, and as a result I still walk with a slight limp. Recently I read an article by one of the ten thousand windbags who vent their views about me in the newspapers: they say that my ape nature has not yet been entirely repressed; the proof is supposed to be that whenever I have company, I am inclined to lower my pants to show the bullet's path of entry. Every tiny finger of that guy's writing hand ought to be blown off, one by one. I, I have the right to lower my pants in front of anyone I like; there is nothing to see there other than a well-groomed pelt and the scar left by a—let us choose here a specific word for a specific purpose, a word, however, that should not be misunderstood—the scar left by a profligate shot. Everything is open and above board; there is nothing to hide; where it is a question of truth, every large-minded person casts off the fanciest manners. If, on the other hand, that scribbler were to lower his pants whenever he has company, things, I assure you, would look very different, and I will let it stand as a sign of his good sense that he does not do so. But that being so, let him keep his delicate sensibility off my back!

After those shots I awoke—and here my own memory gradually takes over—in a cage in steerage of the Hagenbeck freighter. It was not a four-sided cage with bars; instead, only three barred sides were attached to a crate, which thus formed the fourth wall. The whole was too low for me to stand and too narrow to sit down. Hence I squatted with bent, continually trembling knees; and since at first I may not have wanted to see anyone and was eager only to remain in the dark, I faced the crate while the bars of the cage cut into the flesh of my backside. This way of keeping wild animals during the first few days of their captivity is considered effective; and today, with my experience, I cannot deny that from a human point of view this is, in fact, the case.

2. Kafka very likely knew of the vaudeville act titled "Peter, the Human Ape," which opened at the Ronacher Theater in Vienna in December 1908. Advertisements claimed that Peter acted "just like a human being, has better table manners than most people, and behaves so well that even more highly evolved creatures would do well to model themselves on him." He smoked, drank, ate on stage, pedaled a bicycle, and rode a horse.

At the time, however, I did not think about these matters. For the first time in my life I had no way out; at the very least, there was no moving forward; directly in front of me was the crate, board joined firmly to board. Admittedly, a continuous gap ran between the boards; upon my first discovery of the gap, I greeted it with the blissful howl of unreason; but this gap was not by a long shot big enough to stick even my tail through, and all an ape's might could not widen it.

Later I was told that I had made unusually little noise, from which the others concluded that either I would soon expire or that, should I succeed in surviving the first critical period, I would be eminently trainable. I survived this period. Glumly sobbing, painfully searching for fleas, wearily licking a coconut, knocking my skull against the wall of the crate, sticking out my tongue whenever someone came near me—these were the first occupations in my new life. In all that, however, still only one feeling: no way out. Naturally, today I can use human words only to sketch my apish feelings of the time, and so I misstate them; but even if I cannot arrive at the old apish truth, my recital at least leans in that direction, there can be no doubt.

I had had so many ways out before, and now I was left with none. I was stuck. If they had nailed me down, I would have had no less freedom of movement. Why was that? Scratch open the flesh between your toes, and you will not find the reason. Crush your backside against the bars of your cage until they almost cut you in two, and you still won't find the reason. I had no way out but had to provide myself with one, for I could not live without it. Always up against the wall of this crate—I would inevitably have croaked. But at Hagenbeck, apes belong up against the wall—well, so I stopped being an ape. A clear, beautiful thought that I must somehow have hatched with my belly, for apes think with their belly.

I am afraid that what I mean by "a way out" will not be clearly understood. I am using it in the most common and also the fullest sense of the word. I deliberately do not say "freedom." I do not mean that great feeling of freedom on all sides. Perhaps I knew it as an ape, and I have known human beings who long for it. But as far as I am concerned, I did not ask for freedom either then or now. By the way: human beings all too often deceive themselves about freedom. And just as freedom counts among the most sublime feelings, so too the corresponding delusion counts among the most sublime. Often, in the vaudeville theaters, before I go on, I have seen some artiste couple up at the ceiling fooling around on their trapezes. They swung, they rocked, they jumped, they floated into each other's arms; one carried the other by the hair with his teeth. "That, too, is human freedom," I would think, "high-handed movement."

You mockery of holy Nature! No building could stand up to ape-dom's laughter at such a sight.

No, it was not freedom I wanted. Just a way out; to the right, to the left, wherever; I made no other demands; even if the way out should only be a delusion; my demand was small, the delusion would not be greater. To move on, to move on! Anything but standing still with my arms raised, pressed flat against a crate wall.

Today I see it clearly: without the utmost inner calm I would never have been able to escape. And in fact, I may owe everything I have become to the calm that came over me after the first days on board ship. And this calm, in turn, I very likely owed to the ship's crew.

They are good men, despite everything. To this day I enjoy recalling the sound of their heavy strides that reverberated in my light sleep. They had the habit of going about things extremely slowly. If one of them wanted to rub his eyes, he would lift his hand like a weight on a pulley. Their jokes were crude but hearty. Their laughter was always mixed with a dangerous-sounding cough that did not, in fact, mean anything. They always had something in their mouth to spit out, and they didn't care where their spit landed. They were always complaining that my fleas jumped on them; and yet they were never seriously angry with me on that score; they were aware that fleas thrived in my pelt and that fleas are jumpers; they came to terms with this fact. When they were off duty, a number of them would sometimes sit in a semicircle around me; hardly speaking but merely making cooing sounds to each other; stretched out on crates and smoking their pipes; slapping their knees as soon as I made the slightest movement; and every so often one of them would take a stick and tickle me where I liked to be tickled. If I were invited today to take part in a cruise on this ship, I would certainly decline the invitation, but it is equally certain that, lying there in steerage, the memories I could indulge in would not all be ugly.

It was above all the calm I acquired within the circle of these people that held me back from any attempt to escape. Now, in retrospect, it seems to me as if I had at least suspected that I needed to find a way out if I wanted to stay alive, but that this way out was not to be attained by running away. I no longer know whether escape was possible, but I believe it was; it ought always to be possible for an ape to escape. With my teeth the way they are today, I have to be careful even at ordinary nutcracking; but at that time I could probably have managed eventually to bite through the door lock. I did not do it. What good would it have done me anyway? The minute I stuck out my head, they would have caught me and locked me up in an even worse cage; or I might have been able to slip away unnoticed to the other animals—for example, to the giant snakes opposite—and in their embraces breathed my last; or I might even have been successful in stealing my way to the upper deck and jumping overboard, and then I would have rocked for a little while on the great ocean before drowning. Desperate deeds. I did not calculate in such a human way, but under the influence of my environment I behaved as if I had calculated.

I did not calculate; but I did observe matters with great calm. I saw these men walk back and forth, always the same faces, the same movements: it often seemed to me that only one man was involved. So, this man or these men went unmolested. An exalted goal dawned on me. No one promised me that if I became like them, the cage door would be raised. Promises of that kind, for seemingly impossible fulfillment, are not given. But if fulfillment is achieved, the promises also appear subsequently, just where they had earlier been sought in vain. Now, in themselves these men had nothing that especially appealed to me. If I were a devotee of the above-mentioned freedom, I would certainly have preferred the great ocean to the way out that showed itself to me in the dull gaze of these men. In any case, I observed them for a long time before I thought about such things; in fact, it was the accumulation of observations that first urged me in this definite direction.

It was so easy to imitate these people. Within a few days I had learned to spit. We then spat in one another's faces, the only difference being that afterward I licked my face clean and they did not. Before long I was smoking a pipe like an old hand, and when in addition I pressed my thumb into the bowl of the pipe, all of steerage cheered; it was only the difference between the empty pipe and the filled bowl that I could not grasp for a long time.

It was the brandy bottle that gave me the greatest trouble. The smell was torture for me; I forced myself with all my might; but weeks went by before I overcame my revulsion. Curiously, the men took these inner struggles more seriously than anything else about me. In my recollections, too, I cannot tell these people apart, but there was one of them who came again and again, alone or with his comrades, by day, by night, at all hours; set himself down in front of me with the bottle and gave me lessons. He could not make head or tail of me: he wanted to solve the riddle of my being. He slowly uncorked the bottle and then looked at me to see if I had understood; I confess, I always watched him with wild, hectic attention; no human teacher will find such a human student in the whole wide world; after the bottle was uncorked, he raised it to his mouth; my glances follow him down into his gullet; he nods, satisfied with me, and puts the bottle to his lips; I, ecstatic with gradually dawning understanding, squealing, scratch the length and the breadth of me, wherever my hand lands; he is pleased, puts the bottle to his mouth, and takes a swig; I, impatient and desperate to emulate him, soil myself in my cage, an act that once again gives him great satisfaction; and now, holding the bottle at arm's length and with a swoop bringing it back up again, he leans back with exaggerated pedantry and in one gulp empties it. Exhausted from excessive desire, I can follow no longer and hang weakly onto the bars while he ends the theoretical instruction by rubbing his belly and grinning.

Only now does the practical exercise begin. Hasn't the theoretical teaching exhausted me too much? Very likely I'm far too exhausted. That is part of my fate. Nonetheless, I reach as well as I can for the bottle that is held out to me; trembling, uncork it; with this success my strength gradually returns. Already barely different from my model, I lift the bottle, put it to my lips, and—and with revulsion, with revulsion, even though it is empty and filled only with the smell—throw it on the ground with disgust. To the sadness of my teacher, to my own greater sadness; nor do I make things better either with him or myself when, even after throwing away the bottle, I do not forget to rub my belly brilliantly and grin.

All too often the lesson went this way. And to my teacher's credit, he was not angry with me; true, sometimes he held his burning pipe against my fur until it began to glow at some spot I could reach only with difficulty, but then he would extinguish it himself with his huge, kindly hand; he was not angry with me, he understood that we were on the same side, fighting my ape nature, and that my job was the more difficult one.

What a victory, then, for him as for me, when one evening, before a large group of spectators—perhaps a party was underway, a phonograph was playing, an officer was strolling among the men—when, on this evening, when no one was looking, I grabbed a bottle of brandy that had accidentally been left outside my cage, amid the increasing attention of the company uncorked it very correctly, put it to my lips, and without dawdling, without grimacing, like a professional tippler, with round, rolling eyes and swashing throat, really and truly drank down the entire contents; tossed away the bottle, no longer like someone in despair but like an artist; I did forget to rub my belly; but in return, because I could not help it, because I felt the urge, because all my senses were in an uproar, in short, I shouted "Hello!," broke out in human speech, with this cry leaped into the human community and felt its echo, "Just listen to that, he's talking!" like a kiss on my whole sweat-soaked body.

I repeat: I was not attracted to the idea of imitating men; I imitated because I was looking for a way out, for no other reason. Besides, I accomplished little with this victory. My voice failed again immediately; it returned only after several months; my disgust with the brandy bottle returned, even stronger. But my course was irrevocably set.

When I was handed over to my first trainer, in Hamburg, I quickly recognized the two choices available to me: the zoo or vaudeville. I did not hesitate. I said to myself: try with all your might to get into vaudeville; that is the way out; the zoo is only a new cage with bars; once you get into it, you're lost.

And, gentlemen, I learned. Oh, you learn when you have to; you learn when you want a way out; you learn relentlessly. You supervise yourself, whip in hand; you tear yourself to pieces at the least sign of resistance. Ape nature, falling all over itself, raced[3] madly out of me and away, so that I practically made a monkey of my first teacher, who was soon forced to give up training and had to be delivered to a sanatorium. Fortunately he was soon released.

But I used up many teachers, indeed, even several teachers simultaneously. When I had become more confident of my abilities and the public world followed my progress, I had glimmerings of a future; I myself hired teachers, seated them in five adjoining rooms, and managed to study with them all at the same time by leaping incessantly from one room to the other.

This progress! This penetration of rays of knowledge from all sides into the awakening brain! I do not deny it: it made me happy. But I also admit: I did not overestimate it, not then, even less today. Through an effort that has hitherto never been repeated on this planet, I have reached the average cultural level of a European. That by itself may be nothing at all, but it is something to the extent that it helped me out of the cage and gave me this particular way out, this human way out. There is an excellent German expression, "to slip off into the bushes":[4] that is what I did, I slipped off into the bushes. I had no other way, presupposing that freedom was never an option.

When I review my evolution and its goal so far, I can't complain, but neither am I satisfied. My hands in my pants pockets, the wine bottle on the table, I half-lie, half-sit in my rocking chair and look out the window. When company comes, I play host as is proper. My manager sits in the anteroom; when I ring, he comes and listens to what I have to say. In the evenings there is almost always a performance, and I enjoy successes that can scarcely be surpassed. If I return late at night from banquets, from learned societies, from convivial occasions, a little half-trained chimpanzee is waiting for me, and I have my pleasure of her in the way of all apes. In the daytime I do not want to see her; she has the lunatic look of the bewil-

---

3. The German verb *rasen* means both to "race" and to "rave."
4. The German expression *sich in die Büsche schlagen,* means, literally, "to smash a path (sideways) through the brush or bushes" and hence retains the jungle image.

dered trained animal; I am the only one who recognizes it, and I can't stand it.

By and large, I have achieved what I wanted to achieve. Let no one say that it hasn't been worth it. For the rest, I do not seek the judgment of any man, I merely want to disseminate knowledge; I am merely making a report; to you, too, exalted gentlemen of the Academy, I have merely made a report.

A STARVATION ARTIST • FOUR STORIES

First Distress

A trapeze artist—it is generally acknowledged that this art form, practiced high in the cupolas of the great variety theaters, is one of the most difficult of those attainable by human beings—had so organized his life, at first only from striving for perfection but later from the growing tyranny of habit as well, that as long as he was employed at the same place, he spent night and day on his trapeze. All his needs, which were actually very modest, were provided for by orderlies, who took turns keeping watch below and using specially constructed containers to hoist up and down whatever was needed above. This way of life caused no special difficulties for those around him; it was merely somewhat distracting that during the other numbers on the program he remained floating above, which could not be hidden from sight, and although he mainly kept still at such times, now and again a glance from the public would stray up to him. But the directors forgave him, because he was an extraordinary, an irreplaceable artist. It was, of course, also understood that he lived this way not out of wilfullness and that this was the only way he could keep himself continually in form, the only way he could keep his art at the level of perfection.

Certainly it was also healthy up above, and when during the warmer months the side windows were opened all around the vaulted ceiling and along with the fresh air the sun powerfully penetrated the dusky arena, it was even beautiful. Of course his interactions with others were limited: sometimes an acrobat colleague of his would climb up to him on the rope ladder, and both of them would sit on the trapeze, chatting while bracing themselves to the right and left on the ropes; at other times maintenance men, fixing the roof, might exchange a few words with him through an open window; or the fire inspector, checking the emergency lighting on the topmost balcony, would call out a few respectful though virtually unintelligible words. Otherwise the quiet all around him was unbroken; now and then a worker who might have wandered one afternoon into the empty theater would look up thoughtfully into heights the eye could barely make out, where the trapeze artist, who could not know that someone was watching him, was practicing his skills or resting.

The trapeze artist could have lived happily this way had it not been for the unavoidable journeys from town to town; these placed a great burden on him. To be sure, the manager took pains to spare the trapeze artist any unnecessary prolongation of his suffering; they used racing cars for traveling in the cities, and whenever possible they ran at top speed through the deserted streets at night or in the earliest morning hours, but of course this was too slow for the yearning of the trapeze artist; a whole train compartment was reserved for him, where he spent the trip lying up in the netting of the baggage rack—certainly a miserable substitute for his customary way of life, but at least some sort of approximation; in the next town on the tour, the trapeze was in its place long before the trapeze artist arrived at the theater; all the doors that led into the performance space were thrown wide open, all the corridors kept free—but the happiest moments in the manager's life always occurred whenever the trapeze artist set his foot on the rope ladder and in a flash, at last, was once again hanging up above from his trapeze.

No matter how many trips the manager had successfully managed by now, each new one was still an ordeal, since, aside from everything else, the tours always damaged the trapeze artist's nerves.

And so one day the two of them were once again traveling together; the trapeze artist lay in the baggage rack dreaming, the manager was leaning back in the window seat opposite, reading a book, when the trapeze artist quietly spoke to him. The manager was immediately at his service. The trapeze artist, biting his lips, said that instead of the one trapeze he had used up until now, from now on he would need two trapezes for his acrobatics—two trapezes, one across from the other. The manager consented at once. But as if to show that in this case the manager's agreement carried as little weight as, say, his objection, the trapeze artist said that from now on he would never again and under no circumstances use only one trapeze in his act. At the thought that something of the sort might happen, he seemed to shudder. The manager, hesitant and watchful, once again declared his complete agreement that two trapezes were better than one and that the new arrangement would have the advantage of adding more variety to the performance. At that the trapeze artist suddenly burst into tears. Deeply shaken, the manager jumped up and asked what had happened, and since he received no answer, he climbed up on the seat, stroked the artist, and pressed his face against his own, so that his face grew wet with the trapeze artist's tears. It was only after a great many questions and flattering words that the trapeze artist said, sobbing: "Only this one bar in my hands—how can I live that way?" Now it was somewhat easier for the manager to console the trapeze artist; he promised that at the very next station he would send a telegram about the second trapeze to the next town on their tour; reproached himself for having permitted the trapeze artist to perform on only one trapeze for so long; and thanked him and praised him warmly for finally calling attention to the mistake. In this way the manager succeeded in slowly reassuring the trapeze artist, and he could again return to his corner. But he himself was not reassured; it was with severe concern that he secretly watched the trapeze artist over the edge of his book. Once such thoughts had begun to obsess him, could they ever come to an end? Would they not continue to become more and more intense? Weren't they a threat to his livelihood, life-threatening? And the manager believed that, during the seemingly calm sleep in which the trapeze artist's weeping had ended, he could make out the first wrinkles beginning to etch themselves into the artist's smooth, childlike forehead.

A Starvation Artist

In the past few decades the interest in starvation artists has greatly declined. Whereas earlier it was very profitable to stage independent productions of such grand performances, today that is completely impossible. Times were different then. In those days the whole city was preoccupied with the starvation artist; from one day of starving to the next, interest mounted; everyone wanted to see the starvation artist at least once a day; later on, some subscription-ticket holders sat all day long before the little barred cage; but viewings took place even at night, when the effect was heightened by torchlight; on clear days the cage was carried out into the open, and then it was the children, especially, for whom the starvation artist was exhibited; while for the grownups it was often only a joke, in which they joined because it was all the rage, the children looked on in open-mouthed wonder, for safety's sake holding each other's hands, as, pale in a black leotard, with strongly protruding ribs, even disdaining a chair, he sat on spread straw, now nodding politely, now answering questions with a strained smile, stretching his arm through the bars in order to let them feel how thin he was; then again, he shrank completely into himself once more, concerned with no one, not even with the striking of the clock, so important to him, which was the sole piece of furniture in the cage; instead he merely stared straight ahead with eyes half-shut, now and then taking sips from a tiny glass of water to moisten his lips.

Aside from the spectators, who made up the ever changing crowd, there were also permanent watchmen, chosen by the public—oddly enough, usually butchers—whose job it was, always three at a time, to watch the starvation artist day and night so that he did not, perhaps in some secret way, manage to take nourishment. But that supervision was a mere formality, introduced to satisfy the masses, for initiates knew well enough that during starving times the starvation artist had never, under any circumstances, even under compulsion, taken in even the slightest morsel: the honor of his art forbade such an action. Of course not every watchman could understand this concept: sometimes watchmen on the night shift were very lax in the performance of their duties, deliberately sitting in a remote corner and immersing themselves in card games, with the obvious intention of permitting the starvation artist to take a little refreshment, which they supposed he could produce from some secret store. Nothing tormented the starvation artist more than such watchmen; they made him melancholy; they made his starving terribly difficult; sometimes during the hours of the watch, overcoming his weakness, he sang for as long as he could so as to show these people how unjust their suspicions were. But that ploy helped little; they were merely amazed at his dexterity in managing to eat even while singing. He much preferred those watchmen who sat close to the bars and, not content with the dim lighting of the hall at night, shone on him the electric flashlights with which the manager had provided them. The glaring light did not disturb him in the least: he could not sleep anyway; and he could always doze briefly under any sort of illumination and at any time, even in the noisy, overcrowded hall. He was very glad to spend the night with such watchmen without sleeping a wink; he was prepared to joke with them, to tell them stories from his journeyman years, and in turn to listen to their stories, anything just so as to keep them awake, to be able to show them again and again that he had nothing edible in the cage and that he starved in a way that not one of them could. But he was happiest when morning came and an opulent breakfast, for which he had paid, was brought to them, on which they threw themselves with the appetite of healthy men who had spent a strenuous, sleepless night. True, there were people who wanted to interpret this breakfast as a piece of undue influence on the watchmen, but that was going too far; and when they were asked whether they might be ready to take over the night watch without breakfast for the good of the cause alone, they slipped away, though they continued to harbor suspicions.

This, of course, was just one of the suspicions that were inevitably connected with starving. Since no one was able to spend all the days and nights beside the starvation artist uninterruptedly playing watchman, no one could know, on the strength of his own perceptions, whether the fast had truly been performed uninterruptedly, faultlessly; only the starvation artist himself could be certain, and so only he could also be the perfectly assured spectator of his fast. However, there was yet another reason why he was never satisfied; perhaps it was not entirely from fasting that he was so emaciated that many people, to their regret, had to stay away from the performances because they could not stand the sight of him; no, he was so emaciated only from dissatisfaction with himself. For he alone, and no other initiate, knew how easy it was to starve. It was the easiest thing in the world. He did not keep this fact a secret, but no one believed him; at best he was considered modest, but for the most part he was regarded as a publicity hound or even a charlatan, for whom starving was indeed easy because he knew how to make it easy for himself and who had the nerve to halfway admit it. He had to put up with all of this, and in the course of the years he did grow used to it, but inwardly his dissatisfaction continued to gnaw at him, and never, after any period of starving—you had to grant him this distinction—had he ever left the cage of his own free will. The manager had set forty days as the maximum starving time; he never permitted the starving to go on longer, not even in the great metropolitan centers, and indeed, for a very good reason. Experience had proven that for about forty days, through gradually intensified publicity, you could go on stimulating a city's interest, but beyond that time there was no audience, a significant decline in attendance could be registered; of course there were slight differences between cities and countries in this regard; as a rule, however, forty days was the maximum. On the fortieth day, then, the door of the cage, garlanded with flowers, was opened, an enthusiastic audience filled the amphitheater, a military band played, two doctors entered the cage to take the necessary measurements of the starvation artist, the results were announced to the hall through a megaphone, and finally two young ladies appeared, overjoyed to have won the lottery, and intending to lead the starvation artist out of his cage down a few steps, where a carefully chosen invalid's meal had been laid out on a little table. And it was at this moment that the starvation artist always began to resist. Though he would willingly rest his bony arms on the outstretched hands of the ladies who, bending down, offered him their help, he refused to stand. Why should he stop right now, after forty days? He could have held out for a long time, for an unlimited time; why stop right now, when he was in his starving prime—indeed, not yet even in his prime? Why did they want to rob him of the glory of continuing to starve, the glory not only of becoming the greatest starvation artist of all time, which he probably was already, but in addition, of topping his own efforts to an inconceivable point, for he felt no limits to his ability to starve. Why did this crowd, which pretended to admire him so much, have so little patience with him; if he could hold out and continue to starve, why wouldn't they hold out? Furthermore, he was tired, he was sitting comfortably in the straw, and now he was supposed to stand tall and proceed to his meal, the very thought of which was enough to make him feel queasy and nauseous, though he strenuously suppressed all signs of this condition solely out of consideration for the ladies. And he looked up into the eyes of the ladies who seemed so friendly but in reality were so cruel, and he shook his head, which was too heavy for his weakened neck. But what happened next was what always happened. The manager came and silently—the music made talking impossible—raised his arms above the starvation artist as if inviting the heavens to look down at its handiwork, here on the straw, this pitiable martyr, which the starvation artist admittedly was, but in a quite different sense; grasped the starvation artist around his thin waist, intending through exaggerated caution to produce a convincing impression of how fragile a creature he was dealing with here; and handed him over—not without surreptitiously shaking him a little, so that the starvation artist's legs and torso wobbled back and forth uncontrollably—to the ladies, who meanwhile had turned deathly pale. Now the starvation artist was ready to endure anything; his head rested on his chest, as if it had come rolling in from somewhere and, for some inexplicable reason, stuck there; his body was hollow; his legs, from an instinct of self-preservation, pressed themselves tightly against each other at the knees, while his feet scrabbled at the ground as if it were not the real one, they were still looking for the real one, and the entire burden of his body—admittedly very light—rested on one of the ladies, who, imploringly, with fluttering breath—this was not how she had imagined her position of honor—at first stretched her neck as far as it would go, at least to protect her face from any contact with the starvation artist; but then, when this proved impossible and her more fortunate companion did not come to her rescue but contented herself with tremulously carrying before her the hand of the starvation artist, that little bundle of bones, she broke into tears amid the delighted laughter of the hall and had to be replaced by a servant who had been ready and waiting long in advance. Then came the meal, a small amount of which the manager poured down the starvation artist's throat in his swoonlike half-sleep, amid some comic banter, designed to distract attention from the artist's condition; a toast to the public, which had allegedly been whispered to the manager by the starvation artist, was then proposed; the orchestra backed the entire proceedings with a great flourish, the crowd broke up, and no one had any reason to be dissatisfied with what he had seen—no one, that is, except the starvation artist, he alone, always.

And so he lived with regular short rest periods for many years, in apparent glory, honored by the world, but for all that usually in a melancholy mood, which grew increasingly so because no one was able to take it seriously. And how could he be consoled? What more could he want? And if at times some well-meaning person came along who felt sorry for him and tried to tell him that his sadness probably came from his fasting, it could happen, especially during an advanced stage of the fast, that the starvation artist might respond with an outbreak of rage and, to everyone's horror, begin to rattle the bars of his cage like an animal. But the manager had a punishment for such fits that he rather enjoyed applying. Before the assembled audience he would apologize for the starvation artist, admitting that only the irritability provoked by starving, something not easy for well-fed persons to understand, could excuse his behavior; in this connection he then came to speak of the starvation artist's claim that he could go on starving much longer, a belief that could be explained in exactly the same way; praised the lofty striving, the good will, the immense self-denial that was obviously present in this claim; then sought to refute the claim simply enough by showing photographs, which were simultaneously put on sale, for in the pictures the starvation artist could be seen on a fortieth day of starving, in bed, enfeebled to the point of extinction. This twisting of the truth, which, although it was already well known to the starvation artist, always freshly unnerved him, was too much for him. The effect of the premature ending of his fast was being represented here as its cause! To struggle against this stupidity, against this universe of stupidity, was impossible. Up to this point he had always been ready at the bars of his cage to listen eagerly and in good faith to the manager, but as soon as the photographs appeared, he always let go of the bars, sank, sighing, back into the straw, and the audience, reassured, could once again approach and view him.

When, a few years later, witnesses to such scenes recalled them, they were often unable to understand their own reactions. For in the meantime the previously mentioned shift had occurred; it had happened almost overnight; there might have been deeper reasons, but who had any interest in discovering them? In any case, one day the pampered starvation artist found himself abandoned by the crowds of pleasure seekers, who preferred to go streaming off to other shows. Once more the manager raced with him through half of Europe to see if the old interest might still be found here or there; all in vain; as if by a secret understanding, what was practically an aversion to public displays of starving had developed everywhere. Of course, in reality it could not have happened so suddenly, and now, after the event, people began to recall a number of early warnings, which at that time, in the ecstasy of success, had not been adequately noted and not adequately suppressed, but now it was too late to do anything about them. Certainly the time for starving, as for all things, would come again, but that was no consolation to the living. What, now, should the starvation artist do? The man whom thousands had once wildly acclaimed could not exhibit himself in booths at small village fairs, and as for taking up another vocation, the starvation artist was not only too old but above all much too fanatically devoted to starving. So he dismissed the manager, the companion of a career without compare, and accepted an engagement with a great circus; and to spare his feelings, he did not even glance at the terms of the contract.

A great circus with its innumerable performers and animals and contraptions, forever balancing and supplementing one another, can find work for anybody at any time—even a starvation artist—if, of course, his demands are correspondingly modest, and in this particular case, it was not only the starvation artist himself who was hired but his old, time-honored name as well; indeed, it could not even be said that, given the peculiar nature of this artistry, which does not diminish with the artist's increasing age, in this instance an artist who had put in his time and was no longer at the height of his powers was seeking refuge in a quiet circus job; on the contrary, the starvation artist gave assurances—entirely credible ones—that he could starve just as well as before; indeed, he maintained that if he could have his way, and this he was promised without further ado, he would really and for the first time give the world a true reason to be astonished, although his claim, considering the mood of the times, which the starvation artist in his zeal was quick to forget, merely produced a smile among the experts.

Deep down, however, even the starvation artist did not lose sight of reality and accepted it as perfectly natural that he, with his cage, should not be placed as, let us say, a showstopper in the center ring but installed outside at a quite easily accessible spot, close to the animal sheds. Huge, brightly colored posters framed the cage, proclaiming what could be seen there. When, during the intermissions, the audience rushed to the menagerie to see the animals, it was almost unavoidable that they would pass by the starvation artist and stop for a moment: they might have continued to stay at his cage if other spectators, crowding in from behind in the narrow passage and not understanding why they were being held up on the way to the animals they longed to see, had not made extended quiet contemplation impossible. This was also the reason why the prospect of these visiting hours, for which the starvation artist naturally yearned, since they were the meaning of his life, also made him shudder. In the beginning he could hardly wait for the intermissions; thrilled, he had watched the crowd come surging in, until all too soon he became convinced—even the most stubborn, almost deliberate self-deception could not stand up to experience—that every time and without exception it was made up, at least to judge by the people's intention, solely of visitors to the animal sheds. And it was this view from afar that remained the most attractive. For when the crowd had reached him, he was immediately surrounded by the shouts and curses of raging, continually re-forming groups, those—the starvation artist soon found them the more insufferable—who wanted to take their time looking at him, not with any appreciation but merely on a whim and from spite, and the second group, who began by clamoring for the animal sheds. Once this great mob had gone past, the stragglers arrived, and these people, whom nothing prevented from lingering as long as they liked, hurried past with long strides, almost without a sideward glance, to get to the animals on time. And it was a none too frequent godsend when a family man arrived with his children, pointed his finger at the starvation artist, explained in detail what it was all about, and told of years gone by, when he had been present at similar but incomparably more splendid performances; and then the children who, because school and life had insufficiently prepared them, admittedly stood uncomprehending—what was starving to them?— but the radiance of their searching eyes betrayed something of new, more merciful times to come. Perhaps then the starvation artist sometimes told himself that everything would be a little better if only he were not located so close to the animal sheds. The choice was thus made too easy for the visitors, not to mention that the stench of the stalls, the restlessness of the animals at night, the carrying past of raw chunks of meat for the carnivores, and the roaring at feeding time caused him intense suffering and continual depression. But he did not dare to complain to the management; after all, it was the animals he had to thank for the crowd of visitors, among whom there might be found an occasional spectator intended for him; and who knew where they would tuck him away if he tried to make them aware of his existence and therefore also of the fact that, strictly speaking, he was nothing more than an obstacle on the way to the animal sheds.

A small obstacle, to be sure, an ever shrinking obstacle. People

grew used to the sheer oddity of wanting to draw attention to a starvation artist nowadays, and their adaptation spelled his doom. He
could starve as best he could, and he did so, but nothing could save
him any longer; people passed him by. Try to explain the art of
starving to someone! Those who have no feel for it can never be
made to understand. The handsome posters became dirty and illeg-
ible, they were torn down, no thought was given to replacing them;
the little board indicating the number of days he had spent starving, which at the beginning had been carefully retabulated every
day, remained unchanged for a long time, for after the first few
weeks, the staff had grown sick of performing even this small
chore; and so, while the starvation artist went on starving the way
he had once dreamed of doing, and he succeeded effortlessly in exactly the way he had prophesied at that time, no one counted the
days, no one, not even the starvation artist himself knew how great
his achievement really was, and his heart grew heavy. And when
once in a while an idle passerby stopped to make a joke about the
outdated number and spoke of cheating, this was the stupidest lie
that indifference and innate cruelty could devise, for it was not the
starvation artist who was cheating, he performed his work honorably, it was the world that cheated him of his reward.

But many more days went by, and that phase came to an end as
well. One day a supervisor noticed the cage, and he asked the attendants why this cage full of rotting straw was left standing here
when it could be put to good use; no one knew the answer until
someone, prompted by the board with the number, remembered
the starvation artist. They poked around in the straw with sticks
and found the starvation artist underneath. "You're still starving?"
asked the supervisor. "When will you stop at last?" "Forgive me, all
of you," the starvation artist whispered; only the supervisor, who
held his ear against the bars of the cage, heard him. "Of course,"
said the supervisor and tapped his forehead with his finger to indicate to the staff the starvation artist's condition, "we forgive you." "I
always wanted you to admire my starving," the starvation artist said.
"We do admire it," said the supervisor, obligingly. "But you should
not admire it," said the starvation artist. "Well, then we don't admire it," said the supervisor. "Why shouldn't we admire it?" "Because I have to starve, I can't help it,"[1] said the starvation artist.
"Well, how about that!" said the supervisor. "So why can't you help
it?" "Because I," said the starvation artist, lifting his tiny head a lit-

1. *Weil ich hungern muss,* says the starving-artist, *ich kann nicht anders.* When the great
Protestant reformer Martin Luther was challenged and asked to desist from his then
heretical actions, he replied, using these very words, *ich kann nicht anders,* literally, "I
cannot [do] otherwise."

tle, his lips pursed as if for a kiss, and speaking right into the ear of the supervisor, so that nothing would go unheard, "because I could not find the food I liked.[2] If I had found it, believe me, I would not have caused a sensation, and I would have stuffed myself just like you and all the others." Those were his last words, but his shattered gaze retained the firm, if no longer proud, conviction that he was still starving.[3]

"Let's go, clean up this mess!" said the supervisor, and they buried the starvation artist together with the straw. But into the cage they put a young panther.[4] Even the dullest minds felt relief at seeing this wild animal bounding around in a cage that had for so long been barren. The animal lacked for nothing. The food he liked was brought to him without long reflection by his keepers; he did not even seem to miss his freedom; this noble body, equipped just short of bursting with everything it needed, seemed to carry its freedom around with it; it seemed to lodge somewhere in the jaws; and the joy of life sprang from its maw in such a blaze of fire that it was not easy for the spectators to withstand it. But they controlled themselves, crowded around the cage, and would not be budged from the spot.

Josefine, the Singer or The Mouse People

Our singer is named Josefine. Anyone who has not heard her does not know the power of song. There is no one who is not carried away by her singing, a fact deserving of all the more appreciation since, by and large, people of our kind are not music lovers. For us the best music is peace and quiet; our life is hard; even when we try to shake off our daily cares, we can no longer rise to matters as remote from our ordinary life as music. But we do not complain too much—even that is beyond our reach; we consider our greatest virtue to be a certain practical shrewdness, which, of course, we need most urgently; and we use the smirk of our shrewdness to comfort ourselves about everything, even when we might feel the yearning—though that does not arise—for the hap-

2. Cf. the concluding lines of "The Knock at the Courtyard Gate": "Could I still sense any air other than that of a prison? That is the great question—or rather, it would be the question if I had any prospect of being released."
3. Cf. the dying look of the officer in *In the Penal Colony*: "It [the face] was as it had been in life; no sign of the promised deliverance could be discovered; what all the others had found in the machine the officer did not find; his lips were firmly pressed together; his eyes were open, had an expression of life, their look was full of calm and conviction, the forehead was pierced by the point of the great metal thorn."
4. See the Norton Critical Edition of Kafka's *The Metamorphosis*, in which Gregor Samsa, the hero, is also discarded like trash, his room/cage cleaned, and a new, flourishing source of life (his sister Grete) put on center stage.

piness that can flow from music. Josefine is the one exception; she loves music and knows how to convey it; she is the only one; with her passing, music—who knows for how long?—will vanish from our lives.

I have often considered what this music is really all about. After all, we are totally unmusical; how is it that we understand Josefine's singing or, since Josefine denies this, that we at least think we understand it? The simplest answer would be that the beauty of her song is so great that even the dullest minds cannot resist it, but this answer is not satisfactory. If it were really so, her singing would always produce an immediate feeling of something extraordinary, the feeling that something rang from this throat which we had never heard before and which we are not even capable of hearing, something that only this one individual, Josefine, and no one else enables us to hear. Precisely this, in my opinion, is not the case; I do not feel it nor have I noticed anything like it in others. In our private circle we openly admit to each other that Josefine's song as such does not represent anything extraordinary.

Is it really song? Despite our lack of musicality, we have traditions of song; in the early days of our people there was song; legends tell of it, and songs have even been preserved though, of course, no one can sing them anymore. So we do have an inkling of what song is, but Josefine's artistry really does not correspond to it. Is it even song, then? Isn't it perhaps just squeaking?[1] And squeaking, of course, is something all of us are familiar with; it is the characteristic artistic skill of our people or, rather, not a skill at all but a typical manifestation of life. All of us squeak, but of course no one dreams of passing it off as art; we squeak without paying attention, without even noticing, and in fact, there are many of us who don't even realize that squeaking is one of our traits. Hence, if it were true that Josefine does not sing but merely squeaks, and even perhaps, as it seems at least to me, barely exceeds the bounds of ordinary squeaking—indeed, perhaps her strength does not even completely suffice for this usual squeaking, whereas an ordinary laborer can produce it effortlessly all day long at his work—if all that were true, then Josefine's alleged artistry would be disproved, but precisely then we would truly have to solve the puzzle of its huge effect.

But it actually isn't mere squeaking that she produces. If you station yourself a good distance from her and listen or, better still, submit yourself to the following test: let Josefine sing among others and assign yourself the task of recognizing her voice, then you will

1. The German word translated throughout this story as "squeaking" is *pfeifen*, which, for human beings, means "whistling."

invariably single out only an ordinary squeak, at most a sound somewhat striking in its delicacy or weakness. But if you stand in front of her, it really is not just squeaking; to understand her art, you must not only hear but also see her. Even if the sound were merely our everyday squeaking, we are confronted right from the start with the oddity of someone who stands up ceremoniously to perform only the usual. It does not take any great artistry, after all, to crack a nut, and so no one would dare to summon an audience and crack nuts for its entertainment. But if someone does that and he succeeds in his intent, then it cannot be, after all, just a matter of mere nutcracking. Or it is a matter of nutcracking, but it turns out that we have ignored this art because we are past masters at it and this new nutcracker is the first to reveal its authentic nature to us, in which case it could even contribute to the effect if this person were a little less competent at nutcracking than most of us.

Perhaps it's the same where Josefine's song is concerned; we admire her for what we do not admire in ourselves; in regard to the latter, by the way, she agrees with us entirely. Once I was present when someone—as often happens, of course—drew her attention to the squeaking of the common folk and did so only in a very understated way, but for Josefine even that was too much. I never saw so insolent, so arrogant a smile as she then assumed; she, who appears to be the true epitome of gentleness, strikingly gentle even among a people as rich in such feminine types as our own, seemed at that moment downright mean; given her great sensitivity, she surely must have felt this immediately and composed herself. And so, at all events, she denies any connection between her art and squeaking. She has nothing but scorn, and probably unacknowledged hatred, for anyone who has a different opinion. That is not ordinary vanity, for this opposition, to which I too half-belong, surely admires her no less than does the majority, but Josefine wants not only to be admired but to be admired in exactly the way she decides; admiration as such is of no concern to her. And when you are sitting in front of her, you understand her; opposition can be offered only at a distance; when you sit in front of her, you understand: what she is squeaking here is no squeaking.

Since squeaking is one of our unconscious habits, you might imagine that there will be some squeaking among Josephine's audience as well; her artistry gives us a sense of well-being, and when we feel well, we squeak; but her audience does not squeak, we are as quiet as mice; as if we were partaking of the peace we long for, which at least our own squeaking prevents us from attaining, we keep quiet. Is it her singing that enchants us, or is it rather the ceremonious quiet that surrounds her weak little voice? Once it happened that during Josefine's concert some silly young pipsqueak began in all innocence to pipe up. Now, it was the very same thing that we were hearing from Josefine; there, in front, her squeaking, still bashful despite all the routine, and here, in the audience, an unself-conscious, childlike squeaking; it would have been impossible to specify the difference; but still we immediately booed[2] and whistled for this disturbing element to pipe down, although none of it would have been necessary, for she would surely have crept away on her own in fear and shame, while Josefine struck up her squeak of triumph and was in total ecstasy, her arms stretched out and her neck extended as high as it would go.

This, by the way, is how she always is: every trivial detail, every happenstance, every bit of unruliness, a creak in the wooden floor, a gnashing of teeth, a lighting failure, all strike her as an opportunity for heightening the effect of her singing; in her opinion she sings to deaf ears anyway; there is no lack of enthusiasm and applause, but she has long since learned to give up on what she considers genuine appreciation. Hence, all disturbances greatly suit her; anything coming from outside that confronts the purity of her song, everything that can be subdued in easy battle—indeed, even without a battle but merely by this very confrontation—can contribute to arousing the crowd, teaching it not understanding, of course, but awe-filled respect.

But if small things serve her so well, then how much more so do great things. Our life is a very unsettled one: every day brings surprises, anxieties, hopes, and terrors, so that it would be impossible for any individual to bear all of it if he did not have the support of his fellows all day and all night; but even so, life often becomes very difficult; sometimes even the shoulders of a thousand tremble under a burden that was originally meant for just one individual. Then Josefine believes that her time has come. At once she stands there, this gentle being, vibrating in a terrifying way, especially below her breast: it is as if she had gathered all her strength in song; as if everything in her that does not immediately serve song had been drained of all power, almost all life force, as if she were stripped bare, exposed, entrusted only to the protection of good spirits, as if, while she is thus dwelling in song, totally removed from herself, a cold breeze blowing past could kill her. But it is precisely at such a sight that we, her alleged opponents, are accustomed to saying to ourselves, "She can't even squeak; look what a terrible strain it is for her just to eke out not song—we're not talking about song—but something resembling our usual squeaking." So it seems to us; yet, as we've already mentioned, this impression, though inescapable, is

---

2. The word for "to boo" in German is *zischen*, "to hiss," which is also the famous noise in *The Burrow*; hence it can be construed there as an expression of felt universal disapproval for Kafka's own literary construction.

also transient, swiftly fleeting. Soon we, too, are plunged into the sensation of the crowd as, body warmly pressed on body, breathing with awe, it listens.

And to gather around her this crowd of our people, who are almost continually in motion, shooting off here and there for purposes that are often not very clear, Josefine generally needs to do no more than assume that stance—her little head tilted back, mouth half-open, eyes turned toward the heights—that indicates that she intends to sing. She can do so wherever she likes, it does not have to be a place visible from afar, any sort of hidden corner chosen at a casual moment's whim will do as well. The news immediately spreads that she is setting up to sing, and soon entire processions are on their way to her. Sometimes, it is true, obstacles do intrude, for Josefine prefers to sing in troubled times; multiple cares and needs compel us to take a multitude of different routes; even with the best will in the world we cannot assemble as quickly as Josefine would like, and at such times she may stand there in her grand attitude for some length of time without an adequate audience— then, of course, she grows angry, then she stamps her feet, curses in a most unmaidenly manner, indeed, she even bites. But not even such behavior damages her reputation; instead of restraining her excessively grand pretensions a little, people struggle to adapt to them; messengers are sent to bring the listeners in; she is kept in ignorance of what is happening; you can see sentinels posted on the surrounding roads, waving to the newcomers and urging them to hurry; this goes on for as long as it takes, until, finally, a passable number has gathered.

What drives the people to take such pains on Josefine's behalf? A question no easier to answer than the question of Josefine's song, with which, in fact, it is connected. You could cross it out and fuse it completely with the second question if it could be asserted, say, that the people are unconditionally devoted to her for the sake of her song. But this is not the case; unconditional devotion is all but unknown to our people; this people that loves shrewdness above all, harmless shrewdness, of course, childish whispering, gossiping, innocent, of course, with barely moving lips, such a people cannot finally devote itself unconditionally; Josefine may well be aware of this; it is what she is fighting against with all the might of her feeble throat.

Except, of course, that one must not go too far in making such general judgments; the people are indeed devoted to Josefine, but not unconditionally. They would never, e.g., be capable of laughing at Josefine. You have to admit: there are a number of things about Josefine that can make you laugh; and by and large, we are always on the verge of laughing; despite all the grief in our lives, a quiet

laughter always has a place in our lives; but we do not laugh at
Josefine. Sometimes it seems to me that the people think of their
relation to Josefine as one in which she, this fragile, vulnerable,
somehow distinguished being, who, in her own opinion, is distinguished for her song, has been entrusted to them, and she is their
responsibility; the reason for this is not clear to anyone, yet the fact
seems to have been established. But you do not laugh at something
that has been entrusted to you; to laugh would be a dereliction of
duty; it is the absolute limit of spite that the most spiteful of us inflict on Josefine when they sometimes say: "One look at Josefine
and you lose all desire to laugh."

So the people take care of Josefine the way a father looks after a
child who stretches out her little hand—you cannot tell whether
pleading or demanding—to him. You might think that our people
were not suited to perform such fatherly duties, but in reality we
carry them out exemplarily, at least in this case; no individual could
do what the people as a whole are able to do in this respect. Of
course, the difference in power between the people and the individual is so enormous that they need only draw their ward into the
warmth of their intimacy and the ward is sufficiently protected. No
one, however, dares to speak of such things to Josefine. "I don't give
a squeak for your protection," she would say. "Squeak away, Josefine," we think. Besides, it isn't really a refutation when she rebels:
it is more like an altogether childish way of being and a childish
way of showing gratitude, and it is the father's way to pay no attention to it.

Something else is involved, however, that is harder to explain in
terms of the relationship between the people and Josefine. Josefine,
that is, holds the opposite opinion, she thinks that she is the one
who protects the people. Her singing allegedly rescues us from
grim political or economic situations, it accomplishes no less than
that; and if it does not banish misfortune, at least it gives us the
strength to endure it. This is not how she puts it, but she does not
put it any other way, either; she rarely has anything to say, she is
silent among the blabbermouths, but it flashes from her eyes, you
can read it off her tightly shut lips—among us only a few can keep
their lips shut, but she can. Whenever we get bad news—and some
days it rushes in pell-mell, falsehoods and half-truths included—
she rises up immediately, although normally she is drawn wearily to
the ground, rises up and cranes her neck and strives to oversee her
flock like the shepherd before the storm. It is true that in their
wild, unruly way children make similar demands, but Josefine's are
not as unreasonable as theirs. Of course she does not save us, and
she does not give us strength; it is easy to give yourself airs, claim
to be the savior of this people—a people that, accustomed to pain,

unsparing of itself, quick to decide, well acquainted with death, only apparently anxious in the daredevil atmosphere in which it continually lives, and furthermore, as fertile as it is daring—it is easy, I say, to give yourself airs after the event and claim to be the savior of this people that has always managed to save itself one way or another, even if sacrifices were required that make the historian—in general we completely neglect historical research—freeze in horror. And yet it is true that it is precisely in times of trouble that we listen to Josefine's voice with even greater intensity. The threats that hang over us make us quieter, more humble, more submissive to Josefine's domineering ways; we are glad to join together, glad to huddle up against one another, especially because the occasion lies so far from the tormenting principal issue; it is as if we were drinking hastily—yes, we are in a hurry, that is something that Josefine all too often forgets—a communal goblet of peace before the battle. It is not so much a song recital as a popular assembly and, what is more, a meeting that, except for the bit of squeaking at the front, is entirely quiet; the hour is too solemn for anyone to want to waste it with babbling.

Now, such a relationship could not, of course, satisfy Josefine. Despite all the nervous discontent that fills her because her position has never been properly defined, there is a good deal that Josefine, blinded by self-confidence, does not see, and with no great effort she can be brought to overlook a good deal more; a swarm of flatterers is continually busy to this end and hence really engaged in a public service—but merely singing to one side, unnoticed, in a corner of a popular assembly, for such a thing she would hardly give up her singing, though in reality it would not be easy to ignore.

But she does not have to, for her art does not go unnoticed. Although basically we are preoccupied with quite different matters and the silence that reigns is by no means only for the sake of her singing, and many who are present do not bother to look up, instead pressing their faces into the fur of their neighbors, so that Josefine seems to be exhausting herself in vain, all the same, something of her squeaking—this cannot be denied—inevitably forces its way to us. This squeaking that arises where silence is imposed on everyone else comes almost as a message from the people to the individual; Josefine's thin squeak in the midst of grave decisions is almost like the wretched existence of our people amid the tumult of a hostile world. Josefine asserts herself, this nothing of a voice, this nothing of an achievement asserts itself and makes its way to us; we do well to remember this. If ever a true virtuoso of song were found among us, we would certainly not put up with him at such a time, we would unanimously reject the absurdity of such a performance. May Josefine be protected from the knowledge that our very listening to her is an argument against her song. She probably suspects such a thing, otherwise why would she deny so passionately that we listen to her? But time and again she sings, squeaking herself past this suspicion.

But she might have another consolation: to some extent we genuinely listen to her, probably in much the same way you listen to a virtuoso; she achieves effects that a virtuoso among us would strive in vain to achieve, effects she owes only and alone to her inadequate abilities. This is probably connected mainly with the way we live.

Among our people youth is unknown, there is barely any childhood. It is true that demands are regularly made to grant the children special privileges, special indulgences, to grant them the right to some carefree days, some meaningless romps, some time to play—this right should be acknowledged and efforts made to realize it; such demands are made, and almost everyone approves of them, there is nothing that one could approve of more, but given the reality of our lives, there is also nothing that could be less readily granted; the demands are approved, attempts are made to meet them, but soon everything is back to where it was before. The truth is that our life is such that just when a child can run around a little and can begin to make out its surroundings, it must also look after itself like an adult; dispersed as we must be for economic reasons, the areas where we live are too vast, our enemies too numerous, the dangers that confront us on all sides too incalculable— we cannot shelter our children from the struggle for existence, and if we did so, it would mean their premature end. Along with these sad reasons, there is also, of course, an uplifting one: the fertility of our tribe. One generation—and each is numerous—shoves up against the next, the children do not have time to be children. Among other peoples, children may be carefully provided for; schools may be set up for the little ones; children may come rushing out of these schools every day, the future of the people; but for some period of time it is the same children who day after day come out. We do not have schools, but countless crowds of our children come rushing out of our people at the shortest possible intervals, cheerfully squealing or peeping as long as they cannot yet squeak, tumbling or rolling away from the pressure at their backs as long as they are too young to run, clumsily tearing everything along with them in their mass as long as they cannot yet see—our children! And not, as in those schools, the same children: no, again and again, always new ones, endlessly, without interruption; hardly does a child appear than it is a child no longer, and crowding behind it already are the faces of the new children, indistinguishable in their quantity and their haste, rosy with happiness. Of course, as beautiful as this all may be and however much others may rightly envy us, the outcome is that we cannot give our children a real childhood. And this situation has consequences. A certain unfading childishness—a trait that cannot be wiped out—pervades our people; directly contradicting our finest qualities, our unerring practical reason, we sometimes behave with utter foolishness, with exactly the same kind of foolishness as children: we are absurd, extravagant, generous, reckless, and all this often just for the sake of a little fun. And naturally, while our enjoyment of this state no longer possesses the full force of a child's enjoyment, something of it certainly remains alive. And from the very beginning Josefine has also profited from this childishness of our people.

But as a people we are not only childish: in a certain sense we are also old before our time; childhood and old age manifest themselves differently among us than they do among others. We have no youth; we are adults from the outset, and then we are adults for too long: this situation results in a certain weariness and hopelessness that cuts a broad swath through the soul of our people, who on the whole are tough and strong in hope. This is very likely connected with the fact that we are unmusical; we are too old for music, its excitement, its uplift does not suit our gravity: wearily we shoo it away; we have fallen back on our squeaking; some squeaking here and there, that is what suits us. Who knows whether there are any musical talents among us; but if there were, the nature of our comrades would be bound to suppress their gift before it ever unfolded. On the other hand, Josefine may squeak or sing or whatever she prefers to call it to her heart's content: that does not bother us, that suits us, that is something we have no difficulty putting up with; but if there is supposed to be anything musical about it, then it is reduced to the lowest possible nothingness; a certain musical tradition is preserved but without weighing us down in the least.

But Josefine brings even more to people of such a disposition. At her concerts, especially in grave times, only the very young continue to be interested in the singer as such; only they gaze with amazement at the way she purses her lips, expels the air between her dainty front teeth, fades away with admiration of the notes that she herself produces, and uses her swooning to fire herself up to new feats that become ever more incomprehensible to her; but the true body of her audience—as is clear to see—has withdrawn into itself. Here, in the scant pauses between battles, the people dream; it is as if each individual relaxed his limbs, as if each restless soul might indulge for once his desire to unwind and stretch out in the big, warm, communal bed. And here and there into these dreams comes the sound of Josefine's squeaking; she calls it rippling, we call it bumping; but whatever it is, this is where it belongs more than anywhere else, in the way that music hardly ever finds the moment that is waiting for it. Something of our poor, brief childhood is in it; something of lost, irretrievable happiness; but something of the active present-day life is in it as well, its small measure of incomprehensible but nonetheless enduring and irrepressible cheerfulness. And all this is really proclaimed, not in a booming voice, but rather lightly, in whispers, intimately, sometimes a little hoarsely. Naturally, it is a squeaking. How could it be anything else? Squeaking is the language of our people, except that many squeak their whole life long without knowing it; in this case, however, squeaking is freed from the bonds of daily life and frees us for a little while as well. These are performances we certainly don't want to miss.

But it is a far cry from this to Josefine's claim that at such times she gives us new strength, etc., etc. Ordinary people think so, at least, not Josefine's flatterers. "How could it be otherwise?"—they say with sheer brazen impudence—"how else do you explain the full houses, especially at times of imminent danger, full houses that have sometimes even prevented adequate and timely defense against this very danger?" Well, the latter claim is, unfortunately, correct, but it still does not amount to one of Josefine's claims to fame, especially considering that when such gatherings were unexpectedly blown apart by the enemy and as a result many of our people lost their lives, Josefine, who was to blame for all of it and, indeed, whose squeaking might have attracted the enemy, always managed to get to the safest nook and very quietly under the protection of her escorts was the first to disappear with all possible speed. But this, too, is something everyone knows at heart, and still they rush in the next time Josefine gets up to sing, anywhere, anytime she pleases. One might conclude that Josefine is almost above the law, that she can do whatever she likes, even when it endangers the entire community, and that all will be forgiven. If such were the case, even Josefine's pretensions would be fully understandable; indeed, in a certain sense you could see this freedom the people would grant her, this extraordinary gift granted to no one else and in fact running counter to the law, as recognition of the fact that the people, as Josefine maintains, do not understand, gape helplessly at her art, feel unworthy of it, use literally desperate measures to try to make up for the suffering they thus inflict on her; and just as her art lies beyond their power of comprehension, they place her person and her wishes outside their power to command. Now, all of this is simply, absolutely untrue, perhaps in lesser matters the people capitulate too easily to Josefine, but just as they do not capitulate unconditionally to anyone, they do not capitulate to her.

For a long time, perhaps since the beginning of her artistic career, Josefine has fought to be excused from all work in consideration of her song; she expects to be relieved of the cares of earning her daily bread and everything else connected with our struggle for existence and—presumably—shift the burden to the whole populace. Anyone prone to enthusiasm—such types do exist—could, merely from the very oddness of this claim, from a mental constitution capable of thinking up such a claim, conclude that it is intrinsically justified. Our people, however, draw different conclusions and calmly reject the claim. Nor do they go to great lengths to refute the justifications for her appeal. Josefine points out, e.g., that the strain of working harms her voice—that though the effort involved in working is slight in comparison with the effort of singing, it nonetheless robs her of the possibility of resting adequately after singing and gathering strength for new song: thus she would be completely exhausted and under these circumstances would never be able to attain her highest achievement. The people hear her out and pay no attention. This people, so easily moved, is sometimes utterly unmovable. The rejection is sometimes so harsh that even Josefine staggers, she appears to accept it, works properly, sings as well as she can, but all that only for a while until, with renewed strength—her strength in this respect appears to be unlimited—she once again takes up the struggle.

Now it is perfectly clear that Josefine does not actually aspire to what she literally demands. She is reasonable, she is not work shy—indeed, among us shirking is utterly unknown; even if her demands were granted, she would surely not change her way of life, her work would never get in the way of her song, and her song would surely not grow any more beautiful—hence, what she strives for is simply the public acknowledgment of her art, an acknowledgment that is unambiguous, that will last for all time, rising far above everything known to this day. But while practically everything else strikes her as within reach, this goal stubbornly eludes her. Perhaps she should have aimed her attack in another direction from the very beginning, perhaps she herself now recognizes her mistake; but now she cannot retreat, retreating would mean to become untrue to herself, and it is with this demand that she must now stand or fall.

If she really had enemies, as she says, they could watch the struggle with amusement, without having to lift a finger. But she has no enemies, and even if at times some people have objected to her, no one finds this struggle amusing. Even if only because here our people show their cold, judgmental side, something we rarely display. And even if in this case someone approved of this attitude, any trace of pleasure vanishes at the mere idea that the people might at some time behave toward him in a similar way. No, what is at stake in the rejection, just as in the claim, is not the thing itself but rather the fact that the people can cut themselves off so inscrutably from a comrade, and all the more inscrutably when you consider that otherwise they look after this very comrade with fatherly—and more than fatherly, with humble—concern.

If one individual stood in the place of the people here, you could imagine that all this time he had given in to Josefine with a continually burning desire to stop once and for all being so indulgent; that he had made a superhuman effort to give in, in the firm conviction that this indulgence would somehow find its proper limit; indeed, that he had given in more than was necessary merely to speed things up, merely to spoil Josefine and drive her on to ever new desires, until she would make a final demand; and now, having long been prepared, he would curtly deliver this final rejection. Well, this is not how matters really stand; the people don't require such subterfuges; moreover, their admiration of Josefine is genuine and proven, and Josefine's demands are so extreme that any simple child could have foretold her the outcome; nonetheless, it may be that in Josefine's conception of the matter, such presentiments also play a role, adding a bitterness to the pain of someone who has been rejected.

But even if she has such presentiments, she does not allow them to frighten her off the struggle. Lately the struggle has grown even more critical; if so far she has fought it only with words, she is now beginning to employ other methods, which in her view are more effective but in our view hold greater danger for her.

Many believe that Josefine has grown so insistent because she feels herself growing older, her voice is showing signs of weakening, and so she thinks it high time to launch her final struggle for recognition. I do not believe this. Josefine would not be Josefine if this were true. For her there is no such thing as growing older or signs of weakness in her voice. When she demands something, she is not motivated by externals but rather by an inner logic. She reaches for the highest laurels, not because at some moment they happen to be hanging down a little lower, but because they are the highest; if it were in her power, she would hang them even higher.

This contempt for external problems does not, however, keep her from employing the most unworthy methods. Because her rights strike her as beyond all doubt, what does it matter how she attains them? Especially when in this world, as she figures, worthy methods must always fail. Perhaps it is for this very reason that she has shifted the struggle for her rights from the domain of song to another area, one that means less to her. Her followers have circulated statements of hers claiming that she feels quite capable of singing in a way that would be a true delight to the people on every level, down to the most covert opposition—a delight not in the popular sense, since the people maintain that they have always been delighted by Josefine's song, but in the sense of Josefine's longing. But she adds that since she cannot counterfeit the lofty or flatter the base, everything must remain just as it is. It is another matter, however, with her struggle to be excused from work; true, this struggle also concerns her song, but here she is not fighting directly with the precious weapon of her song, and therefore every method she employs is good enough.

And so, e.g., the rumor spread that unless her demands were accepted, Josefine intended to shorten the coloraturas.[3] I know nothing about coloraturas, and I have never noticed any sign of coloratura in her song. But Josefine intends to shorten the coloraturas, for the present not eliminate them but merely shorten them. She has allegedly carried out her threat; as for me, I have, of course, noticed nothing different from her previous performances. The people as a whole listened as usual, without saying anything about the coloraturas, and its treatment of Josefine's demand has not changed either. Incidentally, like her physical form, Josefine's thinking also undeniably has quite a graceful aspect. And so, e.g., as if her decision with respect to the coloraturas had been too harsh or abrupt for the people, after that performance she announced that the next time she would again sing the full coloraturas. But following the next concert she thought better of it again; now she declared that the great coloraturas were definitely over and that they would not be resumed unless there was to be a decision favorable to Josefine. Now the people simply ignore all these announcements, decisions, and changes of decision, the way an adult who is thinking his own thoughts ignores the chattering of a child—fundamentally well disposed but unreachable.

But Josefine does not relent. And so, e.g., she recently maintained that she had hurt her foot at work, which would make it difficult for her to sing standing up; but since she could sing only standing up, she would now have to curtail the tunes as well. Despite the fact that she limps and leans on her followers, no one believes that her injury is real. Even granting the special sensitivity of her little body, we are, after all, a working people, and Josefine is one of us; but if we began to limp every time we suffered a scrape, there might be no end to the entire people's limping. But even if she lets herself be led around like a cripple, even if she displays herself in this pitiful condition more often than usual, the people

3. Elaborate vocal ornamentation containing improvised or written running passages and trills.

continue to listen to her singing, grateful and enchanted as before, but they make no great fuss over the abridgements.

Since she cannot limp forever, she invents other ploys; she feigns fatigue, bad temper, weakness. So now, in addition to a concert, we have drama. Behind Josefine we see her followers begging and imploring her to sing. Oh, how much she wants to, but she can't. They comfort her, flatter her, almost carry her to the spot already picked out beforehand where she is supposed to sing. Finally, with inexplicable tears, she relents, but now, as she makes a show of beginning to sing with her last ounce of will power, limp, her arms not extended as usual but hanging lifelessly at her sides, creating the impression that they might be a little too short—as she tries to begin her song, no, it won't work, an involuntary jerk of her head indicates as much, and she collapses before our eyes. But then, look, she pulls herself together and sings, not, I think, so very differently than otherwise, perhaps if you have an ear for the subtlest shadings, you'll detect a marginally unusual excitement, but that only enhances the effect. And at the end she is actually less tired than before; with a firm gait, to the extent that such a description applies to her affected little scamper, she moves off, refusing all help from her retinue and coldly eyeing the crowd that, awestruck, parts for her to pass.

This is how it was last time; the latest news, however, is that she had disappeared just at a moment when she was expected to sing. It is not only her followers who are looking for her, many others are enlisted in the search, all in vain: Josefine has disappeared, she does not want to sing, she does not even want to be begged to sing, this time she has abandoned us entirely.

Strange how badly she calculates, our clever Josefine, so badly that you have to think she doesn't calculate at all, that she is only driven on by her fate, which in our world can only be a very sad one. It is she herself who withdraws from song, she who destroys the power she has acquired over our feelings. How could she ever have acquired this power, knowing our feelings so little? She hides and does not sing, but the people, calm, showing no disappointment, imperious, an immovable body, which, despite appearances to the contrary, can only bestow gifts and never receive them, not even from Josefine, this people continues on its way.

Josefine, however, can only go downhill. Soon the time will come when her last squeak peals out and falls silent. She is a brief episode in the eternal history of our people, and the people will recover from this loss. Certainly it will not be easy for us; how can we possibly hold gatherings in complete silence? But weren't these gatherings silent even when Josefine attended? Was her actual squeaking notably louder and livelier than the memory of it will be?

Even during her lifetime was it ever more than a mere memory? Didn't the people, in their wisdom, value Josefine's song so highly precisely because in this way it could never be lost?

And so perhaps we will not miss very much at all, but Josefine, released from earthly torments, which, however, in her opinion are reserved for the chosen ones, will joyfully lose herself in the incalculable mass of our people's heroes, and soon, for we practice no history, she will enjoy the heightened redemption of being forgotten, like all her brethren.

[POSTHUMOUSLY PUBLISHED STORIES]

The Bridge

I was stiff and cold, I was a bridge, I spanned an abyss; my toes were dug in one side, my hands in the other; I had clamped[1] myself in crumbling clay. The tails of my coat fluttered at my sides. In the depths the icy trout stream blustered. No tourist strayed to this trackless height; the bridge was not yet marked on the maps. And so I lay, waiting; I had to wait; without falling, no bridge, once erected, can stop being a bridge. One day, toward evening—was it the first, was it the thousandth, I cannot tell, my thoughts were always racing in confusion, always, always in circles—toward evening in the summer, the brook was roaring with a darker sound, I heard the footstep of a man! Toward me, toward me. Stretch out, bridge, get into position, beam without a railing, hold the one who has been entrusted to you; invisibly lend evenness to the uncertainty of his steps; but if he stumbles, then show who you are and, like a mountain god, fling him across to land. He came, he knocked on me all over with the iron tip of his cane, then he lifted my coat-tails with it and folded them back on me; he thrust his spike into my bushy hair and let it stay there for a long time while probably gazing around into the distance. But then—just as I was following him

---

1. *Festgebissen*, past participle of *sich festbeißen*, a keyword in Kafka's lexicon. It means, literally, "to bite into something with clenched jaws so as to become, along with one's body, immovably attached to it." In an extended sense, it means to attach oneself to something (a project, an idea) with an unsurpassable intensity. In the Norton Critical Edition of *The Metamorphosis*, the hero, Gregor Samsa, who has been transformed into a verminous bug, "clamps his jaws," literally "bites himself" into the lock on the door of his bedroom in an effort to escape his room and explain his predicament to his parents and his boss (p. 11). In "Jackals and Arabs," two young jackals "bite themselves" [or "fasten their teeth"] into the narrator's coattails: it is said, according to the jackals' protocol, to be a sign of exceptional courtesy (p. 70). Perhaps the word meant so much to Kafka because it suggests the intensity with which he attached himself to his writing destiny, to the huge stakes involved, believing that he had sacrificed so much for it.

in a revery over mountain and valley—he jumped with both feet onto the middle of my body. I shuddered in wild pain, totally uncomprehending. Who was it? A child? A gymnast? A daredevil? A suicide? A tempter? A destroyer? And I turned to look at him. Bridge turns around! I had not yet turned around when I was already falling; I fell, and in a moment I was torn apart and impaled on the sharp stones that had always gazed up so peacefully at me from the raging water.

The Hunter Gracchus

[*Two Fragments*]

I

Two boys were sitting on the wall of the wharf playing a game with dice. A man was reading a newspaper on the steps of a monument in the shadow of the sword-waving hero. A girl at the fountain was filling a tub with water. A fruit seller was sprawled beside his wares, looking out at the lake. The empty door and window frames of a bar revealed two men in the back, drinking wine. The proprietor was sitting at a table in the front, dozing. A sailboat glided gently, as if carried across the water, into the little harbor. A man in a blue smock climbed ashore and drew the rope through the rings. Behind the boatman two other men in dark coats with silver buttons carried a bier on which, under a large, floral-patterned, fringed silk cloth, a man was apparently lying. No one on the wharf paid any attention to the new arrivals, even when they put down the bier to wait for the boatman, who was still working on the ropes; no one approached; no one questioned them; no one took a closer look at them.

The boatman was held up a little longer by a woman with loosened hair who, a baby at her breast, now appeared on deck. Then he came, pointed toward a yellowish two-story house that rose sharply to the left near the water; the bearers took up their burden and carried it through the low door framed by slender columns. A little boy opened a window, noticed the troop just as it was disappearing into the house, and hurriedly closed the window again. The door was now closed as well, it was made of heavy oak carefully joined. A flock of doves, which until now had been flying around the clock tower, now settled outside the house. As if their food were stored in the house, they flocked together outside the door. One flew up to the second floor and pecked at the windowpane. They were brightly colored, well-cared-for, lively creatures. The woman on the sailboat flung grain to them in a wide arc; they picked it up and flew toward the woman.

An old man in a top hat with a mourning ribbon came down one of the narrow, steep little alleyways descending to the harbor. He looked around attentively, everything troubled him, the sight of garbage in a corner made him grimace, fruit peelings were scattered on the steps of the monument; as he went past, he pushed them aside with his cane. He knocked on the columned door, at the same time taking his top hat into his black-gloved right hand. The door was opened at once, easily fifty small boys formed a line in the long hallway and bowed.

The boatman came down the stairs, greeted the gentleman, led him upstairs, on the second floor walked him around the delicate, airy loggia surrounding the courtyard, and while the boys crowded after them at a respectful distance, both men entered a cool, large room at the rear of the house from where no other houses were visible, only a bare, grayish-black rock wall. The bearers were busy placing and lighting several long candles at the head of the bier, but these gave off no light; it was only as if the shadows that had been at rest had been startled awake and flickered across the walls. The cloth on the bier was folded back. A man lay there with wildly matted hair and beard, tanned skin, looking something like a hunter. He lay motionless, seemingly without breathing, with closed eyes; but only the surroundings hinted that he might be a dead man.

The gentleman went up to the bier, laid his hand on the brow of the man who lay there, then knelt and said a prayer. The boatman signaled to the bearers to leave the room; they went out, drove away the boys who had gathered outside the room, and shut the door. But even this quiet did not seem to satisfy the gentleman; he looked at the boatman, who understood and went through a side door into the next room. At once the man on the bier opened his eyes, with a pained smile turned his face to the gentleman, and said, "Who are you?" Without visible astonishment the gentleman got up from his kneeling position and answered: "The mayor of Riva."

The man on the bier nodded, pointed with a weakly outstretched arm to a chair, and after the mayor had accepted his invitation, said: "I knew that, of course, Mayor, but in the first moments I always forget everything, it all goes around in my head, and it's better if I ask, even if I know all the answers. You also probably know that I am the hunter Gracchus."[1]

---

1. The Hunter Gracchus, in bed and always delirious "in the first moments" after being awakened, here addresses the Mayor with the intimate pronoun *du* ("Who are you?"). Thereafter he shifts to the polite form *Sie*. It is evidently a custom of Kafka's to use the intimate pronoun in conversations with any person who lands in or near the bed of his heroes—and hence appears to them as in a kind of dream. Cf. the intimate pronoun that the wounded boy addresses to the country doctor (of "A Country Doctor") after he has been put into the boy's bed (n. 3, p. 63).

"Certainly," said the mayor. "Your arrival was announced to me late last night. We had already been asleep for some time. Then, toward midnight, my wife cried out: 'Salvatore'—that's my name—'look at the dove at the window!' It really was a dove but as big as a rooster. It flew up to my ear and said: 'Tomorrow the dead hunter Gracchus is coming, receive him in the name of the city.' "

The hunter nodded and drew the tip of his tongue between his lips: "Yes, the doves fly ahead of me. But do you think, Mayor, that I ought to remain in Riva?"

"It's too soon to say," the mayor answered. "Are you dead?"

"Yes," said the hunter, "as you see. Many years ago, indeed it must be an inordinately large number of years ago, I fell off a cliff in the Black Forest—that's in Germany—while hunting a chamois. Since then I've been dead."

"But you're also alive," said the mayor.

"In some sense," said the hunter, "in a sense I'm alive at the same time. My death barge went off course, a wrong turn of the tiller, the momentary inattentiveness of the boatman, a distraction by my beautiful homeland, I don't know what it was, I only know this, that I remained on earth and that since then my barge sails on earthly waters. So I, who wanted only to live in my country's mountains, travel through all the countries on earth after my death."

"And you have no share in the hereafter?" asked the mayor with furrowed brow.

"I am always on the grand staircase," replied the hunter, "that leads up to it. On this infinitely wide and open stairway I drift, now toward the top, now toward the bottom, now to the right, now to the left, always in motion. But when I attempt the greatest vaulting swing upward and can already see the gleaming gate above me, I awaken on my old barge, drearily stranded somewhere in earthly waters. The basic mistake of my erstwhile death grins at me from all around my cabin. Julia, the boatman's wife, knocks and brings to my bier the morning drink of the country whose coastline we happen to be passing at the moment."

"An awful fate," said the mayor, lifting his hand defensively. "And is it in any way your fault?"

"In no way," said the hunter; "I was a hunter, does that mean I bear some sort of guilt? I was assigned the post of hunter in the Black Forest, at a time when there were still wolves. I lay in wait, pulled the trigger, hit my target, removed the pelt, does that make me guilty? My labors were blessed. I was known as the great hunter of the Black Forest. Does that make me guilty?"

"I'm not competent to decide that," said the mayor, "but I can't see any guilt in that either. But then whose fault is it?"

"The boatman's," said the hunter.

"And now you intend to stay with us in Riva?"

"I do no intending," said the hunter with a smile, and to excuse his mockery, he laid his hand on the mayor's knee. "I am here, that's all I know, that's all I can do. My barge has no tiller, it is driven by the wind that blows in the nethermost regions of death."

II

No one will read what I write here; no one will come to help me; if the task of helping me were set, all the doors of all the houses would remain shut, all the windows shut, everyone would lie in his bed with his blankets pulled over his head, the whole earth one nighttime hostel. That makes sense because no one knows about me, and if anyone did know about me, he would not know where I sojourn, and if he did know where I sojourn, he would not know how to keep me there, and if he did know how to keep me there, he would not know how to help me. The thought of wanting to help me is a sickness and requires bed rest.

This I know, and so I am not writing to call for help, even when in moments, undisciplined as I am, e.g. right now, I think very seriously of it. But it is probably enough to drive out all such thoughts for me to look around and remember where I am and—this is something I can say with certainty—where I have been living for centuries.

As I write this, I am lying on a wooden plank; I am wearing—it is not pleasant to look at me—a dirty shroud; hair and beard, gray and black, are inextricably tangled together; my legs are covered with a large, floral-patterned, silk shawl with long fringes. At my head a sacramental candle illuminates me. On the opposite wall is a small picture, apparently of a bushman who is aiming his spear at me while taking cover as best he can behind a gorgeously painted shield. You find many stupid depictions on board ships, but this is one of the stupidest. Otherwise my wooden cage is quite empty. The warm air of the southern night comes in through a porthole in the side, and I hear the water beating against the old sailboat.

I have been lying here ever since the time when I, still the living hunter Gracchus, at home in the Black Forest, chased a chamois and fell. Everything went in order. I gave chase, fell, bled to death in a gulch, was dead, and this sailboat was supposed to carry me into the hereafter. I still remember how cheerfully I stretched out on this plank for the first time; never before had the mountains heard such song from me as these four walls, still dusky at that time. I had been happy to live and was happy to die; before coming on board I joyfully threw down that ragbag of a rifle, knapsack, and hunting coat that I had always proudly carried, and I slipped into

my shroud like a girl into her wedding dress. Here I lay and waited.
    Then there happened * * *

Building the Great Wall of China

The northernmost point of the Great Wall of China was finished. The construction[1] was brought to this point from the southeast and the southwest and the sections joined. This system of partial construction was also followed on a smaller scale by the two great armies of workers, the eastern and the western. It was arranged by forming gangs of about twenty workers, each of which was given the task of completing a part of the Wall of about five hundred yards; the adjoining work gang then constructed a wall of equal length to meet it. But then, after the juncture was accomplished, the construction was not continued at the end of these thousand yards, as you might expect; instead, the groups of workers were sent into quite different regions to continue work on the Wall. In this way, of course, numerous large gaps came about, and these were only gradually and slowly filled in, many only after the construction of the Wall had already been announced as completed. Indeed, it is said that there are gaps that have not been filled in at all; according to some people these are much larger than the completed sections, although this assertion may be only one of the many legends that have grown up around the Wall and which, given the length of the Wall, is not something one person can verify, at least with his own eyes and by his own standards.

Now, one would think that it would have been more advantageous in every way to build continuously, or at least continuously within the two main sections. After all—a fact generally circulated and known—the Wall was conceived of as a defense against the peoples of the north. But how can a wall that is not a continuous structure offer protection? Indeed, not only can such a wall not protect, but the construction itself is in perpetual danger. Those sections of the Wall left abandoned in barren regions can easily be destroyed, over and over, by the nomads, especially since at that time these people, made anxious by the construction of the Wall, changed their dwelling places with incomprehensible rapidity, like locusts, and so perhaps had a better overview of the progress of the Wall than even we ourselves, its builders. Nevertheless, construction could probably not have proceeded by any other method than the one we used. To understand this, one has to consider the fol-

---

1. The German word for "construction" is *Bau*, the same word as "burrow." Like *The Burrow* (p. 162), this story deals with the perils of construction.

lowing: the Wall is supposed to provide protection for centuries; hence the most painstaking construction, the application of the architectural wisdom of all known ages and peoples, and the permanent sense of personal responsibility in the builders were indispensable prerequisites for the work. For the smaller jobs, certainly, it was possible to employ ignorant day laborers from among the people—men, women, children, anyone prepared to work for decent pay; but to supervise as few as four day laborers, a knowledgeable man with architectural training was needed, a man able to feel in the depths of his heart the purpose of this undertaking. And the loftier the charge, the greater the demands, of course. And such men were in fact available, and if not in the quantity this construction could have employed, yet in a considerable number.

The work had not been undertaken lightly. Fifty years before the construction began, throughout the whole area of China that was supposed to be surrounded by a wall, architecture was declared to be the most important field of study, and masonry in particular, and all other fields were recognized only to the extent that they related to it. I remember very clearly when, as small children, hardly steady on our legs, we stood in our teacher's small garden and were told to build a kind of wall out of pebbles; and our teacher, tucking up his robe, ran against the wall, making the whole thing tumble down, of course, and he reproached us so fiercely for the weakness of our construction that we scattered in all directions, sobbing, and ran to our parents. A small incident, but characteristic of the spirit of the times.

I had the good fortune, when I passed the highest test of the lowest school at the age of twenty, that the Wall was about to be built. I say good fortune because many who had previously reached the apex of the education that was available to them were unable to apply their knowledge to anything for years, knocked around uselessly with the grandest blueprints in their heads, and wasted their lives in droves. But those who finally came in to lead the construction, even those at the bottom, were truly worthy of their responsibilities; these were men who had given a great deal of thought to the Wall and never stopped thinking about it, who, on sinking their first stone into the ground, felt that they were virtually one with the Wall. But such men were driven, of course, not only by a passion to perform the most thorough work but also by impatience to see the construction finally rise up in its perfection. The day laborer knows nothing of this impatience, he is driven only by pay; the upper level of leaders, indeed even the leaders of the middle rank, saw enough of the manifold growth of the Wall to sustain their intellectual and moral strength; but the men of the lower ranks who stood intellectually far above their outwardly petty tasks had to be provided for differently.

They could not be expected, e.g., to spend months, let alone years, setting one stone next to another in an uninhabited mountainous region, hundreds of miles from home; the hopelessness of such work, which, however industriously performed, would not achieve its goal even at the end of a long life, would have driven them to despair and, most important, diminished their usefulness to the work. And that is why the system of partial construction was chosen: five hundred yards of wall could be finished in roughly five years; by that time, of course, the leaders were generally exhausted and had lost all confidence in themselves, the construction, and the world; but while they were still ecstatic from the festival when the sections of the thousand-yard wall were joined, they were sent far, far away. On the journey they saw, here and there, finished sections of the Wall looming up; they paused at the compounds of higher-ranking leaders, who bestowed medals on them; they heard the cheers of new armies of workers streaming in from the hearts of the provinces; they saw the felling of forests destined for Wall scaffolding; they saw mountains being hammered into stones for the Wall; at sacred sites they heard songs of the pious pilgrims begging for the completion of the Wall. All this soothed their impatience, the quiet life of their homeland, where they spent some time, strengthened them; the respect enjoyed by those engaged in building, the unquestioning humility with which their reports were heard, the trust the simple, silent citizen placed in the eventual completion of the Wall—all these tensed the strings of their souls; like eternally hopeful children they left their homeland, the desire to labor once again at this national mission became uncontrollable; they left home sooner than necessary, half the village accompanied them for long stretches; on all the roads, greetings, pennants, and flags: never before had they seen how great and rich and beautiful and lovable their country was; every fellow countryman was a brother for whom they were building a protective wall and who was thankful all his life, thankful with everything that he had and was: unity! unity! breast on breast, a round dance of the people, blood no longer confined in the meager circulatory system of the body but rolling on sweetly and yet returning to its source through the infinity of China.

And in this way the system of partial construction makes sense, but there may well have been additional reasons. Nor is it some eccentricity on my part that makes me dwell so long on this question; it is a crucial question relating to the entire building of the Wall, as unimportant as it may seem at first. If I am to convey and explain the intellectual perspectives and experiences of that time, I cannot dig deeply enough into this question.

First of all, you must admit that deeds were accomplished at that time that fall just short of the building of the Tower of Babel, although they were the very opposite when it comes to being pleasing to God—at least according to human reckoning. I mention this fact because during the early stages of construction a scholar published a book that explicated the parallels very precisely. He sought to prove that it was not for the generally stated reasons that construction of the Tower of Babel failed to accomplish its goal, or at least that these familiar reasons did not include the principal ones. His proofs consisted not only of documents and reports; he also claimed to have conducted investigations on the site and to have discovered that the construction foundered, and was destined to founder, on the weakness of its foundations. In this respect, admittedly, our own time was far superior to that long-vanished age; almost every educated contemporary was a skilled mason and was unerring in the matter of laying a foundation. But this was not the scholar's point at all; instead he maintained that the Great Wall would create, for the first time in human history, a solid foundation for a new Tower of Babel. Ergo: first the Wall and then the Tower. At the time, his book was in everyone's hands, but I admit that even today I do not really know how he thought this tower would be built. The Wall, which did not even describe a circle but only a sort of quarter- or semicircle, was supposed to provide the foundation for a tower? Plainly, that statement could only have been meant in a spiritual sense. But then, what was the use of the Wall, something that was a tangible fact, the result of the labor and the lives of hundreds of thousands of workers? And why were there plans of the Tower—granted, quite sketchy ones—included in this book, as well as detailed suggestions as to how the national power was to be harnessed to this future work? There were many addled minds at that time—the book is merely one example—perhaps precisely because so many people were seeking to rally as much as possible around a single purpose. Human nature, giddy at heart, a thing of flying dust, cannot endure being fettered; if it fetters itself, it will soon go mad, begin to rattle its chains, and tear to pieces wall, chain, and itself, scattering them to the winds.

It is possible that even these considerations, which actually speak against building the Wall, were not left unexamined by our leaders when they decided on partial construction. We—here I am very likely speaking on behalf of many—have really only come to know ourselves as a result of poring over the decrees of the highest leadership; and here we have discovered that without the leadership, neither our book learning nor our common human understanding would have sufficed for even the small tasks we perform within the great whole. In the leadership office[2]—where it was lo-

---

2. For "office," Kafka actually writes *Stube*, which connotes a rather ordinary room in a home, evoking the often shabby surroundings of Kafka's figures of highest authority.

cated and who occupied it, no one I have ever asked knows or knew—in this office there surely revolved all human thoughts and desires and, in countercircles, all human goals and fulfillments; but through the window the reflection of divine worlds fell on the hands of the leaders as they drew their plans.

And therefore to any unprejudiced observer the idea will be unacceptable that the leaders, if they had seriously wanted to, could not have overcome the difficulties that stood in the way of a continuous Wall construction. And so the only remaining conclusion is that the leaders purposely chose partial construction. But partial construction was only a makeshift and unsuited to its purpose. The conclusion that remains is that the leaders wanted something unsuited to their purpose. An odd conclusion, certainly. And yet in another respect there is a good deal of justification for it. Nowadays it may be safe to discuss such matters. In those days the secret principle held by many, even the best, was: Try with all your might to understand the decrees of the leadership, but only up to a certain point; then stop thinking about the subject. A very reasonable principle, which was further elaborated into an often repeated parable: Stop thinking about it not because it could harm you, since it is not at all certain that it will harm you. What we have here is neither a matter of doing nor not doing harm. You will be as the river in spring. It rises, becomes more powerful, nourishes more richly the land bordering its long banks, keeps its own essence intact as it runs into the sea, and becomes more nearly equal and more welcome to the sea. Think this far about the decrees of the leadership. But then the river overflows its banks, loses its outline and its shape, slows in its downward course, tries to run counter to its destiny by forming little inland seas, damages the fields, and yet, since it cannot continue spreading itself so thin, instead runs back into its banks and in the hot season that follows even dries out dismally. Do not think this far about the decrees of the leadership.

Now this parable may have been right on point during the building of the Wall, but for my current report it is of limited value at most. My investigation is purely historical; lightning no longer quivers from thunderclouds that blew away long ago, and I may therefore look for a way to explain the partial construction that goes beyond what was considered satisfactory at that time. The limits set for me by my intellectual capacity are certainly narrow enough, but the domain one would have to run through here is infinite.

From whom is the Great Wall supposed to protect us? From the people of the north. I come from southeastern China. No northern people can threaten us there. We read about them in the books of our elders: the cruelties they commit in accordance with their nature make us gasp aloud in our peaceful arbor; in artists' paintings, faithful to the truth, we see these faces of damnation, the gaping maws,[3] the jaws equipped with long, pointed teeth, the scrunched-up eyes that seem to squint at the victim whom their maws will crush and rend. When the children misbehave, we show them these pictures, and at once they fly, weeping, into our arms. But we know nothing more about these people of the northern lands; we have never seen them, and if we stay in our village, we will never see them, even were they to rush and race straight at us on their wild horses; the country is too great and will not let them come to us, they will run awry into the empty air.

And so, if this is how matters stand, why do we leave our homeland, the river and the bridges, our mothers and fathers, our wives in tears, our children who need instruction, and go away to school in a faraway city; and why are our thoughts even farther away, with the Wall in the north? Why? Ask the leaders. They know us. They, whose minds are roiled with enormous worries, know about us, know our unimportant work, see us sitting together in the low huts, and the prayer that the head of the household recites in the evening amid his family is found pleasing to them or displeases them. And if I may be allowed such a thought about the leadership, I have to say that in my opinion the leadership existed before this time, did not come together like, let us say, exalted mandarins who, inspired by a beautiful morning dream, hurriedly convene a session, hurriedly pass resolutions, and the same evening drum the populace out of their beds to carry out the resolutions, even if it were only to organize an illumination in honor of a god who had shown himself favorable to the lords the day before and, the following day, the lanterns having hardly been extinguished, give them a sound thrashing in some dark corner. Rather, the leadership has very likely always existed, and the same for the decision to build the Wall.

To some extent while the Wall was being built and afterward to this day, I have been occupied almost exclusively with comparative ethnography—there are certain questions whose nub, so to speak, one can get to only by this method—and here I have found that we Chinese possess certain public and state institutions that are uniquely clear and still others that are uniquely obscure. To trace the reasons, especially for this latter phenomenon, has always appealed to me and still appeals to me, and the building of the Wall, too, is essentially affected by these questions.

Among our most obscure institutions is certainly the empire. In

---

3. Kafka writes *Mäuler*, literally, "muzzles," the mouths and jaws of animals and used only pejoratively of human beings.

Peking, of course, especially in the court, there is some clarity on this matter, although even that is more apparent than real; the teachers of public law and history at the academies of higher learning also pretend to have precise knowledge of these subjects and to be able to impart this knowledge to their students; and the further down one goes to the lower schools, the more, understandably enough, people's doubts about their own knowledge vanish and a wave of half-education surges up high as mountains around a few theorems that have been rammed into the students' minds for centuries; and although these have lost nothing of their eternal truth, they also remain eternally unknown amid this vapor and fog.

But it is precisely this question concerning the empire that, in my opinion, the people should be asked about first, since in the end the empire is supported by the people. Here, admittedly, I can again speak only of my homeland. Outside of the rural divinities and their rituals, which fill the entire year with such variety and beauty, all our thoughts went to the emperor. But not to the current one, or rather, they would have gone to the current one if we had known who he was or anything definite about him. Of course, we were always bent on finding out something of the sort; it was the sole curiosity that occupied us. But, as remarkable as it sounds, it was virtually impossible to find out anything, not from pilgrims, although they roam through many lands; in neither the nearby nor the remote villages; not from sailors, although they sail not only our little streams but also the sacred rivers. We certainly heard a good deal, but we could not take anything from this abundance.

Our country is so vast that no fairy tale can do justice to its size, the heavens barely span it. And Peking is only a dot, and the emperor's palace only a smaller dot. The emperor as such, to be sure, is for his part great through all the hierarchies of the world. But the living emperor, a man like us, rests as we do on a couch that, while generously proportioned, is still comparatively narrow and short. Like us he sometimes stretches his limbs, and when he is very tired, he yawns with his finely chiseled mouth. How were we to learn anything about all this, thousands of miles to the south; after all, our lands almost border on the Tibetan highlands. And besides, every piece of news, even if it were to reach us, would come much too late, would be long obsolete. The emperor is surrounded by the brilliant and yet shadowy mass of the court, the counterweight to imperial power, always ready with poisoned arrows to shoot the emperor from his authority. The empire is immortal, but the individual emperor falls and crashes, even entire dynasties finally sink and breathe their last in a single death rattle. The people will never know anything of these struggles and sufferings; like latecomers, like strangers in the city, they stand at the outlets of the densely crowded side streets, peacefully consuming the provisions they have brought with them, while way out in front, in the middle of the marketplace, the execution of their lord and master proceeds apace.

There is a legend that expresses this relationship well. The emperor, so it goes, has sent a message to you, one individual, a puny subject, a tiny shadow who has fled from the imperial sun into the most distant of distances, to you alone the emperor has sent a message from his deathbed. He has made the messenger kneel down beside the bed and has whispered the message to him; it mattered so much to him that he made him repeat it in his ear. He has nodded to confirm the accuracy of what was said. And in front of all the spectators at his death—all walls that might block the view are ripped down, and the great personages of the empire stand in a circle on the wide and vaulting open staircase—in front of them all he dispatched the messenger. The messenger began his journey at once; a strong man, a tireless man, a swimmer without equal; now thrusting out one arm, now the other, he makes his way through the crowd; when he encounters resistance, he points to his breast, which bears the sign of the sun; and he advances easily, like no other. But the crowd is so deep, their dwelling places are without end; if he could only reach open land, how he would fly, and soon you would be sure to hear the wonderful beat of his fists at your door. Instead, how uselessly he exhausts himself; he is still forcing his way through the chambers of the innermost palace; he will never get to the end of them; and if he did succeed, nothing would have been gained; he would have to fight his way down the stairs; and if he succeeded, nothing would have been gained; he would have to cross the courtyards, and after the courtyards the second, outer palace, and more stairs and courtyards, and another palace, and so on through the millennia; and if he did finally crash out of the outermost gate—but that can never, never happen—the imperial capital would now lie before him, the center of the world, heaped to the top with its sediment. No one can penetrate this, let alone with the message of a dead man addressed to a nonentity. But you sit at your window and envision it as in a dream when evening comes.

Just so, as hopelessly and hopefully, our people view the emperor. They do not know which emperor is reigning, and there is even doubt about the name of the dynasty. A lot of this sort of thing is learned by rote at school, but the general uncertainty in this respect is so great that even the best students are drawn into it. In our villages, long-dead emperors are set up on thrones, and one who lives on only in song has recently issued a decree that the priest reads aloud in front of the altar. Battles from our most ancient history are just now being fought, and with glowing cheeks your neighbor bursts into your house with the news. The emperor's wives—overfed among their silk cushions, estranged from noble custom by cunning courtiers, swollen with lust for power, irascible in their greed, expansive in their lust—commit their villainies again and again anew; the more time that passes, the more terribly do all the colors glow, and with loud lamentations the village learns one day how millennia ago an empress drank her husband's blood in long drafts.

This, then, is how the people deal with past emperors, although they mingle the current ones with the dead ones. If once, once in a lifetime, an imperial official touring the provinces accidentally comes into our village, makes certain demands in the name of the ruler, examines the tax rolls, visits schools, questions the priest about our doings, and then, before climbing back into his sedan chair, summarizes everything in long admonitions to the assembled community, a smile flickers across all our faces, each man looks furtively to the next and bends down to the children so as not to be observed by the official. What, you think, he is speaking about a dead man like someone who is alive, this emperor died a long time ago, the dynasty was wiped out, the official is making fun of us, but we will act as if we did not notice, so as not to hurt his feelings. But we will seriously obey only our present ruler, for to do otherwise would be a sin. And behind the sedan chair of the official, as it races off, some figure who has been arbitrarily elevated climbs out of his crumbling urn and stamps his foot as master of the village.

[Similarly, as a rule our people are scarcely affected by political upheavals, by contemporary wars. Here I recall an incident from my youth. A rebellion had broken out in a neighboring but nonetheless far removed province. I can no longer remember what caused it; anyway, in this context it is unimportant: reasons for uprisings present themselves with every dawning day, these are an excitable people. And now at one point a flyer from the rebels was brought to my father's house by a beggar who had traveled through that province. That very day was a holiday, our rooms were filled with guests, the priest sat in the center and studied the paper. Suddenly everyone began to laugh, in the confusion the flyer was torn to bits, the beggar, who had already been showered with gifts, was kicked and shoved out of the room, everyone scattered and ran off into the beautiful day. Why? The dialect spoken in the neighboring province is basically different from ours, and this difference expresses itself as well in certain forms of the written language that for us have a somewhat old-fashioned ring. Hardly had the priest read two sentences of this sort than we had made up our minds. Old things, heard long ago, calamities long since recovered from.

And—so it seems to me in my recollection—although the horrors of living life spoke irrefutably from the beggar, people shook their heads, laughing and refusing to hear more. That is how eager are we to wipe out the present.][4]

Anyone intent on concluding from such phenomena that we basically have no emperor at all would not be far from the truth. Again and again I need to assert: there is perhaps no people more loyal to the emperor than our people in the south, but this loyalty does not benefit the emperor. True, the sacred dragon stands on the little pillar at the end of the village, and within living memory it has always blown its flaming breath in homage in the exact direction of Peking, but Peking itself is more foreign to the people of the village than life in the great beyond. Is there really supposed to be a village where the houses jostle up against each other, eclipsing fields that extend farther than the view from our hills; and between these houses people stand day and night, head to head? It is harder for us to imagine such a city than to believe that Peking and its emperor are one single thing, say, a cloud peacefully changing shape under the sun in the course of the ages.

Now, the result of such opinions is, to a certain extent, a free, ungoverned life. By no means immoral; on my travels I have hardly ever encountered such purity of morals as in my homeland. But still, a life that is subject to no current law and follows only directives and warnings that extend to us from ancient times.

I am on guard against generalizations, and I do not maintain that things are the same in all ten thousand villages of our province or, indeed, in all five hundred provinces of China. But still, on the basis of the many texts I have read on this subject, as well as my own observations—the building of the Wall in particular, with its wealth of human material, gave anyone of sensibility the opportunity to journey through the soul of almost all the provinces—on the basis of all this I may perhaps be permitted to say that the dominant attitude toward the emperor again and again and everywhere exhibits certain features in common with the attitude in my homeland. Now, I have no intention of accepting this attitude as a virtue, on the contrary. And while it is mainly the fault of the regime, which in this most ancient empire on earth has always been unable, perhaps through neglect of this concern in favor of other matters, to develop the institution of empire with such clarity that it would exercise its influence immediately and incessantly as far as the realm's most distant frontiers. On the other hand, this attitude also exhibits a weakness of imagination or conviction among the people, who are

---

4. The passage in brackets was crossed out by Kafka; but the editor of this Norton Critical Edition, like some other editors, considers it too valuable to leave out.

unable to embrace the empire obediently, in all its liveliness and presence, raising it from its submersion in Peking; and yet the subjects wish nothing more than just for once to feel this connection and drown in it.

Thus this attitude is unlikely to be a virtue. It is all the more striking that precisely this weakness appears to be one of the most important means of unifying our people; indeed, if one may be so forward as to employ such an expression, it is the very ground on which we live. To supply detailed reasons for a reproach here would not mean assaulting our conscience but, what is far worse, assaulting our legs. And for this reason I will for the moment go no further into the investigation of this question.

Into this world news of the building of the Wall now penetrated. It, too, was delayed by some thirty years since its proclamation. It was on a summer evening. I, ten years old, was standing with my father on the riverbank. As suits the importance of this frequently discussed occasion, I can recall the smallest details. Father was holding me by the hand, something he loved to do right up into his old age, and running his other hand along his long, very thin pipe as though it were a flute. His long, sparse, stiff beard was raised into the air, for while he was enjoying his pipe, he was looking across the river at the mountains. At the same time his pigtail, the object of the children's awe, sank lower, rustling faintly on the gold-brocaded silk of his best gown. At that moment a sailboat came to a halt before us; the boatman signaled to my father to come down the embankment; he himself climbed up toward him. They met halfway; the boatman whispered in my father's ear; to get close enough, he put his arms around him. I could not understand what they were saying; saw only that my father did not seem to believe it; the boatman tried to corroborate its truth; my father still could not believe it; then, with a sailor's passion, he practically tore his gown to shreds at his chest to warrant the truth; my father became quieter and the boatman leaped with a thump into the boat and sailed away. My father turned thoughtfully to me, banged out his pipe, stuck it into his belt, and stroked my cheek while pulling my head to him. That is what I liked best, it made me very cheerful, and in this way we went home. There the congee was already steaming on the table, a number of guests had gathered, the wine was about to be poured into the cups. Without taking any notice of this activity, still on the threshold, my father began to report what he had heard. Of course, I do not remember the exact words, but because of the extraordinary circumstances, which engrossed me even as a child, the meaning made so deep an impression on me that I trust my memory to give a version of what he said. I am doing so because it was very characteristic of the people's way of understanding. My father then said something like: * * *

[A strange boatman—I know all those who usually sail by here, but this one was a stranger—has just told me that a great wall is going to be built to protect the emperor. For infidel tribes, with demons among them, often gather in front of the imperial palace and shoot their black arrows at the emperor.][5]

The Knock at the Courtyard Gate

It was in the summer, a hot day. On the way home with my sister, I passed a courtyard gate. I don't know whether she knocked at the gate out of mischief or distraction or whether she merely made a threatening gesture with her fist and did not knock at all. A hundred steps farther down the road, turning off to the left, there was the beginning of a village. We did not know this place, but people came out of the very first house and waved to us in a friendly but warning way, themselves terrified, cowering in terror. They pointed to the courtyard that we had passed and reminded us of the knock at the gate. The owners of the courtyard would lodge a complaint against us; the investigation would begin immediately. I was very calm and calmed my sister down as well. She had probably not even knocked, and if she had, nowhere in the world would such an action become a court case. I also tried to make the people around us understand this, they listened to me but withheld their opinion. Later they said that not only my sister but I, too, as her brother, would be prosecuted. I nodded, smiling. All of us looked back at the courtyard the way one watches a cloud of smoke in the distance and waits for the flames. And in fact, we soon saw horsemen riding in through the wide-open courtyard gate. Dust rose, shrouding everything; only the tips of their high lances glittered. And no sooner had the troop disappeared into the courtyard than it seemed to have turned the horses around and started on its way to us. I pushed my sister away, I would smooth things over all by myself; she refused to abandon me; I said that in that case she should at least change her clothes so as to appear before the gentlemen in a nicer dress. Finally she obeyed and began the long walk home. The horsemen were already alongside us; from high up on horseback they asked where my sister was; she was not here at the moment came the anxious reply, but she would return later. The answer was accepted almost with indifference; it seemed most important that they had found me. There were primarily two gentlemen: the judge, a lively young man, and his quiet assistant, who was called Assmann. I was summoned to the parlor of the village tavern. Slowly,

5. This valuable paragraph was also crossed out by Kafka.

turning my head from side to side, adjusting my suspenders, I began to move along under the piercing glances of the gentlemen. At this moment I still almost believed that a word would be enough to free me, a city person, even free me honorably from this peasant breed. But when I had crossed the threshold to the parlor, the judge, who had run ahead and was waiting for me, said, "I'm sorry for this man." There was no doubt that he meant not my present situation but what would happen to me. The room looked more like a prison cell than like a tavern parlor. Large flagstones, a dark gray, bare wall, an iron ring cemented somewhere into it, at the center something that was half plank bed, half operating table.

Could I still sense any air other than that of a prison? That is the great question—or rather, it would be the question if I had any prospect of being released.

A Crossbreed

I have a peculiar animal, half-kitten, half-lamb. It is an heirloom from my father's estate, but it is only during its time with me that it has developed; formerly it was far more lamb than kitten, but now it has about the same amount of each. From the cat, head and claws; from the lamb, size and shape; from both, its eyes, which are flickering and mild, the hair of its coat, which is soft and lying close to the skin, its movements, which are at once skipping and slinking; in the sunshine on the window sill it curls up into a ball and purrs; on the meadow it rushes around like mad and can scarcely be caught; it runs away from cats, it tries to attack lambs; on moonlit nights the roof gutters are its favorite promenade; it cannot meow and loathes rats; it can lie in wait for hours beside the hen coop, but it has never yet seized an opportunity for murder; I feed it sweetened milk, which is what most agrees with it; it sucks it down in long drafts through its carnivore's teeth. Naturally it is a great spectacle for children. Sunday morning is visiting time; I have the little creature on my lap, and all the children from the neighborhood stand around me. Then the most amazing questions are asked, ones that no human being can answer. [Why is there only one such animal, how come I am the one who has it, whether there was ever an animal like it before and what will happen after it dies, whether it feels lonely, why doesn't it have babies, what is its name?][1] I don't make any effort to answer but confine myself to exhibiting what I

---

1. The lines enclosed in brackets were crossed out by Kafka in manuscript but retained as too good to lose by Kafka's first editor, Max Brod, in its first German publication. The editor of this Norton Critical Edition agrees with Brod's decision.

have without further explanation. Sometimes the children bring cats with them; once they even brought two lambs; but contrary to their expectations, no recognition scenes ensued; the animals looked at each other calmly with their animal eyes and evidently accepted one another's existence as a divinely ordained fact.

On my lap the creature knows neither fear nor the desire to hunt others. It feels happiest cuddled up against me. It sticks to the family that has raised it. This is probably not some extraordinary loyalty but the correct instinct of an animal that, though it has countless in-laws on earth, may not have a single close blood relative; for that reason it holds sacred the protection it has found with us. Sometimes I have to laugh when it sniffs me all over, wriggles between my legs, and cannot be separated from me by any means. Not content with being lamb and cat, it comes close to wanting to be dog as well. I seriously believe something of the sort. [Once, as can happen to anyone, I could no longer see a way out in my business dealings and everything connected to them, and I wanted to let everything go to ruin; in such a mood I sat at home in my rocking chair, with the creature on my lap, and as I happened to look down, there were tears dripping from its giant whiskers—Were they mine, were they the creature's? Did this cat with the soul of a lamb also have the ambition of a man?—I have not inherited much from my father, but this heirloom is nothing to be ashamed of.] It has the restlessness of both creatures, the cat's and the lamb's, different as they are. That is why it feels unhappy in its own restricting skin. [Sometimes it jumps up on the armchair next to me, braces itself with its front legs against my shoulder, and puts its muzzle to my ear. It is as if it were telling me something, and in fact it then leans over and looks into my face to see the impression that its communication has made on me. And to be agreeable, I act as if I had understood and nod. Then it jumps friskily down onto the floor and dances around. I am almost convinced that it would not know how to contain itself for envy if I were ever to show it how the butcher sticks his knife into the young lambs.] Perhaps for this animal the butcher's knife would be a release, [but I cannot slaughter an heirloom] but because it is an heirloom, I must deny it that. [So it must wait until its breath leaves it of its own accord, even though it sometimes looks at me as if through eyes full of human reason, demanding that I do the reasonable thing].

A little boy had a cat as the sole inheritance from his father and by means of it became the Lord Mayor of London.[2] What will I be-

2. This is the story of Dick Whittington, a poor country boy, who came to London with his cat to seek his fortune. When he reached Highgate Hill, he became discouraged and turned to go back home, but then he heard the bells of London pealing and saying, "Turn again, Dick Whittington, three times Lord Mayor of London."

come because of my creature, my heirloom? Where does this huge city lie?

An Everyday Event

An everyday event; putting up with it, everyday heroism: A has to negotiate an important business transaction with B from the neighboring village of H. He goes to H for preliminary consultations, covering the distance there and back in ten minutes each way, and at home he boasts of this remarkable speed. The following day he again goes to H, this time to close the deal; since this will presumably take several hours, A leaves very early in the morning; but although all the surrounding circumstances, at least in A's opinion, are exactly the same as the day before, this time it takes him ten hours to get to H. When, exhausted, he arrives in the evening, he is told that B, annoyed at A's failure to appear, left for A's village half an hour earlier; they should have run into each other on the road. A is advised to wait since B is sure to return immediately. But A, anxious about the transaction, sets off for home in a hurry. This time, without paying special attention, he completes the journey in the blink of an eye. At home he learns that B had arrived bright and early, even before A left; indeed, he had met A at the gate and reminded him of the deal, but A had replied that he did not have time just then, he had to leave at once. Despite this incomprehensible behavior on A's part, however, B had remained to wait for A. Though he had repeatedly asked whether A had not returned yet, he had remained upstairs, in A's room. Happy at being able to see B after all and explain everything to him, A runs upstairs. He is already near the top when he stumbles, strains a tendon, and almost fainting from the pain, incapable even of shouting, only whimpering in the dark, hears and sees B—it is unclear whether at a great distance or right next to him—stamping furiously downstairs and disappearing once and for all.

The Silence of the Sirens

Proof that inadequate, even childish stratagems can also serve as a means of rescue.

In order to withstand the Sirens, Odysseus stuffed wax into his ears and had himself chained to the mast. All voyagers from the beginning of time could, of course, have done something of the sort (except for those the Sirens lured from a great distance); but it was known throughout the world that this could not possibly help. The song of the Sirens penetrated all materials, even wax, and the passion of those they seduced would have burst more than chains and mast. But Odysseus did not think of that, although he had probably heard as much; he had complete faith in the handful of wax and the bundle of chains, and taking an innocent pleasure in his little stratagems, he sailed out to meet the Sirens.

The Sirens, however, have an even more terrible weapon than their song—namely, their silence. Though it has never actually happened, it is conceivable that someone could have escaped from their singing but never from their silence. Nothing on earth can resist the feeling of having defeated them by one's own powers and the ensuing ecstasy of hubris[1] that pulls everything along with it.

And in fact, when Odysseus came, these powerful singers did not sing, whether because they believed that it was only silence that could defeat this adversary or because the sight of bliss on the face of Odysseus, who was thinking of nothing except wax and chains, made them forget to sing.

But Odysseus did not hear their silence, so to speak; he thought they were singing and that only he was safeguarded from hearing it; first he glimpsed the turnings of their necks, their deep breathing, their tearful eyes, their half-open mouths; but he believed that these were part of the arias that resounded, unheard, around him. But soon everything slipped from the gaze he was aiming into the distance; the Sirens literally vanished from his consciousness, and just when he was closest to them, he no longer knew of them.

But they, more beautiful than ever, stretched and twisted their limbs, let their ghastly hair blow freely in the wind, spread their claws on the rocks; they no longer wanted to seduce, they wanted only to grasp the luster of Odysseus's great eyes for as long as possible.

If the Sirens possessed consciousness, at that moment they would have been annihilated; as matters stood, they remained, it was only that Odysseus eluded them.

There is, moreover, an appendix to this story that has come down to us. Odysseus, it is said, was so full of tricks, was such a fox, that not even the goddess of destiny could penetrate his innermost self; perhaps, although this can no longer be grasped by human reason, he really did notice that the Sirens were silent and held up to them and the gods the semblance of the events above only as a kind of shield.

---

1. Excessive pride; presumption, originally toward the gods.

Prometheus

Legend attempts to explain the inexplicable; because it arises from a ground of truth, it must end again in the inexplicable.

Four legends tell of Prometheus. According to the first, he was chained fast to the Caucasus because he betrayed the gods to men, and the gods sent eagles who fed off his liver, which perpetually grew back.

According to the second, Prometheus pressed himself deeper and deeper into the rock to escape the pain of the hacking beaks, until he became one with the rock.

According to the third, in the course of the millennia his betrayal was forgotten, the gods forgot it, the eagles, he himself forgot.

According to the fourth, everyone became weary of what had become meaningless.[1] The gods grew weary, the eagles grew weary. The wound closed wearily.

There remained the inexplicable mountains of rock.

On the Question of the Laws

Unfortunately, our laws are not generally known, they are the secret of the small group of nobles who rule us. We are convinced that these ancient laws are being strictly upheld, but it is still an extremely tormenting thing to be ruled by laws that we do not know. I am not thinking here of the various possibilities of interpretation and the disadvantages that are entailed when only individuals and not the entire nation may participate in the interpretation. These disadvantages may not be so great. After all, the laws are so ancient, centuries have labored over their interpretation; this interpretation has probably also become law; and though a possible freedom of interpretation still exists, it is very limited. Moreover, the nobles evidently have no reason to allow their personal interests to influence their interpretation to our disadvantage, since from the very beginning the laws have been determined for the nobility; the nobles stand outside the law, and it is for this reason that the law seems to have put itself exclusively into their hands. In this, naturally, there is wisdom for us—who doubts the wisdom of the ancient laws?—but equally misery as well; there's probably no getting around that.

By the way, the existence of these apparent laws can only be sur-

---

1. Kafka's word is *grundlos*, literally, "ground-less"; this image returns to the opening sentence, which speaks of a "ground of truth."

mised. It is a tradition that they exist and have been entrusted to the nobility as a secret, but this is not nor cannot be anything other than an old tradition to which age lends credence; for the nature of these laws also demands that their continued existence be kept secret. And so, if we the people have been following attentively the actions of the nobility from the most ancient times and possess records of this made by our ancestors, which we have conscientiously continued, and if we think that we have discerned certain guiding principles in the innumerable facts, allowing us to draw a conclusion as to this or that legal decision; and if, following these conclusions, which have been most carefully sorted and filed, we seek to make some little arrangements for our lives for the present and the future—then all this is extremely uncertain and may be no more than an intellectual game, for the laws that we are trying to figure out may not even exist. There is a small party that is firmly of this opinion and that seeks to prove that, if any law exists, it can only be this: What the nobles do is the law. This party sees only arbitrary actions in the nobility and rejects the popular tradition that, in its opinion, produces only very small, accidental benefits, and on the other hand, mostly serious damage, since it gives the people a false, deceptive sense of security that leads to recklessness with respect to coming events. Such damage cannot be denied, but the overwhelming majority of our people sees its cause in the fact that the tradition is still far from being sufficient and much more of it must be researched, as well as in the fact that its content, huge as it seems to us, is still much too small and that centuries must still pass before it will be sufficient. What is dismal at present in this prospect is brightened only by the belief that one day the time will come when both the tradition and our research of it arrive, with a sigh of relief, so to speak, at their conclusion, when everything has become clear, when the law belongs to the people, and when the nobility disappears. This statement is certainly not made with hatred of the nobility, not in the least and not by anyone; we are more readily inclined to hate ourselves because we cannot yet be deemed worthy of the law. And that is the real reason why that party that does not believe in authentic law—certainly a very tempting party— has remained so small, because it also fully acknowledges the nobles and their right to continued existence. Only a sort of contradiction can express the situation properly: a party that would also repudiate the nobility along with the belief in the laws would immediately have the entire people behind it, but such a party cannot come into existence because no one dares to repudiate the nobility. We live on this knife's edge. A writer once summed up the matter thus: The only visible, indubitable law that is imposed on us is the nobility, and should we want to deprive ourselves of our only law?

Poseidon

Poseidon sat at his desk doing the accounts. Administering all the waters meant that he had an endless task. He could have had assistants, as many as he wanted, and he did have a great many, but because he took his office very seriously, he did the accounts over again, and so his assistants were of little use to him. It cannot be said that the work gave him pleasure; really, he did it only because it was imposed on him; indeed, he had often applied for what he called more cheerful work[1] but, then, whenever various proposals were made to him, it turned out that nothing really appealed to him so much as his present office. It was also very difficult to find something else for him to do. After all, he could not possibly be put in charge of, let us say, one particular ocean; apart from the fact that here, too, the work of doing the accounts would be not less but only more small-minded, the great Poseidon could only be given a superior position. And if he was offered a position unrelated to the waters, the very idea made him feel sick, his divine breathing became irregular, his bronzed chest began to heave. And his complaints were not really taken seriously; when a mighty man pesters, one must try to seem to accommodate him, even when his case has absolutely no prospect of success; no one really thought of removing Poseidon from his office, he had been fated to be the God of the Seas from the beginning of time, and that was how it had to be.

What mostly annoyed him—and this was the main reason for his dissatisfaction with his office—was hearing about the ideas that people held of him: how, for example, he continually went dashing over the waves with his trident. Meanwhile he was seated in the depths of the world's ocean, continually doing the accounts; an occasional trip to Jupiter was the sole interruption of the monotony—a trip, by the way, from which he usually returned in a rage. As a result he had hardly seen the oceans, except fleetingly during his hasty ascent to Olympus, and had never really traveled through them. He used to say that he was waiting until the end of the world, then there might come a quiet moment when, just before the end and after going over the final reckoning, he could still make a quick little tour.

---

1. Kafka's word is *fröhlich* (gay, cheerful), and "gay" might be the more precise translation. In light of Kafka's ongoing involvement with the works of Friedrich Nietzsche (see n. 4, p. 26), one should hear the allusion to Nietzsche's great philosophical work *Die fröhliche Wissenschaft* ("la gaya scienza"). Nietzsche's eminent translator Walter Kaufmann titles this book *The Gay Science*.

Researches of a Dog

How my life has changed, and how, at heart, it has not! If I now think back and summon up remembrance of the times when I was still living in the midst of dogdom, taking part in all its concerns, a dog among dogs, on closer scrutiny I soon find that something was not quite right from the very beginning, that a little fracture was in place, a slight uneasiness would come over me in the midst of the most venerable of public occasions, sometimes even among my closest friends; no, not sometimes, but actually quite often, the mere sight of another dog, someone dear to me—the mere sight of him, as if I were seeing him for the first time somehow, filled me with embarrassment, fright, helplessness, even despair. I tried to calm myself as best I could; friends to whom I confessed helped me; more peaceful times returned, times in which such surprises did not stop occurring but were accepted more equably, fitted more equably into my life, perhaps making me sad and weary but also allowing me to go on coping as an admittedly somewhat cold, reserved, timid, calculating dog but, all in all, a regular one. Without these periods of rest and recovery, how could I ever have reached the age I now enjoy? How could I have fought my way to the calm with which I contemplate the terrors of my youth and endure the terrors of age? How could I have arrived at the point of drawing conclusions from my admittedly unhappy—or to express the matter more carefully, not very happy—disposition and to live in accord with them to the extent of my abilities? Withdrawn, solitary, preoccupied only with my hopeless, dilettantish, but for me, indispensable little researches, which despite everything probably do provide me with a secret hope—thus I live; but, for all this, I have not lost a general overview of my kind from this distance: news sometimes makes its way to me, although gradually less and less frequently, and sometimes I, too, let myself be heard from. The others treat me with respect; they do not understand my way of life, but neither do they hold it against me, and even young dogs, whom I sometimes see running by in the distance, a new generation whose childhood I can just dimly remember, do not withhold a deferential greeting.

For the fact should not be overlooked that for all my peculiarities, which are as plain as day, I am by no means entirely different from my family. When I think about it—and for this I have the time, the desire, and the ability—dogdom does have some truly strange characteristics. Besides us dogs there are many different kinds of creatures all around—poor, meager, mute beings, whose speech is limited only to certain cries; many of us dogs study them, have given them names, seek to help them, educate them, improve them, etc.; except in cases where they try to upset me, or when there is a chance that they might furnish me with a tasty morsel (where we live that happens very rarely), they leave me cold, I mix them up, I look right through them; but one thing is too striking to have escaped me—namely how little, compared with dogs, they stick together, how they pass each other by in so alienated a way, silently and with a secret hostility, how only the most ordinary common interest can superficially unite them slightly, and how even this common interest can give rise to animosity and disputes. We dogs, on the other hand! Surely it can be said that we live together practically in a large huddle, all of us, however much we may differ in other ways as a result of the countless and profound differences that have arisen over time. All in one large huddle! Something urges us toward one another, and nothing can prevent us from expressing this urge, over and over again; all our laws and institutions, the few that I still know and the countless ones that I have forgotten or never knew, stem from the longing for the greatest happiness we are capable of: warm togetherness. But now the other side of the coin. No species, to my knowledge, lives so widely dispersed as we dogs do, none has so many differences of class, of kind, of vocation—so many that they cannot be surveyed. We who want to hold together—and again and again, in spite of everything, we do succeed, if only on a small scale and even then only in exuberant moments—it is precisely we who live far apart from one another, in peculiar professions often incomprehensible to the next dog, clinging to rules that are not those of dogdom, indeed, are more truly opposed to it.

What difficult things these are, things that one would do better to leave unexamined—I understand that point of view as well, understand it better than my own—and yet these are things that completely fascinate me. Why won't I behave like the others, live in harmony with my kind, silently accept whatever disturbs that harmony, overlook it as a little mistake in the great reckoning, and turn forever toward what binds us happily together and not toward what, time and time again, irresistibly, of course, tears us out of the circle of our kind?

My disquiet, which can never be entirely stifled, began after various sorts of earlier indications with a particular incident in my youth. At that time I was in one of those blessed, inexplicable states of excitement that everyone probably experiences as a child; I was still a very young dog, roughly at the end of my puppyhood; I liked everything, I felt connected to everything; I believed I was the ringleader of all great things going on around me, to which I had to add my voice; things that would have remained miserably inanimate had I not given them legs, not gamboled for them; well, children's fantasies that evaporate with the years, but at that time they were very strong, I was completely under their spell; and then something admittedly extraordinary happened that appeared to justify my wild expectations. In itself it was nothing extraordinary—since then I have often enough seen such things, and even more remarkable ones—but at that time it made a strong, original, indelible, formative impression on me.

That is, I met a little company of dogs—or rather, I did not meet with it, it came toward me. At that time I had long been running through the darkness with a premonition of great things—a premonition that, of course, could easily prove deceptive, for I had always had it—had been running for a long time through the darkness, hither and yon, blind and deaf to everything, guided only by my uncertain craving, when I suddenly came to a stop with the sense that here was the right place; I looked up and there was brilliant, bright daylight, merely a bit misty, everything full of intoxicating smells swelling up in confusion; I greeted the morning with chaotic barks; then—as if I had conjured it—out of some darkness, producing a terrible clamor the likes of which I had never heard before, seven dogs stepped into the light.

Had I not clearly seen that they were dogs and that they themselves brought this clamor with them—although I could not see how they produced it—I would have run away this minute, but as matters stood, I stayed. At that time I knew almost nothing about the creative musicality with which only the race of dogs is endowed; it was something that until now had escaped my powers of observation, which were only slowly developing; naturally, ever since infancy, music had surrounded me as a self-evident, indispensable vital element, but nothing had compelled me to separate it from the rest of my life; others had attempted to call my attention to it through hints suited to the mind of a puppy; all the more surprising then, even shocking, were those seven great musical virtuosi.

They did not speak, they did not sing, in general they held their tongue with almost a certain doggedness, but they conjured forth music out of that empty space. Everything was music. The way they raised and set down their feet, certain turns of their heads, their running and their resting, the attitudes they assumed toward one another, the combinations they formed with one another like a round dance, as when, for example, one braced his front paws on the other's back and then they all positioned themselves so that the first dog, erect, bore the weight of all the others, or as when, their bodies slinking close to the ground, they formed intertwined figures and never made a mistake—not even the last one, who was a little unsure of himself, did not always immediately hook up with the others, staggered a little, as it were, when the melody struck up, but was unsure only by comparison with the magnificent certainty of the others, and even had he been much more unsure, indeed utterly unsure, he would not have ruined anything, since the others, great masters, were keeping time so steadily.

But it is too much to say that you actually saw them, you hardly saw any of them. They had appeared, you welcomed them silently as dogs; true, the clamor that accompanied them was very confusing, but in the end they were dogs, dogs like you and me; you observed them in the usual way, like dogs that you meet on the street; you wanted to go up to them, exchange greetings, for they were also very close—dogs, certainly much older than me and not of my long-haired, woolly variety but also not too unusual in size and shape, really rather familiar; I knew many of such a breed, or a similar one, but while you were still caught up in such reflections, the music gradually took over, practically seized hold of you, swept you away from these real little dogs, and quite against your will, resisting with all your might, howling as if pain were being inflicted, you could attend to nothing but this music that came from all sides, from the heights, from the depths, from everywhere, pulling the listener into its midst, pouring over him, crushing him, and even after annihilating him, still blaring its fanfares at such close range that they turned remote and barely audible. And again you were released, because you were already too exhausted, too annihilated, too weak to hear any more, you were released and saw the seven little dogs doing their marches, performing their leaps; you wanted to call out to them, as dismissive as they looked, beg for instruction, ask them what they were doing here—I was a child and believed I was allowed to ask anybody anything—but I had hardly started to speak, hardly felt the good, familiar doggish connection with the seven when their music started up again, driving me out of my mind, spinning me around in circles, as if I myself were one of the musicians, when I was only their victim, hurling me, however I begged for mercy, this way and that, and finally saved me from its own violence by forcing me into a tangle of timbers[1] that were standing all around that area, though I had not noticed them before, and that now held me firmly, pressing my head down and giving me the opportunity to catch my breath a little even if the music was still thundering out there.

To tell the truth, I marveled less at the art of the seven dogs—it was incomprehensible to me, quite outside my abilities and hence something I could in no way relate to—than at their courage in ex-

1. One could think of these "timbers" as the puppy's impression of the chair legs of the gallery seats (see Hargraves's essay, p. 321).

posing themselves wholly and openly to the thing they produced and at their power to endure it calmly without its breaking their spine. Of course, I now realized, as I began to observe them more closely from my hideout, that it was not so much calm as extreme tension with which they worked—their legs, seemingly moving with such assurance, twitched at every step with an incessant anxious trembling; these dogs gazed at each other rigidly, as if in despair, and their tongues, which they forever tried to control, after each attempt immediately protruded slackly from their muzzles again. It could not be fear of their success that so excited them; whoever dared such things, accomplished such things, could no longer be afraid—what, then, could they be afraid of? Who was forcing them to do what they were doing here? And I could no longer resist, especially now that they seemed so incomprehensibly in need of help, and so, through all the clamor, I cried out my questions, loud and demanding. But they—incredible! incredible!—they did not answer, acted as if I did not exist; dogs who do not respond in any way when they are called offend against good manners, a transgression for which the smallest as well as the largest dog is under no circumstances forgiven. Might they possibly not even be dogs? But then, how could they not be dogs, when listening more intently, I could now hear even the tiny cries with which they fired each other up, calling attention to difficult spots, warning against mistakes; I even saw the last, the smallest dog, for whom most of the calls were intended, often peering in my direction, as if he were longing to answer me but controlled himself because it was not allowed. But why was it not allowed, why wasn't the thing that our laws always unconditionally require not allowed this time? My heart rebelled, I almost forgot the music. These dogs before me were violating the law. Great magicians they might be, but the law applied to them as well: that was something that I, a child, already knew very well. And from this point I saw even more. They really had good reason to remain silent, assuming that it was from feelings of guilt that they did so. For what a way to behave; because of the loud music I had not noticed until now that they had truly cast off all shame; these miserable creatures were doing something that was at once most ridiculous and most obscene—they were walking upright on their hind legs. Ugh! They were exposing themselves and openly flaunting their nakedness, they prided themselves on it, and whenever they obeyed their better instincts for a moment and lowered their front legs, they were literally horrified, as if it were a mistake, as if nature were a mistake, and once again they rapidly raised their legs, and their eyes seemed to be asking forgiveness that they had had to desist a little from their sinfulness.

Had the world turned upside down? Where was I? What had

happened? Here, for the sake of my own existence, I could no longer hesitate, I worked my way out of the clasp of the timbers and with one bound leaped out, heading for the dogs; I, the boy pupil, must be the teacher, I had to make them understand what they were doing, had to stop them from sinning further. "Such old dogs, such old dogs!" I kept repeating. But hardly had I freed myself, and only two or three bounds separated me from the dogs, when the clamor once more exerted its power over me. Perhaps in my eagerness I might have been able to resist, since I already knew it well enough, but its fullness, which was terrible, might still be combated—a clear, vigorous, continuous tone, arriving unchanged literally from a great distance, perhaps the true melody in the midst of the clamor—but this sound rang out and forced me to my knees. Oh, what a bewitching music these dogs made! I could not proceed, I no longer wanted to instruct them, they could go on spreading their legs, committing sins, and luring others to the sin of silent observation, but I was such a small dog, who could require such a difficult act from me? I made myself even smaller than I was, I whimpered, and if at that moment the dogs had asked me my opinion, I might have given them my approval. Besides, it was not long before they vanished, with all the clamor and all the light, into the darkness from which they had come.

As I said, the entire incident does not contain anything out of the ordinary, in the course of a long life you will encounter many things that would be even more astonishing if taken out of context and seen through the eyes of a child. Furthermore, you can also, of course—as the apt expression goes—"rationalize" it, as with everything else; then it is clear that this time seven musicians had met together to play music in the still of the morning, that a little dog had strayed into their midst, a tedious listener whom they had tried to drive away, unfortunately in vain, with particularly terrible or sublime music. He pestered them with his questions; were they, who had already been disturbed enough by the mere presence of this stranger, also supposed to respond to this nuisance and exaggerate it by answering? And even if the law does require you to reply to everyone, is such a tiny stray dog someone even worth mentioning? And perhaps they did not even understand him, for he probably stuttered his questions quite unintelligibly. Or perhaps they did understand him and, overcoming their reluctance, did answer, but he, this little dog, unaccustomed to music, could not distinguish the answer from the music. And as far as hind legs are concerned, perhaps as an exception they did really walk on them alone; true, it's a sin! But they were alone, seven friends, among friends, in intimate togetherness, so to speak, within their own four walls, so to speak, entirely private; for friends, after all, are not the public, and where there is no public, a nosy little street dog does not constitute one; in this case then, isn't it as if nothing at all had happened? It is not entirely so, but nearly so, and parents ought to teach their little ones not to run around so much and, better, to hold their tongues and respect their elders.

Once having arrived at this point, the case is settled. Of course what has been settled for grownups has not quite been settled for the little ones. I ran around telling my story and asking questions, making accusations and doing research; I wanted to drag everyone to the spot where it had happened, I wanted to show everyone where I had stood and where the seven had been and where and how they had danced and made music; and if anyone had come with me, instead of shaking me off and making fun of me as everyone did, I would probably have sacrificed my sinless state and tried to get up on my hind legs to make the whole event transparently clear. Well, we always disapprove of whatever a child does, but in the end we forgive him everything. But I have kept my childlike nature, and while keeping it, I have become an old dog. Just as at that time I never stopped discussing that incident out loud—to which today I admittedly give a much lower value—analyzing its components, testing it on those present without consideration for the nature of my company, constantly occupied only with this question, which just like all the other questions, I did find tiresome but which—this was the difference—I wanted for this very reason to solve absolutely by dint of research, so as finally to gain a new view of ordinary, quiet, happy, everyday life. I have subsequently worked the same way, even if with less childish means—but the difference is not very great—and I persist stubbornly to this day.

But it was with that concert that it began. I am not complaining, what is at work here is my innate nature, which would surely have found another opportunity to emerge even without the concert, except that the fact of its happening so soon used to cause me a great deal of pain: it robbed me of a good deal of my childhood; the blissful life of young dogs, which many are able to prolong for years, lasted only a few short months for me. But what of it! There are more important things than childhood. And perhaps there is a greater quantity of childlike happiness, earned by a life of hard work, beckoning to me in my old age than a real child would have had the strength to bear, but which I'll have by then.

I began my investigations at that time with the simplest things; there was no lack of material, unfortunately; it is its very abundance that, in the darkest hours, makes me despair. I began to investigate what dogdom took as nourishment. Now that is, if you will, not a simple question, it has occupied us from primordial times, it is the main object of our reflections; the observations and

experiments and viewpoints in this field are innumerable, it has become a science whose enormous scope not only exceeds any individual's powers of comprehension but even that of the sum of all
scholars and can be borne exclusively by no less than the whole of
dogdom, and even then only partially, and even they groan under its
burden; again and again it crumbles into bits of ancient cultures,
long assimilated, and must be laboriously supplemented, not to
mention the difficulties and prerequisites of modern research that
are hard to meet. Do not raise all these objections to me, I am just
as aware of them as your average dog, it never occurred to me to
meddle in real science, I have all due respect for it, but as for ex-
panding it, I lack the knowledge, industry, quiet and—not least, especially for several years now—the appetite. I gulp down my food
whenever I find any, but I don't think it's worth the slightest preliminary systematic agricultural reflection. In this respect I am satisfied with the essence of all science, the terse rule with which
mothers discharge their little ones from their teats and into life:
"Wet on everything, as much as you can." And doesn't this rule really contain almost everything? What does scientific research, ever
since our forefathers began it, have to add that is of crucial importance? Details, details, and how uncertain they all are; but this rule
will continue for as long as we are dogs. It concerns our main food
staple; certainly we have other resources as well, but in an emergency, and when the years are not too bad, we could live off our
main food staple; we find this food on the ground, but the ground
needs our water, it feeds on it and only at this price gives us our
food, the emergence of which—however, and this is not something
to forget—can be speeded up through certain incantations, songs,
and movements. But this, in my opinion, is everything; from this
aspect there is nothing fundamental to be said further about it. In
this, too, I am one with the great majority of dogdom, and I strictly
dissociate myself from all heretical views in this regard. To tell the
truth, I am not interested in pointing out peculiarities or in having
the last word; I am only too happy when I can agree with my fellows, and in this case I do. But my own researches run in a different direction. The evidence of my eyes teaches me that when the
earth is sprinkled and cultivated according to the rules of science,
it yields food and indeed in such quality, in such quantity, in such a
manner, in such places, and at such hours as required by the laws
in whole or in part established by science. This I grant; however,
my question is: "From where does the earth get this food?" A question that generally others pretend not to understand and which
they answer at best with: "If you don't have enough to eat, we'll give
you some of ours." Consider this answer. I know: It does not belong
to the virtues of dogdom to share with others the food we have

once obtained. Life is hard, the earth is stubborn, science is rich in knowledge but poor enough in practical results; whoever has food, keeps it; that is not self-interest but its opposite, it is dog law, it is the unanimous decision of our kind, arrived at by overcoming self-ishness, for the haves are indeed always in the minority. And that is why the answer, "If you don't have enough to eat, we'll give you some of ours," is a standing figure of speech, a joke, a tease. I haven't forgotten that. But it was all the more meaningful for me, at a time when I was trotting all over the world with my questions, that the others put aside all jokes at my expense; no one, of course, actually ever gave me anything to eat—where could anyone get it from, just like that? And if by chance anyone did happen to have a morsel, in the frenzy of his hunger he naturally forgot every other consideration; but the offer was meant seriously, and now and then I did actually get a bite whenever I was quick enough to grab it for myself. Why was it that the others gave me such special treatment? Went easy on me, allowed me privileges? Because I was a weak, skinny dog, malnourished and too little concerned about food? But many malnourished dogs make their way through our world, and the others grab even the most miserable scraps out from under their noses whenever they can, often not from greed but usually on principle. No, I was privileged, it was not a fact I could demon-strate with details so much as a definite impression. Was it, then, that they were delighted by my questions, that they considered them especially clever? No, they were not delighted by my ques-tions, and they considered all of them stupid. And yet it could only have been the questions that attracted their attention. It was as if they would rather do that monstrous thing of stuffing my mouth with food—none of them did it, but all of them wanted to—than put up with my questions. They would have done better to chase me away and refuse to put up with my questions. No, they did not want to do that; they certainly did not want to listen to my ques-tions, but it was precisely because of these questions of mine that they did not want to chase me away.

That was the time when, as much as they laughed at me, treated me like a silly little creature and pushed me around, I really en-joyed the greatest public esteem; nothing of this kind ever recurred: I was admitted everywhere, nothing was denied me; under the pre-text of treating me roughly, I was actually fawned over. And all, fi-nally, because of my questions, because of my impatience, because of my lust for research. In this way they wanted to lull me to sleep, to divert me without using force, almost lovingly, from a path whose falsity was not so much beyond all doubt that it would have justified the use of force; in addition, a certain awe and fear kept them from using force. By that time I already had an intimation of something of the sort; today I see it very clearly—much more clearly than those who were doing it at the time: the truth is that they wanted to lure me away from my path. They were not successful; they achieved the opposite: my awareness grew more acute. I even came to realize that it was I who wanted to lure the others and that to a certain extent this temptation actually succeeded. It was only with the help of the rest of dogdom that I began to understand my own questions. When, for example, I asked: "From where does the earth get this food?" was I concerned, as it could seem judging by appearances, about the earth? Was I at all concerned about the earth's problems? Not in the least; that, as I soon realized, was far from my interests; I cared only about dogs, and nothing else. For what else is there besides dogs? Who else can you call upon in this vast, empty world? All knowledge, the totality of all questions and all answers, resides in dogs. If only this knowledge could be made effective, if only it could be brought into the light of day, if only dogs did not know so infinitely much more than they admit, than they admit to themselves! Even the most garrulous dog is a greater secret than the places where the best food is found. You slink around your fellow dog, foaming at the mouth with desire, you thrash yourself with your own tail, you ask, you plead, you howl, you bite, and achieve—well, you achieve what you could have achieved effortlessly: loving attention, friendly contact, honorable sniffings, passionate embraces. My howling and yours mingle and unite, everything aims at finding oblivion in ecstasy, but the one thing that you wanted to achieve above all—admission of knowledge—remains denied to you; in the best case, after you have taken your powers of seduction to the extreme, your request, whether mute or audible, is answered only by opaque grimaces, odd looks, veiled, dim eyes. It is not very different from the way it was when as a child I cried out to the music dogs, and they kept silent.

Now it might be said: "You complain about your fellow dogs, about their reticence on crucial matters, you claim that they know more than they admit, more than they want to accept in life; and this concealment, the reason and secret for which they naturally also continue to keep silent, poisons your life, makes it intolerable, so that you will either have to change it or leave it; that may be, but after all, you are a dog yourself, you also have dog knowledge: now, say it, not only in question form but as an answer. If you say it, who will stand up to you? The great chorus of dogdom will chime in as if it had been waiting for this. Then you will have truth, clarity, admission: as much of it as you want. The roof of this low-lying life, about which you say such nasty things, will open, and all of us, dog arrayed with dog, will ascend into that high freedom. And if we should not attain the absolute, if things should become worse than before, if the whole truth turns out to be more intolerable than the half-truth, if it should be confirmed that those who keep silent are in the right as the upholders of life, if the gentle hope that we still have should turn into complete hopelessness—uttering the word is still worth the effort, since you refuse to live the way you are permitted to live. Well, then, why do you reproach the others for their silence while you yourself keep silent?" Easy answer: Because I am a dog. Essentially just as rigorously uncommunicative as the others, resistant to my own questions, rigid from anxiety. Have I been questioning dogdom, then, strictly speaking, at least since I've grown up, so that it will answer me? Do I have such foolish hopes? Can I see the foundations of our life, intuit their depth, see the workers engaged in building, laboring in the dark, and still expect that all this will be brought to an end, destroyed, abandoned in answer to my questions? No, I truly no longer expect this.

With my questions I harass only myself, want to fire myself up with the silence that is the only thing that still replies to me. How long will you put up with the truth that your research makes you realize more and more: that dogdom keeps silent and will always keep silent? How much longer will you put up with it?—that is the authentic question of my life, sounding above all particular questions; it is asked only of me and need not bother anyone else. Unfortunately, I can answer it more easily than the particular questions: I expect to hold out until my natural end; more and more the calm of old age resists these unsettling questions. I will probably die peacefully, keeping silent and surrounded by silence, and I look forward to it almost with composure. An admirably strong heart, lungs that cannot be worn out prematurely, have been given us dogs as if out of malice; we stand fast against all questions, even our own, bulwarks of silence that we are.

Lately I have been reflecting more and more on my life, looking for when I might have made the crucial mistake that is to blame for everything, but I cannot find a mistake. And yet I must have committed some error, for if I had not committed it and still failed to achieve what I wanted by the honest work of a long life, that would prove that what I wanted was impossible, and complete hopelessness would follow. Look at your life's work! Starting off with the investigations of the question: From where does the earth get our food? A young dog, naturally greedy and full of lust for life, I renounced all pleasures, shunned the full panoply of amusements, buried my head between my legs in the face of temptation, and settled down to work. It was not scholarly work or remotely related to scholarship or its methods or its intent. Those were probably mistakes, but they could not have been crucial. I have had little learning, for I left my mother at an early age, soon grew accustomed to independence, led a life of freedom; and premature independence is the enemy of systematic learning. But I have seen and heard a good deal, spoken with many dogs of the most disparate kinds and vocations, and, I believe, grasped everything reasonably well and connected my individual observations reasonably well: that has made up a bit for my lack of erudition; and besides, independence, though it may work to the disadvantage of learning, is of great advantage to an individual's research. In my case, it was all the more necessary, since I was not able to follow the true scientific method, which would have meant utilizing the work of my predecessors and forming relationships with contemporary researchers. I was completely dependent on myself, beginning at the very beginning and with the awareness, delightful for youth but extremely depressing in old age, that the final punctuation mark that I arbitrarily set down will also be my ultimate conclusion. Have I really been so alone with my researches, now and always? Yes and no. It is impossible that now and then there were no individual dogs who were, and are today, in my situation. My situation cannot be as bad as all that. I am not a hair's breadth distant from canine nature. Every dog feels as I do, feels the urge to ask questions, and like every dog, I feel the urge to keep silent. Everyone feels the urge to ask questions. How else could my questions have produced even the slight shocks that I was often granted to note with rapture—admittedly, with exaggerated rapture? And that I feel the urge to keep silent does not, unfortunately, require any special proof. I am, therefore, not fundamentally different from any other dog, and that is why, despite all differences of opinion and aversions, everyone basically respects me, and I would not behave otherwise toward any other dog. Only the mixture of elements is different—a difference that is of very great importance to the individual but insignificant from the standpoint of the species. And should the mixture of these elements, which are always at hand, in the past and in the present, never have turned out to be like mine and, if you want to call my mixture unfortunate, be even more unfortunate? That would run counter to the rest of experience. We dogs are engaged in the most outlandish vocations—vocations that would beggar belief if we did not have the most reliable reports concerning them. I am thinking here above all of the example of the air dogs. When I first heard of one, I laughed, I would not allow myself be convinced. What? There was supposed to be a dog of the smallest breed, not much bigger than my head, even in advanced age not much bigger; and this dog, naturally a weakling, to judge by appearances an artificial, immature, overcarefully coiffed creature, incapable of taking an honest jump—this dog, the story went, was supposed to move about most of the time high in the air while doing no visible work, just resting.[2] No, to attempt to convince me of such things would be to exploit excessively the unbiased mind of a young dog, I thought. But shortly thereafter I heard from another quarter about another air dog. Had they joined forces to make a fool of me? But then I saw the music dogs, and from that time on I considered anything possible, no prejudices limited my conceptual powers; I tracked down the most senseless rumors and followed them as far as I could; in this senseless life the most senseless things seemed to me more probable than anything sensible and especially productive for my research. So too the air dogs. I found out a great deal about them; true, so far I have never succeeded in seeing one, but I have long been convinced of their existence, and in my worldview they occupy a position of importance. As in most cases, here too it is naturally not their art that above all sets me thinking. It is wonderful, who can deny it, that these dogs are able to float on air; I am one with the whole of dogdom in my amazement. But my feeling is that the absurdity, the silent absurdity of these beings, is far more wonderful. Generally, no reasons are given; they float on air, and that's all there is to it, life goes on, here and there you hear talk of art and artists, that's all. But why, great-hearted dogdom, why do these dogs float? What is the meaning of their vocation? Why can't you get one word of explanation out of them? Why are they floating around up there, allowing their legs, the pride of dogs, to wither, cutting themselves off from the nourishing earth: they sow not and yet they reap, and they are even, I hear, especially well nourished at the expense of dogdom.

I can flatter myself that my questions brought some slight movement into these matters. People begin to produce reasons, to piece together some sort of rational foundation, they make a beginning, although they will not go beyond this beginning. But that is still something. And in the process something comes to light that, while not the truth—we will never get this far—intimates the deep-rootedness of the lie. All the senseless phenomena of our life, and quite particularly the most senseless, can be rationalized in this way. Not completely, of course—that is the devilish joke—but just enough to ward off awkward questions. Take the air dogs again, for example. They are not arrogant, as one might think at first, but rather especially dependent on their fellow dogs: if you try to put yourself in their place, you will understand. They must try to be pardoned for

2. "Air dog" is a neologism for Kafka's better neologism *Lufthund*, which is immediately understandable in German and is brilliantly funny. German has the expression *Luftmensch*—literally, "air man"—a man (or, less often, woman) whose natural habitat is the air of idealism, speculation, illusion—and who, as a result of his or her "vocation," may find it difficult to be employed and so is obliged to "live on air." In this story the dog narrator is thinking of lapdogs—who are carried around and who almost never touch the ground—as playing a similar role to that of *Luftmenschen* in the human sphere.

their way of life, or at least distract attention from it, make others oblivious to it, and indeed, if not openly—that would be a violation of the obligation to silence—then they must do it in some other way, and they do it, so I am told, by an almost insufferable talkativeness. They always have something to tell, partly their philosophical reflections, in which, since they have completely dispensed with physical exertion, they can forever be absorbed, partly the observations that they make from their elevated vantage point. And although they are not highly distinguished for their intellectual powers, something that is perfectly understandable considering their dissolute life, and their philosophy is as worthless as their observations, and science can hardly make use of any of it and never depends on such miserable sources, nevertheless, when you ask what it is about these air dogs, time and again you are told that they contribute a great deal to science. "That's right," you then say, "but their contributions are worthless and tedious." The answer to that is a shrug of the shoulder, a change of subject, vexation, or laughter; and a little while later, when you ask again, you hear once more that they contribute to science, and finally, when you yourself are next questioned, if you are not very careful, you will give the same answer. And perhaps it is also better not to be too stubborn and to acquiesce, not in acknowledging the life of these air dogs as justified, which would be impossible, but in tolerating them. But more should not be required, that would be going too far, and yet more is required. You are asked to put up with ever new air dogs that are forever appearing on the scene. It is not at all clear where they come from. Do they multiply by reproducing? Are they strong enough to do that? After all, they are not much more than a pretty pelt, so what is supposed to be reproducing itself here? And even if the improbable were possible, when is it supposed to take place? For they are always seen alone, self-sufficient up there in the air, and if for once they condescend to run, the activity lasts for only a minute or two, a few mincing steps, and always only in strict solitude and allegedly lost in thought, from which, even when they make an effort, they cannot tear themselves away, or so, at any rate, they claim. But if they do not reproduce, is it conceivable that there are dogs who would willingly give up life at ground level, willingly become air dogs, and for the sake of comfort and a certain technical skill choose the sterile life on the cushions? That is not conceivable, neither reproduction nor willing accession is conceivable. But the reality is that new air dogs appear all the time; from which it follows that even if the obstacles appear to our minds to be insurmountable, any breed of dog, once it exists, however odd it may be, will not die out, at any rate not easily, at any rate not without there being in every breed something that puts up an effective defense for a long time.

Surely I must assume this to be the case for my breed as well when it holds true for a breed of dog, the air dog, so eccentric, absurd, absolutely odd-looking, and unfit for life. Besides, I'm not odd-looking at all, I'm an ordinary middle-class dog, very common at least here, in this neighborhood, especially outstanding in nothing, in nothing especially contemptible: in my youth and even to some extent in my manhood, I was even quite a handsome dog as long as I did not neglect my appearance and had plenty of exercise; my front view was particularly admired, my slim legs and the handsome way I carried my head; and my gray, white, and yellow coat, curly only at the tips, was also very pleasing, none of that is unusual, only my nature is odd; but this, too, as I must never fail to remember, is well-founded in the general nature of dogs. Now, if even the air dog is not unique, and here and there in the great world of dogs another one of his breed can always be found, and if they continue to manufacture new generations out of the void, then I can also be confident that I have not been abandoned. Of course, the destiny of the fellow members of my species must be very special, and their existence will never be of obvious help to me, if for no other reason than that I would seldom recognize them. We are those whom silence oppresses, who long to break through because of a literal hunger for air; others appear to be flourishing in their silence, although this only appears to be so, just as in the case of the music dogs, who appeared to make music calmly but were really intensely excited; but this appearance is strong, you try to master it, but it defies every attempt.

How, then, do my fellow members of the species cope? What do their attempts to go on living despite everything look like? They can take different forms. As long as I was young, I tried with my questions. Perhaps I could team up with those who ask lots of questions, then I would have fellows of my species. I actually tried that for a time while practicing self-mastery, a necessary self-mastery, for the ones with whom I am concerned, after all, are mainly those who are supposed to answer, and the ones who continually interrupt me with questions that for the most part I cannot answer I find repugnant. And, then, who does not like to ask questions when he is young; so how will I pick out the right ones from among all the questioners? One question sounds like any other, what counts is the intention, but that is hidden, often even from the questioner. And in a fundamental sense, questioning is a peculiarity of dogdom, they all ask questions at the same time, as if by doing so they intended to erase all trace of the genuine questioners. No, I do not find fellows of my species among the young questioners any more than among the old ones, those who keep silent, to whom I now belong. But what good are all these questions anyway? I, for one, have run aground on them; my fellows are probably much smarter than I am and employ other excellent methods to put up with this life—methods, of course, that, I will add from my own experience, may help them in a pinch, calm them, put them to sleep, have a mutating effect, but that in general are just as impotent as mine, for no matter where I look, I see no sign of their success. I am afraid that the last thing by which I would recognize fellows of my species is their success.

Where, then, are the fellows of my species? Yes, that is my complaint, that's it. Where are they? Everywhere and nowhere. Perhaps one of them is my neighbor, three jumps away from me; we often call to one another, and he comes to me as well, I do not go to him. Is he a fellow of my species? I don't know; to tell the truth, I don't recognize anything of the sort in him, but it's possible. It's possible, and yet nothing is more improbable; when he's away, with the aid of all my imagination, just for a lark, I can discover in him much that is suspiciously familiar; but when he stands before me, all my fantasies are a joke. An old dog, even somewhat smaller than I am—and I am barely medium-size—brown, short-haired, with head lowered wearily, with shuffling steps; in addition he drags his left hind leg a little as a result of some illness. For a long time now I have related to no one as intimately as I have to him; I am glad that I still find him somewhat tolerable, and when he leaves, I shout the friendliest things after him—not, of course, out of affection but in a rage at myself, because, as I watch him go, I simply find him completely repulsive again, the way he slinks off with his leg dragging behind and his hind parts much too low. Sometimes it seems to me as if I were intent on mocking myself when in my private thoughts I call him fellow. Nor does he betray any sort of fellowship in our conversations; certainly he is intelligent and, given what we have here, cultured enough; I could learn a lot from him, but are intelligence and culture what I am looking for? We usually talk about local issues, and here I am amazed—my solitude has made me more insightful in this respect—how much intellect is necessary, even for an ordinary dog, even in average, not too unfavorable circumstances, just to live his life and protect himself against the worst of the usual dangers. Science provides the rules, true, but to understand them even at a distance and in their roughest major outline is not easy; and even when one has understood them, there comes the real difficulty, that of applying them to local conditions; in this almost no one can help, nearly every hour gives rise to new tasks, and every new patch of earth presents its particular challenge; no one can claim that he is settled in somewhere for the duration and that his life more or less runs by itself—not even I, whose needs literally grow less every day. And all this interminable effort—to what end? Only to bury oneself deeper and deeper in silence, never again able to be hauled out by anyone.

People often boast of the universal progress of dogdom through the ages, and they probably mean mainly the progress of science. Certainly, science marches on, it is unstoppable, it even marches on at an accelerated pace, faster and faster, but what is there to praise in this? It is as if you were to praise someone because he grows older as the years go by and as a result death comes ever closer. That is a natural and also an ugly process in which I find nothing to praise. I see only decline, although I do not mean that previous generations were essentially better, they were just younger, that was their great advantage, their memory was not yet as over-burdened as ours is today, it was easier to get them to speak out, and even if no one ever succeeded, the possibility was greater; this greater possibility is indeed what so affects us when we listen to those old, really simple stories. Here and there we hear a suggestive word, and we would jump to our feet if we did not feel the weight of the centuries upon us. No, whatever I have to reproach my age with, earlier generations were not better than the newer ones; in a certain sense, in fact, they were much worse and much weaker. Even then, of course, miracles did not run freely through the streets for just anyone to catch, but dogs were—I cannot put this any differently—not so currish as today; the structure of dogdom still had some play in it; at that time the true word could still have intervened, determined the construction, changed its tune, changed it at will, turned it into its opposite, and that word was there, or at least was near, hanging on the tip of everyone's tongue, everyone could receive it; where has it gone today? Today you could dig into your bowels and still not find it. Our generation may be lost, but it is more innocent than the former one. I can understand the hesitation of my generation; indeed, it is no longer hesitation, it is the forgetting of a dream dreamed a thousand nights ago and for-gotten a thousand times: who will scold us merely for forgetting for the thousandth time? But I also believe I understand the hesitation of our forefathers; we would probably not have acted any differ-ently; I'm tempted to say: it is fortunate for us that it was not we who had to take on the guilt, that in a world already darkened by others, we might instead rush toward our death in almost guiltless silence. When our forefathers went astray, they were hardly think-ing of eternal wandering, they still saw the crossroads, as it were; it was easy for them to turn back whenever they wanted, and if they hesitated to turn back, it was merely because they wanted to enjoy their dog's life for a little while longer; it was not in any sense a genuine dog's life yet, and it already seemed to them intoxicatingly beautiful, so how would it be a little later, at least a little bit later?

and so they went on wandering. They did not know what we could divine by observing the course of history, that the soul changes sooner than life does and that when they began to enjoy the dog's life, they must already have had a very old dog's soul and were not nearly as close to the creation as it seemed to them or as their eyes, reveling in all the dog's joys, tried to persuade them. Who can still speak of youth today? They were the genuinely young dogs, but their sole ambition was unfortunately aimed at becoming old dogs, an ambition at which, of course, they could not fail, as all succeeding generations prove and ours, the last, proves most clearly.

Of course, these are not matters that I discuss with my neighbor, but I often think of them when I am sitting opposite him, this typically old dog, or burying my snout in his coat, which already has a whiff of the smell that you find in skinned pelt. It would be pointless to discuss such things, with him as with anyone else. I know how the conversation would run. Here and there he would have a few objections to make, finally he would agree—agreement is the best weapon—and the matter would be buried, so why then worry it out of its grave in the first place? And yet, perhaps I do have a deeper understanding with my neighbor, one that goes beyond mere words. I cannot stop maintaining as much, though I have no proof and perhaps am only prey to a simple delusion, just because for a long time now he is the only one I see, and so I have to stick with him. "Are you perhaps my fellow after all? In your own way? And are you ashamed because you've failed at everything? Look, it's the same with me. When I'm alone, I howl about it; come, it is sweeter to howl together." Sometimes I have such thoughts and meanwhile give him a hard look. He does not lower his gaze, but at the same time there is nothing I can read in it; he looks at me dully, puzzled that I am silent and have broken off our conversation. But perhaps this very look is his way of asking questions, and I disappoint him in the same way he disappoints me. In my youth, if other questions had not been more important for me at that time and I had not been abundantly self-sufficient, I might have asked him aloud and would have received some sign of weak agreement, hence less than today, when he is silent. But aren't we all silent in the very same way? What keeps me from believing that everyone is a fellow of mine, that not only do I have an occasional fellow researcher, lost and forgotten along with his paltry findings, whom I cannot reach anymore in any way whatever through the darkness of the ages or the crush of the present, but instead that from the beginning of time all dogs have been my fellows, all of them have striven in their own way, all of them unsuccessful in their own way, all of them silent or babbling craftily in their own way, just as these hopeless researches entail? But then I would not have had to cut myself off at all, I could have remained quietly among the others, would not, like some badly behaved child, have had to force my way out through the ranks of the grownups, for, just like me, they want to find a way out, and the only thing about them that perplexes me is their understanding that tells them that no one gets out and that all such urging is foolish.

Such thoughts, however, are clearly the effect of my neighbor, he confuses me, he makes me melancholic; and yet in himself he is cheerful enough, at least I hear him, when he is in his own territory, shouting and singing such that it annoys me greatly. It would be best to renounce this last bit of social intercourse, not to pursue vague reveries of the kind that are unavoidably generated by every sort of social intercourse with dogs, however jaded one thinks one is, and to apply the little time that remains entirely to my researches. The next time he comes I will creep away and pretend to be asleep, and I will repeat that for as long as it takes for him to stop coming.

My researches have also become disordered, I grow slack, I grow weary, I merely trot mechanically where once I enthusiastically raced. I recall the time when I first began to investigate the question, "From where does the earth get our food?" Then, of course, I lived amid my people, forced my way up to where the crowds were thickest, tried to turn everyone into witnesses to my work; having witnesses was even more important to me than my work, since I was still expecting to have some sort of general effect. Naturally this filled me with enthusiasm, which now that I am solitary has fled. But at that time I felt so strong that I did something unheard of, that contradicts all our principles, and surely everyone who was an eyewitness then remembers it as something uncanny.

Though science normally strives toward endless specialization, I discovered in it a remarkable simplification in one respect. It teaches as its major tenet that the earth produces our food; and then, having made this preliminary hypothesis, it indicates the methods of obtaining various kinds of food of the best quality and the greatest abundance. It is, of course, correct that the earth produces our food, there's no doubt about that; but the matter is not as simple as it is usually presented, as simple as to exclude all further investigation. Let us consider merely the most primitive occurrences that happen each day. If we were to be entirely inactive, as I come close to being nowadays, and after perfunctory cultivation of the soil were to curl up and wait for whatever happens, we would indeed find food on the ground, provided that anything would come of it at all. But that is not what happens as a rule. Anyone who has remained even slightly open-minded about science—and there are, of course, very few of them, for the circles that science draws are

becoming ever wider—will readily recognize, even when he does
not attempt special observations, that the main part of our food
found lying on the ground in such instances comes down from
above; indeed, we catch most of it, each according to his dexterity
and greed, even before it touches the ground. In saying this I am
not saying anything against science; of course the ground also produces this food, and does so in a natural way; whether it draws the
one kind out of itself or calls down the other from above may not
be an essential difference, and science, which has determined that
cultivation of the soil is necessary in both cases, may not have to be
concerned with those distinctions, for we have the saying, "Grub in
your muzzle, all questions solved for the nonce." Now it seems to
me that science does concern itself in a veiled way, at least to some
extent, with these things, since it acknowledges two principal methods of obtaining food—genuine cultivation and supplementation
and refinement in the form of incantation, dance, and song. Here I
find a division, admittedly incomplete but still sufficiently clear,
that corresponds to the distinction I have made.[3] Cultivation
serves, in my opinion, to bring about both sorts of food and remains
indispensable, whereas incantation, dance, and song apply less to
ground food in the narrower sense, instead serving mainly to attract
food from above. Tradition supports me in my view of the matter.
In this instance it seems that the people are rectifying science without knowing it and without science's daring to offer resistance. If,
as science claims, those ceremonies are supposed merely to serve
the ground, perhaps to give it the strength to fetch food from
above, then, logically, they would have to be carried out entirely on
the ground, everything would have to be whispered to, sung before,
and danced in front of the ground. Nor, to the best of my knowledge, does science require anything different. And now the odd element: the people direct all their ceremonies upward. This is not a
violation of science, science does not forbid it, it grants the farmer
freedom in this matter; its teachings have only the soil in mind, and
if the farmer carries out the teachings of science relating to the
soil, science is satisfied, but in my opinion its train of thought really
ought to demand more. And I, who have never been deeply initiated
into science, simply cannot imagine how scholars can let our people, in that passionate way of theirs, chant the magic incantations
skyward, wail the old folk songs into the air, and perform their leaping dances as if, oblivious of the soil, they wanted to vault upward
forever. Stressing these contradictions was my starting point; when-

3. Cf. the two modalities of script inflicted on the body of the prisoner in *In the Penal
Colony*: "The genuine script has to be surrounded by many, many ornaments; the real
script encircles the body only in a narrow belt; the rest of the body is meant for adornments" (p. 43).

ever scientific doctrine stated that harvest time was approaching, I concentrated entirely on the soil, I scrabbled it in a dance, I twisted my head in order to get as close as possible to the soil, later I dug a hole for my snout, and thus I sang and declaimed so that only the ground heard it and no one else near or over me.

The results of my research were minimal; sometimes I received no food, and I was ready to exult at my discovery, but then food did come again, as if my strange performance had produced some bafflement at first but now its advantages had been recognized and my barks and jumps could be happily dispensed with; often the food came even more abundantly than before, but then again it completely failed to materialize. With a diligence hitherto unknown in young dogs, I kept exact lists of all my experiments; I thought that here and there I'd found a track that could lead me further, but then it would once again run off into uncertainty. I was unquestionably thwarted by the inadequacy of my scientific preparation. I had no guarantee, for example, that the failure of the food to materialize was caused by my experiments rather than by unscientific cultivation of the soil, and if that was so, then there was no proof for any of my conclusions. Under certain circumstances I could have produced an almost perfectly accurate experiment—if, that is, I had been successful just once in inducing a descent of food without soil cultivation and solely by means of ceremonies directed upward, and then a failure of food to materialize solely by means of soil-based ceremonies. True, I did attempt something of this kind but without firm conviction and under less than perfect experimental conditions, for it is my unshakeable opinion that a certain amount of cultivation is always necessary; and even if the heretics who do not think so were right, their theory could certainly never be proved, since watering of the soil occurs under pressure and within certain limits cannot be avoided. I had greater success with another, admittedly slightly eccentric, experiment that caused something of a sensation. Reasoning from the usual method of snatching food from the air, I resolved not to let the food fall down, of course, but also not to catch it. To this end, whenever food came, I jumped up a little, but I made sure the jump fell short; but the food generally fell to the ground, dull and indifferent, and I threw myself on it furiously, furious not only with hunger but also with disappointment. But in isolated cases something else did occur, something actually wonderful; the food did not fall but followed me through the air; the food pursued the hungry. It did not happen for long, just for a short stretch, and then it fell or completely disappeared, or—the usual case—my greed ended the experiment prematurely, and I gobbled up the object.

Nonetheless, I was happy in those days, a murmuring ran through my surroundings, the others had become restive and attentive, I found my acquaintances more open to my questions, I saw in their eyes a gleam that seemed to search for guidance; even if it was only the reflection of my own glances, I wanted nothing more, I was satisfied. Until I learned, of course—and others learned it along with me—that my experiment had been described a long time ago in the scientific literature and had already been successfully carried out on a much grander scale than in my case; and although it had not been attempted for a long time because of the rigors of self-discipline required, owing to its alleged lack of scientific value, it did not need to be repeated. It only proved something that was already known—that the ground fetches food not only straight down but also on a slant, indeed, even in spirals. That is where I now stood, but I was not discouraged, I was still too young; on the contrary, I was encouraged to attempt perhaps the greatest accomplishment of my life.

I did not believe in the scientific devaluation of my experiment, but in such cases what matters is not belief but only proof, and I wanted to get started on proof and in so doing, expose this originally somewhat eccentric experiment to the full glare of daylight, at the center of research. I wanted to prove that when I shrank back from the food, it was not the ground that attracted it slantwise but rather that it was I who lured it into following me. True, I could not develop this experiment further: to see the grub in front of you and at the same time perform scientific experiments on it is something you cannot endure for any length of time. But there was something else I wanted to do: I wanted to fast for as long as I could, at the same time avoiding all sight of food, every temptation. If I withdrew in this way, remained lying down day and night with my eyes closed, and concerned myself neither with picking up nor with snatching food in midair, and if, as I did not dare to claim but still mildly hoped, without my taking any further measures except for the inevitable irrational sprinkling of the ground and the silent recitation of incantations and songs (I wanted to leave out the dancing, so as not to weaken myself), food would spontaneously fall from above and, without paying any attention to the ground, come knocking on my teeth for admittance—if this were to happen, then science would not, admittedly, have been refuted, for it has enough elasticity to admit exceptions and individual cases, but what would be the reaction of the common people, who fortunately do not have so much elasticity? For this would by no means be the kind of exceptional case that history records, where because of physical sickness or of melancholy someone refuses to prepare, look for, or take in his food, and then dogdom comes together to incant conjuring formulas, and in this way succeeds in having food deviate from its usual path directly into the muzzle of the invalid. On the contrary, I was at my full strength and in perfect health, my appetite was so splendid that it prevented me for days at a time from thinking of anything else, I submitted myself to fasting voluntarily, believe it or not; I could make the food come down by myself, I was ready to do so, and so I required no help from dogdom, even refusing such help in no uncertain terms.

I looked for a suitable spot in some outlying bushes, where I would hear no talk of food or smacking of chops and crunching of bones; I stuffed myself to the gills for one last time and then lay down. I wanted, if possible, to spend the entire time with my eyes closed; for as long as no food came, it would be one unbroken night for me, even if it should go on for days and weeks. In this situation, however—something that made matters very difficult—I allowed myself only little sleep or, at best, none at all, for not only did I have to conjure down the food but I also had to be on guard that I did not sleep through the arrival of the food; on the other hand, sleep was very welcome, for I would be able to fast much longer asleep than awake. For these reasons I resolved to apportion the time very carefully and sleep a good deal but always only for brief periods. I achieved this by always sleeping with my head propped up on a frail twig, which soon cracked and in this way awakened me. Thus I lay, sleeping or waking, dreaming or singing quietly to myself. The first period passed uneventfully; perhaps there, in the place where food comes from, it had remained somehow unnoticed that here I was, resisting the normal course of things, and so everything remained quiet. My exertions were a little roiled by the fear that the other dogs would miss me, soon locate me, and try to do something to hinder me. My second fear was that, as a result of a mere besprinkling, the ground would produce so-called chance-food, although according to science it wasn't fertile, and the aroma would tempt me. But for the time being nothing of the sort happened, and I could go on fasting. Apart from these fears, I felt calm at first in a way that I had never noticed in myself before. Although I was really at work here negating science, I was filled with contentment and almost the proverbial calm of the scientific worker. In my reveries I was pardoned by science, there was room in science for my researches as well; a comforting voice sounded in my ears proclaiming that, even if my researches were successful, and especially then, I would never be lost to the common life of dogs; science looked kindly on me, science itself would undertake the interpretation of my findings, and this promise already signified fulfillment; while until now in my innermost being I had felt cast out and had run up against the walls of my species like a savage, I would now be received with great honor, the sought-after warmth of the collective dogs' body would flow around me; praised to the skies, swaying from side to side, I would be carried on the shoulders of my species.

Remarkable effect of the initial fast. My achievement seemed to me so great that I began to weep from emotion and self-pity even there in the quiet bushes; this was, I admit, not entirely understandable; for if I was awaiting my well-deserved reward, why was I weeping? Probably merely from contentment. I have never liked my own weeping. I have always wept only when I've been content, and that was rarely enough. Of course, this time it was soon over. The beautiful images gradually dissipated as my hunger grew more grievous; it was not long before my fantasies and higher feelings swiftly took leave of me, and I was alone with hunger burning in my guts. "That is hunger," I said to myself countless times, as if I were trying to persuade myself that hunger and I were still two distinct entities and I could shake it off like a tiresome lover, but in reality we were utterly, painfully one, and when I said to myself, "That is hunger," it was really the hunger that was speaking, and this was its way of mocking me.

An evil, evil time! I shudder when I think of it, not only, of course, because of the suffering that I lived through but above all because at that time I did not finish, because I will have to go through this suffering all over again if I hope for any achievement, for today I still consider fasting the ultimate and most powerful instrument in my research. The way goes through fasting; the ultimate goal can be attained only through the ultimate effort, if it is attainable, and among us this ultimate effort is voluntary fasting. And so when I think over those times—and above all else I enjoy pawing through them—I also think through the coming times that threaten me. It seems that almost a lifetime must pass before you recover from such an experiment; all the years of my maturity separate me from that fast, and I have still not recovered. The next time I begin fasting, I might have more determination than before as a result of my greater experience and better insight into the necessity of the experiment, but as a result of my previous effort, my powers are diminished; at the very least I will grow faint in mere anticipation of the familiar terrors. My weaker appetite will not help me; it only devalues the experiment a little and will probably force me to fast for a longer period than was necessary at that time. I think I am clear about these and other presuppositions; there has certainly been no lack of trial experiments during this long interval; often enough I have literally taken a bite at fasting but have not yet felt strong enough to go all the way, and youth's guileless pleasure in the attack has naturally disappeared forever. It had already vanished by the middle of my first fast. A number of considerations plagued me. Our forefathers appeared before me in threatening guise. Although I consider them to blame for everything, even if I do not dare to say so publicly, hold them guilty of our life as dogs, and so could easily answer their threats with counterthreats, I bow down before their knowledge; it came from sources that we no longer know; hence, as much as I feel the urge to fight them, I would never directly transgress their laws; it is only through their loopholes, for which I have a specially developed nose, that I come swarming out.

With respect to fasting, I refer to the famous dialogue in the course of which one of our sages expressed his intention of banning fasting, whereupon a second sage advised against this move with the question, "But who would ever fast?" and the first allowed himself to be convinced and rescinded the ban. But now the question again arises: "Well, isn't fasting, after all, forbidden?" The great majority of commentators deny this, consider fasting permitted, side with the second sage, and thus fear no ill effects even from an erroneous commentary. I had, of course, made sure of this before beginning to fast. But now as I lay contorted with hunger, in my mental confusion continually seeking relief in my own hind legs and desperately licking, chewing, sucking on them right up to my anus, the generally accepted interpretation of that dialogue seemed to me completely false; I cursed the science of commentary, I cursed myself for having let myself be led astray by it; the dialogue contained, in fact, as any child—a starving one, of course—could not fail to see, more than just one single prohibition against fasting; the first sage wished to forbid fasting, and whatever a sage wishes is as good as done, so fasting was forbidden; the second sage not only agreed with him but also considered fasting impossible, thus shunting onto the first prohibition yet a second, the prohibition stemming from the very nature of dogs; the first sage acknowledged as much and withheld his express prohibition, i.e. he commanded dogs, after laying out all this, to use their intelligence and prohibit their fasting. Hence a triple prohibition instead of the usual single one, and I had violated it.

At this point I might have tardily obeyed and stopped fasting, but in the midst of the pain there was also the temptation to continue, and I followed it, lusting after it as if after strange dogs. I could not stop; I might also have been too weak to stand up and find help in inhabited regions. I heaved myself back and forth on the forest litter, I could no longer sleep, I heard noises everywhere; the world that had been asleep all my life so far seemed to have been awakened by my fasting; I was assailed by the idea that I would never again be able to feed, for then I would have had to silence the liberated, thundering world once again, and I would not be able to;

but the loudest noise of all I heard in my belly; I often laid my ear against it and must have rolled my eyes in horror, for I could hardly believe what I heard. And now that everything was becoming so awful, the tumult seemed to seize hold of my very nature, which made senseless attempts to save itself: I began to smell dishes, exquisite dishes that I had not eaten for the longest time, joys of my childhood, yes, I smelled the aroma of my mother's teats; I forgot my resolution to resist all smells or, more truly, I did not forget it; together with this resolution, as if it were a resolution that belonged to what I was doing, I dragged myself in every direction, but always only for a few steps, and I sniffed, as if looking for dishes only to beware of them. The fact that I found nothing did not disappoint me; the dishes existed, but they were always a few too many steps away; before I could get to them, my legs folded under me. But at the same time I knew there was nothing at all there and that I went through these little motions simply from fear of a final breakdown at a spot that I would never leave again. My last hope, my last temptation vanished: I would perish miserably here; what was the sense of my researches, childish experiments hatched in childishly happy times; this, now, was the moment of seriousness, here research could have proven its worth, but where had it gone to? Here there was only a dog, helplessly snapping his teeth at the empty air, who all unaware went on convulsively and hurriedly besprinkling the ground though he could no longer conjure up even the slightest magic incantation out of the huge jumble of them in his memory, not even the little verse with which newborn pups duck down under their mother. I felt as though I were not only cut off by a short sprint from my brothers but as if I were infinitely far off from everyone and that I would die not from hunger but as a result of my desolation. It was perfectly evident that no one cared about me, no one below ground, no one above ground, no one in the air: I was perishing of their indifference; their indifference said, "He is dying," and so it would happen. And didn't I agree? Didn't I say the same thing? Hadn't I wanted to be forsaken like this? Very well, you dogs, but not so as to perish here in this way but to go over to the truth, out of this world of lies, where there is no one from whom we can learn the truth, not from me either, native citizen of the lie. Perhaps the truth was no longer so very far away, only too far away for me, who failed and died. Perhaps it was not so very far away, and hence I was not as forsaken as I thought, not forsaken by the others, only by me, who failed and died.

But we do not die as rapidly as a nervous dog imagines. I merely fainted; and when I awoke and lifted my eyes, a strange dog was standing over me. I did not feel hungry, I felt very strong, my joints seemed to me full of elasticity, even if I made no attempt to test them by standing. I did not actually see more than usual: a handsome but not very extraordinary dog stood before me; I saw that and nothing else, and yet I believed that I saw something more in him than usual. There was blood under me; for a minute I thought it was food, but then I realized at once that it was blood that I had vomited. I turned away from it and toward the strange dog. He was a lean, long-legged brunet, flecked here and there with white, and he had a beautiful, strong, searching gaze. "What are you doing here?" he said, "You must leave this place." "I cannot leave now," I said, without further explanation, for how could I have explained everything to him, and anyway he seemed to be in a hurry. "Please, go away," he said and restlessly lifted one leg after the other. "Leave me alone," I said; "go, and don't worry about me; the others don't worry about me either." "I'm asking you for your own sake," he said. "Ask me for whatever reason you like," I said; "I can't go[4] even if I wanted to." "That's not where the trouble lies," he said smiling. "You can go. It's just because you seem to be weak that I'm asking you now to walk away slowly; but if you hesitate, you'll have to run later on." "Let that be my problem," I said. "It's mine too," he said, saddened by my stubbornness and so evidently ready to leave me for the time being but also to take the opportunity to approach me lovingly. At any other time I would have gladly accepted the advance from this beauty; at that time, however, I don't know why, I was seized by horror of it. "Away," I shouted, all the louder since I had no other means of defending myself. "All right, I'll leave you," he said, slowly backing off. "You are strange. Don't you like me?" "I'd like you if you'd go away and leave me in peace," I said, but I was no longer as sure of myself as I wanted him to believe. My senses sharpened through fasting, I saw or heard something in him; it was just beginning, it grew, it came toward me, and already I knew: this dog clearly has the power to drive you away, even if you cannot imagine at the moment how you will ever be able to get up off the ground.

And I looked with ever increasing desire at this dog who, in response to my rude answer, had only gently shaken his head. "Who are you?" I asked. "I am a hunter," he said. "And why won't you let me stay here?" I asked. "You're disturbing me," he said. "I cannot hunt while you're here." "Try," I said, "maybe you will still be able to hunt." "No," he said, "I'm sorry, but you must go." "Don't hunt today," I pleaded with him. "No," he said, "I have to hunt." "I have to go away, you have to hunt," I said, "nothing but have to's. Do you understand why we have to?" "No," he said, "but there's nothing to

---

4. The German verb *gehen* can mean "to go" and also "to walk." This explains the pun in the handsome stranger dog's following remarks.

understand here: these are self-evident, natural things." "Not so," I said; "you're sorry you have to chase me away, and yet you're doing it." "That's the way it is," he said. "That's the way it is," I repeated angrily, "that's no answer. What would be easier for you to do without—doing without hunting or doing without driving me away?" "Doing without hunting," he said with no hesitation. "Well, then," I said, "there's a contradiction here." "What kind of a contradiction?" he said. "My dear little dog, do you really not understand that I have to? Don't you understand things that are self-evident?" I no longer answered, for I noticed—and at this, new life ran through me, such life as is conferred by terror—I noticed through intangible details, which perhaps no one besides me could have detected, that from the depths of his chest this dog was getting ready to sing. "You are going to sing," I said. "Yes," he said gravely, "I am going to sing; soon, but not yet." "You are already beginning," I said. "No," he said, "not yet. But get ready." "I can already hear your song in spite of your denials," I said, trembling. He was silent. And then I believe I perceived something that no dog had ever experienced before me; at any rate, cultural memory does not contain even the slightest hint of it; and in infinite anxiety and shame I hurriedly lowered my face into the puddle of blood in front of me. What I seemed to perceive was that the dog was already singing without his being aware of it—no, more than that: that the melody, detached from him, was floating through the air and then past him according to its own laws, as if he no longer had any part in it, floating at me, aimed only at me.[5]

Today, of course, I deny any such perceptions and attribute them to my overstimulation at the time, but even if it was an error, it nevertheless had a certain grandeur and is the sole reality, even if only an apparent reality, that I salvaged and brought back into this world from the time of my fast, and it shows, at least, how far we can go when we are completely out of our senses. And I really was completely out of my senses. Under ordinary circumstances I would have been seriously ill, incapable of moving, but I could not resist the melody that the dog now quickly seemed to adopt as his own. It grew stronger and stronger, there may have been no limits to its power to increase, it was already on the verge of shattering my eardrums. But the worst of it was that it seemed to be there for my sake alone, this voice, whose sublimity made the woods grow silent, for my sake alone; who was I that I still dared to remain here, sprawled out before this music in my filth and blood? My body shaking, I rose, looked down at myself, "This will not run," I still

---

5. Since the narrator—this dog—refuses to see or cannot see the human world, the music may very well be the sound of hunting horns (see Hargraves's essay, p. 321).

thought but soon I rushed off, hotly pursued by the melody, with the most splendid leaps and bounds. I did not say anything to my friends; immediately on my arrival I would probably have told the entire story, but then I was too weak; and later it seemed to me something that could not be communicated. Hints that I could not force myself to repress vanished without a trace in the general conversation. As it happened, I recovered physically in a few hours; mentally, I bear the consequences even today.

But I widened my researches to include the music of the dogs. Certainly here, too, science had not been idle; the science of music is, if I have been correctly informed, perhaps even wider in scope than that of food and in any case more firmly grounded. The matter is explained by the fact that you can work more passionately in the field of music than you can in the field of nutrition; in music it is more a matter of pure observations and systematizations; there, on the other hand, it is above all one of practical consequences. Connected to this is the fact that the science of music enjoys greater respect than the science of nutrition, though the former could never affect the people as deeply as the latter. Before I had heard the voice in the woods, my relation to the science of music was also more remote than my relation to any other science. It is true that my experience with the music dogs had already drawn my attention to it, but at that time I was still too young; furthermore, it is not easy even to approach this science, it is considered especially difficult and becomes aristocratically impenetrable to the crowd. Furthermore, while in the case of the air dogs, music had been the first thing to strike me, their secretive nature seemed to me more important than the music; their terrible music was probably like nothing else in the world, and so I could neglect it more readily, but from that time on it was their nature that I encountered in all dogs everywhere. To penetrate into the nature of dogs, however, research into nutrition seemed to me most suitable as the means to lead unerringly to the goal. Perhaps I was wrong on that count. Of course, there is some overlap between the two sciences that even then aroused my suspicions. I mean the doctrine of the song that calls down food from above. Here again I am severely handicapped by the fact that I have never seriously penetrated into the science of music either, and in this respect I cannot count myself even one of the half-educated whom science has always particularly despised. This is something I have to be aware of, always. Faced with even the easiest science test administered by a genuine scientist, I would do very poorly—a circumstance of which, sadly, I have proof. The reasons, apart from the circumstances of my life that I have already mentioned, lie, of course, mainly in my lack of propensity for science, scant intellectual power, poor memory and, above all, inability to focus consistently on a scientific goal. I admit all this openly to myself, even with a certain delight. Because the deeper reason for my incapacity for science seems to me to be an instinct, and to tell the the truth, it is not a bad instinct. If I wanted to brag, I would say that precisely this instinct has destroyed my scientific skill, for it would certainly be a very remarkable phenomenon, to say the least, if I, who display a passable intelligence in the ordinary business of daily life, which is certainly not so simple, and above all who, even though I do not understand science, nevertheless understand scientists very well—something my results confirm—if I were from the very beginning unable to raise my paw to even the first rung of science. It was my instinct that, perhaps precisely for the sake of science but a different science than is practiced today, an ultimate science, led me to value freedom above all else. Freedom! Of course, the freedom that is possible today—a stunted growth. But nevertheless freedom, nevertheless a possession.

A Comment

It was very early in the morning, the streets clean and deserted, I was going to the railroad station. When I compared a tower clock with my watch, I saw that it was already much later than I had thought, I had to rush, the shock of this discovery made me unsure of the way, I did not yet know my way around this city very well, luckily a policeman was nearby, I ran up to him and, out of breath, asked him for directions. He smiled and said, "You want me to tell you the way?" "Yes," I said, "since I can't find it myself." "Forget about it! Forget about it!" he said, and with a broad swing of his body he turned away, like people who want to be alone with their laughter.

On Parables

Many complained that the words of the wise are over and over again merely parables, of no use in everyday life, and that's all we have. When the wise man says, "Go across," he does not mean that you ought to cross the street to the other side, something that you could manage if the result were worth the trip. But what he means is some fabulous Beyond, something we have never known, which he cannot describe more accurately and therefore can be of no help to us in this case. In effect, all these parables merely attempt to say that the inconceivable is inconceivable, and we knew that already. But the matters we truly struggle with every day are different.

In response, someone said, "Why do you resist? If you'd follow the parables, you'd become parables yourselves and with that, free of the everyday struggle."

Someone else said, "I bet that is a parable too."

The first one said, "You win."

The second one said, "But unfortunately only in a parable."

The first one said, "No, in reality; in the parable you lost."

The Burrow[1]

I have established my burrow, and it seems to be a success. From the outside all that is visible is a large hole, but in fact it leads nowhere: after just a few steps you hit natural hard rock. I will not boast of having accomplished this trick by design, it is simply a remnant of one of my many abortive attempts at building, but in the end I thought it advantageous to leave this one hole unfilled. Of course, trickiness of so fine a weave can be suicidal, I know that better than anyone, and it is certainly risky to let this hole call even the slightest attention to the possibility that there is something here worth investigating. But you do not know me if you think I am a coward and that it is simply out of cowardice that I have built my burrow. About a thousand steps from this hole, covered with a removable layer of moss, is the burrow's real entrance; it has been made as safe as anything in this world can be made safe; true, someone can step on the moss or poke into it, then my burrow would lie open; and whoever so desires—let it be noted, though, that certain skills, not all too commonly found, would be needed—can break in and destroy the whole thing forever. I fully understand as much, and even now at its high point my life hardly knows an hour of complete peace: there, at that one place on the dark moss,

---

1. Kafka's title *Der Bau*, a word that recurs throughout his work, poses an insuperable difficulty for the translator: the German word means "building, construction," but since in this story we are obviously dealing with an underground construction produced by a badgerlike animal, the word of choice would seem to be "burrow." Once we have committed ourselves to this "burrow," however, we have sacrificed an element of tension that is a constitutive part of the story: the doubleness of a structure that is built horizontally underground but is represented in the mind of the badger-narrator in "higher" terms, terms more suitable to a structure built vertically above ground. This tension is concretely conveyed in the word the narrator chooses for the nodal points of his construction—*Platz* (square)—a word I have translated with "court" (you will soon see why). For what is disconcerting is that these "squares" are also vaulted chambers and in the most important instance constitute a *Burg*, a castle—an underground castle! Previous translators have rendered this *Burgplatz* (literally, "castle square") as "castle keep," employing the old-fashioned word "keep," which means a castle stronghold. But this word conceals the disorientating tension of an underground structure that is perpetually misconceived by the animal-narrator as an above-ground building. In a word, this "discourse" of architecture conveys the vanity of the creature that persists in imagining itself to be of an altogether higher evolutionary type. (This note is owed to a suggestion by Benno Wagner.)

I am mortal, and often in my dreams a lascivious snout sniffs incessantly around it. It can be argued that I could have filled in this
real entrance hole as well—at the top with a thin layer of firmly
packed dirt, farther down with loose soil, so that it would never
take me more than a slight effort to excavate the exit whenever I
wanted. That, however, is not feasible, caution demands that I
should have an immediate possibility of escape, true prudence demands—as, unhappily, it does so often—that you should risk your
life; all these are very laborious calculations, and the delight that
the sharp-witted mind takes in itself is sometimes the sole reason
why it continues its calculations. I must have the immediate possibility of escape, since, despite all my vigilance, isn't it possible that
I could be attacked from a completely unexpected quarter? I live
peacefully in the innermost part of my burrow, and meanwhile
slowly and quietly from somewhere or other the enemy is boring his
way toward me; I don't mean to say that his scent is better than
mine, perhaps he knows as little about me as I do about him, but
there are frenzied brigands who blindly rummage their way through
the earth, and given the huge extent of my burrow, even they can
hope to crash into one of my passages in one place or another.
True, I have the advantage of being in my own house, of knowing
every one of the routes and where each one leads; a brigand can
very easily become my victim and a sweet-tasting one at that; but I
am growing old, many others are stronger than I am, and my enemies are countless, and it could well happen that in fleeing from
one enemy, I run into the clutches of another, oh, so many things
could happen, but always I must feel assured that somewhere there
might be an exit that is easy to reach and entirely unobstructed,
where I do not have to do anything to get out so that, for one thing,
as I am desperately digging, even through earth that heaps up easily, all of a sudden—heaven protect me!—I do not feel the teeth of
my persecutor in my thigh. And it is not only enemies from outside
who threaten me, there are also enemies in the bowels of the earth;
until now I have never seen them, but legends exist about them,
and I firmly believe in them. They are creatures of the inner earth,
not even legend can describe them, even those who have become
their victims barely glimpsed them, they come, you hear the
scratching of their claws just below you in the earth, which is their
element, and already you are lost. You realize that you are not in
your own house, you are in theirs. Not even my exit will save me
from them, as indeed it probably will not save me at all but rather
ruin me; but it is a hope, and I cannot live without it.

Apart from the main passage, I am connected with the outer
world by other very narrow, relatively safe passages that provide me
with good, breathable air: they were built by the wood mice; I have

managed to incorporate them properly into my burrow, they also allow me to catch the scent of faraway things and hence protect me; furthermore, through them all sorts of little creatures come running to me, which I devour, so that I can have a hunting preserve adequate to a modest standard of living without leaving the burrow at all; that is, of course, a great advantage.

But the best thing about my burrow is its silence; of course this is deceptive, at any time the silence can suddenly be shattered, and then everything is at an end, but at present, it is still there, I can slip through my passages for hours on end and hear nothing but the occasional rustling of some lesser creature, which I then immediately silence between my teeth, or the trickling of the soil, which indicates to me the need for repairs; otherwise everything is quiet. The air of the woods wafts in, at once warm and cool; sometimes I stretch out and whirl around in the passage for sheer contentment. It is a beautiful thing to have such a burrow in advancing age, to have put a roof over your head at the approach of fall.

Roughly every hundred yards I have widened the passages into small round chambers, where I can curl up comfortably, enjoy the warmth of my own body, and rest. That is where I sleep the sweet sleep of peace, of gratified desire, of the achieved goal of home ownership. I don't know whether it is habit from the old days or whether the dangers in even this house are serious enough to wake me, but from time to time at regular intervals I am startled out of deep sleep and listen, listen into the silence that reigns unchanged day and night, smile, comforted, and with relaxed limbs sink into still deeper sleep. Poor wanderers, without a home, on the highways, in the woods, crept into a cranny in a heap of leaves at best, or in a pack of their comrades, exposed to all the harms of heaven and earth. I lie here in a little chamber secured on all sides—there are more than fifty like it in my burrow—and between dozing and unconscious sleep, for which I choose the hours as my moods dictate, time passes.

Not quite at the center of the burrow, carefully planned for the case of utmost danger, not exactly a pursuit but a siege, lies the main chamber. While all the rest of the burrow may be more a product of rigorous reasoning than of physical effort, this castle court is the result of the most arduous labor of my body, using all its parts. More than once in the despair of physical exhaustion, I wanted to give up, heaved myself on my back and cursed the burrow, dragged myself outside and let the burrow lie open; after all, I could do so, since I no longer wanted to return to it, until at last, some hours or days later, I regretfully returned, on the verge of lifting up my voice in rejoicing to find the burrow unharmed, and with genuine cheerfulness began the work all over again. My work on the castle court became needlessly more difficult: needlessly because the burrow gained no real advantage from the additional work since, just at the spot where the chamber should be according to plan, the earth was very loose and sandy; the earth had to be practically hammered solid to form this great, beautifully vaulted and rounded chamber. But for this kind of work I have only my forehead.[2] And so with my forehead I ran against the wall thousands and thousands of times, all day and all night long, and I was glad when I banged myself bloody, for this was proof that the wall was beginning to harden, and in this way, as you may perhaps grant me, I fully earned my castle court.

In this castle court I collect my provisions, here I heap up everything I catch inside the burrow that exceeds my needs of the moment and everything that I bring back from my hunting expeditions outside. The chamber is so big that provisions for half a year do not fill it. Therefore I can easily spread them out, move around among them, play with them, enjoy their great quantity and various smells, and always have an accurate overall view of what is on hand. Then I can always make fresh arrangements and do the necessary preliminary calculations and hunting plans depending on the season. There are times when I am so well provided for that out of general indifference to food I leave the small fry who scamper around here completely untouched—a policy that, for other reasons, might prove unwise. My frequent preoccupation with preparations for defense means that at least in small-scale matters my views on how the burrow can best be used for such purposes change or evolve. Then it sometimes seems dangerous to me to base my defense entirely on the castle court; after all, the variousness of the burrow offers me various possibilities, and it seems to me to accord more closely with prudence to distribute the provisions slightly and to fill a number of small chambers with them. I then designate about every third chamber as a reserve larder or every fourth one as a principal larder and every second one as an auxiliary larder, and so forth. Or, for purposes of deception, I exempt a number of passages entirely from piles of provisions, or I choose only a few chambers, quite impulsively, each depending on its position relative to the main exit. Of course, each of these new plans requires heavy, hod-carrying labor; I have to recalculate the situation and then carry the loads back and forth. Of course, I can do this at my leisure, without rushing, and it's not such an unpleasant thing to carry these goods

---

2. This last phrase, *die Stirn haben*, which literally means "to have the forehead," also means, more colloquially, "to have the nerve" or "to have the gall." A somewhat freer reading of this sentence—one that is syntactically possible though rhetorically odd—would produce the meaning: "And only I have the nerve to undertake such a project." In this case the sentence would be a coded reference to the author, a "semi-private game," reflecting back on the audacity of Kafka's enterprise as a writer.

between your teeth, to lie down and rest wherever you want, and to nibble on whatever appeals to you at that moment. It is worse at times when, usually after I have been startled out of my sleep, it seems that the current distribution of provisions is completely wrong, that it can lead to great dangers, and that immediately, in all haste, without regard for sleepiness and fatigue, the situation must be corrected; then I hurry, then I fly, then I have no time for calculations, I, the one who is bent on carrying out a new and quite precise plan, arbitrarily seize whatever lands between my teeth, dragging, carrying, moaning, groaning, stumbling, and any random change in the present situation, which seems to me so extremely dangerous, is the only thing that will satisfy me. Until gradually, on becoming fully awake, sobriety returns: I can hardly understand my panic haste, breathe in deeply the peace of my house, which I myself have disturbed, return to my sleeping quarters, fall asleep at once in new-found weariness, and on awakening find still hanging from my teeth a rat, perhaps, as incontrovertible proof of night work that already seems almost dreamlike. Then there are other times when I believe that the best plan of all would be to gather all my provisions into a single chamber. What good are the provisions in the little chambers, how much, after all, can each one hold, and besides, whatever I place there blocks the passage and is more likely to hinder me when I try to run if I should ever have to go on the defensive. It may be stupid, furthermore, but it's true that your self-confidence suffers when you can't see all your provisions assembled together and know at a single glance exactly what you own. Also, in the course of these various distributions, can't a good deal be lost? I can't always be galloping crisscross through all my passages to check that everything is as it should be. The idea behind distributing my provisions is certainly correct, but really only if you have several chambers like my castle court. Several such chambers! Of course! But who can manage that? Also, being late additions, they can't be fitted into my burrow's master plan. But I will admit that therein lies a fault in the construction, the way a fault is always bound to arise whenever you have only one specimen of anything. And I also confess that during the entire construction work, the demand for several castle courts stirred in my consciousness, obscurely, true, but plain enough had I had been willing to acknowledge it; I have not yielded to this necessity, I felt too weak to face the vast amount of work involved, I even felt too weak to envision the necessity of the work; somehow I consoled myself with feelings no less obscure, suggesting that something otherwise not good enough would, in my case, just for once, as an exception, through an act of mercy, be good enough, probably because providence is especially interested in preserving my forehead, this battering ram, from harm. Well, that is why I have only one castle court, but the vague sense that just this once, the one would be good enough, has been lost. However that may be, I have to be content with the one, the small chambers cannot possibly replace it, and so, once this conviction has matured in me, I begin once more to drag everything out of the small chambers and back to the castle court. For some time after that, it is a source of great comfort to me to have all the chambers and passages bare, to see the quantities of meat heaped up in the castle court, projecting far into the outermost passages the mixture of many smells, each one of which delights me in its own way and each one of which I can distinguish clearly at long range. Then, especially peaceful times tend to follow, when I slowly and gradually shift my sleeping quarters from the outer circles toward the inner, diving ever more deeply into the smells, until I can't stand it any longer and on a given night, storm into the castle court and wreak havoc among the provisions, gorging myself to the point of total torpor on the greatest delicacies I have. Happy but perilous times: anyone who knew how to take advantage of them could easily annihilate me at no danger to himself. Here, too, the absence of a second or a third castle court has a damaging effect, it is the great, singular total amassing of provisions that allures me. I try in various ways to protect myself from this, the distribution among the small chambers is certainly also one of these measures; unfortunately, like other similar measures, it leads through deprivation to still greater greed, which then overwhelms reason and arbitrarily transforms my plans for defense to satisfy its own ends.

After such moments I am in the habit of collecting my thoughts by inspecting the burrow and often, after the necessary improvements have been made, by leaving it, though never for longer than a brief period. The punishment for doing without the burrow for longer periods seems too severe to me even then, but the necessity of occasional excursions is something I can agree to. It is always with a certain ceremonious air that I approach the exit. During periods of domesticity I stay away from it: I avoid using even the last turns of the passage that leads to it; nor is it an easy matter to wander near it, for in this area I have built a crazy zigzag structure of passages; that was where my burrow began; at that time I could not hope that I would ever be able to complete it as my plan dictated. I began half-playfully at this little corner, and in this way my initial joy in the work was wildly expressed in building a labyrinth; at the time, this seemed to me the acme of all constructions, but today I judge it, probably more accurately, as overly fussy puttering, not really worthy of the burrow as a whole; and though it might certainly be exquisite in theory—here is the entrance to my house, I said at that time ironically to my invisible enemies, and I imagined the whole lot of them suffocating in the labyrinth at the entrance—in reality it represents a far too flimsy[3] fantasy that would be hard put to resist a serious attack or an enemy desperately fighting for his life. Should I rebuild the sector for this reason? I keep postponing the decision, and it will very likely remain as it is. Apart from the enormous amount of work I would be taking on, it would also be the most dangerous job imaginable; at the time I began the burrow, I could work at that spot in relative calm, the risk was not much greater than at any other time. But today it would imply a nearly deliberate intent to draw the attention of the entire world to the burrow: today that action is no longer possible. I am almost glad; admittedly, I still have a certain sentimental attachment to this first effort, the work of a beginner. And if a major attack were actually to come, what opening layout could save me? The entrance can deceive, distract, torment the attacker, as mine can do in a pinch. But I would have to try to respond immediately to any really major attack with all the resources of the entire burrow and with all the powers of my body and soul—so much is truly self-evident. And so this entrance may as well remain as it is. So many weaknesses are imposed on the burrow by nature that it might as well retain this shortcoming that was created by my own hands, one I recognize clearly, even if only after the fact. All this, however, is not to say that this flaw does not make me uneasy from time to time, or perhaps always. If I avoid this part of my burrow as I make my usual rounds, it is mainly because I find the sight unpleasant, because I do not always want to be forced to see a flaw in the burrow when I am already all too often aware of this flaw rumbling in my consciousness. Even if the flaw at the entrance exists ineradicably, I nevertheless prefer to be spared the sight of it as long as possible. I need only go in the direction of the exit, and even though I am still separated from it by passages and chambers, I already have the sense of having landed in an atmosphere of great danger; sometimes it seems to me as if my coat were growing thin, as if I might soon be standing there in my bare flesh, greeted at that moment by the howls of my enemies. Certainly, the simple act of exiting produces such unhealthy feelings, this cessation of domestic protection, but it is still the mazy construction at the entrance that particularly torments me. Sometimes I dream that I have reconstructed it, altering it completely, swiftly, with titanic powers, in a

3. "Flimsy" here translates Kafka's word *dünnwändig*, literally "thin-walled," which plays on both the hero's architecture and his internal doubt as to the solidity of his project.

single night, entirely unobserved, and that now it is impregnable; the sleep when this happens is the sweetest sleep of all: when I awaken, tears of joy and release still glitter on the hairs of my beard.

Whenever I go out, therefore, I must physically overcome the torments of this labyrinth as well, and it is both irritating and moving sometimes when I go astray for a moment in my own creation,[4] so that the work seems to be forever straining to prove its right to exist to me, its maker, whose judgment has long been established.[5] But then I am beneath the covering of moss, which I sometimes allow—so rarely do I stir from the house—to grow into the rest of the forest floor; and now all it takes is a jerk of my head and I am in foreign territory. For a long time I do not dare to perform this little movement; if I did not have to face conquering the labyrinth all over again, I would certainly quit today and wander back. Why? Your house is protected, a compact unit. You live in peace, you are warm, well-nourished, master, sole master of an abundance of passages and chambers; and all this you are willing—not to lose, let us hope—but in a certain sense to wager; though you have the confidence to win it back, you have agreed to play a game for lofty, all too lofty stakes. Are there rational reasons for this decision? No, for something like this there can be no rational reasons. And yet I cautiously lift the trap door, and I am outside; cautiously I let it drop and race away as fast as I can, away from the telltale spot.

Yet I am not really out in the open: though I am no longer squeezing my way through the passages but hunting in the open woods, feeling in my body new strengths for which there was, so to speak, no room in the burrow—not even in the castle court, even if it were ten times bigger. Furthermore, the food outside is better; while the hunting is more difficult and success more rare, the result must be rated higher in every respect. I deny none of that, and I can appreciate and enjoy it at least as much as anyone else, and probably much better, for I do not hunt like some vagrant, out of recklessness or desperation, but calmly and with a sense of purpose. Nor am I destined or delivered over to a life outdoors; rather, I know that my days are numbered, that I need not hunt here for all time but that, somehow, when I feel like it and when I am weary of this life, I will be summoned by someone whose invitation I will not be able to resist. And so I can enjoy my time here to the fullest and spend it without a care—or I could, and yet I cannot. I am too deeply occupied by my burrow. I have run swiftly out through the entrance, but soon I return. I look for a good hiding place and

4. Feel the self-reflexiveness of this, of Kafka's thinking of his own position vis-à-vis his writing.
5. Read this as "whose story *The Judgment* has long been established" (p. 3).

stealthily watch the entrance to my house—in this instance from the outside—for days and nights at a time. You may call it foolish, but it gives me ineffable pleasure; even more, it consoles me. It feels to me, then, not as if I were standing outside my house but outside myself while I am asleep and knew the joy of sleeping deeply and at the same time of being able to keep a close watch on myself. In a certain sense I am privileged, not only to see the ghosts of the night in the helplessness and blissful trust of sleep, but also to encounter them in reality with the full strength of wakefulness and the calm capacity to form judgments. And, strangely enough, I find that matters are not proceeding as badly as I had often thought and as I will probably think again when I go back down into my house. In this respect—very likely also in another, but in this respect especially—these excursions are truly indispensable. Certainly, as carefully as I have chosen an entrance off the beaten track—though the overall plan imposed certain restrictions on me—when you sum up the observations of a week or so, the traffic past the entrance is still very heavy, but such is perhaps common in all habitable regions; and it may be even better to expose yourself to heavier traffic, which precisely because it is heavy, carries itself along, than to live in complete solitude and be at the mercy of the first arbitrary intruder who comes shuffling by. There are many enemies here, and even more of these enemies' cronies, but they are also at war with each other, and while they are thus engaged, they race past the burrow. During all this time I have never seen anyone actually exploring at the entrance, to my and his good fortune, for out of my senses with worry for my burrow, I would surely have hurled myself at his throat. Of course, some of the passers-by have been creatures in whose vicinity I did not dare to remain and from whom I had to flee whenever I had a mere foreboding of them in the distance; I can hardly speak with certainty about their attitude toward the burrow, but it's comfort enough that I returned soon afterward and found none of them still lurking there and the entrance undamaged. There were happy times in which I could almost make myself believe that the world's hostility had ceased or subsided or that the burrow's strength had raised me above the war of annihilation that had been raging so far. Perhaps the burrow does protect me more than I had ever thought or dared to hope when I was inside. Matters went so far that at times I was seized by the childish desire not ever to go back to the burrow but to settle down here, near the entrance, and spend my life observing it, finding my happiness in perpetually realizing how securely the burrow, were I inside it, would protect me. Well, there comes a terrible, swift awakening from childish dreams. What does this kind of security actually amount to? From the experience I have gathered

here, outside the burrow, can I possibly judge the dangers surrounding me inside it? Can my enemies sniff the correct scent of
me when I am not in my burrow? Certainly they have something of
my scent, but not the full effect. And isn't the existence of the full
scent often the precondition for normal danger? Hence, the attempts I make here are only half-, only one-tenth-hearted, suited to
reassure me and through false reassurance to endanger me to the
extreme. No, I'm not the one, though I thought I was, who watches
me sleeping; rather, I am the one who sleeps while the one who
wants to deprave me watches. Perhaps he is among those who are
always casually sauntering past the entrance just to make sure, just
as I do myself, that the door has not yet been violated and is waiting for their attack, and who walk past only because they know that
the master of the house is not at home, or perhaps only because
they know that he is innocently lurking in the nearby bushes. And I
abandon my observation post, having had my fill of life in the open:
it seems to me that there is nothing more for me to learn here, not
now and not later. And I want to take my leave of everything here,
descend into the burrow, and never come out again, letting matters
take their course and not delaying them with useless observations.
But now, spoiled from having watched all the goings-on at the entrance for so long, it is a huge torment for me to start the descent,
which in itself positively creates a sensation, not knowing what will
happen all around me behind my back and then behind the trap-
door once it has been put back in place. I begin the attempt on
stormy nights, by quickly tossing in my catch; that ploy appears to
be successful, but whether it is truly successful will come to light
only after I have gone down myself; it will come to light, but no
longer to me, or not only to me, but too late. And so I stop and do
not go down. I dig a trial tunnel no longer than I am myself, naturally at a sufficient remove from the real entrance, and also shut off
by a moss covering. I creep into the tunnel, cover it behind me,
wait there for carefully calculated shorter and longer periods at different times of day, then I throw off the moss, come out, and register my observations. I have the most varied experiences, some good,
some bad, but I cannot discover a general law or an infallible
method of descent. As a result, I am happy not to have gone down
yet into the real entrance and am desperate about having to do so,
and do so soon. I am not very far from deciding to go a long way
away from here, to resume my old, desolate life that lacked all security, that was a single, monolithic abundance of dangers and
therefore did not allow the separate dangers to be so distinctly seen
and feared, as the comparison between my safe burrow and life
elsewhere continually teaches me. Such a decision would, admittedly, be complete madness, the result only of having lived far too

long in senseless freedom, the burrow still belongs to me, I need to take only a single step and I am safe. And I tear myself away from all doubts, and in broad daylight I run straight for the door, quite sure now about wanting to lift it up, but I can't do it, I run past it and deliberately throw myself into a thorn bush as punishment, as punishment for a wrong I do not understand. Then at last I have to admit that I was right after all and that it is impossible to go down without openly exposing my dearest possession, at least for a little while, to everyone all around, on the ground, in the trees, in the air. And the danger is not imaginary but very real. And it need not be a real enemy in whom I arouse the desire to follow me, it can just as easily be some innocent little thing, some repulsive little female who pursues me out of curiosity and so becomes, quite unawares, the leader of the whole world against me, nor does it have to be that way, perhaps—and that is no less bad than the other, in many respects it is the worst—perhaps it is someone of my own kind, an expert, a connoisseur of burrows, a fellow member of a woodland order,[6] a peace lover, but a depraved thug who wants to dwell where he has not built. If he were actually to appear now, if his filthy craving were actually to lead him to discover the entrance, if he were actually to set to work lifting up the moss, if he were actually to succeed, if he were actually to adroitly force himself in and had now disappeared so far into it that only his backside still popped up for a second, if all that were actually to happen, so that finally, in a frenzy of pursuit, free of all scruples, I could leap on him, bite into his flesh, tear him limb from limb, rip him to pieces, and drink his blood, cram his corpse down to the rest of my catch, but above all—this would be the main thing—I would finally be in my burrow again, this time ready to take pleasure in admiring the labyrinth but first of all wanting to pull the moss cover over me and rest, I think, for the rest of my life. But no one arrives, and I remain entirely dependent on myself. Being continually occupied with the difficulty of the thing, I lose much of my nervousness, I no longer avoid the entrance even outside the burrow; prowling around it in circles becomes my favorite occupation, it is almost as if I were the enemy, spying out a suitable opportunity for a successful break-in. If only I had someone whom I could trust, to whom I could delegate my observation post, I might indeed go down confidently. I would arrange

6. Kafka says all this with one marvelous neologism—*Waldbruder*—literally, "woodsbrother," where "brother" suggests at once fraternal kinship and, in the sense of "friar," membership in a secret order. In light of Kafka's cultural background, the word also suggests the Hussite "brotherhood" of Bohemian history; hence, the word "brother" would point to the exclusiveness of a fraternal order and, furthermore, to a specific (Bohemian) national identity. The Hussites were followers of the Bohemian religious reformer Jan Hus (1370–1415), who created a schism from the Roman Church; he was condemned and burned at the stake but was regarded for centuries as a martyr and a founding figure for the independent Czech nation to be born.

with this being, whom I trust, to keep a strict lookout on the situation during my descent and for a long time afterward, and in case of signs of danger to knock on the moss cover, but not otherwise. Thus the decks above me would be cleared, nothing would be left, at most my trusty confidant. For won't he demand a favor in return, won't he at least want to have a look at the burrow? Even this much, voluntarily letting someone into my burrow, would be extremely painful for me, I built it for myself, not for visitors, I don't think I would let him in; even as a reward for his enabling me to enter my burrow, I would not let him in. But I could not let him in anyway, for then either I would have to let him go down by himself, and that is beyond the pale of the imaginable, or we would have to go down at the same time, in which case the very advantage that he is supposed to bring me, of manning the observation post behind me, would be lost. And what is the value of such trust? Can someone I trust when we are face to face still be trusted just as much when he is out of sight, when the moss cover separates us? It is relatively easy to trust someone when you are keeping him under surveillance or at least can keep him under surveillance, it might even be possible to trust someone at a distance; but to trust completely from a point inside the burrow—hence inside another world—someone who is outside, is, I think, impossible. But it is not even necessary to have such doubts; indeed, it is enough just to consider that during or after my descent any one of all the countless contingencies of life could prevent my trusty confidant from doing his duty and the incalculable consequences that the slightest accident befalling him might have for me. No, all in all I have no reason to complain about being alone and without anyone I can trust. I am sure that I'm not losing any advantage by it, and probably I'm sparing myself problems. Trust, however, is something I can have only in myself and the burrow. That is something I should have considered sooner, and I should have made provisions for the instance that is so much on my mind now. It would have been possible, at least in part, at the outset of my construction. I should have had to lay out the first passage in such a way as to have two entrances at a suitable distance from one another. In that way I could have gone down with all unavoidable circumspection through the one entrance, swiftly run through the front passage to the second entrance, lifted the moss cover slightly—it would have had to be appropriately structured for this purpose—and tried to survey the situation for several days and nights from that vantage point. That's the only way it could have been done properly, though two entrances double the danger, but I would have had to silence this objection, especially since the one entrance, conceived merely as an observation post, could have been quite narrow. And with this thought I lose myself in technical considerations, I begin to dream the dream of a perfect burrow again, and that calms me a little; with delight I see, eyes closed, clear and less clear designs that would enable me to slip in and out unnoticed. When I lie there thinking, I rate these possibilities very high but nevertheless only as technical achievements, not as real advantages, for this ability to slip in and out unhindered—what good is it? It points to a restless mind, uncertain self-worth, unclean desires, bad qualities that seem still worse given that the burrow indeed stands firmly in place and is capable of flooding you with peace if you only open yourself to it altogether. Now, of course, at this moment I am outside it and seek a way to get back; and for this the requisite technical devices would be highly desirable. But perhaps not so very highly. Aren't you grievously underestimating the burrow in the nervous anxiety of the moment when you see it as merely a cavity to creep into for the greatest possible security? It is this safe cavity for certain, or it ought to be, and when I imagine myself in the midst of danger, then I wish, with clenched teeth and all the strength of my will, that the burrow were nothing else than the hole destined to save my life and that it might fulfill this clearly defined task with the greatest possible perfection, and I am ready to exempt it from every other task. Now, however, matters are such that in reality—and in a state of high emergency you have no aptitude for seeing reality, and even in nonthreatening times you must first acquire this aptitude— in reality, though the burrow provides a great deal of safety, it is by no means enough; will worries, then, ever come to rest in it? For these are worries of a different kind, prouder, more substantial, of- ten deeply repressed, but their corrosive workings are perhaps the same as those of the worries that life outside produces. If I had constructed the burrow only to safeguard my life, the result would certainly not have defrauded me, but a comparison between the monstrous amount of labor and the actual degree of security pro- vided, at least insofar as I am able to feel it and insofar as I can profit from it, would not have come out in my favor. It is very painful to admit as much to yourself, but it has to be done, espe- cially in view of the entrance, which is now shut off from me, its ar- chitect and owner; indeed it positively goes into cramps resisting me. But the burrow is more than merely some life-saving hole! When I stand on the castle court, surrounded by my piles of meat, my gaze turned toward the ten passages that lead outward from there, each one, specifically according to the overall plan of the court, sunken or raised, elongated or curving, growing wider or nar- rower, and all equally quiet and empty and ready, each in its own way, to lead me to my many chambers and all of these, too, quiet and empty—then the thought of safety is far from my mind, then I know clearly that here is my castle, which, through scratching and biting, battering and banging, I have reclaimed from the obstinate ground, my castle that can never belong in the slightest to anyone else and that is so much mine that here in the end I can even calmly accept the fatal wound from my enemy, for here my blood seeps into my own soil and will not be lost. And what else than this is the meaning of the lovely hours that, half peacefully sleeping, half happily wakeful, I am accustomed to spend in the passages, in passages that are designed precisely for me, for comfortable stretching, childish tumbling, dreamy sprawling, blissful falling asleep. And the small chambers, each one so familiar, each one, though they are exactly alike, can be clearly distinguished by me with my eyes closed, merely by the curvature of the wall; they embrace me more peacefully and warmly than any nest embraces any bird. And everything, everything quiet and empty.

But if this is how matters stand, why do I hesitate, why am I more afraid of an intruder than of the possibility that I may never see my burrow again? Well, fortunately this last is an impossibility, there is no way that it would be necessary for me to reflect in order to understand what the burrow means to me, I and the burrow belong together to such an extent that I could calmly settle here, calmly despite all my anxiety, I would have no problem persuading myself to open the entrance in spite of all my doubts, it would be quite enough for me to wait and do nothing, for in the long run nothing can drive us apart and somehow, in the end, I am bound to get back. But of course, how much time can pass before that moment, and how much can happen during this time, up here no less than down below? And yet it depends entirely on me to cut this interval short and do what's necessary at once.

And so, already too tired to think, my head lowered, unsteady on my legs, half asleep, more groping than advancing, I approach the entrance, slowly lift the moss, go down slowly, in my distraction allow the entrance to remain uncovered for an unnecessarily long time, remember, then, what I have failed to do, go upward again to repair the oversight, but why am I going up? I am only supposed to pull the moss cover closed, fine, so I go down again, and now I finally do pull up the moss cover. It is only in this state, exclusively in this state, that I can carry out this operation. And so I lie there under the moss on the catch I have brought in, blood and meat juices flowing around me, and could begin to sleep the sleep that I have longed for. Nothing disturbs me, no one has followed me; above the moss everything seems to be quiet, at least up until now, and even if it were not quiet, I don't think I could stop now to make additional observations; I have changed my position, I have come down into my burrow from the upper world, and I feel the effect immediately. It is a new world, one that confers new strength, and what is weariness above does not count as such here. I have returned from a journey, too tired to think or feel after my exertions; but seeing my old home again, the work of settling in that is waiting for me, the necessity of rapidly inspecting all the rooms at least superficially, but above all, making my way hurriedly, at top speed, to the castle court: all this transforms my weariness into restlessness and zeal, it is as if the minute I entered the burrow, I had had a long, deep sleep. The first part of the work is very laborious and requires all my energy: that is, bringing my catch through the labyrinth's narrow passages with their thin walls. I push forward with all my might, and this works, but much too slowly for me; to speed things up, I tear back a piece of this mass of meat and push my way over the top, right through it, now I have only some of it in front of me, now it is easier to advance, but I am so deep in the midst of this profusion of meat here, in these narrow passages, through which it is not always easy to pass even by myself, that I could easily suffocate in my own provisions, there are times when I can save myself from the crush of plenty only by feeding and drinking. But the transport is successful, it does not take all too long before I have completed it, the labyrinth is behind me; drawing a deep breath, I find myself in a passage with regular walls, drive my catch through a connecting passage into a main passage that has been especially designed for such situations and that leads steeply downward to the castle court. Now it is no longer work, now everything rolls and flows downward almost by itself. At my castle court at last! At last I'll be allowed to rest. Everything is unchanged, no disaster seems to have occurred, the slight damage noticed at first glance will soon be repaired. But first comes my long march through the passages, but that is no trouble, it is a chat with friends, the way I used to chat with friends in the olden days or—I am still not very old at all, but my memory of many things has already become murky—the way I used to, or the way I heard that it used to be. I begin now on the second passage, deliberately taking my time, once I have seen the castle court, I have infinite amounts of time; I always have infinite amounts of time inside the burrow, for everything that I do there is good and important and sates me, so to speak. I begin on the second passage and break off my revisions in the middle and go over to the third passage and let it lead me back to the castle court, and now, of course, I have to begin the second passage all over again, and so I play with my work and add to it and chuckle to myself and am delighted and become totally confused by so much work but do not stop doing it. It is for your sake, you passages and chambers, and you above all, castle court, that I have come, that I have counted my life as nothing after having been stupid enough for such a long time as to tremble about it and to delay my return to you. What do I care about danger now that I am with you? You belong to me, I to you, we are bound together, what can happen to us? Even if up above the creatures are already crowding forward and the snout is poised that will pierce the moss. And now even the burrow, mute and empty, welcomes me, confirming what I say.

Now, however, I am after all overcome by a certain lassitude, and I curl up a little in one of my favorite chambers; I am far from having inspected everything, and instead I want to continue my inspection to the end, I don't want to sleep here, I am only giving in to the temptation of settling in as if I did want to sleep, I want to check whether it would work here much as it did before. The test is successful, but I am not successful at tearing myself away, I remain here in a deep sleep. I must have slept for a long time, roused only from the last sleep that already dissolves of its own accord; this sleep must be very light, for a hardly audible hissing wakes me. I know immediately what it is: the small fry, whom I have supervised much too little and spared much too much, have bored a new tunnel somewhere in my absence; this tunnel has run into an old one, air is being trapped in there, and that is what is producing the hissing sound. What indefatigably active creatures they are, and how annoying their industry. I must first determine the location of the disturbance by making experimental excavations while listening attentively at the walls of my passage, only then will I be able to eliminate the noise. Besides, if the new tunnel fits into the structure of the burrow somehow, I'll gladly welcome it as a new air vent. But from now on I mean to pay much more attention than before to these creatures, not one of them can be spared.

Since I have had a good deal of practice in such investigations, the job will probably not take long, and I can begin at once, though other tasks are at hand; but this one is the most urgent, I must have silence in my passages. This noise, as it happens, is a relatively innocent one; I did not hear it at all when I arrived, although it must already have been there; I had to feel completely at home again in order to hear it; it is, so to speak, only audible to the ear of the homeowner who is truly exercising his authority. And it is not even constant, the way such noises are as a rule; there are long pauses, which are evidently due to blockages in the air flow. I begin my investigation, but I cannot find the spot where intervention is called for; though I make several excavations, I dig only at random and naturally nothing comes of it, and the heavy labor of digging and the even greater effort of putting back the dirt and leveling it is completely futile. I come no closer to the source of the noise; unvaryingly thin, it sounds at regular intervals, now like hissing, now more like squeaking. For the time being I could surely just leave matters be; the noise is certainly very disturbing, but there can be little doubt about what I assume to be its source, and so it will also hardly get any louder; on the contrary, it can also happen— although so far I have never waited long enough to find out—that in the course of time the further labors of these little borers will cause such noises to disappear by themselves; and apart from that, a coincidence can often put you handily on the track of the disturbance while systematic searching can fail for a long time. Thus I console myself and would much prefer to go on wandering through the passages, visiting the chambers, many of which I haven't seen even once since returning, and in between always romping a little in the castle court, but the noise does not let me be, I must go on searching. The small creatures are costing me a lot of time, a lot of time that could be better spent. In such cases it is usually the technical problem that attracts me; for example, on the basis of the noise— which my ear is skilled in discerning in all its fine distinctions— I imagine the cause with registerable precision, and then I feel driven to test whether my theory corresponds to reality. With good reason, for as long as a finding has not been made, I cannot feel secure, even if it were only a matter of knowing where a grain of sand falling down a wall will roll. And in this respect such a noise is by no means an unimportant matter. But important or unimportant, however much I search, I find nothing, or rather, I find too much. And this had to happen right in my favorite chamber, I think; I move a good distance away from there, almost halfway down the path to the next chamber, the whole thing is really a joke, as if I intended to prove that it was not just my favorite chamber that had produced this disturbance but that there are disturbances elsewhere, and smiling I begin to listen, but soon I stop smiling, for it is true, the same hissing occurs here as well. It is really nothing, sometimes I think that no one except me heard it; I hear it now, of course, more and more distinctly with an ear grown more acute by practice, although in reality it is exactly the same noise everywhere, something I can prove to myself by the comparative method. Nor is it growing louder, as I realize when I listen attentively at the center of the passage without pressing my ear to the wall. At that point it is really only by dint of straining—yes, of total submersion—that I divine rather than hear the breath of a sound now and again. But it is exactly this steady equivalence at all the spots that bothers me most, for it cannot be squared with my initial hypothesis. Had I guessed the reason for the noise correctly, it would have had to emanate most audibly from one definite spot, which merely had to be located, and from there the noise would have to grow fainter and fainter. But if my explanation was not on target, what was I dealing with? The possibility remained that there were two noise centers, that up until now I had been listening only at some distance from both centers, and that as I approached the one center, its noise increased, but as a result of the decreasing noise from the other center, the net result to the ear remained about the same. And already I was close to believing that if I listened very carefully, I could make out differences of tone, even if very indistinctly, that agreed with my new hypothesis. In any case, I must extend the scope of the experiment much farther than I have done so far. And so I head down the passage to the castle court, where I begin to listen. Strange, the same noise here as well. It is a noise produced by the digging of some trivial creatures, who have infamously exploited my absence; whatever it is, they are far from harboring any sort of hostility toward me, they are completely preoccupied by their own work, and as long as they encounter no obstacle in their path, they keep on in the direction they started in; I know all that and yet the fact that they have dared to come as close as the castle court is incomprehensible to me and disturbs me and muddles the intellectual clarity that is crucial to my work. In this matter I will not introduce distinctions: whether it was the not inconsiderable depth at which the castle court lies, whether it was its immense extent and its correspondingly strong drafts that scared off the diggers, or whether it was simply the fact that it was the castle court—the existence of which had penetrated their dull minds through some sort of report—the very solemnity of the place. In any case I had never before noticed any sign of digging in the walls of the castle court. Though creatures, drawn in droves by the powerful odors, have come here—this was where my hunts were most profitable—they had always dug their way through my upper passages from somewhere and then fearful, yes, but powerfully attracted, come running down the passages. Now, however, they were also boring within the walls. If only I had carried out the most important plans of my youth and early manhood—or rather, if I had only had the strength to carry them out, for there was no lack of will. One of my favorite plans had been to disengage the castle court from the earth surrounding it, that is, keep its walls to a thickness more or less equal to my height but over and beyond this, to create all around the castle court a hollow space the width of the wall, leaving intact a small foundation that, unfortunately, could not be detached from the ground. I had always imagined this hollow space, probably not without some justice, as the most wonderful abode I could ever have. To hang from this dome, to pull yourself up, to slide down, to turn a somersault, and once again to feel the ground under your feet, and to play all these games literally on the body of the castle court and yet not in its own true chamber; to be able to avoid the castle court, to give your eyes a rest from it, to postpone until later the joy of seeing it and yet not to have to do without it but instead literally hold it tight between your claws, something impossible to do if you have only the one ordinary open access to it; but above all to be able to watch over it, to be so richly compensated for being deprived of the sight of it that if you had to choose between staying in the castle court or in the hollow space, you would certainly choose the hollow space for all the days of your life so as always to roam up and down there forever and protect the castle court. Then there would be no noises in the walls, no insolent excavations right up to the court itself; then peace would have been guaranteed there, and I would be its guardian, I would have to listen, not with revulsion to the excavations of the little creatures but with delight to something that fully eludes me now: the rustle of silence in the castle court.

But all this beauty is exactly what does not exist, and I must get to work, I must almost be glad that my investigation is now directly connected to the castle court, since that quickens my pace. Of course it becomes more and more evident that I need all my resources for this work, which at first seemed to be merely trifling. I now tap on the walls, and wherever I listen, high and low, at the walls or on the ground, at the entrances or in the interior, everywhere, everywhere, the same noise. And how much time, how much concentration is required for this long listening to a noise that comes and goes. You can, if you want, take the small consolation of self-delusion from the fact that, here at the castle court, as opposed to the passages, if you lift your ear from the ground, you hear nothing because of its great size. Solely for relaxation, solely to take stock of myself, I frequently make this experiment, strain to listen, and am happy to hear nothing. But this aside, what has really happened? Faced with this phenomenon, my initial explanations fail completely. But other explanations that suggest themselves are ones I promptly have to reject as well. You might think that what I hear is simply the small creatures themselves at their work. But that would run counter to all my experience; I cannot suddenly begin to hear something that has always been present but that I have never heard before. My sensitivity to disturbances might have increased over the years in the burrow, but my sense of hearing has surely not grown keener. It is precisely in the nature of the small fry that you do not hear them: would I have ever put up with them otherwise? At the risk of starving, I would have exterminated

them. But perhaps—this thought also sneaks into my reflections—
I am dealing here with an animal with whom I am not yet familiar.
It is possible, though I have been observing life here below long
and carefully, but the world is manifold and never lacks for nasty
surprises. But as it would not be a single animal, it would have to
be a great herd that has suddenly invaded my territory, a great herd
of small animals that can only be of a higher order than the small
fry, since they are audible, but not much higher, for the noise their
work makes is itself slight. Hence they could be unknown creatures, a migrating herd merely passing through that disturbs me but
whose procession will soon be over. So I could merely wait without
doing any work, which would in the end prove to have been unnecessary. But if they are these unfamiliar animals, why do I never
manage to see any of them? By now I have made a number of excavations to catch one of them, but I don't come across any. It occurs
to me that they might be quite tiny animals, much smaller than
those I know, and that it is only the noise that they make that is
greater. Accordingly I pore over the soil I have dug up, I toss the
clumps into the air so that they disintegrate into the most minute
particles, but the noisemakers are not among them. Gradually I realize that I can achieve nothing by such random small excavations,
by doing so I am merely plowing up the walls of my burrow; I hurriedly scrabble here and there, I have no time to fill in the holes, at
many spots there are already heaps of earth that block my path and
my view; of course, all that bothers me only incidentally, I cannot
roam or look around or rest now, sometimes while working I have
even fallen briefly asleep in some hole, the claws of one paw stuck
over my head in the soil, from which I was trying to tear a piece
just as I was falling asleep. From now on I am going to change my
methods. I will build a regular large tunnel in the direction of the
noise, and I will not stop digging until, independent of all theories,
I find the real cause of the noise. Then I will eliminate it if it lies in
my power to do so, but if not, I will at least have certainty. This certainty will bring me either contentment or despair, but whichever it
may be, the former or the latter, it will be unquestioned and justified. This decision makes me feel better; everything I have done so
far seems to me overly hasty; in the excitement of my return, not
yet free of the worries of the upper world, not yet fully absorbed
into the peace of the burrow, I have become oversensitive from having had to be without it for so long, I have let an admittedly remarkable phenomenon rob me of my composure. What is it, then?
A slight hissing, audible only after long pauses, a nothing, though I
don't mean to say that you could get used to it, no, you could not
get used to it, but you could notice it for a while without for the
present taking any steps against it, e.g., every few hours listen for it

occasionally and patiently register the results but not, like me, drag
your ear along the walls and tear open the soil almost every time
the noise became audible, not really to find anything but to do
something that matches your inner disquiet. That will now change,
I hope. And then again, I hope it won't—as I admit, my eyes shut,
furious with myself—for my disquiet still trembles in me as it has
done for hours, and if reason did not hold me back, I would probably want to start digging at any given spot, whether I could hear
anything there or not, insensibly, spitefully, merely for the sake of
digging, almost like the little creatures who dig either for no reason
whatever or only because soil is their food. My new rational plan
tempts me and fails to tempt me. There are no objections to it, at
least I know of none; as best as I can tell, it should lead to my goal.
And yet, basically, I don't believe in it, I believe in it so little that I
am not even afraid of the possible horrors of its outcome, I don't
even believe that the outcome will be horrible; indeed, it seems to
me that I've had the idea of digging systematically ever since the
noise first arose, and it is only because I have no faith in it that I
haven't started on it before. But of course I'll start on the tunnel, I
can't see any other possibility, but I won't start right away, I'll put
off the job for a while; if reason is to be respected once again, it
must be fully respected, I will not hurl myself into this work. In any
case, I'll first repair the damage I have done to the burrow by my
senseless rooting around; that will cost me a fair amount of time,
but it is necessary; if the new tunnel is really to lead to its goal, it
will probably turn out to be a long one, and if it should not lead to
its goal, it will be endless, in any case the job means a longer absence from the burrow, though an absence that's less grievous than
the time spent in the upper world, I can stop the work whenever I
like and pay a visit home, and even if I don't do so, the air of the
castle court will blow gently over me and surround me as I work,
and yet this means leaving the burrow and submitting myself to an
uncertain fate; that is why I want to leave the burrow in good
shape, I don't want it said that I, who fought for its peace, shattered its peace myself and did not restore it immediately. So I begin
scraping the soil back into the holes, a job that I know how to do
expertly, something that I have done countless times almost without considering it work and that, especially as far as the final pressing and smoothing down is concerned—it is certainly not mere
self-praise, it is simply the truth—I am able to do with unsurpassed
skill. But this time I find it hard, I am too distracted, again and
again in the midst of my work I press my ear to the wall and listen
and, indifferent, let the soil that I have just picked up trickle back
again into the passage under my feet. The final work of embellishment, which requires greater concentration, is almost too much for

me. Ugly humps, disturbing cracks remain, not to mention that the old sweep and verve of the whole will never reemerge in so patched a wall. I try to console myself with the thought that the job I am doing is only provisional. When I return, when peace has been restored, I will put the final touch on everything, and everything will be done in a flash. Yes, in fairy tales everything is done in a flash, and this consolation belongs to the world of fairy tales as well. It would be better to finish the work right now, that would be much more useful than to keep on interrupting it to go on journeys through the passages, establishing new sources of noise; which is really very simple, for all it takes is standing wherever you like and listening. And I make other useless discoveries. I sometimes think that the noise has stopped; in fact, there are long pauses between sounds, and sometimes you fail to hear the intermittent hissing because all too often your own blood is beating in your ear, and then again two pauses come together as one, and for a while you think the hissing has stopped forever. You no longer listen, you jump up, your whole life is transformed, it is as if the source from which the stillness of the burrow flows were opened. You are careful not to test the discovery immediately, you look for someone to confide in before it has been questioned, and so you go galloping to the castle court; since you have been awakened to new life in every part of your being, you are reminded that for a long time you have not had anything to eat, you rip something from the provisions that lie half-buried under the soil, and you are still gulping it down while racing back to the site of the incredible discovery; first you want to convince yourself of it again, just casually, just for a fleeting instant as you eat; you listen, but the slightest instant of attention at once reveals that you have made a deplorable mistake; far away, in the distance, the imperturbable hissing persists. And you spit out the food and would like to stomp it into the ground, and you return to your work, not knowing what that might be, anywhere where it seems necessary and there is no lack of such places; you begin mechanically doing something, as if a supervisor were present and you had to put on a show for him. But no sooner have you set to work for a little while, it may happen that you make a new discovery. The noise seems to have grown louder—not, of course, a good deal louder, here it is always a matter of the finest distinctions, and yet a little louder, clearly perceptible to the ear. And this increased sound seems to be coming nearer; you can practically see the steps by which it is approaching even more distinctly than you hear the increase in sound. You leap back from the wall, you try to grasp in a flash all the possible consequences of this discovery. You feel as if you had never really organized the burrow for protection against an attack; you had meant to, but contrary to all your life experience, the danger of an attack and therefore organizing a defense against it seemed remote, or not remote (how could that be possible!) but, on a scale of relative importance, way below the arrangements for a peaceful life and so, for this reason, you gave that life first priority throughout the burrow. Much could have been organized in this respect without upsetting the overall plan; it is truly baffling to me how these details have been neglected. I have had a lot of good luck during all these years, my good luck has spoiled me, I had been anxious, but anxiety in the midst of good luck leads nowhere.

What needs to be done first now would surely be to inspect the burrow minutely with a view to its defense and all conceivable attendant possibilities, work out a plan of defense and the appropriate building plan, and then immediately set to work as vigorously as a youngster. That would be the essential task, which, incidentally, comes much too late, but it would be the essential task rather than digging some huge research tunnel, which has no other purpose than to divert me, defenseless, into using all my energies to seek out the danger, in the foolish fear that it would not arrive soon enough on its own. Suddenly, I fail to understand my earlier plan, I cannot find the slightest reason in what used to seem so reasonable, again I stop my work, and I stop listening as well, I don't want to discover any further increase of sound at this moment, I have had enough of discoveries, I drop everything, I would be satisfied just to settle my inner conflict. Again I let myself be led away by my passages, entering passages ever more remote—not yet seen since my return, still utterly untouched by my scrabbling paws—whose stillness is aroused by my coming and sinks down over me. I do not surrender to it, I hurry on past, I do not know what I am looking for, probably only a way to pass time. I wander so far afield that I arrive at the labyrinth, I am tempted to listen at the moss cover; such remote things, for the moment so remote, capture my interest. I push upward until I am there and listen. Deep silence; how lovely it is here, no one outside is concerned with my burrow, everyone goes about his own business, which has no connection with me, how did I manage to achieve this? Here at the moss cover is now perhaps the only spot in my burrow where I can listen for hours and hear nothing. A complete reversal of the situation in the burrow, the previous place of danger has become a place of calm, while the castle court has been dragged into the clamor of the world and its dangers. Even worse, here, too, there is no peace in reality, here nothing has changed, whether silently or noisily, the danger above the moss threatens as before, but I have become insensitive to it, I am much too preoccupied with the hissing in my walls. Am I preoccupied with it? It is growing louder, it is coming closer, but I wriggle my way through the labyrinth and camp up here under the moss, it is almost as if I had already abandoned my house to the hisser, content just to have a little peace up here. To the hisser? Do I have a new, definitive opinion about the source of the noise? Surely the noise stems from the channels that the little creatures dig? Isn't that my definitive opinion? I don't seem to have given up this belief yet, after all. And if the noise doesn't stem directly from the channels, then it does so indirectly in some way. And if it turned out to have no connection whatever with them, then it is not likely that anything can be assumed a priori, and you have to wait until you might discover the source or until it reveals itself. Of course, you could still continue to play with hypotheses, it could be proposed, e.g., that somewhere in the distance water has flooded in, and what seems to me to be hissing or squealing is actually a rushing sound. But apart from the fact that I have absolutely no experience of such things—I immediately drained the groundwater I found here in the beginning, and it has not returned in this sandy soil—aside from this, it is actually a hissing sound and cannot be reinterpreted as a rushing one. But what good are all these admonitions to keep calm when my imagination will not keep still, and I have actually come to believe—it is pointless to deny this to myself—that the hissing stems from one animal and not from many animals or small animals, but from one single, large one. There is a good deal of evidence to the contrary: that the noise can be heard everywhere and always at the same volume, and moreover, regularly, day and night. Certainly, at first you would rather be inclined to the hypothesis of a number of small animals; but since I would have had to find them in the course of my excavations and I have found nothing, the only remaining hypothesis is the existence of the one, large animal, especially since all the elements that appear to contradict the hypothesis do not make the animal impossible but only dangerous beyond all imagining. That is the only reason why I have resisted this hypothesis. I am now abandoning all self-deception. For a long time now I have been toying with the idea that it can be heard even at a great distance because it is working frantically, it is digging its way through the soil as quickly as someone walking freely out in the open, the ground all around its tunnel rumbles even after it has moved on, these reverberations and the sound of the digging itself unite in the far distance, and I, who hear only the last waning of the sound, hear it everywhere as the same. Contributing to this is the fact that the animal is not heading for me, that is why the sound does not change, instead a plan is in operation whose purpose I cannot grasp, I merely assume that the animal—and I am by no means saying that it is aware of my existence—is encircling me; it has probably already circled my burrow a number of times since I became aware of it. And now the sound is, in fact, becoming louder, and hence the circles tighten. The nature of the sound, a hissing or squealing, gives me a lot to think about. If I scratch and scrabble the ground as I do, the sound I make is a very different one. The only way I can explain the hissing is that the animal's principal tool is not its claws—which may only serve as an aid—but rather its muzzle or snout, which aside from its clearly enormous force, must be sharp in some way. The animal probably bores its snout into the earth with a single mighty thrust and tears out a huge chunk; during that time I hear nothing, that is the pause, but then it breathes in again preparatory to a new thrust—this inhaling, which must make an earthshaking racket not only because of the animal's strength but also because of its haste, its frenzy as it works, and this is the sound I hear as a faint hissing. But what remains utterly incomprehensible to me is the animal's ability to work without cease, perhaps the short pauses provide an opportunity for a moment's rest, but it never appears to have taken a truly substantial break. It digs day and night, always with the same force and vigor, the plan that dances before its eyes demanding the swiftest possible execution, and it has all the skills needed to carry it out. Now, I could never have anticipated such an enemy. But apart from its peculiar characteristics, what is happening now is no more than something I should have been afraid of from the outset, a contingency I should always have prepared for: someone is coming at me. How did it happen that for so long everything ran quietly and smoothly? Who guided the paths of my enemies so that they engaged in wide detours around my property? Why was I protected for so long, only to be so terrorized now? What were all the small dangers, which I spent my life brooding over, compared to this single one! Did I, as the owner of the burrow, hope to be superior to anyone who might come? It is precisely because I am the owner of this great and vulnerable work that, we can agree, I am defenseless against any more serious attack, I have been spoiled by the bliss of ownership, the vulnerability of the burrow has made me vulnerable, the injuries it suffers pain me as if they were my own. This is exactly what I should have foreseen; instead of thinking only about defending myself—and how lightly and fruitlessly did I do even that!—I should have been thinking about defending the burrow. Above all, precautions should have been taken, in case of an enemy attack, for sealing off individual sections, and as many individual sections as possible, from the less endangered sections by making landslides, which would have to be operational in the shortest possible time, and indeed, using huge masses of earth so effectively that the aggressor would never even suspect that the real burrow began only behind him. And more than that, these landslides would have to be designed not only to conceal the burrow but to bury the aggressor as well. I never made the slightest start on anything of the sort, absolutely nothing has been done in this direction, I was as thoughtless as a child; I spent the years of my manhood on childish games, even when I considered danger, I merely toyed with the idea, I failed to think genuinely about the genuine dangers. And there was no lack of warnings.

Admittedly, nothing that would come close to what is happening now has ever happened before, though something like it did happen in the early days of the burrow. The main difference is simply that those were the early days. At that time I was what you might call a young apprentice, still working on the first passage, the labyrinth had only been roughly outlined, and though I had already dug out a small chamber, its scale and the wall-treatment were a complete failure; in a word, everything was so primitive that it could be considered an experiment only, something you could suddenly drop with no regrets the minute you lost patience. Then one day it happened that I was lying among my heaps of earth during a break—throughout my life I have always taken too many breaks—when I suddenly heard a distant sound. Being young at the time, I was more curious than frightened. I abandoned my work and assumed a listening attitude; note that I listened rather than running up under the moss to stretch out there in order not to have to listen. I did at least listen. I had no trouble realizing that it was the sound of digging, similar to mine; it sounded fainter, but it was hard to tell how much of that was due to distance. I was tense but otherwise cool and collected. Perhaps, I thought, I am in someone else's burrow, and the owner is now digging his way toward me. If this assumption had proved true, I would have moved away to build a burrow elsewhere, since I was never bent on conquest or eager for a fight. But, of course, I was still young, I still did not have a burrow, I could still be cool and collected. Even subsequent developments did not really trouble me, although they were not easy to interpret. Supposing that whoever was doing the digging was really heading for me because he had heard me digging, it was impossible to know now whether, when he changed direction—as in fact happened—he did so because my rest period deprived him of any points of reference for his path or rather because he had changed his mind. But perhaps I was basically deluded, and he had never headed directly for me; in any case the sound grew stronger for a while, as if he were approaching; being young at the time, I might not have been displeased to see the digger suddenly pop up out of the ground, but nothing of the sort happened, at a certain point in time the digging sound began to grow weaker, it became fainter and fainter, as if the digger had gradually swung off his original course;

and all of a sudden it broke off completely, as if he had decided to take a completely opposite course and were moving directly away from me into the distance. For a long time I continued to listen for him in the silence before returning to my work. Well, this warning was clear enough, but I soon forgot about it, and it had barely any influence on my building plans.

Between that time and now lie the years of my manhood, but isn't it as if nothing lay between them? Today I am still taking a rather long break and listening at the wall, and the digger has recently changed his mind, he has turned around, he is returning from his journey, he thinks that he has given me sufficient time to prepare to receive him. But on my side everything is arranged less well than it was then, the great burrow stands undefended, and I am no longer a young apprentice but an old master builder, and what powers I still have fail me when it comes to making a decision. But no matter how old I am, it seems to me that I would very gladly be even older, so old that I can no longer rise from my pallet under the moss. For the truth is that I really cannot flourish here, I rise and once more I race down into the house as if my stay up here had filled me not with peace but only with new worries. How do matters stand below at last count? Had the hissing become fainter? No, it had become louder. I pick ten listening posts at random and clearly register my mistake, the hissing has remained the same, nothing has changed. Over there no changes take place, there you are at peace and transcend time, while here every instant jars the listener. And again I take the long road back to the castle court, all around everything seems agitated along with me, seems to be looking at me and then instantly to be looking away so as not to upset me, and yet tries again to read from my expression the decisions that will save us. I shake my head, I still have none. Nor am I going to the castle court to carry out some plan. I pass the spot where I had wanted to build the investigation tunnel, I check it again, it would have been a good spot, the tunnel would have led in the direction where most of the small air vents are, it would have made my work very much easier, perhaps I would not have had to dig very far at all, would not have had to dig all the way to the source of the sound, perhaps listening at the vents would have been enough. But no reflection is strong enough to inspire me to this labor of digging. This tunnel is supposed to bring me certainty? I have reached the point where I do not even want certainty. In the castle court I pick out a nice piece of skinned red meat and take it with me deep into one of the piles of dirt: there at any rate there will be silence insofar as real silence still exists here at all. I lick and nibble at the meat, thinking in turn about the strange animal that is making its way in the distance and that I ought to enjoy my provisions to the hilt while I still have the chance. This latter is probably my sole practicable plan. For the rest, I try to decipher the animal's plan. Is it passing through, or is it working on its own burrow? If it is passing through, then it might be possible to come to an understanding with it. If it really breaks through to me, I will give it some of my provisions, and it will move on. Surely it will move on. In my pile of dirt I can dream of everything, even of coming to an understanding, though I know very well that something of this sort does not exist and that the minute we see each other—no, just sense the other's presence—we will immediately show each other our claws and teeth in a mutual frenzy, one not a second sooner or later than the other, both filled with a new and different sort of hunger, even if we are otherwise full to bursting. And as always so here too, with complete justification, for who, even if he were only passing through, would not change his itinerary and all his future plans on catching sight of the burrow? But perhaps the animal is digging its own burrow; then I cannot even dream of arriving at an understanding with it. Even if it were such an unusual animal that its burrow would tolerate a neighbor, my burrow cannot tolerate one; at least, it cannot tolerate a neighbor who can be heard. At the moment the animal does seem very far away, if only it would withdraw just a little bit farther, the sound might disappear altogether, perhaps then everything would be all right, like in the old days; in that case it would be only an unpleasant but instructive experience, inspiring me to all sorts of improvements; once I have peace of mind and no danger is immediately pressing, I am fully capable of all sorts of respectable work. Perhaps the animal, in light of the countless possibilities that its capacity for work appears to create for it, will give up the idea of extending its burrow in the direction of mine and instead head in the direction of the other side. This outcome cannot, of course, be achieved by negotiation either but only by the animal's own good sense or by some compulsion I can exercise. In either case the decisive factor will be whether the animal knows of my existence and what it knows. The more I think about it, the less likely it seems to me that the animal has heard me at all, it is possible—though I can't imagine it—that it has heard reports of me from other sources but very unlikely that it has heard me. As long as I knew nothing about it, it cannot have heard me at all, for I was quiet then, there is nothing more quiet than reunion with my burrow; later, when I undertook experimental excavations, it might have heard me, though my style of digging makes very little noise; but if it had heard me, then I, too, would have noticed some sign of it; it would at least have had to stop work often to listen, but everything remained unchanged, the * * *.

[Here the story breaks off.]

BACKGROUNDS
AND CONTEXTS

FRANZ KAFKA

[Letters, Diaries, and Conversations]

Letter to Oskar Pollak[1]

January 27, 1904

I think one ought to read nothing but books that bite and sting. If the book we are reading does not wake us up with the blow of a fist against the skull, then why are we reading that book? So that it will make us happy * * *? My God, we would be happy even if we had no books. And in a pinch we could write such books as make us happy ourselves. No, we need those books that affect us like a misfortune, that cause us a lot of pain, like the death of someone whom we loved better than ourselves, as if we were cast out in the forests, cut off from all human beings, like a suicide; a book must be the ax for the frozen sea in us.

Diary: Fragment of a Story[2]

between July 19 and November 6, 1910

There is at the moment hardly any difference between me and the bachelor, except that I can still think of my youth in the village and perhaps, when I want to, perhaps even if my situation alone demands it, I can cast myself back there. But the bachelor has nothing ahead of him and therefore nothing behind him either. In the moment there is no difference, but the bachelor has only the moment. At that time—which no one can know today, for nothing can be so annihilated as that time—at that time he missed the mark when he constantly felt the ground of his being, the way one suddenly notices an ulcer on one's body that until that moment was the slightest thing on one's body—yes, less than the slightest, for it did not even seem to exist, and now it is more than everything else that our body has possessed since birth. If until this time our entire

---

1. *Franz Kafka, Briefe 1900–1912*, ed. Hans-Gerd Koch (Frankfurt a.M.: Fischer, 1999), 36. All selections from this volume are translated by the editor of this Norton Critical Edition. Oskar Pollak (1883–1915) was a fellow student of Kafka's at the Old Town Gymnasium (advanced high school); their friendship continued throughout their university years. Pollak studied Baroque art in Rome but at the outbreak of World War I volunteered to fight for Austria, achieved officer's rank, and was killed in action on June 11, 1915.
2. These are story fragments of the second version of Kafka's novella *Description of a Struggle*, which he was struggling to complete. *Tagebücher in der Fassung der Handschrift*, ed. Michael Müller (Frankfurt a.M: Fischer, 1990), 114–118, 125; all selections from this volume are translated by the editor of this Norton Critical Edition. For American translations of Kafka's diaries, consult *The Diaries of Franz Kafka, 1910–1913*, trans. Joseph Kresh (New York: Schocken, 1948) and *The Diaries of Franz Kafka, 1914–1923*, trans. Martin Greenberg (New York: Schocken, 1949).

being was directed to the work of our hands, to whatever was seen by our eyes, heard by our ears, down to the steps of our feet, now we suddenly turn completely in the opposite direction, like a weathervane in the mountains. Now, instead of having run away at that moment, even in this latter direction—for only running away could have kept him on the tips of his toes, and only the tips of his toes could have kept him on the earth—instead of that, he lay down, as children now and then lie down in the snow in winter so as to freeze to death * * *. Once and for all, this man stands outside our people, outside our humanity, he is continually starved, only the moment belongs to him, the everlasting moment of torment that is never followed by the spark of a moment of elevation; he always has only the one thing: his pain, but in the whole wide world no second thing that could serve as a cure; he has only as much ground as his two feet need, only as much of a hold as his two hands span, and hence so much less than the trapeze artist in a variety theater, for whom a safety net has been suspended below. * * *

Already my protective essence seemed to dissolve here in the city; I was beautiful in the early days, for this dissolution takes place as an apotheosis, in which everything that sustains our life flies from us but even in flying away, illuminates us for the last time with its human light.

To Max Brod[3]

December 17, 1910

I won't come this evening; I want to go on being by myself until early Monday, up until the last minute. This being hot on my own heels is still a joy that excites me and that, in spite of everything, is a healthy joy, for it produces in me that general restlessness from which arises the only possible equilibrium.

Diary[4]

December 20, 1910

What excuse do I have for not yet having written anything today? None. Especially as my state of mind is not at its worst. An invocation sounds continually in my ear, "If you would come, invisible judge (*Gericht*: also, court)!"

---

3. *Briefe 1900–1912*, 131. Max Brod (1884–1968), Kafka's closest friend and literary executor, was himself a prolific writer.
4. *Tagebücher*, 135.

Diary[5]

February 19, 1911

The special nature of my inspiration * * * is this, that I can do everything, not only with respect to a particular piece of work. If I write a sentence at random, for example, "He looked out the window," it is already perfect.

Diary: from "My Visit to Doctor Steiner"[6]

March 28, 1911

My happiness, my skills, and every possibility of being useful in any way have always been located in the literary field. And here I have certainly experienced states * * * in which I dwelled completely in every idea but also fulfilled every idea and in which I not only felt myself at my boundaries but at the boundaries of the human as such.

Diary[7]

August 20, 1911

Is it so difficult, and can an outsider understand that you experience a story within yourself from its beginning, from the speck in the distance, up to the approaching locomotive of steel, coal, and steam, and you don't abandon it even then but want to be pursued by it and have time for it, and so you are pursued by it, and of your own momentum you run before it wherever it may impel and wherever you may lure it?

Diary[8]

October 3, 1911

Again, it was the power of my dreams, shining into wakefulness even before I fall asleep, that did not let me sleep. In the evening and the morning the consciousness of my poetic abilities can hardly be surveyed. I feel loosened down to the ground of my being and can lift up out of myself whatever I want. * * * It is a matter of more mysterious powers, of something absolute in me.

5. Ibid., 30.
6. Ibid., 34. Rudolf Steiner (1861–1925), an Austrian polymath and sage, was the founder of a spiritual movement called anthroposophy (wisdom of the human being). He wrote a doctoral dissertation on Fichte's theory of knowledge and edited Goethe's scientific writings; his most important philosophical work was *The Philosophy of Freedom* (1894).
7. *Tagebücher*, 38.
8. Ibid., 53.

Diary[9]

November 20, 1911

My antipathy to antitheses is certain. They come unexpectedly, true, but not as a surprise, since they have always been very close by; if they were unconscious, then they were so only at the extreme edge. Admittedly, they generate thoroughness, fullness, completeness, but only like a figure on the "wheel of life";[1] we have chased our little idea around the circle. As different as they can be, they also lack nuance; they grow under one's hand as if bloated by water, beginning with a prospect onto boundlessness and always ending up the same medium size. They curl up, they cannot be straightened, they offer no leads, are holes in wood, do double time marching in place, draw antitheses onto themselves, as I have shown. May they draw down all of them onto themselves and forever.

Diary[2]

January 3, 1912

It is easy to recognize in myself a concentration on writing. When it had become clear in my organism that writing was the most productive direction of my being, everything rushed in that direction and left empty all those abilities that were directed first and foremost toward the joys of sex, eating, drinking, philosophical reflection on music.[3] I starved in all these directions * * *.

Diary[4]

March 24, 1912

In the next room * * * they are talking about vermin and corns. * * * It is easy to see that such conversations inhibit any real progress. It is information that will be forgotten again by both parties, and even now it proceeds in self-forgetfulness, without any sense of responsibility. But just for that reason, because such conversations are unthinkable without absence of mind, they reveal empty spaces that, if one stays with the topic, can be filled only by reflections or, better, by dreams.

9. Ibid., 259–60.
1. A toy with a revolving wheel.
2. *Tagebücher*, 341.
3. There is no comma in Kafka's manuscript between the phrase "philosophical reflection" and "music." The editor of this Norton Critical Edition holds that the text must stand as it is written, in which case Kafka is saying, somewhat unexpectedly, that the joy that writing starves is the joy of philosophical reflection on music or the philosophical reflection that music provokes. Other scholars point to the fact that Kafka often omitted commas in his unpublished writings and that in this case, too, he must have left out the comma purely by chance. This argument produces the more familiar idea that Kafka deprived himself of the joys of philosophical reflection *and* music.
4. *Tagebücher*, 412–13.

Diary[5]

September 23, 1912

I wrote this story, *The Judgment*, in a single push during the night of the 22nd–23rd, from ten o'clock to six o'clock in the morning. My legs had grown so stiff from sitting that I could just barely pull them out from under the desk. The terrible strain and joy as the story developed in front of me, as if I were advancing through a body of water. Several times during the night I carried my own weight on my back. How everything can be risked, how a great fire is ready for everything, for the strangest inspirations, and they disappear in this fire and rise up again. * * * The confirmed conviction that with my novel I am in the disgraceful lowlands of writing.[6] It is only in this context that writing can be done, only with this kind of coherence, with such a complete unfolding of the body and the soul. * * * Many emotions borne along in the writing—for example, the joy that I will have something beautiful for Max's *Arkadia*; thoughts of Freud, of course; in one passage, of *Arnold Beer*; in another, of Wassermann; of a (smashing to pieces) in Werfel's giantess; naturally also of my "The Urban World."[7]

Diary[8]

September 25, 1912

Yesterday I held a reading [of *The Judgment*] at Baum's. * * * Toward the end, my hand flew around in front of my face, uncontrollably and truthfully. I had tears in my eyes. The inarguable quality of the story was confirmed.

---

5. Ibid., 460.
6. At the same time that Kafka was writing the story *The Judgment*, he was at work on the novel he called "the America novel" or at other times *Der Verschollene* (The boy who was never heard from again). The novel was never finished, although the bulk of it is familiar to American readers as the novel *Amerika*.
7. The title of an unpublished story of Kafka's found in his diaries following February 21, 1911 (*Tagebücher*, 151). *Arkadia*, an annual literary magazine edited by Max Brod, who had published his novel *Arnold Beer: The Destiny of a Jew* earlier that year. Jakob Wassermann (1873–1934) was very likely known to Kafka from various "literary evenings" in Prague. Wassermann wrote shrewdly psychological, realistic narratives under the influence of Dostoyevsky; his heroes are idealists in pursuit of absolute moral values. For "smashing to pieces," see p. 11. Franz Werfel (1890–1945) enjoyed a wide popular success for his many novels published in Europe (e.g., The *Forty Days of Musa Dagh* [1933], a historical novel of the Armenian resistance to the Turks) and after his forced emigration in America (e.g., *The Song of Bernadette* [1941]). Kafka is here referring to Werfel's story "The Giantess," published earlier that year in *Arkadia*.
8. *Tagebücher*, 463.

Conversation with Max Brod[9]

end of *1912*

Franz himself provided three comments to this story [*The Judgment*] * * *, the first in conversation with me. He once said to me—quite without provocation—as I recall, "Do you know what the concluding sentence [of *The Judgment*] means?—I was thinking here of a strong ejaculation." The two other comments are found in the *Diaries*.

Diary[1]

February 11, 1913

After correcting proofs of *The Judgment*, I will write up all the connections that have dawned on me, as best as I now remember them. This is necessary because the story came out of me like a regular birth, covered with filth and mucus, and only I have the hand that can penetrate to the body of it and the desire to do that:

The friend is the connection between father and son, he is the major thing they have in common. Sitting alone at his window, Georg takes a passionate pleasure in plunging into and stirring up what they have in common, he believes that he contains his father inside himself, and he regards everything as peaceful except for a fleeting, sad mood of reflection. As the story develops, it shows the father rising up above what they hold in common—the friend—and setting himself up as Georg's opposite, reinforced by other small things held in common, that is, the love, the tender devotion of Georg's mother, the loyal memory of her, and the customers, whom the father did in fact originally gain for the business. Georg has nothing; his fiancée, who lives in the story only through the connection with the friend—therefore, to what is held in common—and who, since there has not yet been a wedding, cannot enter into the blood circle that encloses the father and the son, is easily expelled by the father. All the things held in common are amassed around the father, Georg feels them only as something strange, something that has become autonomous, never sufficiently protected by him, exposed to Russian revolutions, and only because he himself has nothing more than his father in his sights, the judgment that completely closes off the father from him has so powerful an effect on him.

"Georg" has as many letters as "Franz." In "Bendemann" "mann" [man] is only an intensification of "Bende" undertaken for all the potential possibilities of the story. But "Bende" has the same num-

---

9. Max Brod, *Über Franz Kafka* (Frankfurt a.M.: Fischer Bücherei, 1966), 114. This selection translated by the editor of this Norton Critical Edition.
1. *Tagebücher*, 491–92.

ber of letters as "Kafka," and the vowel "e" is repeated in the same positions as the vowel "a" in "Kafka."

"Frieda" has as many letters as "Felice" and the same initial; "Brandenfeld" has the same initial as "Bauer" [farmer], and through the word "Feld" [field] it also has some connection through the meaning.[2] Perhaps even the thought of Berlin is not without influence and the memory of the Electorate of Brandenburg may have been suggestive.[3]

To Kurt Wolff[4]

April 11, 1913

The Stoker, *The Metamorphosis* * * * and *The Judgment* belong together outwardly and inwardly: there is an overt and, even more important, a covert connection between them, and I would not like to abandon the idea of making this connection clear by gathering them together in a book titled, let us say, *The Sons*.

To Felice Bauer[5]

June 2, 1913

Do you find any meaning at all in *The Judgment*, I mean any direct, coherent, meaning that you could follow? I don't, nor can I explain anything in it. But a lot of strange things are involved. Just look at the names! It was written at a time when, although I knew you and the value of the world was heightened by your existence, I still had not yet written to you.[6] And now look * * * [Kafka repeats the gist of the last two paragraphs of his diary entry for February 11, 1913, but adds the following:] "Mann" [man] in the name "Bendemann" is there probably out of pity, to strengthen this poor

2. "Felice" refers to Felice Bauer (1887–1960), with whom Kafka conducted a passionate correspondence from 1912 to 1917. She became Kafka's fiancée in the year 1914 (the engagement was dissolved) and then again in 1917 (the engagement was again dissolved). During this period she lived in Berlin and worked as executive secretary to a manufacturer of dictating machines. Kafka described her once as a "happy, healthy, self-confident girl." After their relationship ended, Felice married and had two children. She lived with her family in Switzerland and then in the United States until her death.

3. The Mark or Electorate of Brandenburg is a vast land area of Prussia including Berlin.

4. *Franz Kafka, Briefe 1902-1924*, ed. Max Brod (Frankfurt a.M.: Fischer, 1958), 116. All selections from this volume are translated by the editor of this Norton Critical Edition. Kurt Wolff (1887–1963), head of a Leipzig publishing house, published Max Brod's yearbook *Arkadia*, in which *The Judgment* appeared in 1913. He also published Kafka's short novels *The Stoker* and *The Metamorphosis*, among others. After emigrating to the United States in 1942, he founded Pantheon Books.

5. This letter to Felice Bauer and all subsequent letters were originally published in *Briefe an Felice*, ed. Erich Heller and Jürgen Born (Frankfurt a.M: Fischer, 1967). This letter is found on page 394. All extracts from this volume of letters are translated by the editor of this Norton Critical Edition, who consulted *Letters to Felice*, trans. James Stern and Elizabeth Duckworth (New York: Schocken, 1973).

6. This is untrue. Kafka's first letter to Felice was written two days *before* he wrote *The Judgment* (see n. 5, p. 223).

"Bende" in his battles. * * * And there are several more of this sort; those are all things, of course, that I discovered only later. Incidentally, the whole story was written in one night, from eleven o'clock until six in the morning. When I sat down to write, I wanted * * * to describe a war; from his window a young man was supposed to have seen a crowd of people approaching over the bridge, but then everything turned around in my hands.

To Felice Bauer[7]

June 10, 1913

The Judgment cannot be explained. * * * The story is full of abstractions that are never admitted. The friend is hardly a real person, he may rather be what Georg and his father have in common. The story is perhaps a tour of inspection around father and son, and the changing shape of the friend is perhaps the change in perspective in the relations between father and son.

To Felice Bauer[8]

June 26, 1913

My relation to writing and my relation to people are unchangeable and grounded in my being, not in temporary relations. For my writing I need seclusion, not "like a hermit," that would not be enough, but like a dead man. Writing, in this sense, is a deeper sleep, ergo, death; and just as you will not and cannot drag a dead man from his grave, so you will not and cannot drag me from my desk in the night.

Diary[9]

December 4, 1913

Seen from the outside, it is a terrible thing for someone who is an adult but still young to die or, worse, to kill himself. To leave the scene in complete confusion—which would make sense in the course of further development—without hope or with the sole hope that in the great reckoning this appearance in life will be seen as something that never happened. I would be in such a situation now. To die would mean nothing more than to surrender a nothing to a nothing, but that would be impossible for the senses, for how could you, even as a nothing, consciously surrender yourself to the nothing, and not only to an empty nothing but rather to a roaring nothing, whose nothingness consists only in its incomprehensibility.

7. *Briefe an Felice*, 396–97.
8. Ibid., 412.
9. *Tagebücher*, 604.

Diary[1]

August 6, 1914

From the standpoint of literature my fate is very simple. My feeling for the representation of my dreamlike inner life has made everything else trivial, and these other things have withered horribly and do not stop withering. Nothing else can ever satisfy me. But my strength for that representation cannot be counted on at all, perhaps it has already vanished forever, perhaps it actually will come over me once again, though the circumstances of my life are not favorable to that end. And so I waver, I fly incessantly to the peak of the mountain, but I can barely stay on top for an instant. Others waver as well, but in lower regions, with greater powers; if they risk falling, they are caught up by the kinsman who walks beside them for that purpose. But I waver up there; it is not death, alas, but the eternal torments of dying.

Diary[2]

December 13, 1914

The best things I have written have their basis in this ability of mine to die contentedly. All these good and strongly persuasive passages always deal with someone's dying, that it is very hard for him, that there is an injustice or at least a harshness in it for him, and that this, at least in my opinion, is moving for the reader. But for me, who believe that I will be able to feel contentment on my deathbed, such scenes are secretly a game; indeed, I take pleasure in dying in the one who dies, hence, calculatingly exploit the attention that the reader concentrates on death, have a great deal more lucidity than he, who I assume will lament on his deathbed, and for these reasons my lament is as perfect as possible, nor does it suddenly break off, as with a real lament, let us say, but takes its course beautifully and purely.

To the Kurt Wolff Publishing House[3]

October 15, 1915

My wish would really be to publish a largish book of novellas (let us say, the novella from *Arkadia*, *The Metamorphosis*, and one more novella[4] under the general title of *Punishments*) * * *.

---

1. Ibid., 546.
2. Ibid., 708–09.
3. *Briefe 1902–1924*, 134.
4. *In the Penal Colony.* "Novella from *Arkadia*": *The Judgment.*

To the Kurt Wolff Publishing House[5]

August 14, 1916

I ask for your kind courtesy in publishing *The Judgment* in a separate little volume. Although *The Judgment*, of which I am especially fond, is very short, it is also more of a poem than a story: it needs free space around it and is also not unworthy of getting it.

To the Kurt Wolff Publishing House[6]

October 11, 1916

I received your kind words about my manuscript [of *In the Penal Colony*] with great pleasure. Your critique of what was painful in it coincides entirely with my view, though I must admit that I feel something similar about almost everything I have hitherto done. Notice how little is free of this or that form of this painful impression! In explanation of this latter story, I shall add only that it is not alone in being painful but that our times in general and mine in particular are and were similarly very painful, and mine in particular even more painful than the universal. God knows how far along this way I would have come if I had continued to write or, better, if my circumstances and my condition had allowed the sort of writing that, with my teeth biting my lips, I longed for. But they did not do that. In my present condition the only thing left for me to do is to wait for calm, in saying which I surely reveal myself, at least outwardly, to be incontestably a contemporary. * * *

To Felice[7]

December 7, 1916

I have misused my writing as a "vehicle" to get me to Munich, with which I don't otherwise feel the slightest spiritual connection, and after two years in which I wrote nothing have had the fantastic arrogance to do a public reading [of *In the Penal Colony*] when for 1½ years in Prague I read nothing aloud to my friends. By the way, back in Prague I continued to recall Rilke's words. After some very kind remarks about *The Stoker*, he thought that neither *The Metamorphosis* nor *In the Penal Colony* had the coherence that that [first] piece had achieved. The remark is not easy to understand, but it is insightful.

5. *Briefe 1902–1924*, 148.
6. Ibid., 150.
7. *Briefe an Felice*, 744.

Diary[8]

August 7, 1917

The traveler felt too tired to give an order or even to do anything at all. The only thing he did was pull a handkerchief from his pocket, make a move as if to dip it into the distant pail, press it against his forehead, and put it down next to the pit. This is how he was found by the two gentlemen whom the commandant had sent to find him. As if refreshed, he jumped up when they spoke to him. With his hand on his heart he said, "I'll be a damned dog if I allow this." But then he took himself at his word and began to run around on all fours. A few times he jumped up, literally tore himself loose, clung to the neck of one of the gentlemen, shouted in tears, "Why does all this have to happen to me," and hurried back to his post.

Diary[9]

August 8, 1917

And even if everything was unchanged, the spike was there, all right, thrusting out crookedly from the shattered forehead.

As if all that brought to mind for the traveler that what was to follow would be solely his affair and that of the dead man, with a wave of his hand he dispatched the soldier and the condemned man, they hesitated, he threw a stone at them, they still went on deliberating, then he ran up to them and punched them with his fists.

"What?" the traveler suddenly said. Had something been forgotten? A crucial word? A movement? A handshake? Who can make sense of this confusion? Damned vile air of the tropics, what are you doing to me? I don't know what's happening. My power of judgment has remained at home in the north.

"What?" the traveler suddenly said. Had something been forgotten? A word? A movement? A handshake? Highly possible. Most probably. A crude error in the reckoning, a fundamental misconception, a screaming, ink-spurting stroke of the pen runs right through the whole. But who will correct it? Where is the man to correct it? Where is the good old compatriot Müller [Miller] from the north, who will stuff the two grinning fellows over there between the millstones?

8. *Tagebücher*, 822–23. All the entries shown from the diaries between August 7 and 9, 1917, are part of Kafka's attempt to produce an ending to *In the Penal Colony* that would satisfy him.
9. Ibid., 823–25.

"Make way for the snake!" someone called. "Make way for the great Madame." "We are ready," someone shouted in reply, "we are ready." And we pathfinders, widely praised stone-breakers, marched out of the bushes. "Let's go," called our commandant, cheerful as ever, "Let's go, you snake fodder." Whereupon we raised our hammers, and for miles around the busiest banging began. No rest breaks were allowed, only a change of shift. The arrival of our snake was announced for this very evening, until then everything had to be banged and shattered into dust, our snake cannot bear even the tiniest pebble. The fact is that she is a single snake, incomparably spoiled thanks to our labor, therefore shaped into a singular character as well. We do not understand it, we regret it, that she still calls herself snake. At least she ought always to call herself Madame, even though, of course, as Madame she is also incomparable. But that is not our worry, our business is to make dust.

Hold the lamps high, you up front! You others quietly behind me! Everyone single file. And be still. That was nothing. Don't be afraid. I take full responsibility. I'll lead you out.

Diary[1]

August 9, 1917

The traveler gestured vaguely, stopped making any further effort, shoved the two of them away from the corpse, and pointed out to them the colony where they were to go at once. With gurgling laughter they showed that they gradually understood the order, the condemned man pressed his face, which had been smeared a number of times over, against the hand of the traveler, the soldier slapped the traveler's shoulder with his right hand—in his left hand he waved his rifle—now all three belonged together.

The t[raveler] had to forcibly resist the feeling that came over him that in this case a perfect order had been established. He grew tired and abandoned his plan of burying the corpse now. The heat, which was continuing to increase—the t[raveler] did not want to lift his head toward the sun just so as not to begin staggering—the officer's sudden final silence, the sight of the two of them over there, staring at him strangely, with whom he had lost all contact through the death of the officer, finally this sheer mechanical refutation that the officer's opinion had suffered here—all this—the t[raveler] could no longer remain standing and sat down on the cane chair. Had his ship thrust itself through these pathless sands and come here to pick him up—that would have been best. He

1. Ibid., 825–27.

would have gone aboard, only after reaching the stairs would he have reproached the officer for the cruel execution of the condemned man. "I will report what happened when I get home," he would have said, his voice raised so that the captain and the sailors, leaning over the railing above, full of curiosity, would also hear. Whereupon the officer would justifiably have asked, "Executed?" "But he's right here," he would have said and pointed to the traveler's luggage carrier. And in fact it was the condemned man, a fact that the t[raveler] confirmed by peering sharply at his features and carefully examining them. "My compliments," the t[raveler] would have had to say, and say gladly. "A conjuror's trick?" he asked. "No," said the o[fficer], "I have been executed thanks to a mistake on your part, on your orders." The captain and the sailors listened even more attentively. And all of them now saw the officer run his hand across his brow, uncovering a spike protruding crookedly from his shattered forehead.

To Kurt Wolff[2]

September 4, 1917

Perhaps there is some misunderstanding about *In the Penal Colony*. I have never been entirely of one mind in asking for it to be published. Two or three of the final pages are botched, and their presence points to some deeper flaw; there is a worm somewhere that hollows out even what is substantial in the story.

Diary[3]

September 25, 1917

I can still get fleeting satisfaction from works like "A Country Doctor," with the proviso that I can still manage something of the sort (very unlikely). But happiness only in case I can raise the world into purity, truth, immutability.

Notebook "H" (Aphorisms)[4]

October 1917 to February 1918

For everything outside the sensate world, language can be used only in the manner of an allusion but never even approximately in the manner of an analogy, since corresponding to the sensate world, it is concerned only with property and its relations.

---

2. *Briefe 1902–1924*, 159.
3. *Tagebücher*, 838.
4. Franz Kafka, *Nachgelassene Schriften und Fragmente II*, ed. Jost Schillemeit (Frankfurt a.M.: Fischer, 1992), 126. All selections from this volume are translated by the editor of this Norton Critical Edition.

To Max Brod[5]

early April 1918

When we write something, we have not coughed up the moon [*den Mond ausgeworfen*], whose origins might then be investigated. Rather, we have moved to the moon with everything we have. * * * The only separation that can be made, the separation from the homeland, has already taken place. * * * Any criticism that deals in concepts of authenticity and inauthenticity and seeks to find in the work the will and feelings of an author who isn't present—any such criticism seems to me to make no sense and follows only from the critic's also having lost his homeland.

Notebook "H"[6]

February 7, 1918

I feel too tightly constricted in everything I signify; even the eternity that I am is too tight for me. But if, for instance, I read a good book, say a travel account, it rouses me, satisfies me, suffices me. Proof that previously I did not include this book in my eternity or had not pushed forward far enough to an intimation of the eternity that necessarily includes this book as well.—From a certain stage of knowledge on, weariness, insufficiency, constriction, self-contempt must disappear: that is, where I have the strength to recognize as my own being something that previously, having been alien, refreshed me, satisfied, liberated, exalted me.

Letter to His Father[7]

November 1919

My writing was about you: there I only bemoaned what I could not bemoan on your breast. It was an intentionally long drawn out leave-taking from you except that, although it was forced by you, it took its course in the direction determined by me.

Diary[8]

January 13, 1920

Though whatever he does seems to him extraordinarily new, at the same time, corresponding to this impossible plenitude of new things, it seems extraordinarily dilettantish, hardly even tolerable, incapable of becoming historical, bursting the chain of the generations, breaking down for the first time into all its depths the music

5. *Briefe 1902–1924*, 240–41.
6. *Nachgelassene Schriften* II, 84–5.
7. Ibid., 192.
8. *Tagebücher*, 848–49.

of the world, which until now could at least be divined. Sometimes, in his arrogance, he is more afraid for the world than for himself.

Diary[9]

February 15, 1920

The matter is as follows: one day, many years ago, I sat, certainly sad enough, on the slopes of the Laurenziberg.[1] [I examined the wishes that I had for my life. The most important or the most delightful turned out to be my wish to attain a view of life (and—this was, to be sure, necessarily bound up with it—to be able to convince others of it in writing), in which life, while still retaining its natural, heavy rise and fall, would also be recognized with the same clarity as a nothing, a dream, a floating. Perhaps a beautiful wish, if I had wished it correctly, let us say, as the wish to hammer a table with painfully methodical, technical competence and simultaneously not to do it and not in such a way that people could say, "Hammering a table is nothing to him" but rather, "Hammering a table is a true hammering and at the same time a nothing to him," whereby the hammering would surely have become still bolder, still more determined, still more real, and if you will, still more insane. But he could not wish in this fashion at all, for his wish was not a wish, it was only a defense of nothingness, a granting of protection and civil rights to nothingness, a breath of cheer that he wanted to lend to nothingness, into which at that time he had scarcely taken only his first few conscious steps but which he already felt as his element.] At that time it was a sort of farewell that he took from the illusive world of youth; it had, incidentally, never directly deceived him but only caused him to be deceived by the utterances of all the authorities around him. The necessity of his "wish" had come about as a result.

Diary[2]

February 15, 1920

He does not live for his personal life; he does not think for his personal thought. It seems to him that he lives and thinks under the compulsion of a family, which is surely itself overabundant in the power of life and thought but for which he signifies, in accordance with some law unknown to him, a formal necessity. For this unknown family and these unknown laws he cannot be released.

9. Ibid., 854–55.
1. In today's Prague it is known as Petrín, a hilly park on the side of the Vltava (Moldau) River opposite the Old Town. The following passage was enclosed in brackets in the original.
2. *Tagebücher*, 857.

Loose Pages[3]

early 1921

Writing denies itself to me. Hence plan for autobiographical investigations. Not biography but investigation and detection of the smallest possible components. Out of these I will then construct myself, as someone whose house is unsafe wants to build a safe one next to it, if possible out of the material of the old one. What is bad, admittedly, is if in the midst of building, his strength gives out and now, instead of one house, unsafe but still complete, he has one half-destroyed and one half-finished house, therefore nothing. What follows is insanity, something like a Cossack dance between the two houses, whereby the Cossack scrabbles and throws aside the earth with the heels of his boots until his grave is dug out under him.

Diary[4]

October 19, 1921

Anyone who cannot come to terms with his life while he is alive needs one hand to ward off his despair over his fate a little—it occurs very imperfectly—but with his other hand he can note down what he sees among the ruins; for he sees other things and more than what others see; in fact, he is dead during his own lifetime and the real survivor. This presupposes that he does not need both hands, and more hands than he has, for his struggle with despair.

Diary[5]

December 6, 1921

From a letter: "During this sad winter I warm myself by it." Metaphors are one of the many things that make me despair of writing. Writing's lack of independence, its dependence on the maid who makes the fire, on the cat warming itself on the stove; it is even dependent on the poor old human being warming himself. All these are independent activities ruled by their own laws; only writing is helpless, it does not live by itself, it is a joke and a despair.

The Castle: Kafka's last novel[6]

ca. January 1922

There [on the floor with Frieda, in a puddle of beer] hours passed, hours of breathing together, of hearts beating together,

3. *Nachgelassene Schriften II*, 373.
4. *Tagebücher*, 867.
5. Ibid., 875.
6. *Das Schloß, Roman*, ed. Malcolm Pasley (Frankfurt a.M.: Fischer, 1982), 68–9. This selection translated by the editor of this Norton Critical Edition.

hours in which K. again and again had the feeling that he was going astray or so deep in a foreign place as no man ever before him,
a foreign place [or: a foreign woman] in which even the air had no
ingredient of the air of home, in which one must suffocate of for-
eignness and in whose absurd allurements one could still do no
more than go farther, go farther astray.

Diary[7]

January 16, 1922

The clocks do not agree; the inner one races in a devilish or de-
monic—at any rate inhuman—way, the outer one goes haltingly at
its usual pace. What else can happen except that the two different
worlds come apart, and they do come apart or at least tear at each
other in a dreadful way. There may be various reasons for the wildness of the inner working; the most visible one is introspection,
which will not allow any idea to come to rest but chases each one
upward, itself become idea again, to be chased further by renewed
introspection. Second, this chasing takes the direction [that leads]
away from mankind. The solitude that for the most part has all
along been forced on me, in part was voluntarily sought by me—
but what was this, too, if not compulsion?—is now becoming completely unambiguous and is heading for the extreme. Where is it
leading? The most compelling [thought] seems to be that it can
lead to insanity; nothing further can be said about it, the chase
goes through me and tears me to bits. Or I can—can I?—bear up,
if only for the most minute part, hence allow myself to be carried
along by the chase. To what place, then, do I come? "Chase,"
"hunt," is, after all, only a metaphor, I can also say, "assault on the
last earthly boundary," an assault from below, from mankind, and
since this too is only a metaphor, I can replace it by the metaphor
of an assault from above down on me.

This whole literature is an assault on the boundary; and if Zionism had not intervened, it could easily have developed into a new
secret doctrine, a kabbalah. Beginnings of such a thing exist. Admittedly, what is required is something like an incomprehensible
genius that drives its roots into the old centuries anew or creates
the old centuries anew and does not expend itself on all that but
only now begins to expend itself.

7. *Tagebücher*, 877–78.

Diary[8]

January 27, 1922

The necessity of being independent of the unhappiness mixed with awkwardness of the double sled, the broken suitcase, the wobbling table, the poor light, the impossibility of having quiet in the hotel in the afternoon, and such. This cannot be achieved by neglect, since it cannot be neglected; it is only to be achieved through the summoning of new powers. Here, it is true, there are surprises; even the most disconsolate person must admit as much; as experience shows, something can come out of nothing: the coachman with the horses may crawl out of the dilapidated pigsty.

Diary[9]

January 27, 1922

The strange, mysterious, perhaps dangerous, perhaps saving comfort of writing: the leap out of murderer's row of deed followed by observation, deed followed by observation,[1] in that a higher type of observation is created, a higher, not a keener type, and the higher it is and the less attainable from the "row," the more independent it becomes, the more obedient to its own laws of motion, the more incalculable, the more joyful, the more ascendant its course.

To Max Brod[2]

July 5, 1922

I am, to put it first in quite general terms, afraid of the trip. * * * But it is not fear of the trip itself. * * * Rather, it is fear of change, fear of attracting the attention of the gods to myself by what is, for my circumstances, a great act.

When I let everything run back and forth again and again between my aching temples during last night's sleepless night, I became aware again of what I had almost forgotten in the relative calm of the past few days—what a weak or even nonexistent ground I live on, over a darkness out of which the dark power emerges when it wills and, without bothering about my stammers, destroys my life. Writing maintains me, but isn't it more correct to say that it maintains this sort of life? Of course, I don't mean by this that my life is better when I don't write. Rather, it is much worse then and wholly intolerable and must end in insanity. But that [is true], of

8. Ibid., 891–92.
9. Ibid., 892.
1. No punctuation in original.
2. *Briefe 1902–1924*, 383–86.

course, only under the condition that I, as is actually the case, even when I don't write, am a writer; and a writer who doesn't write is, admittedly, a monster asking for insanity.

But how do things stand with this being a writer? Writing is a sweet, wonderful reward, but for what? During the night it was clear to me with the vividness of childish show-and-tell: it is the reward for service to the devil. This descent to the dark powers, this unfettering of spirits bound by nature, dubious embraces, and whatever else may go on below, of which one no longer knows anything above ground when one writes stories in the sunlight. Perhaps there is another kind of writing, I know only this one; in the night, when anxiety does not let me sleep, I know only this. And what is devilish in it seems to me quite clear. It is vanity and the craving for enjoyment, which is forever whirring around one's own form or even another's— the movement then multiplies itself, it becomes a solar system of vanities—and enjoys it. What the naive person sometimes wishes, "I would like to die and watch the others cry over me," is what such a writer continually realizes: he dies (or he does not live) and continually weeps about himself. From this comes a terrible fear of death, which does not have to manifest itself as the fear of death but can also emerge as the fear of change * * * .

The reasons for his fear of death can be divided into two main groups. First, he is terribly afraid of dying because he has not yet lived. By this I do not mean that wife and child and field and cattle are necessary to live. What is necessary for life is only the renunciation of self-delight: to move into the house instead of admiring it and decking it with wreaths. Countering this, one could say that such is fate and is not put into any man's hands. But then why does one feel remorse, why doesn't the remorse stop? To make oneself more beautiful, more attractive? That too. But why, over and beyond this, in such nights, is the keyword always: I could live and I do not.

The second main reason—perhaps there is, after all, only one, at the moment I can't quite tell the two apart—is the consideration, "What I have played at will really happen. I have not ransomed myself by writing. All my life I have been dead, and now I will really die. My life was sweeter than that of others, my death will be that much more terrible. The writer in me will, of course, die at once, for such a figure has no basis, has no substance, isn't even made of dust; it is only slightly possible in the maddest earthly life, it is only a construction of the craving for enjoyment. This is the writer. But I myself cannot live on, since I have not lived, I have remained clay, I have not turned the spark into a fire but have used it only for the illumination of my corpse." It will be a peculiar burial: the writer, hence a thing without existence, consigns the old corpse, corpse all along, to the grave. I am enough of a writer to want to enjoy it with all my senses, in total self-forgetfulness—not wakefulness but self-forgetfulness is the first prerequisite of being a writer—or what amounts to the same thing, to want to tell the story of it, but that will no longer happen. But why do I speak only of real dying? It's the same thing in life. I sit here in the comfortable attitude of the writer, ready for anything beautiful, and must watch idly—for what can I do besides write—as my real self, this poor defenseless being (the writer's existence is an argument against the soul, for the soul has indeed evidently abandoned the real self, but has only become a writer, has not been able to go any further; should its parting from the self be able to weaken the soul so much?) for any old reason, now, for a little trip * * *, is pinched, thrashed, and almost ground to bits by the devil. What right have I to be shocked, I who was not at home, when the house suddenly collapses; for I know what preceded the collapse: didn't I emigrate, abandoning the house to all the powers of evil?

To Max Brod[3]

end of July 1922

A son incapable of marriage, who produces no carriers of the name; pensioned at 39; occupied only with an eccentric writing that aims at nothing else than the salvation or damnation of his own soul * * * .

Loose Pages[4]

October/November 1922

"What are you talking about? What is it about? What is that—literature? Where does it come from? What use is it? What questionable things! Add to this questionableness the further questionableness of what you say, and a monstrosity arises. How did you get on these lofty, useless pathways? Does that deserve a serious question, a serious answer? Perhaps, but not yours, that is a matter for loftier rulers. Quick, retreat!"

Diary[5]

June 12, 1923

More and more fearful as I write. It is understandable. Every word twisted in the hand of the spirits—this twist of the hand is their characteristic gesture—becomes a spear turned against the

3. Ibid., 401.
4. *Nachgelassene Schriften II*, 527–28.
5. *Tagebücher*, 926.

speaker. Most especially a remark like this. And so ad infinitum. The only consolation would be: It happens whether you want it to or not. And what you want is only of infinitesimally little help. What is more than consolation is: You too have weapons.

Conversation with Max Brod[6]

undated

He often spoke of the "false hands that reach out toward you in the midst of writing"—and also of the fact that what he had written and even what he had published had made him go astray in the work he did afterward.

Notebook "G"[7]

November 25, 1917

Before setting foot in the Holiest of Holies, you must take off your shoes, but not only your shoes but everything, traveling clothes and luggage, and under that, your nakedness and everything that is under the nakedness and everything that hides beneath that, and then the core and the core of the core, then the remainder and then the residue and then even the gleam of the imperishable fire. Only the fire itself is absorbed by the Holiest of Holies and lets itself be absorbed by it; neither can resist the other.

6. *Der Prozeß, Franz Kafka, Gesammelte Werke*, ed. Max Brod (Frankfurt a.M.: Fischer, 1965), 316. This selection translated by the editor of this Norton Critical Edition.
7. *Nachgelassene Schriften II*, 77. Here, the chronological order of composition is being broken deliberately.

CRITICISM

STANLEY CORNGOLD

[Preface to an Understanding of Kafka]†

Franz Kafka was born on July 3, 1883, into a German-speaking Jewish family in Prague, the capital of the Czech Lands of the Austro-Hungarian Empire. This piling up of ethnic particulars right from the start should suggest something of the complexity of Kafka's predicament as it is reflected in his stories, novels, and confessional writings. Kafka's situation, like his city's, is mazy, intricate, and overly specified by history, lending his life an exceptional danger and promise: the danger of becoming lost in impenetrable contradiction that finally flattens out into anxiety, apathy, nothingness; and the promise, too, of a sudden breaking open under great tension into a blinding prospect of truth. At various times you see Kafka laying weight on one or the other of his identity elements in an effort to mark out his way—he understood Yiddish, learned Hebrew, toyed with Zionism; he espoused socialist ideals that aligned him with the aspirations of the Czech-speaking working class; and he sought literary fame by competing with masters of German literature living and writing in the German-speaking capitals (chiefly Berlin, hardly at all Vienna, which he disliked).[1] But the way he took—and to judge from his posthumous fame, found—was, with few interruptions, the way of writing.[2]

The "way" is a figure of speech that is meant to confer a special distinction on Kafka's decision to write. The work that he actually produced and published in his lifetime is not huge by ordinary standards of literary greatness, consisting of seven small volumes, four of them devoted to single stories. Yet on the strength of "The Judgment" ("Das Urteil"), "The Stoker" ("Der Heizer"), and *The Metamorphosis* (*Die Verwandlung*), all of which he published early, in single volumes, in the years 1913–15, Kafka enjoyed an indubitable literary esteem. His stories were admired by writers of the order of Robert Musil and Rainer Maria Rilke, and publishers like Ernst Rowohlt and Kurt Wolff pressed him for more of his work. There stood in his way, however, for most of his life, the mass and difficulty of his professional duties: he was a high official—Senior Le-

---

† Adapted from *Lambent Traces: Franz Kafka* (Princeton, NJ: Princeton University Press, 2004), xi–xv. Used by permission of the publisher, Princeton University Press. Copyright © 2004 by Princeton University Press. Page numbers to this Norton Critical Edition appear in brackets.

1. Hartmut Binder, " 'Man muss die Nase dafür haben': Kafka und seine Bücher," *Kafkas Bibliothek: Expressionismus* (Stuttgart: Antiquariat Herbert Blank, 2001), 6.
2. For an illuminating discussion of the metaphor of "the way," from the pre-Socratic philosophers to Heidegger, Blanchot, and, especially, Kafka, see David Schur, *The Way of Oblivion* (Cambridge, Mass.: Harvard University Press, 1998).

gal Secretary—at the partly state-run Workers' Accident Insurance
Institute.

Kafka's writing arose as an empirical practice, at a place—a
desk—at a time—between eleven at night and three in the morning. To accomplish what he did, he had to construct a kind of
salient around this time and place: he required an almost unimag-
inably deep degree of protection for his writing. Yet for as long as
he was employed by "the office," he could not feel free of its demands. His best known story, *The Metamorphosis*, which recounts
the transformation of a traveling salesman into a verminous beetle,
suggests the omnipresence of just this office as a threat. Soon after
Gregor Samsa wakes at four (read: just as Kafka "wakes" from his
creative "dream" spent writing), the household is invaded by the office head, who knocks on his door, demanding Gregor's loyalty and
attention to his job. The imposition on the hero of a verminous
body connects in Kafka's imagination with the "monstrous" reduction of himself at the instant his private redoubt is invaded. In this
story the daily logic of cause and effect is reversed: here the monstrosity is the harbinger, and not the result, of the invasion. Kafka
wrote that if he did not write, there would be nothing left of him;
and if he were not let in peace, there would indeed be nothing left
of him. At the end of *The Metamorphosis*, the charwoman says,
"Look, you don't have to worry about getting rid of the stuff next
door. It's already been taken care of" (M 42).

Kafka prepared for his profession from early on: he attended the
German National Altstädter Gymnasium; took his law exams at the
German Charles University; and, thereafter, on his own account a
token Jew among Germans (and after 1918 a token German among
Czechs), worked, and was advanced, for fourteen years in the office
that released him only after his tuberculosis asserted the greater
claim. With almost pathological modesty, he suppressed the knowledge of his achievement on behalf of workmen's compensation (his
activity is not to be confused with that of "little" clerks like the
young Italo Svevo or Fernando Pessoa). Time and again, he was
obliged to bring home masses of documents to prepare for court
defenses of the Institute's cases. That the writing of *The Metamorphosis* was, to Kafka's mind, ruined by the "business trip" he had to
take while in the throes of composition is well known. Less well
known is the fact that this business trip was a complex legal defense that he won, obtaining a solid settlement for the Institute
(LF 69).

There is, however, another, and altogether productive, sense in
which the world of the office enters his stories, shaping the spaces,
for example, in which the hero of *The Trial* encounters the officials
of the court that has arrested him for an unnamed crime. The at-

tics and personnel of lower-middle-class tenements also contribute to the scene—the rough world that Kafka knew through his erotically charged city walks and the clamor of the beneficiaries of the insurance he helped to disburse. Kafka's literary greatness as an analyst of modernity, of the fusion of bureaucracy and technology as the governing principles of everyday life, would not have been achieved were it not for his immersion in the phantasmagoric hell of office life.[3] And still this burden drained him and threatened to leave nothing over for what finally mattered to him: "literature." It is only from literature and never, to Kafka's mind, the benevolent aspect of his professional work that he could imagine his justification.

Kafka lived his secretly excruciating bachelor's life within a radius of a few miles from the Old Town Center of Prague, held captive until 1923, the year before his death, by the city he called this "old crone" with "claws" (L 5). During this time he made trips, often with friends, fairly far afield—to Paris and London and Como and Berlin, and in the last year of his life did indeed live in Berlin. But what he felt with almost unbearable intensity—leading him, especially at the time of his writing his first important stories and just before beginning *The Castle*, to fear that he was going mad—were the elements of his personality in tension. At best this tension worked to produce a sort of claustral space between himself and the din of the world that did not exclude the entrance of subliminally selected productive atoms. He was responsive to politics and history and public culture, but he sought to translate this polemical complex, for his safety, into a private, recondite, even "dreamlike" writing. In other words, Kafka responded to his culture by looking beyond it, and his writing was his "telescope." He sought to see as far as was humanly possible and was blissful when he felt he was succeeding.

* * *

My Kafka is an ecstatic. This bliss, this feeling himself "at the boundary of the human," is the reward of writing well, even if, as a feeling, it has no immediate linguistic content, since

> for everything outside the sensate world, language can be used only in the manner of an allusion (*andeutungsweise*) but never even approximately in the manner of an analogy (*vergleichs-*

---

3. A number of critics—Jeremy Adler, among others—have recently emphasized this point. "Although Kafka constantly stresses the conflict between his writing and his profession," writes Adler, "this perceived dualism . . . provides the premise for his authorship, enabling him to write about modernity and its discontents from the inside. . . . His job brought him into direct contact with industrialization, mechanization, and bureaucracy, as well as with the struggle between capital and labor, and his official writings antedate his literary breakthrough." Jeremy Adler, "In the Quiet Corners," *Times Literary Supplement*, no. 5140 (5 October 2001), 6–7.

weise)], since corresponding to the sensate world, it is concerned only with property and its relations. [p. 205]

All of Kafka's writing turns on this ecstasy—its hiddenness, its warning, its power to justify a ruined life—but it cannot name directly what is nothing in respect of material things and the signs dependent on them. We know of Kafka's horror of metaphor, his frustration at "writing's lack of independence [of the world]" [p. 208]. Still, there is the call of "real" writing, whose purpose is to bring about a "constructive destruction" of the world of experience.[4] Real writing, however, is not something that Kafka can summon up at will. In times of failure, the good death of ecstatic writing is haunted by terror of the death of a misspent life—misspent, because "God does not want me to write—but I, I must" (L 10). Only a writing that flows from a full immersion could justify the risk. If it is less than wholehearted, it is only a great shame; and, then, for Kafka—like Joseph K., the hero of *The Trial*—it would seem as though nothing more than his shame could survive him (T 231).

There are these two sorts of death in Kafka—the good death of self-loss in writing and the "roaring" ("*brausenden*") death of an unjustified life [p. 200]. One involves the denial of the empirical ego, and survival; the other, the refusal of "the sensate world," and extinction. They separate, come together, split apart, stream into one another, drawing the figure of Kafka's spirit in his work—elliptically. It is in such a manner—elliptically—that I mean to describe Kafka's spirit, recalling Walter Benjamin's view of Kafka's work as an ellipse whose twin foci are profane empirical urbanity, on the one hand, and mystical experience, on the other.[5]

I think of this tension as the tension between two longings, which arise in response to the two kinds of death that disturb him. One strains for the cultural immortality promised by literary works that deserve to survive; but it, too, is not without the ecstatic, the mystical dimension of creation. The other craves to find in death, before or beyond obliteration, a form of the "heightened redemption" ("*gesteigerte Erlösung*") vouchsafed to Kafka's mouse-singer Josefine [p. 108]. Both ecstasies are sought and feared, suspected and affirmed. Neither is simple, and neither is otherworldly. Cul-

---

4. "[A] destruction of the world that is not destructive but constructive" (DF 103, GW 6:220).

5. "Letter to Gershom Scholem on Franz Kafka" (12 June 1938), trans. Edmund Jephcott, in *Walter Benjamin, Selected Writings, Volume 3, 1935–1938*, ed. Howard Eiland and Michael W. Jennings; trans. Edmund Jephcott, Howard Eiland, et al. (Cambridge, Mass.: Harvard University Press, 2002), 325. The approach is caught up in the lustrous words of Theodore Weiss, "[Kafka's] is the microscope that by the bright obliquity reveals in our daily conventions the unsuspected horror." "Franz Kafka and the Economy of Chaos," *The Man from Porlock: Engagements 1944–1981* (Princeton: Princeton University Press, 1982), 254.

tural immortality is also a contingent affair of being published and read by persons who live in cities and feed (on) the media. And real death occurs in a context of tradition shaped by historical Judaism and types of Gnostic teaching rampant in Prague in Kafka's lifetime.[6]

Everything, however, depends on perceiving which of these foci—the worldly matrix or the imagination of redemption elsewhere—exerts the stronger pull. One could misunderstand their relation by simplifying it, since Kafka's mystic refusal of the world also involves its necessary inclusion: "what we call the world of the senses is the evil in the spiritual world" (DF 39, GW 6:236–37). His gnostic élan makes its way through a universe of medial, sensate inscriptions: K.'s visit to the Castle is organized by telephone; Kafka found bliss in trashy movies, just as he devoured pulp novels about colonial exploits in savage lands.[7] But these are cartoon-like reflexes of what truly mattered to him, the inescapable attraction of flexible genius to its own mockery.[8] Kafka's real longings are not local and contemporary and least of all an affair of cultural politics. They are apocalyptic. They seek "the strongest possible light" by means of which "one can dissolve the world"; they would "raise the world into purity, truth, immutability" [p. 205]. They are the dominant motive in this unequal play of forces.

* * *

In the Circle of "The Judgment"

> Kafka's work is dipped in the color of powerlessness. The work develops out of a lifelong diary that keeps going by questioning itself.
>
> —Elias Canetti, *"Dialogue with the Cruel Partner"*

The importance for Kafka of writing his first great story "The Judgment" cannot be overestimated. He composed the piece on the night of September 22–23, 1912, in a single sitting, in a single inspired thrust, and it thereafter became a permanent reference to the stations of his career—his breakthrough and his vindication. What remained crucial was the way the story was written: it came out of him like nothing he had written before, in "a complete unfolding of the body and the soul" [p. 197]. Only work written in this

---

6. See "Introduction: Beginnings."
7. Hanns Zischler, *Kafka Goes to the Movies* (Chicago: University of Chicago Press, 2002). The importance of *Schaffsteins Grüne Bändchen* (Schaffsteins little green books) for satisfying Kafka's imaginative needs is richly discussed in John Zilcosky's *Kafka's Travels: Exoticism, Colonialism, and the Traffic of Writing* (New York: Palgrave, 2003).
8. Think of Stephen Daedalus's stance, in James Joyce's *A Portrait of the Artist as a Young Man*. I have used the edition of R. B. Kershner (Boston: Bedford, 1993).

fashion deserved to survive. Toward the end of that year 1912, after reading "The Judgment" aloud at a circle of relatives and friends, he noted in his journal, "The inarguable quality of the story was confirmed" [p. 197].[1]

The production and reproduction, in the telling, of such ecstasy confirmed for Kafka his earlier promise as an author. The story looks back to many attempts to find the themes and forms that he could acknowledge as his children, offspring of a literary reproduction (he wrote in his journal: "The Judgment" "came out of me like a regular birth" [p. 198]. And the story also looks forward to a time of despondency, marked by such works as *The Metamorphosis* (written in 1912; published in 1915); *The Trial* (1914–1915; 1925); and "In the Penal Colony" (1914; 1919)—works about debasement and the failed promise of justification.

Erich Heller has noted a remarkable coded attestation of the importance of "The Judgment" for Kafka. During that night in which Kafka wrote the story, writes Heller,

> he felt, his diary records, that several times "I heaved my own weight on my back" and knew that "only *in this way* can writing be done." With his novel-writing, interrupted again and again, and stretching over years, he was, as we have heard him lament, "in the shameful lowlands of writing." Anyone having read and pondered these remarks cannot but think of them when the Lawyer in *The Trial* speaks to K. of two classes of lawyers (lawyers are, after all, the professional writers of "petitions" on behalf of the accused): the ordinary type who leads his client "by a slender thread until the verdict is reached" and the superior type who "lifts his client on his shoulders . . . and carries him without once letting him down until the verdict is reached, and even beyond it" (where there is "verdict" in the English translation, there is "*Urteil*" in the German, "judgment"). There is little doubt that Kafka was thinking of the story of that name.[2]

This is only one of a number of such moments in Kafka's writing in which "The Judgment" is commemorated. The story "In the Penal Colony," which Kafka was to write in the midst of composing *The Trial* in 1914, two years after the composition of "The Judgment, also encodes the continuing intensity with which the night of

1. On August 14, 1916, Kafka wrote to Mr. Meyer of the Kurt Wolff publishing house, asking to have "The Judgment" published as a book in its own right. " 'The Judgment,' which means a great deal to me, is admittedly very short, but it is more a poem than a story; it needs open space around it and, moreover, deserves that, I think" (L 125). Five days later, Kafka added, "The story . . . needs open space around it if it is to exert its force. It is also my favorite work and so I always wished for it to be appreciated if possible by itself" (L 126).
2. Erich Heller, *Franz Kafka* (New York: Viking, 1974), 95.

"The Judgment" lived on in him. The German word for the prisoner in "In the Penal Colony" is "der Verurteilte" ("the condemned man") [p. 36]. The explorer, who is visiting the penal colony, asks with amazement: "He doesn't know his own judgment?" (The word for "judgment" is, again, "Urteil.") To this the officer-in-charge replies, "No" [p. 40].[3] A good deal of the mythic autobiography of the writer is packed into these lines. The obvious connection runs between the act of not knowing or no longer knowing—disowning, forgetting—one's story "The Judgment," on the one hand, and the punishment that such forgetfulness will call down. If Kafka has forgotten the promise of future achievement implied in writing "The Judgment," then, in a certain sense, he deserves to be sentenced to death.

The officer then explains why the prisoner has been kept in the dark: "It would be pointless to tell him. After all, he is going to learn it on his own body" [p. 40].[4] Consider that "The Judgment" is about the destruction of the hero's engagement to a woman whose initials are FB (Frieda Brandenfeld). Consider that Kafka actually dedicated "The Judgment" to his future fiancée Felice Bauer with the words "A Story for Ms. Felice B." Kafka, who, only afterwards, in July 1914, was to suffer a broken engagement with his fiancée, would then experience the meaning of the story in actual truth, on his own body, as it were. Part of the mythic greatness of "The Judgment" for Kafka can have been its prophetic character.[5]

*　*　*

3. This point is discussed in Mark Anderson, *Kafka's Clothes: Ornament and Aestheticism in the Habsburg Fin de Siècle* (Oxford: Clarendon Press, 1992), 186.

4. In citing this passage, Heller comments: "The German original alludes to the idiom '*etwas am eigenen Leib zu spüren bekommen*'—'to come to experience something at first hand, i.e., on one's own body.'" And he adds: "Once again Kafka takes a figurative saying literally, and reveals the horror underlying . . . this particular phrase" (*Franz Kafka*, 18–19). But the prisoner will not get to experience his sentence on his own body (see chapter 4); so much for Kafka's alleged "literalization" of metaphor.

5. This point was made earlier by Anderson, *Kafka's Clothes*, 185. The consciousness of this mythic power only dawned gradually to Kafka. At first, in the letter to Felice Bauer dated October 24, 1912, he denied that there was the slightest connection between her and the events and persons of the story. This démenti is not surprising, since at the time Kafka contemplated an affiancement with her, but the bitter truth of the story is that, in the words of his own commentary of February 11, 1913, "The bride, who lives in the story only in relation to the friend, that is, to what father and son have in common, is easily driven away by the father" (D1 278–79). Afterwards, when the thought of the failure of the engagement had become apparent to him with an habitualness that made it no longer terrifying, he was content to change his mind. In the same diary, he wrote: "'Frieda' has as many letters as 'Felice' and the same initial, 'Brandenfeld' has the same initial as 'Bauer' [peasant] and in the word 'Feld' [field] a certain connection in meaning, as well" (D1 279). Furthermore, in a letter to Felice Bauer of June 2, 1913, he repeated this discovery in almost the same words, adding, then, the pleasant observation: "'Friede' [peace] and 'Glück' [happiness] are also closely related" (LF 265). A most suggestive feature of this letter is the error of fact it contains. Kafka says to Felice, "It was written at a time when I had not yet written to you, though I had met you and the world had grown in value owing to your existence" (LF 265). In fact "The Judgment" was written two days *after* his first letter to Felice. It is as if Kafka were in-

Crucial to "The Judgment" is what could be termed its "metaphorical drama." A diary entry for January 19, 1911, details Kafka's discovery of the expulsive power of words when they assume unwonted literal and/or metaphorical meanings. This reminiscence turns on an uncle's judgment (literally, *Urteil*) condemning a literary effort of himself as a child. "The usual stuff," the uncle says—a verdict that grows material enough, in Kafka's recollection, to drive the author out into "the cold space of our world" (D1 44) into which, in his story, he has only fictively condemned both brothers.[6]

A month later Kafka wrote into his diaries a little (unfinished) story called "The Urban World," which advances his coded theorizing of rhetoric. This story centers on an angry, a dangerous conversation between son and elder—here, the father. The son, Oscar, is an "older student," whose father is furious with him (D1 47).[7] In his first harangue the father exhibits the rhetoric of what Kafka will call "family language"—a tissue of threatening banalities in which words stick out like things.

> "Silence," shouted the father and stood up, blocking a window. "Silence, I say. And keep your 'buts' to yourself, do you understand?" At the same time he took the table in both hands and carried it a step nearer to Oscar. "I simply won't put up with your good-for-nothing existence any longer. I'm an old man. I hoped you would be the comfort of my old age, instead you are worse than all my illnesses. Shame on such a son, who through laziness, extravagance, wickedness, and—why shouldn't I say so to your face—stupidity, drives his old father to his grave!" (D1 48)

Compare Kafka's diary entry some months later (March 24, 1912) on the topic of family language:

> In the next room . . . they are talking about vermin and corns. . . . It is easy to see that such conversations prevent any real progress. It is information that will be forgotten again by both parties, and even now it proceeds in self-forgetfulness, without

---

clined to suppress the possibly germinative effect of his (first) letter to Felice on the production of "The Judgment." If letters have a status more or less similar to diary entries, then the thought that his first letter to Felice had preceded the writing of "Das Urteil" would not be subsequently attractive to Kafka, as perhaps impugning the mythic autonomy of its production and condemning all his poetic inspiration in principle to its heteronomous dependence on the preparatory work of diary writing.

6. This piece is discussed incisively by Clayton Koelb, in *Kafka's Rhetoric: The Passion of Reading* (Ithaca: Cornell University Press, 1989), 208–10. Koelb perceives its seminal importance as a treatise on rhetoric.

7. More than once, Kafka was preoccupied by another's irrational, excessive, intransigent hostility. See, for example, his story "A Little Woman" (1923).

any sense of responsibility. But just for that reason, because such conversations are unthinkable without absence of
mind, they reveal empty spaces that, if one stays with the
topic, can be filled only by reflections or, better, by dreams.
[p. 196]

Kafka will insert violent elements of his dreamlike inner life into
the blank spaces of family conversation. Now we are brought to
"The Judgment."

Behind "The Judgment" are the factors of self-division; the cod-
ing of this division as the struggle between the citizen and the
bachelor-writer; and the submission of their struggle to a higher
court, as represented by the father. Kafka's discovery and mastery
of a new device is crucial: the "family language" of "The Urban
World"—the cliché, the dead metaphor, that, as in the diary entry
of January 19, 1911, has the uncanny power to come to life when
taken literally and inserted into the struggle between the litigant-
self and its judge.

To dramatize the struggle between these parties as the struggle to
establish the literal and metaphorical dimensions of words: this
technique is crucial to "The Judgment." The word "dramatize" is
meant to be important. It points once more to the influence on the
composition of "The Judgment" of the Jewish theater that capti-
vated Kafka in the fall of 1911. But beyond this it refers to the
histrionics that flow into and intensify the inner theater of self-
questioning in Kafka's earliest diary entries.

In "The Judgment" the struggle between father and son turns
on the son's effort to make literal his father's words, as if this were
the way to turn him into a thing, and thence to seize and possess him. Their struggle is a contest for the power to make
metaphors.

At the outset it is Mr. Bendemann, the father, who displays his
mastery of this deadly game. The struggle turns on * * * the word
zudecken, meaning, literally, the act of "covering with a blanket."
The father asks his son Georg twice: "Am I completely covered up
now?" seeming, the narrator remarks, "to pay particular attention to
the answer. . . . 'Don't worry, [replies Georg,] you're completely covered up.' 'No!' his father shouted. . . . 'You wanted to cover me up, I
know that, you scamp, but I'm not covered up yet' " [p. 9]. And
here he seems to mean, "I'm not dead and buried yet." The father is
reading the word with elaborate metaphorical stress, which might
also include such secondary meanings of *zudecken* as "to cover" a
subject (so thoroughly as to bury its sense); "to heap meanings of

one sort or another on someone," as "to cover with reproaches"; finally, "to fit words to a meaning" with the negative implication of covering it up.[8] Here, the term *zudecken* has what the philosopher Gilbert Ryle calls "a higher-order function": it is a word connoting the intention of the speaker to "cover" a matter thoroughly, evoking the capacity of words to bury meaning.[9] And it is these various metaphorical senses that the father may be said to have uncovered in his son through the emphasis with which he pronounces the words "cover up."

Observe the sequence of moves in this rhetorical drama. The father's first tactic is to draw Georg into a scene where words seem to mean what they literally say. Georg accedes and reads the act of "covering up" his father in the required, literal way. This is the father's ruse to flush out his son's unconscious desires and then to ridicule them. And so it is with some shock value that the father trumpets out the son's repressed metaphorical meaning: "You wanted to bury me! You wanted to have the last word!" This is the first hostile act in the speech war that will amount to a fatal humiliation of Georg. Georg has been caught out seeming blind to the metaphorical meaning of (his) words.

The father takes fresh confidence from his victory. On attributing to Georg the metaphorical meaning of *zudecken*, he exults to think that Georg can have imagined that he (Georg) could ever have "covered him up." Here, where the word *zudecken* has a higher-order function, to take this figure literally, as the father initially pretends to do, means to deny his son a higher-order consciousness of the son's desire—to bury his father—and also to seem to acquiesce in a literal reading of himself, the father, as a stupid old Herrmanneut.

At this point, we are emphasizing the father's mischief. It is the cruelty of one who would trick or coerce another into taking his own figures literally. Certainly, one could also do "metaphorical violence" to another—crush him precisely by inserting his literal features into a violent metaphor. This, as the novelist Saul Bellow has claimed, would then lead to the sense that the hapless victim is owed "special consideration."[1] The fact, however, that in "The

8. Grimm illustrates the word *zudecken* with the phrase "ein Gedanke, ein Sinn, eine Wahrheit wird durch Worte zugedeckt" (a thought, a meaning, a truth is covered up [or closed off] by words) and further cites a phrase from Goethe: "die verschiedenen Auslegungsarten . . . die man auf den Text anwenden, die man dem Text unterschieben, mit denen man ihn zudecken konnte" (the various kinds of interpretation, . . . which are applied to the text, which are attributed, imputed or stuck on to the text, with which it could be covered-up [or closed off]). *Deutsches Wörterbuch von Jacob Grimm und Wilhelm Grimm* (Leipzig: Hirzil, 1954), 16:319.

9. Gilbert Ryle, *The Concept of Mind* (Chicago: University of Chicago Press, 1984), 195–98.

1. According to the narrator of Saul Bellow's novel *Ravelstein* (for Ravelstein, read: Alan Bloom, or Wolfowitz's mentor): "I had made the discovery that if you . . . spoke of some-

Judgment" so little consideration is shown the victim may follow from the story's self-reflexive reversal of this relation. Instead of the speaker's inflicting "the violence of metaphor," we see the speaker of metaphors—Georg himself—turned into the product of violence—the opaque thing. By reading triumphantly Georg's word *zudecken* as an intended violent metaphor ("you mean to bury me"), the father convicts Georg of opacity, of blindness to his own intention: he makes him consent to his own absence of mind. The narrator confirms this point exactly:

> A long time ago . . . [Georg] had firmly decided to observe everything very exactly so as to avoid being taken by surprise in some devious way, from behind or from above. Now he remembered that long-forgotten decision once again and forgot it, the way one draws a short thread through the eye of a needle. [p. 10]

With this figure we move into a turbulence of metaphors and acts of reading metaphors. The image of a man drawing a short thread through the eye of a needle thrusts itself out, struts as a lure to the reader to enter into this mad game of reading persons to death. And the reading demanded of the reader will be beset, too, by moments of remembering how to understand it and as promptly forgetting it, for it is so elusive. What, otherwise, is the status of *this* figure, inserted into a charged field of metaphorical turmoil by a not so innocent narrator?

Meanwhile, the game between father and son becomes more and more deadly, as Georg turns his father's revelation of the metaphorical underlayer of ordinary language into a parricidal weapon. The father says tauntingly to Georg, "I've got a splendid ally in your friend, and I've got your clientele here in my pocket!" [p. 11]. Georg now seems besotted by the impulse to literalize his father's words—to deny, to refuse the lesson he has just learned: only metaphorize. And yet he must deny this rhetorical lesson because the meaning of his exposed metaphor is so damning—it is the desire to kill his father! For: look how the desire persists. Georg thinks, "He's got pockets even in his nightshirt" and that "with this remark he [Georg] could make his father look ridiculous in front of the whole world" [p. 11]. Here, the aggressiveness of Georg's project is less transparent for the English than for the German reader, who will pick up the implicit metaphor. German knows the proverb "Das letzte Hemd hat keine Taschen" ("the last shirt has no pock-

---

one as a gross, belching, wall-eyed human pike you got along much better with him thereafter, partly because you were aware that you were the sadist who took away his human attributes. Also, having done him some metaphorical violence, you owed him special consideration" (New York: Viking, 2000), 152.

ets"); the last shirt is a funeral shroud. Georg's remark is cruel in a double register: he mocks his father by literalizing the pocket of "in my pocket," and toys with the idea of parricide by literalizing the nightshirt of "the nightshirt without pockets." To this ploy the father responds, as if deliberately to provoke more of the same aggression on Georg's part: " 'How you amused me today, when you came to ask me whether you ought to write to your friend about your engagement. He knows everything a hundred times better than you. . . .' 'Ten thousand times!' said Georg, to make fun of his father," but, as Georg takes his own bait, "while still in his mouth, the words took on a deadly serious note" [p. 11]. Kafka could not have made the point plainer: Whoever reads the metaphor literally—as an image—condemns it to the solitude of a thing; and as whoever reads the metaphor literally, kills it, whoever, as a metaphor, is read literally, turns monstrous or dies. Georg is making the fatal mistake of attempting to read his father as a feeble, toothless, old *thing* in soiled underwear, but his father is more than this!

He calls Georg "a devil." And, indeed, Georg's "devilishness" has been to deprive his father of a necessarily metaphorical existence, for the *father* cannot be defined as an assemblage of literal characteristics—the features of his old body. And now Georg, the literalist, is appropriately disarmed when the father issues him a death sentence: "And therefore know this: I now sentence you to death by drowning!" [p. 12]. Where it would serve Georg to let his father's language assume an only metaphorical resonance, he cannot: he has been turned into a creature who can only make his father's words thinglike. Now he is literally driven to his death by drowning, moist by his own petard.

So much, for the moment, to the mechanism through which the struggle between father and son is fought. What is the meaning of "The Judgment" as a whole?

* * *

Readers feel obliged to produce a hypothesis about the meaning of the end, quite as the philosopher Theodor Adorno warned: not to do so would mean to be destroyed as if by the force of an onrushing locomotive. "Each sentence of Kafka's says 'interpret me,' " and this is especially true of the conclusion of "The Judgment."[2] One needs to get beyond the sense that Kafka's execution of Georg is a mad, unjustifiable destruction of life. For what we have, after all, is hor-

2. "Through the power with which Kafka commands interpretation," Adorno writes, "he collapses aesthetic distance. He demands a desperate effort from the allegedly 'disinterested' observer of an earlier time, overwhelms him, suggesting that far more than his intellectual equilibrium depends on whether he truly understands; life and death are at stake." Theodor W. Adorno, "Notes on Kafka," in *Prisms*, trans. Samuel and Shierry Weber (London: Spearman, 1967), 246.

rendous: a son is condemned to death by his father, a life sentence is revoked and rewritten as a death sentence. Yet, at the end, Kafka, not alone among his readers, felt an ecstatic sense of relief, imagining (as Brod remembers from a conversation with him) "a strong ejaculation"! [p. 198].[3] How can this bliss be squared with the horror of a family execution?

To be entitled to such joy, one must understand Georg as a figure for something not yet alive, something whose value is less than "real life"; he must be an only factitious mask of the author, who arranges Georg's fall and who says, *after* Georg has let himself fall: "At that moment, the traffic going over the bridge was nothing short of infinite" ("In diesem Augenblick ging über die Brücke ein geradezu unendlicher Verkehr") [p. 12].[4] With its multivalent image of "traffics" and its fusion of contradictory temporal ecstasies, the conclusion radiates elements of bliss and horror. One recalls Kafka's aphorism of the drowning man: "The man in ecstasy and the man drowning— both throw up their arms. The first does it to signify harmony, the second to signify strife with the elements" (DF 77).

We need to grasp the threat to Kafka that the personality of Georg represents. Aside from his ugly struggle with his father, Georg has also chosen to stay engaged to his fiancée rather than keep faith with his bachelor friend. As a result, Kafka, the narrator, whose perspective at this point is very nearly identical to Georg's, faces a crisis. The bachelor friend is an inescapable reminder of the writing destiny. And now, as someone who breaks faith with literature, how can the narrator continue? He proceeds, in a perspective distorted by anxiety, to envision the father. This is a coherent move—for the son, too, means to embark on family life. But what follows in this perspective must not be what can actually happen to Kafka in life; the world depicted in "The Judgment" is the world as it must *not* be. The father reveals himself to be the true father of the Russian friend, the semblance of the writer. If Kafka is to grasp the life of literature as sponsored by the father, as his "ideal" offspring, then writing becomes an only compulsive behavior, the neurotic offshoot of the father's vitality. We recall that Kafka did indeed write, in his "Letter to His Father," imagining the worst, "My writing was all about you; all I did there, after all, was to bemoan what I could not bemoan upon your breast."[5] In this perspective, writing

---

3. Max Brod, *Franz Kafka: A Biography*, 129.
4. The standard Muirs' translation is unfortunate since it tends to associate the water in which Georg drowns with the "stream" of traffic going over it. There is no "stream" in the German.
5. Further: "It was an intentionally long-drawn-out leave-taking from you, only although it was brought about by force on your part [note: the vitality, the violence], it did take its course in the direction determined by me" (DF 177). Note that the Muirs actually write, "it did *not* take its course. . . ." This is a bad mistake.

cannot be preferred to marriage. The decision to marry becomes a compelling alternative at the same time that it becomes worthless, for this is the institution that perpetuates neurosis. Being Georg, the narrator cannot turn anywhere and escape guilt: guilt toward the fiancée, guilt toward the friend, and worse, the knowledge that this guilt is itself nothing—a "psychological" event, an instance of family language, and not an essential concern of the self. If this is the case, then Kafka has been sentenced to death.[6]

How, then, could such a crisis turn to ecstasy? It would, by the logic of catharsis. Georg's destruction provides an intense, explosively concentrated relief to a mind "above" him that has arranged the perfect annihilation of a dreaded fate. With this sentence, Kafka identifies and expunges a disastrous inclination of his personality.

But the cathartic route is not the strongest way to read this ending. It is a seductive hypothesis, of course; and it is in fact doubly seductive. The story has presented the father in a stereoscopic perspective. In one respect, he is the empirical father, a reminiscence of Herrmann Kafka; as such, he too crashes to his death. In this case another piece of (illicit) bliss is produced through the logic of purgation: both the negativity of the mask (the bachelor) and the negativity of its sponsor (the real father) are extinguished. But the father can be seen—and felt—otherwise. In another, stronger perspective, his influence works in an entirely positive way. He deals not in curses but in blessings. If the bachelor is the "true son" of the father, then this father is the "true father" of the writer. In this case, the energy of the final scene flows out of a wish-dream come true: the father is splendidly vital. "He beamed with his insight" [p. 10]. And it is this being who loves and approves his son precisely on the condition that he be the bachelor, a condition of the possibility of being a writer. Franz Kafka, the bachelor-writer, is the true son of the loved father. His tormentingly doubled persona having been refined down to its writerly essence, there is no longer any need for such a thing to exist as the genealogical line of Herrmann-father and Georg-son—the practical, marrying businessman. If only Kafka's true father would bless his bachelor-hood—his, in the family sense, sterility, yet, in the extraordinary, literary sense, fertility. In the conclusion to this story, vision becomes event.

This is the core of Kafka's ecstasy, conveyed by the movement following the judgment that drives Georg into the river to drown: Banish the nightmare of an eternal, monotonous, familylike proces-

6. I published the gist of the preceding paragraph in *Franz Kafka's The Metamorphosis* (New York: Bantam, 1972), xv-xvi. I present it now as if it were written by another person, since I no longer hold to its argument.

sion of the will that must not be the case; allow it to transport the wish-dream of the ascetic.

I have said that with this sentence, we have to do with a voice surviving Georg's. In this fictional world, it is a moment occupied entirely by the narrator, the narrator who, from the start, has only pretended to identify his optic with Georg's but has in fact designed his execution.[7] What else does this moment convey?

To answer this question, we must look again at the diary entry that Kafka wrote with a fine elation, the night after he spent composing his story:

> I wrote this story, *The Judgment*, in a single push during the night of the 22nd–23rd, from ten o'clock to six o'clock in the morning. My legs had grown so stiff from sitting that I could just barely pull them out from under the desk. The terrible strain and joy as the story developed in front of me, as if I were advancing through a body of water. Several times during the night I carried my own weight on my back. How everything can be risked, how a great fire is ready for everything, for the strangest inspirations, and they disappear in this fire and rise up again. * * * The confirmed conviction that with my novel I am in the disgraceful lowlands of writing. It is only in this context that writing can be done, only with this kind of coherence, with such a complete unfolding of the body and the soul. * * * Many emotions borne along in the writing—for example the joy that I will have something beautiful for Max's *Arkadia*; thoughts of Freud, of course; in one passage, of *Arnold Beer*; in another, of Wassermann; of a (smashing to pieces) in Werfel's giantess; naturally also of my "The Urban World."

Joy that I will have something beautiful for Max's "Arkadia." This "judgment," conveyed by joy, tends to confirm the jubilant reading of "The Judgment" as the wish-dream that invokes paternal protection of the bachelor-friend at the cost of the destruction of the fiancé-Georg; and here both Kafka's father and Max Brod function as ideal representatives of the public world.[8]

7. Consider Martin Amis's aperçu: "The distance between author and narrator corresponds to the degree to which the author finds the narrator wicked, deluded, pitiful or ridiculous." *Money* (Penguin: New York, 1984), 229.

8. Such a "reader"—the critic I have chiefly in mind—is David Schur, whose lustrous *The Way of Oblivion* (Cambridge, Mass.: Harvard University Press, 1998) concludes with a reading of "The Judgment" that has stimulated my own, especially, his pages 246–65. The flow of traffic, which in the moment of George's drowning goes over the bridge, propels, for Schur, Kafka's afterlife. This is something of which Kafka was aware, to judge especially from the diary entry he wrote the morning after, in which he identifies the aura of ecstatic composition as the fulfilled pledge of literary achievement. The poor immortality (Mallarmé's "faux manoir") imagined by the businessman/fiancé and presumptive father must go under for the sake of the author's craved-for afterlife. A paradoxical fusion of the full time of the Now (*Jetztzeit*) ("at this moment" [in *diesem Augenblick*]) and the historical detachment of the preterite ("*was . . . going* over the bridge" [*ging* über

Consider, further, that the word "judgment," while designating as a synecdoche a certain action within the story world (the sentencing of Georg), also designates the totality of the story's action. And furthermore, it designates the judgment that Kafka twice made on the factual life of the story itself. This tripleness is preserved in his remark, "The inarguable quality of the story was proved." Some of its compact wittiness may have gone unnoticed: the inarguability that was confirmed is not only that of the story, is not only that of Kafka's first diary judgment on the story, it is also that of its afterlife, its survival in the empirical world where stories are read aloud and published.

The critic David Schur stresses the point that, with this story, Kafka would have "something beautiful" for *Arkadia*; here, the empirical reality of publishing has thrust itself in advance into the conclusion of the story.[9] The story intuitively mimes a coming reality; this moment completes the exhilaration of the moment at the outset when the real comet in the telescope thrust itself into the journal—and completes the circle of "The Judgment." With the annihilation of Georg, whose goal is marriage, we have the decisive fictional achievement: the empirical person of the diary entry is extinguished for the sake of the fiction he shall become.

Is this a merely conventional allegorical interpretation? In one sense it is: the story *codes* it. In another sense it is not an imposed or arbitrary allegory. It is a riddle. The story does no more than direct the reading along this allegorical path to an achieved piece of writing, in vivid contradistinction to Georg Bendemann's mendacious letter to a friend. If the story is coded, the code has to be struggled for. The result is driven along by the son's and father's struggle for the friend as a putative figure of authenticity, the "true son" of a "true father."

We have a marker of this consciousness of achievement in the story itself, one clear enough to have provoked the happy verdict that Kafka pronounced after composing the story and then, a few days later, after reading it "at Baum's." The story seemed strong enough to have survived its violent birth. Weight falls again on the bliss of the dream come true that the father be the friend and support of the bachelor's bizarre fertility; for the friend, as "the connection between father and son . . . [and] the major thing they have in common" [p. 198], can mean only: their procreativity. The fa-

---

die Brücke]) that alleges infinitely ongoing process ("nothing short of *infinite* traffic" [ein geradezu *unendlicher* Verkehr]) evokes the afterlife transcending the ecstasies of ordinary temporal distinction: it is the *Zug*, the draught that moved Kafka along as he wrote "The Judgment" in a single sitting, and the flow of the greater traffic of the world—sexual, commercial, epistolary, vehicular. With this "giving birth" of "The Judgment" ("a *regular* birth" [ein regel*rechtes* Geburt]), Kafka shall now enter this flow, truly and for good: the traffic is "ein *geradezu* unendlicher"—the word *geradezu*, difficult to translate, can mean "downright" and contains the word *gerade* (direct, straight).

9. Ibid.

ther, in this wish-dream, wants his son to be the bachelor-writer and wants his first real "offspring"—the story itself—to be born into the world. In the sexual imagery of the closing sentence, "The Judgment" pronounces the judgment on the story itself as a warrant of Kafka the writer's afterlife. Kafka foresees that with this story he will survive Georg, his dreaded antiself, exposed as a false and lying mask; and by his death, Kafka the bachelor, his father's true son, will enter the stream of literary renown. That is the sense of the infinite stream of traffic that flows over the bridge. For all its demotic imagery, it is a being superior to the individual life; it is the confirmation of Kafka's promise as a writer as the promise of cultural immortality. A gnostic truth shelters in a Gnostic text.

* * *

A current of affirmation continues to flow from "The Judgment" into the diary entries written immediately afterwards. We have seen this elation marked in more than one place in the story itself. "The Judgment" creates a father after the son's own heart—the son who is a writer. The father rises up "beam[ing]" with "insight" [p. 10]— a phantasmatic projection of the father who bears the insight that is the son's own and that the son imputes to him: Recognize that you are the father of the writer I am.

The true son of the father is the writer perishing of solitude. The father wants him to write: he is the herald of the new commandant of "In the Penal Colony," no longer the comminatory Jewish God who does not want him to write. "The Judgment" imagines the father as an active principle, the neverceasing author of the son's transformation into the writer. He answers to the god who says: "This man is . . . to come to me" (DF 35). He is the true father, and "The Judgment" is a moment of return to him.

And yet Kafka could not himself assume the patriarchal virility wishfully depicted there. When he reviews his story, some months later, at the beginning of the new year, in a diary entry for February 11, 1913, it is as one who stands outside patriarchy, figuring as the *mother* of the story that "came out of me like a regular birth" [p. 198]. To be neither the good father nor the good father's son will mean to be subject to further coercion, willy nilly, at his actual master's hand, who retains the power to be cruel and false. And now, indeed, in the winter of 1912, Kafka's father is the empirical father Herrmann Kafka with a vengeance, the investor in an asbestos factory, who needs his son for asbestos work: how must Kafka have suffered together the images of the conflagration he was and the dealer in asbestos his father wanted him to be. These are figures in the counterlife to the fiery act of writing: (1) Felice Bauer, (2) the paterfamilias Herrmann Kafka, and (3) asbestos. Kafka was driven to thoughts of suicide.

From November 17 to December 7, 1912, in a period of despondency following the composition of "The Judgment," Kafka wrote *The Metamorphosis*. The monstrosity of the vermin is the measure of its disparity from the son who bathed in his father's radiance, the son who was born some months before as a being who could walk on water. *The Metamorphosis* marks a transformation, indeed; the core transformation is Kafka's being marked negatively as a writer, as a desolate fate. Here, his plan to marry Felice Bauer acquires a higher potency and a higher danger: it can exclude his fulfillment as a writer. Equally, his father's plans for him as a factory manager: what of the plans his other father had for him? The conflict between the two fathers is extreme, is critical. The monster that appears at the outset of *The Metamorphosis* is the transmogrified, the distorted, the damaged form of the new creature he has become: the writer in extremis. And if he is never to fulfill the promise of the new being affirmed in "The Judgment"—his genuine being?—he will remain until his death the monster, the family invalid.

The outcome of *The Metamorphosis* is appalling: Kafka paints the small bliss of the dissolution of Gregor Samsa next to the wide bliss of the dissolution of Georg Bendemann and the apotheosis of the empirical self of Kafka the author. It is as if even the empirical gloom impacted in the vermin were itself so diminished, so abject, that there is little left to burn, and even the elation of death must be dimmed down in a being sunk so low.

Abbreviations

The following abbreviations are used throughout Corngold's text and notes, followed by the appropriate page numbers.

CS   *Franz Kafka: The Complete Stories*, ed. Nahum N. Glatzer. New York: Schocken, 1971.

DF   *Dearest Father*, trans. Ernest Kaiser and Eithne Wilkins. New York: Schocken, 1954.

D1   *The Diaries of Franz Kafka, 1910–1913*, trans. Joseph Kresh. New York: Schocken, 1948.

D2   *The Diaries of Franz Kafka, 1914–1923*, trans. Martin Greenberg (with the assistance of Hannah Arendt). New York: Schocken, 1949.

GW   *Gesammelte Werke in zwölf Bänden, nach der kritischen Ausgabe*, ed. Hans-Gerd Koch. Frankfurt a.M.: Fischer Taschenbuch Verlag, 1992.

L   *Letters to Friends, Family, and Editors*, trans. Richard and Clara Winston. New York: Schocken, 1977.

LF   *Letters to Felice*, trans. James Stern and Elizabeth Duckworth. New York: Schocken, 1973.

M   *The Metamorphosis*, trans. and ed. Stanley Corngold. New York: Norton, 1996.

DANIELLE ALLEN

Sounding Silence†

How admiringly the officer in the penal colony surveys his instrument of execution. With what zeal he explains its mechanism. Curator that he is, he carefully avoids touching the surface of the Old Commandant's drawings. But how lovingly he traces their pattern in the air. The visiting researcher, the voyager, cannot read the script that the officer marks for him, but he understands the performance enough to return the compliment that the officer's gestures demand. He says "evasively," of the drawings and the script, "It's very artistic" (*Es ist sehr kunstvoll*).[1] "Yes," said the officer with a laugh, putting the folder away again, "it's no copy-book lettering [*keine Schönschrift*] for school children" ("IPC" 135 [159]). The officer's gestures establish a context for judging his beloved Commandant's apparatus: it should be viewed, or read, as a work of art. He wants this machine to be seen, however, not merely as one specific artwork but as the very form of art in general. He constantly insists on the transferability of what is "artistic" from one domain of technique to another. The component of the machine that writes on or, better, stabs into the condemned is like a farm implement, a harrow, but with a critical difference. This particular harrow, the officer claims, a piece of glass, performs with far greater artistry than does any ordinary farmer's tool; it is much more artful (*viel kunstgemäßer*) ("IPC" 129 [153]).

Many critics, including Stanley Corngold, have usefully explored how the penal apparatus represents the art of writing itself, but in the story the officer makes an even bigger claim than do the critics.[2] For him, the apparatus represents not merely writing, but "art." Central features of "art-making," he suggests, pertain to widely diverse technical practices: farming, writing, punishment, and drawing. The voyager notices the implication of the officer's

---

† From MODERNISM/*modernity* 8, n. 2 (2001), 325–34. Copyright © 2001 The Johns Hopkins University Press. Reprinted with permission of The Johns Hopkins University Press.
1. Franz Kafka, "In the Penal Colony," in *The Transformation ("Metamorphosis") and Other Stories*, ed. and trans. M. Pasley (London: Penguin Books, 1992), 135; Franz Kafka, "In der Strafkolonie," in *Erzählungen* (Frankfurt am Main: Fischer Taschenbuch Verlag, 1995), 159. The English translation will hereafter be abbreviated "IPC." When both English and German are cited simultaneously, the German citation will follow the English in brackets (or in parentheses after block quotations).
2. Stanley Corngold, *Franz Kafka: The Necessity of Form* (Ithaca, N.Y.: Cornell University Press, 1988).

views and asks of the Old Commandant, "Did he then combine everything in his own person? Was he soldier, judge, engineer, chemist, and cartoonist [*Zeichner*]?" ("IPC" 131 [155]). Indeed, he did. Above all, however, the Commandant was a technician; the officer, curator of his superior's works of art. Kafka's "In the Penal Colony" ruminates on punishment's status as an art, and therefore dwells also, through its insistence on the transferability of "artfulness" between media, on the dismal possibility that all arts contain an element of punishment.

The officer guides the voyager (or hopes to guide him) through an appreciation of the texts and visual signs of the apparatus. He wants him to learn to read the machine. But the officer also regularly and insistently leads the researcher through an experience of sounds, particularly the sound of silence. When the officer describes the sort of reading a condemned man is supposed to do—he is supposed to read his sentence in his body—the officer says that the condemned "purses his lips as if he were listening. You've seen that it isn't easy to decipher the script with one's eyes; but our man deciphers it with his wounds" (Es geschieht ja weiter nichts, der Mann fängt bloß an, die Schrift zu entziffern, er spitzt den Mund, als horche er) ("IPC" 137 [160]). His wounds seem to make some sound to the condemned and so reading becomes listening. But what sound is there in pain? In *The Body in Pain* Elaine Scarry has argued that pain itself is inherently aphasic because it is impossible to vocalize any precise or meaningful calculus of pain.[3]

Momentarily I will analyze the sounds that the condemned hears but first it is crucial to consider how his wounding sounds to the onlookers. As the officer rhapsodizes the process of the execution in the days of the Old Commandant, the focus is as much on what can be heard as on what is seen:

> Before hundreds of pairs of eyes—all the spectators standing on tiptoe right up to the top of the slopes—the condemned man was laid under the harrow by the commandant himself. . . . And then the execution began! No discordant note disturbed the working of the machine [Kein Mißton störte die Arbeit der Maschine]. Many [of the spectators from the penal colony] even ceased to watch and lay with their eyes closed in the sand; all of them knew: Now justice is taking its course [Jetzt geschieht Gerechtigkeit]." ["IPC" 140 (164)]

Justice takes its course quietly and, more importantly, as quiet. Punishment is, Kafka suggests, the art of sounding silence. In the old days, all of the spectators knew, as they lay with their eyes

3. Elaine Scarry, *The Body in Pain: The Making and Unmaking of the World* (New York: Oxford University Press, 1987), 3–11.

closed in the sand, that punishment's point lay also in its sounds. In this, the essential feature of the apparatus is not the bed, not the designer, not the harrow, but the felt stub (*Filzstumpf*), the revolting silencer. In the officer's first description of the felt, he says "it can be easily adjusted to push straight into the man's mouth," and its "object is to prevent screaming." The greatest artfulness in the apparatus lies in precisely its mechanisms for producing silence. And since "In the Penal Colony" insists on the transferability of "artfulness" from one domain of technique to another, Kafka's worries about silence, in this story, must extend to other arts as well.

To return to the officer who manipulates and aspires to produce silence, he too has worries about the silence that is his medium. He suspects that the silence surrounding his machine in the penal colony may no longer reflect acquiescence in, awe at, and fear of the forms of justice enacted by the machine but rather his, and the machine's, complete irrelevance. Indeed, Kafka uses the phrase, *"in der Strafkolonie,"* in the first paragraph of the story in order to report that there is now, under the New Commandant, diminished interest in the inventions of the former regime ["Das Interesse für diese Exekution war wohl auch in der Strafkolonie nicht sehr groß"] ("IPC" 127 [151]). The officer is not only the sole member of the colony to defend the apparatus, but he is also, and more forcefully, solitary in his sustained interest in it.

The officer is not, however, completely convinced that the new kind of silence should be heard as disinterest. Just before he describes how the spectators formerly buried their eyes in the sand to listen to the machine—that is, in the first half of the same paragraph—he addresses this second type, the silence of disinterest, and claims that the people of the colony only *pretend* not to care. He claims that, "although no one will admit it, there are still plenty of supporters of the Old Commandant" ("IPC" 139).

> If you went into the tea-house today, that's to say on an execution day, and listened to what people were saying you'd probably hear nothing but ambiguous remarks [Wenn Sie heute, also an einem Hinrichtungstag, ins Teehaus gehen und herumhorchen, werden Sie vielleicht nur zweideutige Äußerungen hören]. They'd all of them be supporters, but under the present commandant and given his present beliefs they're completely useless as far as I'm concerned. ["IPC" 139–40 (163)]

From silence in the valley to quiet doublemeanings in the tea room; how different these silences are. The artist-officer aspires to reproduce the silence of admiration, fear, and acquiescence, but faces instead the dismaying silence of irrelevance. "In the Penal Colony," then, turns on the equivocal (*zweideutige*) nature of silence, and on the tension between silences that acquiesce or say yes, and those that say no, or, what is the same, it doesn't matter.

Silence is relevant to "In the Penal Colony" in two modes: as yes and as no—the absolutely opposed sounds of silence. This equivocation in silence comes through most clearly in the story's climax, its moment of superlative punishment, when the officer subjects himself to his own justice. Then the machine begins to work on its own, like an apparatus of the divine, yes, a *deus ex machina*. After he strips and is strapped to the bed by the soldier and the condemned man, the officer cannot hit the machine's crank to start it, but it doesn't matter:

> The bed vibrated, the needles danced over the skin, the harrow moved gently up and down. The voyager had been staring at it for some time before it occurred to him that a wheel in the designer should have been grating; and yet all was still, not even the faintest whirring could be heard. As a result of this silent working the machine positively escaped attention [Der Reisende hatte schon eine Weile hingestarrt, ehe er sich erinnerte, daß ein Rad im Zeichner hätte kreischen sollen; aber alles war still, nicht das geringste Surren war zu hören. Durch diese stille Arbeit entschwand die Maschine förmlich der Aufmerksamkeit]. ["IPC" 150 (174)]

Something about the officer's unspoken confession and his decision to punish himself achieves at least the formal perfection of the Commandant's penal regime: total silence. But to know what is perfect about this peculiar punishment, and whether or why Kafka frets about it, it is necessary to understand the judgment that precedes it, for there has indeed been a judgment.

Quite early in the story, the voyager intuits that he has been delegated by the New Commandant of the colony to judge his predecessor's penal apparatus. Nonetheless he worries that any criticism of the machine will provoke the colonists to respond, "You are a stranger, hold your peace." During their discussion at the scene of execution, the officer makes the voyager's status as judge explicit, and he also spells out more precisely the questions of voice and silence at issue in the trial of the machine. He desperately wants the voyager, not to hold his peace, but to call out an appeal on behalf of the officer in the court of public opinion. He wants this in order to prove that the silence around the machine is still definitive of its power, and not a mark of its impotence. It's therefore the machine's production of silence that must be judged by the voyager. He must determine whether the apparatus cranks out yes's or no's.

The officer imagines that the judgment of his machine might

take one of two possible courses. The researcher might return to town after the execution and talk about the machine, or he might return and be silent. The officer expects the respective outcomes of speech and silence to be radically different. If the voyager should return to town and drop a chance remark such as "We only used torture in the Middle Ages," the officer expects to see the New Commandant, upon hearing this remark,

> pushing his chair aside and rushing out on to the balcony, I can see his ladies streaming out after him, I can hear his voice—the ladies call it a voice of thunder [*ich höre seine Stimme—die Damen nennen sie eine Donnerstimme*]—and what he now says goes like this: "A famous researcher from the West . . . has just said that our own procedure . . . is inhumane. Given this verdict [*Urteil*] . . . , I naturally cannot tolerate this procedure any longer. With effect from today I therefore ordain—etc. [*und so weiter*]." ["IPC" 142 (166)]

Kafka need not divulge *what* he will ordain; the content of the Law doesn't matter, only its process, and so the sentence concludes with "and so on." Only the form of verdicts and pronouncements matters.

Should the commandant pronounce his new ordinance, his authoritative voice of power would be laid over the researcher's interpretative voice. About this, the officer says, "You will want to cry out [that you never gave such a verdict] but a lady's hand covers your mouth . . ." ("IPC" 143). In this first account of the course of justice, the voyager's failure to keep his silence about the machine paves the way for the voice of thunder, the sounds that smash (this is Jehovah's voice). The apparatus's brutal silencing power will be replaced by a lady's—also brutal as represented here—palm. In this scenario, the silence produced by the apparatus is one of irrelevance, weaker even than a woman's hand.

In his second scenario of the course of justice, the officer imagines that if the voyager should initially hold his peace, the reverse effects will obtain.

> Unless you are asked directly, you should on no account express an opinion; but what you do say must be brief and non-committal; it should appear that you find it hard to discuss the matter, that you feel embittered, that if you were to speak openly you would almost start cursing and swearing. . . . [*man soll merken, daß es Ihnen schwer wird, darüber zu sprechen, daß Sie verbittert sind, daß Sie, falls Sie offen reden sollten, geradezu in Verwünschungen ausbrechen müßten. . . .*]. Your bitterness, which we want them to recognize, is of course amply justified, but not in the way the commandant imagines. He will

naturally misunderstand it completely and interpret it to suit his own book. That's what my plan depends on [Er natürlich wird es vollständig mißverstehen und in seinem Sinne deuten. Darauf gründet sich mein Plan]. ["IPC" 144 (168)]

The officer's plan rests firmly on silence's shiftiness and equivocation, and on the interchangeability of yes and no. He expects that the New Commandant, taking silence for criticism, will invite the researcher to speak before the assembled public, not recognizing that his silence actually implies an affirmation of the machine. Once given the opportunity to speak, the voyager will, the officer hopes, make a passionate appeal for the machine; this defense of the apparatus will then be followed by the officer's own. The officer promises, "If my speech doesn't drive him out of the hall, it will force him to his knees, so that he has to confess: Old Commandant, to your power I bow" ("IPC" 145). Here the power of the officer's fantasies about voice, silence, and potency become clearer. The officer expects to use silence to prepare an appeal that will in turn silence others. He appeals for a spoken defense that will confirm the power of the silences produced by the machine. But his appeal for an appeal, his call for a voice to set against thunder, is rejected. When the officer asks, "That is my plan; are you willing to help me carry it out?" the voyager responds, simply, "No" ("IPC" 146). This verdict on silence defines the silence around the machine as that of irrelevance and thus convicts the officer, machine, and Old Commandant not of injustice, but of impotence. It is precisely because the story is interested in force—not in justice—that it is difficult to read it politically.

Now condemned, the officer has himself been silenced; his case is closed by a no that came in place of yes. What happens next in the story unfolds "as if" of necessity; silence is, of course, at the heart of it all. In response to the no, the officer is silent, and blinks several times with his eyes fixed on the voyager. The latter asks if the officer wants an explanation. "The officer nods silently" ("IPC" 146). The voyager provides an explanation and

The officer turn[s] towards the machine, grasp[s] one of the brass rods and then, leaning back a little, look[s] up at the designer as if to check that all was in order. . . . It didn't look as if the officer had been listening. "So the procedure hasn't convinced you?" he murmur[s], smiling as an old man smiles at the nonsense of a child. . . . "Then the time has come." ["IPC" 146]

At this point, the officer begins to prepare his own punishment.

Now, one could say that self-imposed punishment, that which is no imposition, is no penalty, and that instinct or intuition whittles the beginning of this scene of punishment to a single detail.

> He only had to stretch out a hand towards the harrow for it to raise and lower itself several times, until it reached the right position to receive him; he merely gripped the edge of the bed and it began at once to vibrate; the felt stub came to meet his mouth, one could see that the officer did not actually want it, but his hesitation lasted only for a moment, he quickly submitted and accepted it. All was now ready, only the straps were still hanging down at the sides, but these were clearly unnecessary, the officer had no need to be fastened down. ["IPC" 150]

Only the felt stub is unwanted. Almost imperceptible is his hesitation before it. Almost imperceptible is the punishment it enforces. The art of the machine is in forcing the convict to take this felt. Remember that the first time the officer had described the felt, he remarked, "Its object is to prevent screaming and biting of the tongue. The man is bound to take the felt of course, since otherwise his neck would be broken by the neck strap" ("IPC" 130). The force of this transaction precedes what "counts" as the force of punishment, the actual inscription of the body. Through the felt, the machine manipulates psychology as well as physiology; it is not merely the body, as so many have argued, that feels the force of the apparatus' punishment; it is also the voice.

What Andreas Gailus calls the "somatization" of the ideologies inscribed by the machine, the transformation of ideologemes, like "honor thy superiors," into bodily matter also involves teaching the psyche, in the form of the voice, that it cannot escape the body. The second time the officer remarks on the felt stub, he says of it, "After two hours, the felt stub is removed, for the man no longer has the strength to scream" ("IPC" 136). This is the point at which the condemned begins listening to his wounds, which means "pursing his lips" as if he were listening. The opaque script is as good as silence, and the condemned comes to know voicelessness, the incapacity to contest meaning. The condemned knows he is beyond the realm of disagreement or acquiescence—here is his enlightenment (*Verstand*).

In focusing on the role of silence in punishment, Kafka has noticed something about the practice of punishment that even the master interpreter of its meaning-making functions missed. In *Discipline and Punish* Michel Foucault famously elaborates the transition from the royal punishments, the spectacles of power and torture of the body of the eighteenth century, to the democratic penitentiary and the discipline of the soul of the liberal nineteenth century.[4] He frames the book's argument with two examples, an account of the 1757 execution of a regicide and a list of rules for young prisoners from 1837. Notable in both stories, although Foucault does not note it, is the amount of attention paid to voice.

The eyewitness to the eighteenth-century execution carefully records when screams, pleas, and curses were expected from the condemned, and when they in fact occurred. Near the end of his account, the witness reports this, "When the four limbs had been pulled away, the confessors came to speak to him; but his executioner told him that he was dead, though the truth was that I saw the man move, his lower jaw moving from side to side as if he were talking" (*DP* 5). The narrative of the execution is structured by a concern for what happens with the man's voice, not merely his body. Similarly, the list of rules for young prisoners begins with the requirement that "At first drum-roll, [they] rise and dress in silence," and concludes with the injunction that after the convicts go to bed at the end of the day, "the cell doors are closed and the supervisors go the rounds in the corridors, to ensure order and silence" (*DP* 6–7). Silence is as central to the punishment Foucault describes, whether royalist or democratic, as to Kafka's, but his own account misses the definitive element of punishment in a variety of Western cultures, though it is institutionalized differently in each.

Punishment seeks to control not merely the body in the one case and the soul in the other, *but always the voice*. The condemned are those and only those who have exhausted their appeals, their calling out, or, as in "In the Penal Colony," have been prevented from calling out at all. They are permitted no defense and are denied even the opportunity to cry out. Their conviction stands, and with it the regime's narrative of who and what they are. Only silence can secure the meaning of a punishment, which always at some level means "a final answer." Silence must therefore fall on a punishment if it is to succeed.

Of course, there are differences in the types of silence demanded by monarchic spectacle and by liberal discipline and observation. The monarchs Foucault describes want silence only after they have extracted particular kinds of sounds—notes of confession, tones of guilt, cries for pardon—but they do in the end wish to still the wagging jaw. Monarchic punishment wants the "quieting" to be *seen* so that royal force will be felt. Democratic punishment, in contrast, wants not a full performance of the death of voice, but, simply, silence. Since democratic punishments, in contrast to monarchic

---

4. Michel Foucault, *Discipline and Punish: The Birth of the Prison*, trans. A. Lane (London: Penguin Books, 1991); hereafter abbreviated *DP*.

ones, rest on the fiction that the polity's laws and punishments reflect the perfect consent of the citizenry (rather than on force), silence is all the more imperative in a democracy. Silence after
punishment signifies the end of contest; it seems to make sensible
a general communal acquiescence in the methods of making meaning that (claim to) have brought closure to the case of a given criminal. Silence implies first acquiescence, then consent. The U.S. has
recently introduced what are being called maxi-maxi prisons, where
prisoners suffer solitary confinement in "administrative segrega-
tion" for violations of prison regulations committed while in other
prisons. The most striking feature of these prisons is the noise that
fills their hallways: a cacophony of shouts, groans, bellows, rattling
of door handles, and banging of possessions against walls. No less
striking to the observer is the silence that falls when the doors to
the prison are closed and one stands outside its walls.[5] In monar-
chies, silence is proof of force; the democratic silence makes all
citizens complicit in punishment.[6] Kafka is indubitably right to represent punishment by depicting silence. And thus music seems to
be exactly the wrong genre for thinking about punishment.

Or does it? Perhaps it seems wrong only if one employs a limited
idea of what silence is. The third time the officer describes the
work done by the piece of felt, he refines his account of silence.
Recall the scene where the officer contrasts the silence of his contemporaries' meaningless chitchat in the tearoom to the sort of silence the colonists used to experience at an execution:

> And then the execution began! No jarring sound [discordant
> note] disturbed the working of the machine. Many even ceased
> to watch and lay with their eyes closed in the sand; all of them
> knew: Now justice is taking its course. In the silence, nothing
> could be heard but the moaning of the condemned man, half
> muffled by the felt. Nowadays the machine cannot wring from
> the man any groans that are too loud for the felt to stifle; but
> in those days a corrosive fluid that we are no longer permitted
> to use dripped from the inscribing needles. ["IPC" 140]

The harrow and the felt do not collaborate merely in order to silence; their art is more diabolical. They first provoke the condemned to voice, and then silence him. When the people in the
penal colony lie down, closing their eyes in the sand, to listen, they
are listening to the performance of silence, to groans stifled. Silence is surely not the absence of sound—aren't there always at
least rattling leaves, scratching pens, and purring hard drives, or

5. "ABC News Special Report," *Nightline*, 20 August 1998.
6. Danielle Allen, *The World of Prometheus: the Politics of Punishing in Democratic Athens*
(Princeton, N.J.: Princeton University Press, 2000), 223–4.

one's own heart—silence must more particularly be the absence of
voices that summon our attention. The penal apparatus therefore
orchestrates the force of voice, and its death, its final descent into
silence. The colonists are listening to an opera. And so music is
not, after all, the wrong art for representing punishment.

But where does this leave writing, for this is the art that most critics believe Kafka to be representing (along with his anxieties about
it) in "In the Penal Colony." I do not mean to erase "writing" with
the word "music," nor to suggest that one mode of perfor-mance can
simply substitute for another. But the story does lead to the conclusion that the art of punishment and the art of music both express
something frightful about art per se. The machine writes not just to
inscribe, but to provoke the very groans that it silences. If writing is
the subject of "In the Penal Colony," then it is specifically the kind
that aspires to silence others and, perhaps, also its author.

Kafka's representation of the penal apparatus lays bare, naked and
acquiescent, as the figure of the officer, the aspiration of art to be
definitive. Over and over we hear in the critical literature that the
term "Kafkaesque" has come to define the modern, or even postmodern situation: "Kafka is in the air," says political theorist Jane
Bennett in a 1994 article.[7] And as Corngold puts it, "the modern
sensibility has become Kafkaesque."[8] The officer punished himself
with the phrase, "Be Just." He may as well have punished himself
with the phrase, "Be definitive," for this is where he has failed, as
Kafka has not. Perhaps Kafka was anxious about the danger of art's
success, about his own potential to silence—or to provide answers.

And yet, if the artist achieves silence in response to her work, is
that good or bad? Is silence a mark of awe and acquiescence or of
apathy? An aspiration to produce silence generates its own contradiction, since silence is also the artist's worst reward. The officer is
one such victim of his decision to work in the medium of silence
and to fall silent in the presence of beauty. The artistry of the machine has worked on him. It is beautiful to him, and therefore definitive and also just. He cannot bear the idea of dismantling the
machine. Kafka's exploration of a problem with art compels a realization that beauty insists on retention. Or rather, when people decide that something is beautiful, they cannot bear the idea of its
destruction. The beauty of the machine seems to the officer to
answer a raft of questions—about monarchy, about justice, about
use—that have never been asked. The officer's obsession with the

7. Jane Bennett, "Kafka, Genealogy, and the Spritualization of Politics," *The Journal of Politics* 56 (1994): 650–70.

8. In *Franz Kafka* Corngold contends that "Kafka helps create the 'description' of an experience of terror whose existence thereupon confirms his work for its clairvoyance"
(2 n. 4). His corpus has "a transparency" that is "the fortuitous result of the great horror
of modern history—the technical application of political terror" (2).

beauty of his machine blocks him from a rigorous ethical analysis of his practices of punishment. Its beauty, definitive to his eyes, constitutes a distraction.

Kafka is famous for defamiliarizing the familiar. One wonders then whether this problem of beauty's distractions is itself meant, finally, to look ordinary. Is the apparatus in the penal colony meant to look like something recognizable in daily life? Is the penal colony meant to look like an ordinary place? Do problems of beauty and of being definitive in fact inhabit the everyday realm of punishment that we see all the time without seeing? I can think of no better illustration of the power of aesthetic force to distract us from ethical questions than the Chicago Metropolitan Correctional Center built by Harry Weese in 1975 at 71 W. Van Buren Street. Extraordinarily beautiful, the prison is triangular and wafer thin, the cream stone almost disappears from some perspectives, body become nothing in a ritual of reverse transubstantiation. Its windows are slits. This is what sets it apart from the rest of the sky-reaching, far-looking buildings of the Chicago Loop. In everything else it conforms to the aesthetic standards of downtown. It is, at the very least, nice for people in nearby buildings to look at.

The American Institute of Architects *Guide to Chicago* offers a description of the building that includes verbal oddities that are symptoms of the aesthetic distraction provoked by the building. The entry includes these remarks:

> Above the tenth-floor mechanical room, identifiable by its angled air intakes, are five-inch-wide windows for the inmates' rooms. The long, thin windows are meant to symbolize an opening that people could not pass through. Not caring much about symbolism, some architecturally disrespectful inmates discovered a way around this design feature and escaped. Lights now wash the exterior, and bars have been added to the interiors of cells."[9]

So strong is the artist's belief in the power of art to be definitive that the building project, as described here, involved a complete confusion of the work that symbols and bars are supposed to do. But symbols and aesthetic objects do do a great deal of work; they may not effectively confine bodies, but they do constrain attention. Their force shows in their ability to distract spectators from questions of ethics, judgment, and practice. Definitiveness is a power to distract. The question, then, that Kafka worries over in "In the Penal Colony" is: to what extremes can aesthetic distraction go? Or, how much power is working against our effort to judge? If silence is

9. *American Institute of Architects Guide to Chicago*, ed. A. Sinkevitch (New York: Harcourt Brace and Company, 1993), 75.

his worry, it is also his relief. The aesthetic object that falls into disregard, or grows stale, grants a furlough to spectators so that they may judge.

Kafka himself concludes his story with a further silence.

> While the voyager was negotiating down below with a ferryman to take him out to the steamer, the pair of them [the soldier and the condemned man] came racing down the steps, in silence, for they did not dare to shout [*rasten die zwei die Treppe hinab, schweigend, denn zu schreien wagten sie nicht*]. But by the time they reached the foot of the steps the voyager was already in the boat and the ferry man was just casting off. They could still have managed to leap into the boat, but the voyager picked up a heavy knotted rope from the deck, threatened them with it and so held them at bay. ["IPC" 153 (177)]

WALTER HINDERER

An Anecdote by Kafka: "A Fratricide"†

Kafka's short narrative "A Fratricide" [p. 73], composed in 1917, has the air of a detective story, asserting beyond a shadow of a doubt that what is to follow has been proved. We have to do here with a murder that is described with painstaking detail but nonetheless remains unexplained. We hear how the murder took place, who the perpetrator was and who the victim; but the motive that led the perpetrator to commit this murder, in contrast with the biblical story of Cain and Abel, is provocatively absent. Aside from the perpetrator and the victim, two others are mentioned: an observer and witness of the murder by the name of Pallas and the wife of the victim, Julia. We hear that the night was moonlit, that the perpetrator, despite the piercingly cold night air, had on only a thin blue suit; that his jacket was unbuttoned; that he gazed at the murder weapon, a remarkable instrument, "half bayonet, half kitchen knife," and indeed struck it "against the bricks of the pavement until it gave off sparks"; and that finally, like a virtuoso, "drew it like a violin bow over the sole of his boot." At the same time he listened to the "sound of the knife" and "the fateful side street," into which his victim must soon turn. But in all this there is not a word about what motivated the deed of the perpetrator—only the question why

---

† Excerpted from " 'Der Kleist bläst in mich, wie in eine alte Schweinsblase': Anmerkungen zu einer komplizierten Verwandtschaft," forthcoming in *Kafka und die Weltliteratur*, ed. Manfred Engel and Dieter Lamping (Göttingen: Vandenhoeck & Ruprecht, 2005). Translated by Stanley Corngold, with permission. Page numbers to this Norton Critical Edition appear in brackets.

"Pallas, a person of private means," who hears everything "with his collar turned up," his dressing gown belted around his broad body, and "shaking his head," observed the event but does not intercede. The victim, Wese, "walks into Schmar's knife" while everything remains in its "senseless, inscrutable place."

To be sure, Schmar comments on his deed, remarking at first, with no great originality, "Julia waits in vain!" and crying out, after his murderous act: "The bliss of murder! Relief, a lightening, won through the flow of another's blood! Wese, old phantom of the night, friend, beer-hall companion, you seep away in the dark earth beneath the pavement" [p. 74]. To judge from these statements, we have to do with the lustful murder of a friend, and the question put to the victim, Wese, reads: "Why aren't you just a bubble of blood, so that I could sit on you and make you disappear for good?" We have to do with the brutal extinguishing of another being, an alien being, yet one very likely familiar enough to be a kind of doppelgänger or double, to judge from the word "brother" embedded in the "Fratricide" of the title. The text's own commentary is scarcely different from the perpetrator's in being as discompassionate as it is laconic: "Water rats, slit open, produce a sound like Wese's." The conclusion offers, as in a drama, a scenic tableau: Frau Wese falls over the body of her husband; "this nightgowned body belongs to him, the fur coat that closes over the couple like the grass of a grave belongs to the crowd" [p. 75]. And then one sees finally how the murderer, "his mouth pressed against the shoulder of the policeman," is led away by the policeman on light feet.

Although it is true that Kafka's novels and many of his longer stories (viz. *The Stoker, The Judgment*) are narrated mainly from a single perspective—all actions reported by a mind that overlaps with that of the main figure—this anecdote, "A Fratricide," represents a departure. Each of the persons is characterized by features of the sort that any number of outside observers could report. The murderer wears a thin jacket; his manipulations of his murder weapon are registered. The reader observes the dressing gown of Pallas, the neighbor, and the fox fur and nightgown of the victim's wife. The victim Wese is seen chiefly as someone wearing a hat who leans on his cane—with one telling exception: he is assigned an inward quality that is given to no other character, but it is done in order to make an objective point. He allows himself to be enticed by the "night sky," by the "dark blue and the gold," as someone evidently susceptible to the moods imparted by nature and aesthetic impressions. But it is for a purpose that these two domains of Wese's life—office and home—are separated from each other; for in this way a boundary is delineated, and it is precisely in this boundary zone that Schmar waits for his prey to stick his knife into him.

Now, in shattering his body, he destroys the "being" that, in his sarcastically spoken "obituary," is alluded to in the "blossoming dreams" that will no more ripen. This same distinction between the body and the higher faculties is also played out in Wese's case in the difference between his "heavy remains" and "the blossoming *dreams.*" Something like the same structure informs the final scene: Frau Wese is said to apportion her intimate "nightgowned body" to her husband but her fox fur to the crowd.

There is no question but that Schmar kills Wese's body while intending to kill his "being" (*Wesen*).[1] Indeed, these names function like abstract signs (the German "Schmarre" means a "slash," "cut," "gash"), and the action of the fratricide remains oddly unreal. Only Schmar's lust for murder stands out and reminds one of the murderous passion of the officer in *In the Penal Colony*. It is typical, too, of the anecdote-form in the hands of Heinrich von Kleist, Kafka's beloved predecessor, that despite the initial detective-story impression made by "A Fratricide," the situation diverges from a possible motivated content, and the (virtual) content has an only schematic character. What Kleist, in one of his anecdotes, has an officer say might have come from the pen of Kafka: "People demand, as the primary condition of truth, that it be probable, and yet probability, as experience teaches, is not always on the side of truth."[2] As a consequence, one may denounce error as much as one wants—thus the figure Antonio, in Kleist's first play *The Ghonorez Family*—"and still it is often the only way to truth."[3] In his notebooks Kafka formulates this paradoxical matter richly: "I go astray. The true path takes its way along a rope that is not stretched up aloft but barely above ground. It appears to be aimed more at tripping one up than to be walked on."[4]

Kleist and Kafka, it can be said, make the principle of opposition and a certain poetics of negation the basic structure of their narratives.[5] Not only the lie, but also error and deception are turned into a universal system.[6] This leads to tautologies as well as contradic-

---

1. The name *Wese* suggests the German word *Wesen*, meaning "being" [*Editor*].
2. Kleist's texts are cited from *Sämtliche Werke und Briefe*, 2 vols, ed. Helmut Sembdner (Munich: Hanser, 1977); here, 2:228.
3. Ibid. 2:3.
4. Franz Kafka, *Nachgelassene Schriften und Fragmente II,* ed. Jost Schillemeit (Frankfurt a.M.: Fischer, 1992), 113.
5. See Karlheinz Stierle, *Text als Handlung* (Munich: Fink 1975), 98–130; Walter Hinderer, "Immanuel Kants Begriff der negativen Grössen, Adam Müllers Lehre vom Gegensatz und Heinrich von Kleists Ästhetik der Negation," in *Gewagte Experimente und kühne Konstellationen*, eds. Christine Lubkoll and Günter Oesterle (Würzburg: Königshausen & Neumann, 2001), 35–62.
6. An allusion to the protest of Josef K., the hero of Kafka's *The Trial*, at the argument of the court priest that "you don't have to consider everything true, you just have to consider it necessary." "A melancholy opinion," said K. "Lies are made into a universal system." Franz Kafka, *Der Proceß. Roman*, ed. Malcolm Pasley (Frankfurt a.M.: Fischer, 1990), 303 [*Editor*].

tions, a situation summed up in a remark by the philosopher Ludwig Wittgenstein: "Tautology and contradiction are the limit-cases of the combination of signs—namely, their dissolution."[7] This thought can be applied to a poetics: Kleist and Kafka develop a technique of representation that bursts the bounds of traditional logic and the world "that is the case" so as to convey new insights and experiences. From the perspective of a poetics of negation, one could indeed say that "the proposition that negates determines a logical position different from that of the negated proposition,"[8] though here, of course, one might begin to ask whether, in dealing with Kleist and Kafka, one is entitled to speak of a logical position at all. For this reason their anecdotes frequently end in paradox, admittedly often taking over the generic structure of the parable but then only to destroy, parody, or transform it. This is true, among other works, for Kafka's variation of the Prometheus legend [p. 129], his novel interpretation of "The Silence of the Sirens" [p. 127], and the parable of the guardian of the Law [p. 129].

"A Fratricide," as mentioned, is underlain, for contrast, by a biblical scene, the fratricide of Cain and Abel; this story Kafka appropriates and restages. Because the motivation to this fratricide is absent or hidden in code, the text admits of many different readings, turning on the topics of professional life versus individual freedom; of self-division resolved by an act of violence; of a doppelgänger or double threatening one's identity; or of the total collapse of a friendship.[9] I wish to stress in the fratricide a variation of the theme of struggle, which could be paralleled with Kafka's intricate (though unfinished) youthful work *The Description of a Struggle*. Here it is relevant that Kafka's influential and beloved precursor Kleist addresses this very theme in his paradox titled "On Reflection."[1] Employing the logic of inversion, Kleist usurps the general view that cold-blooded and lengthy reflection prior to a deed is especially praiseworthy. In a fictive speech he instructs a fictive son that reflection is, in fact, "far more fitting *after* a deed than *before* it." For if it comes into play prior to or during the moment of decision, it would seem only to "confuse, inhibit, or suppress the force necessary for an action, which flows out of a splendid feeling." It is precisely this instruction that the murderer Schmar also follows. In him reflection occurs after the deed; before, only his passionate inner state of mind is shown: "where everything is freezing, Schmar is

7. Ludwig Wittgenstein, *Tractatus logico-philosophicus* (Frankfurt a.M.: Suhrkamp, 1963), 57.
8. Ibid., 40.
9. For interpretations, see *Kafka-Handbuch*, ed. Hartmut Binder (Stuttgart: Kröner, 1979), 317f.
1. Kleist, 2:337f.

on fire." The "splendid feeling," which lends action its necessary force, leads to Schmar's emotional exclamation after his deed: "The bliss of murder!" We have not forgotten that the topic of Kafka's story is an act of murder, but Schmar's exclamation reveals that we have to do here with a *struggle*, which offers "relief, a lightening, won through the flow of another's blood." In his paradox, Kleist asserts that "life itself is a struggle with fate" and hence "acting and struggling" are the same thing. He then goes on to speak of "the wrestler":

> In the moment the wrestler has his opponent in his grip, he simply cannot proceed according to any other consideration than what occurs to him in the moment; and anyone who attempted to calculate which muscles to flex and which limbs to move in order to defeat his opponent would unfailingly adopt the weaker position and be vanquished.[2]

In this perspective we see Schmar behaving like a marionette or an automaton, for consider the following polysyndeton[3] in Kafka's description of his act: "And into the throat from the right, and into the throat from the left, and a third thrust deep into the belly, Schmar sticks his knife" [p. 74]. Note that in this formulation the murderous act occurs first, and only thereafter do we have an indication of its subject. It is also striking that Wese the victim marches along on the above-mentioned line of intersection of his double life as office worker and husband; "in principle it is very sensible," but in doing so he walks "into Schmar's knife." In a word, he runs into the knife of his fate. To be sure, Schmar's "victory," if that is what it is, is a Pyrrhic victory, for at the close he is led away by the police, and in this sense neither has survived the life struggle mentioned in Kleist's paradox:

> Whoever does not hold life, like such a wrestler, in his grip, after all the twists and turns of the struggle—after all the resisting, pressing, eluding, and reacting—feels it and senses it: whatever his intention, he will not prevail in any discussion, let alone in a battle.[4]

In Kafka's "A Fratricide," then, neither Schmar nor Wese can cope with life's struggle. Two aphorisms of Kafka's might serve as commentary: the first, precisely appropriate to our theme, reads: "One of the most effective means by which evil seduces is by summoning to a battle."[5] The other appears to take up indirectly Kleist's remarks and add color to them: "Death is in front of us,

2. Ibid.
3. The deliberate and excessive use of conjunctions in successive words or clauses [*Editor*].
4. Kleist, 2:337.
5. Kafka, *Nachgelassene Schriften*, 114.

more or less like a painting on the classroom wall of Alexander's great campaign at Issus. Everything depends on our darkening the picture or indeed extinguishing it through our actions while we are still alive."[6] Not inadvertently, these aphorisms are part of Kafka's sustained discussion of the Fall of Man, which held a firm position in the discourse on the preparation for Enlightenment and German Idealist thought in the late eighteenth-century from Kant to Schiller, Hegel, and Schelling until it was submitted to a radical revision in such a work, par excellence, as Kleist's "On the Marionette Theater."[7] For Kleist as well as Kafka, the Fall of Man does not promise progress but an unambiguous falling back, a regress of human existence into absurdity and paradox. Kleist's "On the Marionette Theater" speaks of "mistakes ever since we have eaten of the Tree of Knowledge."[8] Kafka also reflected over and over again on the consequences of this loss:

> Ever since the Fall of Man we are essentially equal in the ability to know good and evil; nevertheless, we seek here our particular advantage. But it is only on the far side of this knowledge that the true differences begin. * * * No one can be content with this knowledge alone but must strive to act in accordance with it. But the strength to do this is not given to him, hence he must destroy himself, even at the risk of thus not being able to acquire the necessary strength, but he has no other choice than this last attempt. (That is also the meaning of the threat of death accompanying the prohibition to eat of the Tree of Knowledge; perhaps that is also the original meaning of natural death).[9]

As a consequence, for Kafka, we are not sinful "because we have eaten of the Tree of Knowledge but also because we have not yet eaten of the Tree of Life." And he draws the following conclusion: "The state in which we find ourselves is sinful independent of guilt."[1] There does not appear to be any way of healing this break in human existence. Here Kafka (now unlike Kleist) offers no image of the "concave mirror" in which "knowledge, as it were, could vanish to infinity."[2] And yet one finds the theme of the negation of life in Kafka in all manner of permutations, at times ending even in a

6. Ibid. 133.
7. Also see Manfred Frank/Gerhard Kurz, *ordo inversus. Zu einer Reflexionsfigur bei Novalis, Hölderlin, Kleist und Kafka,*" in *Geist und Zeichen. Festschrift für Arthur Henkel,* ed. Herbert Anton et al. (Heidelberg: Winter, 1977), 95. Peter-André Alt, "Kleist und Kafka," *Kleist-Jahrbuch* (1995), 111ff. In *Negativität der Erkenntnis im Werk Franz Kafkas* (Tübingen: 1981), 19–48, Sabine Kienlecher analyzes in detail Kafka's reflections on the Fall of Man.
8. Kleist, 2:342.
9. Kafka, *Nachgelassene Schriften,* 132f.
1. Ibid. 131.
2. Kleist, 2:345.

fragile victory of logic over despair. "The power of negation," reads a note written in his diaries in 1920, "this most natural expression of the perpetually changing, renewing, dying-away, living-anew of the human fighting-organism—this we always have, but not courage, while life is after all negation, hence negation [is] affirmation."[3] In Kafka's negation of negation a trace of "original, pre-reflective being"[4] appears to be conjured and reproduced, as in the life of the story "A Fratricide," which constructs the struggle *poetically*, and hence negates it. * * *

WALTER SOKEL

Identity and the Individual, or Past and Present

Franz Kafka's "A Report to an Academy" in a Psychoanalytic and a Sociohistorical Context[†][1]

Kafka's "A Report to an Academy" beautifully shows the close connectedness of a Freudian reading with a historical, sociopolitical one. In that respect, it represents a fictional analogue to Horkheimer and Adorno's *The Dialectic of Enlightenment* by bringing to light the full meaning of the Freudian notion of the Ego when it is understood in its relationship to the bourgeois individual of Enlightenment and capitalism. A psychoanalytic reading that does not bring out the—in the broadest sense—political dimension of the link between Kafka and Freud cannot do justice to the richly historical dimension of the "former ape's" report to the Academy. Western colonial imperialism—of which the marauding "hunting expedition" of the "firm" of Hagenbeck, an obviously capitalist enterprise, is a typical example—marks a radical rupture in its victims' lives. As for many other victims of Western colonial imperialism, Rotpeter's subjugation has overturned his existence and cut it into two halves, only tenuously connected with each other.

There are, immediately upon his capture, two threads connecting the temporal halves of his existence before and after capture—an inner and an external one. The former is his memory, the latter is his

3. *Tagebücher in der Fassung der Handschrift,* ed. Michael Müller (Frankfurt a.M.: Fischer, 1990), 861.
4. See Frank/Kurz, 95.
† From *The Myth of Power and the Self: Essays on Franz Kafka* (Detroit: Wayne State University Press, 2002), 268–91. Reprinted by permission of the publisher.
1. * * * A greatly abridged version [of this essay] appeared in German in *Moderne Identitäten. Studien zur Moderne,* ed. Alice Bolterauer and Dietmar Goltschnigg, 212–24. Vienna: Passagen Verlag, 1999.

body, his physical life. In the radically new situation into which he finds himself thrown upon waking up in the cage, his memories of his previous life have become totally useless. His experiences as a "free ape" have lost all bearing upon and cannot help guide him in his unprecedented situation. His past has ceased to have any relevance. "I had had so many ways out before and now none at all" ("Ich hatte doch so viele Auswege bisher gehabt und nun keinen mehr.") (Kafka 1994, 304). If there is to be a "way out," it will have to be totally different from any in the past. There is no example for what he faces.

His memories are not merely useless; they have turned dangerous. For they hold out the temptation of a return to the past that is impossible and, if attempted, might easily be fatal. A conflict has emerged between internal and external continuity in the ape's existence. Memory has become a threat to survival. The continuity of the inner self has turned perilous to the continuation of life. That enduring of the past that is identity threatens to foreclose the organism's future. Incarcerated in his stiflingly narrow cage, the ape desperately needs a "way out" in order to live.

> I had no way out, but had to procure one, for without it I could not live. Crushed forever against that box wall—I would inevitably have croaked.

> Ich hatte keinen Ausweg, musste mir ihn aber verschaffen, denn ohne ihn konnte ich nicht leben. Immer an dieser Kistenwand—ich wäre unweigerlich verreckt. (Kafka 1994, 304)

However, as long as the ape remains tied to his past, his family and species, his identity, he is bound to his cage. For, "at Hagenbeck's apes belong at the box wall" ("Aber Affen gehören bei Hagenbeck an die Kistenwand"). External force has dictated that his species identity must doom him to permanent imprisonment, and thus to early death. His past has become his cage and his executioner. His self-preservation demands the renunciation of his identity: "thus I ceased to be an ape" ("also hörte ich auf, Affe zu sein"). This, as he calls it, "clear beautiful train of thought" ("klarer, schöner Gedankengang") marks an epochal event—the emancipation of the individual from its inherited, collective identity, its "essence" (Kafka 1994, 304). Rotpeter's self-preservation at the cost of his species identity depends, in exact conformity with the Freudian view of the ego's emergence, upon the collaboration of two factors—the organism's narcissistic concern for the body as a separate individual entity and its attunement and adaptation to external reality.

For Freud, the ego develops in opposition to memory that encapsulates and preserves past experience. In his early "Project for a

Scientific Psychology," Freud introduces a sharp dichotomy between memory, the repository of the organism's past, and perception, which is turned toward and attuned to its present surroundings. Being both outward- and present-directed, accurate perception is vital to the individual's survival. It is the origin of both the ego and rational thinking. With the organism's orientation in its present situation, which perception makes possible, the emotional hold or "cathexis" of memory may become distracting and is "not to be carried beyond certain amounts" (Freud 1966, 326). A potential conflict arises between the incipient ego, which, building on perception, is to safeguard the individual's survival, and the organism's remembrance. While memory is freighted with emotion, perception works in the service of quick adaptation to the ever-changing circumstances of the current environment. Its task is to take cognizance of the present, which is also the presence of whatever surrounds the organism and what it encounters at any given moment. Spatial presence and temporal present merge into one. Emotions invested in remembered but no longer present scenes divert the individual's attention from the urgent tasks at hand. Memory evokes a "hallucinatory reality" that might easily interfere with the essential needs of life. Thus the system of perception has to guard against and, to a certain extent, inhibit memory. Descending from perception, the ego has to carry on that task.

The ego's fundamental opposition to fixation on the past characterizes Freud's ego concept throughout his work. In his posthumously published *Outline of Psychoanalysis*, Freud still defines the ego as being determined mainly by "what it has itself experienced, by what has been accidental and current" ("das selbst Erlebte, also Akzidentelle und Aktuelle") (Freud 1991, 69). The ego is concerned with current and recent experience rather than the distant past. It serves the life of the individual rather than that of the species. Reality for the ego is the here and now, the circumstances confronting and affecting the individual in its immediate present.

That turn to the present, to perception and to observation of his new environment, marks the ape's attitude as the initial shock of his trauma, which makes him cling to his past for consolation, yields to the urgent need to deal with his unbearable situation. If he is to find succor in his wretched present, he has to turn his attention to it and not lose himself in dreams of his past. He has to struggle against the lure of memory and inhibit the impulse to return to the past regardless of the impossibility of such an undertaking. Instead he has to begin to survey the scene surrounding his cage and to espy a "way out" consistent with it. His awakening interest in the world of his captors is the sign of his will to live.

As we have mentioned, the ego for Freud has two sources. One is perception. The other is concern for the body, the need of self-preservation. "The ego," says Freud, "is first and foremost a bodily ego" (Freud 1961, 26). What gives rise to the ego as an agency separate from the instinctual and libidinal part of the psyche, later called the Id, is the will to preserve the body. Thus one source of the ego lies in narcissism in its basic nature as channeling of libidinal energy or "love" toward the individual's body. In this original and fundamental form, "narcissism . . . would not be a perversion, but the libidinal complement to the egoism of self-preservation, a measure of which may justifiably be attributed to every living creature" (Freud 1957, 73). The instinct or drive for self-preservation is universal, and the psychic organ entrusted with it is the ego. Thus while one side of the ego is outward-directed, the other side is self-directed. It is solicitous concern for the body, its welfare, its comfort, its safety, and, above all, its continued existence. The first side is a function serving the second. The ego develops as the organism's need to pay close attention to the external world precisely in order to safeguard the body's survival and prosperity to which the instincts and desires of the Id pay no heed. "For the ego, perception plays the part which in the id falls to instinct" (Freud 1961, 25).

The contrast between instinct and perception, the starting point and foundation of consciousness and rational thought, has not only a spatial dimension—instinct being built into the organism while perception mediates with the outside world—but also a temporal one. Instinct is always bound to the past. It directs the organism to repeat again and again the behavior it has always followed. It is inherited from the generic past that precedes the individual. Instincts for Freud are, therefore, always "conservative," indeed reactionary, since they always seek to regain a previous state of affairs. Thus they quite consistently culminate in the death drive that Freud sees inherent in all organic matter as its wish to return to its origin in the inorganic. The system of perception, on the other hand, which serves the individual's self-preservation through observation and adaptation to an ever-changing external reality, compels the organism to adopt at times new and unprecedented behavior. Thus the reality principle is also the motor of progress. It is life-enhancing.

The life that the ego's reality principle safeguards and advances is the life of the individual. The ego is concerned with the survival of the body as a discrete, separate entity, independent of its family and species. The ego's province is the ontogenetic sphere, the sphere of individual existence, rather than the phylogenetic, the life of the species that is transmitted through eros. Individuation, the individual organism's fundamental drive to maintain and assert itself, is for Freud the only means that life possesses to counteract and delay the triumph of the death drive.

> [T]he instincts of self-preservation, of self-assertion and of mastery . . . are component instincts whose function it is to assure that the organism shall follow its own path to death, and to ward off any possible ways of returning to inorganic existence other than those which are immanent in the organism itself. . . . What we are left with is the fact that the organism wishes to die in its own fashion. (Freud 1955, 39)

The confluence of the instinct of self-preservation with the "reality principle," a confluence that explains the Freudian notion of the ego, illuminates Rotpeter's narrative of his mimetic adaptation to an alien species. He insists on surviving as an individual, even at the price of his "natural," his species identity, and he does so by adopting the "reality principle," by literally turning around and changing his outlook. He ceases to be riveted to the back of the cage, behind which he imagines his native jungle, and starts to look outward, into the present surrounding his cage. He begins to search, no longer for a way back to his origin, but for a "way out" of his prison, even though it leads into the realm of his jailers. His absolute will to live compels his concentrated attention to the external presence that he finds just outside the bars that keep him immobilized.

What Rotpeter calls a "way out" marks the turn to the present necessary to individuated life. The present is the temporal aspect of the presence of the new reality that surrounds him. It is a sociopolitical reality formed by his captors and jailers, hitherto instinctively shunned by him. However, life, life as an individual organism, desperately needs a fruitful connection with external reality, no matter how distasteful to one's instinct and "nature." The ape's natural, instinctive, and spontaneous reaction to his capture had, of course, been to recoil from the new world outside his prison and turn backward and inward toward his lost freedom. However, in the situation imposed on him by the power structure of human society, natural instinct would condemn him to die either sooner or later, sooner by a doomed attempt to flee, later by languishing in a cage too cramped to permit survival. His self-preservation demands the "unnatural," the renunciation of his nature. Propelling him forward out of his cage, it will eventually also lift him upward on the evolutionary scale. Rotpeter's story exemplifies Freud's theory of development. Only contingent intervention by external forces that block the instinctive and "natural" ways can, according to Freud, lead to ascent toward a new and higher form of life.

> [T]he phenomena of organic development must be attributed to external disturbing and diverting influences. The elementary living entity would from its very beginning have had no wish to

change; if conditions remained the same, it would do no more than constantly repeat the same course of life. (Freud 1955, 32)

Freud's statement could be a description of the motivating circumstances of Rotpeter's development into a humanlike being that is forced upon him solely by "external, disturbing and diverting influences," and not by any inner drive.

Rotpeter sharply contrasts the lifesaving way out of the cage with freedom, "freedom on all sides." He is at pains to make sure that we do not confuse his way out with freedom:

> I am afraid it will not be exactly understood what I mean by "way out." I use that term in its most common and fullest sense. On purpose I do not say freedom. I do not mean that great feeling of freedom on all sides. Perhaps I had known it as an ape and I have met human beings who yearn for it. But as for myself, I asked for freedom neither then nor now.

> Ich habe Angst, dass man nicht genau versteht, was ich unter Ausweg verstehe. Ich gebrauche das Wort in seinem gewöhnlichsten und vollsten Sinn. Ich sage absichtlich nicht Freiheit. Ich meine nicht dieses grosse Gefühl der Freiheit nach allen Seiten. Als Affe kannte ich es vielleicht und ich habe Menschen kennen gelernt, die sich danach sehnen. Was mich aber anlangt, verlangte ich Freiheit weder damals noch heute. (Kafka 1994, 304)

To understand the significance of Rotpeter's "way out" we should examine the notion of freedom from which he is so intent on distinguishing it. In temporal terms, freedom for him lies in the past. He might perhaps have known it when he had still been nothing else but an ape. He refers to his being an ape as being "free," while calling his becoming human a "yoke" (Kafka 1994, 299). In spatial terms, freedom is situated in a remote distance, immeasurably far beyond the ship that is now carrying him toward Europe, beyond the ocean that stretches between his present captivity and his lost home. Freedom belongs to apedom. Human beings can only long for it, but if they try to attain it, as circus artistes and acrobats, for instance, the pathetic futility of such attempts merely arouses the laughter of apes. Human civilization precludes freedom.

By its great remoteness from the captured ape's present, freedom assumes the aspect of a transcendent Beyond. It has become unreachable to empirical reality. The former ape calls human pretensions at freedom a "mockery of holy Nature" ("Verspottung der heiligen Natur") (Kafka 1994, 305). The adjectival attribute, "holy," alludes to that naturalized version of Christian transcendence associated with Rousseauan Romanticism. "Freedom on all sides" suggests the Infinite, the Absolute, an unbounded unrestricted totality. From the perspective of civilization, however, into which Rotpeter has fallen, it has become synonymous with death. It is an illusion inimical to life, one against which, as we shall see in greater detail, the individual has to be on his guard.

In contrast to absolute freedom, the relative freedom of the "way out" fastens on the immediate present of the lived moment and the immediate presence of the reality in which the subject happens to find himself. Unlike absolute freedom, it is not a way back into memory, but a way out into the world as perceived by the senses. Initially this is a hostile reality, the source of Rotpeter's misery. However, in seeking a way out, he has to accept this reality, monstrously difficult as this seems to his natural instincts, because it is the only one that offers a way out of his cage. The way out into that world demands a colossal sacrifice of dreamed and remembered pleasure and a submission to great unpleasure. However, this unpleasure alone can save him from the infinitely greater unpleasure of slowly dying in the cage. It is an exchange, a payment with a smaller unpleasure for escape from an incomparably greater one.

Very different from freedom, the way out leads into a very limited space, circumscribed by the limits of the ship. Surrounded by the vast ocean, it is a small area, also a kind of cage, but one promising a greatly enlarged room for free movement than the cage in which Rotpeter squats. This difference in degree is enough to amount to one in kind, to a true liberation. Measured against the total impotence of existence in the cramped cage, the scope of movement, the degree of independence and power that the way out will eventually attain for Rotpeter is so considerable that it must be called essential.

In temporal terms, the way out leads forward through the present into the future. Present and future, in fact, are united in it as means are to the end. The present turns into an instrument employed toward the future.

Rotpeter's way out comes about through his looking out, his observing and familiarizing himself with the society of his captors. Preceding and making that possible is his abandonment of his initial hostility. Instead of withdrawing from them, he begins to observe his prison guards and finds: "They are good people, after all" ("Es sind gute Menschen, trotz allem.") (Kafka 1994, 305). This new evaluation of his jailers is decisive to his outward turn, his acceptance and eventual utilization of external reality for the sake of self-preservation and -advancement. Looking out of the cage becomes the preparation for stepping out of it. The sentence following Rotpeter's declaration that finding a way out of his cage is a necessity for his survival sums up his realization of the power structure prevailing at Hagenbeck's: "at Hagenbeck's apes belong at the box wall" ("Affen gehören bei Hagenbeck an die Kistenwand") (Kafka 1994, 304). This insight is the result of the ape's looking out, of his observations, which have made him familiar with the layout and the arrangements of the power structure on the ship. The ape's understanding of these results from deductions drawn from close and thorough observation. As in Freud's theory, rational thought follows from the application of the reality principle, its fastening on sense data and their utilization for and through action. Concentration on external reality leads the ape to reasoning adaptation to it. "But at Hagenbeck's apes belong at the box wall—well, so I stopped being an ape. A clear beautiful train of thought" ("Aber Affen gehören bei Hagenbeck an die Kistenwand—nun, so hörte ich auf, Affe zu sein. Ein klarer, schöner Gedankengang") (Kafka 1994, 304). Through adjustment to it, the ape is ready to use reality for the ego's survival in the only way left to it by prevailing discriminatory power system on board ship—his decision to cease to belong to the disempowered group. We are confronted with a literally fantastic opportunism, a radical submission to reality.

At the same time, the ape's surrender of his species identity is also the birth of the pure unaffiliated individual, an epochal event, which can be regarded as a potentially liberating emancipation of the greatest magnitude. The conflict between the notions of identity and individual emerges here with a particular clarity.

Identity, in this context, is membership in a collective. It is super- and transindividual. The ape possesses his identity through being an ape, offspring and member of an extended family, group, or species—the latter constituting the biological equivalent of what, in ethnographic and sociological terms, would be called ethnicity. Ceasing to be an ape before becoming human—and we must remember, Rotpeter will never be fully human, for he will always retain body, appearance, and sexual behavior of an ape—is to be nothing but a pure, unique individual, abstracted from all group affiliation, cut off from origin, nature, and "being" or "essence," an uprooted, atomized, and, by that very same token, liberated individual, coming as close as conceivable to the concept of the individual as the ultimate unit of society in classical-liberal political thought. To gain a way out into freedom of movement, the ape has to turn himself into a mere individual, unattached to defining and confining heredity, free of identity grounded in the past, and thus utterly open to unprecedented development in the future. Abject adaptation to social reality and its power structure paradoxically entails unparalleled liberation from the fetters of "essential being" or "nature." Yielding identity implies overcoming of stigmatizing essentialism. It is his past that, in the social order in which Rotpeter has been awakened, keeps him caged. In principle, he is already liberated from the cage the moment he stops being an ape and becomes nothing but a "free," i.e., generically unfettered, individual. It is his identity, the superindividual part of his being, that stifles him and threatens his survival. What looks like total surrender to the flagrant injustice and cruelty of social reality emerges, from another perspective, as emancipation from all suprapersonal bonds holding the individual captive to its origin and descent.

The ape's renunciation of his species identity in exchange for liberation from his cage can, in Freudian terms, be read as a narcissism essential to the individual's maturing. The transference of libidinal energy from persons in the child's family—normally his/her mother—to the self leads to sublimation. By way of a rhetorical question, Freud suggests the possibility that "all sublimation . . . [may] take place through the mediation of the ego, which begins by changing sexual object-libido into narcissistic libido" (Freud 1961, 30). Shifting of libidinal attachment from the bosom of the family to the self is for Freud the indispensable condition of the individual's higher development. The price paid by libidinal renunciation will purchase the individual's advance. Narcissism liberates from the retarding tyranny of libidinal desire within the family by rechanneling it toward achievements of the ego. First and foremost, it leads the individual's emancipatory separation, his "weaning," from the mother or mother substitute, toward the formation of a separate independent person.

If we substitute for mother family and species, the "troop" of apes in the midst of which "sinful" shots had felled Rotpeter and separated him forever from the source of his being, his decision to cease to be an ape corresponds precisely to that transfer of libido from the family to the self by which, according to Freud, "the egoism of self-preservation" (Freud 1957, 70) brings about the cultural development Freud calls sublimation. Renouncing his species identity and concentrating on his individual salvation, Rotpeter will advance to a—in evolutionary terms—higher form of life. His self-education into a creature with the mental abilities of a human being depends on his inner abandonment of his family—species being an extension of family. He must sunder the libidinal bonds to the "troop" of apes from which he had sprung, which had sheltered and enwrapped him in the past, and become a solitary, unattached ego in order to free himself from his imprisonment. The original violent separation from his extended family had been his first, his external individuation. Making him a solitary prisoner, it had set him apart and made him an isolated individual. Significantly his remembered consciousness begins with his "awakening" in his prison. There the self that is now writing the memoir was born. But that first, purely external—physical and spatial—individuation has to be completed by a second, a conscious, deliberate, internalized individuation that starts with his turning away from the inner bonds that still attach him to his species and yielding up his fellowship with the "troop" by deciding to stop being one of it. The imperialist social order of Western mankind works upon and through its victim's "egotistical" determination to preserve and improve his life. It forces upon him the severance of his umbilical cord. It is a necessity imposed upon him from without, but one to which he then freely consents. As a "free ape I submitted to this yoke" (Kafka 1994, 299).

Freeing himself from his bonds to his family and origin will set him on the road of freeing himself also from his utter dependence on his jailers. The way out of the cage will allow him not only to survive, but also to support himself by his own efforts and contributions rather than being fed in his cage like an infant or a pet. It will set him on the way to life as an independent self-supporting adult.

That Rotpeter's renunciation of the identity received through his species can be read as liberation receives strong evidence from the context of Kafka's biography. In a letter to Felice, Kafka, as Gerhard Neumann has pointed out, refers to himself as the "ape of my parents" (Neumann 1975, 182 f.), and, in another letter, he refers to his family with the same word, "Rudel" (Kafka 1967, 129), used by his simian protagonist for the "troop" of apes in which he had lived when he was captured. Kafka's use of a term normally reserved for groups of animals is one instance of many that make it clear that, for all his strong emotional ties to his family and his warm esteem of family life in general, Kafka also considered his inability to free himself from his family's powerful hold on him a lifelong prison sentence. His protracted inability, until the final year of his life, to tear himself loose from his family and live away from them as a freelance writer, served as the basis for his worst self-accusations. In such a context, Rotpeter's choice must appear as a desirable alternative, a "way out" into an adulthood his creator seemed unable to attain for himself. What "sinful" bullets, combined with a robust urge to survive, enabled Kafka's simian hero to achieve remained denied to his author. They made him into what Kafka yearned for but could not achieve for himself—an artist able to support himself by his art. Of course, it is a humorous, ironic treatment of an "ideal," filled, as everything in Kafka, with profound ambivalence. Yet, on an intertextual reading of "A Report" and Kafka's life-documents, his identity-shedding protagonist appears more of a "hero" than a "heel," because in him individual self-realization wins out over tribal dependence. The social reality in which the captured ape has to live presents itself as one of glaring self-contradiction. On the one hand, it is a society of horrendous cruelty, injustice, and inequality. Yet, on the other, it is one that holds open literally unprecedented opportunity for the individual willing to free himself from his past. What one might call the psycho-politics of the Freudian concept of the ego, its links to the sociocultural context in which it appears, has been explored in Horkheimer and Adorno's *The Dialectic of Enlightenment*. That work exposes the close inter-connectedness of the psychological concept of the ego with the Baconian-Lockean Enlightenment, the free market economy of capitalism, and the political notion of the autonomous individual underlying the classical theory of modern democracy. "A Report to an Academy" is its analogue in narrative fiction. In it, "healthy" narcissism and the reality principle, which together comprise the ego, operate in a social setting that has the earmarks of Western bourgeois society and help to illuminate its ethos.

The interplay of psychological and sociopolitical elements in Kafka's text can best be seen at that decisive point in the ape's narrative at which his turn toward the world of his captors crystallized into the thought of becoming like them and thereby to be set free eventually. It comes as the culmination of the ape's studious observation of the human beings around him. By making observation the enabling condition for liberation, the ape implicitly uses Francis Bacon's formula for regaining paradise through applying the scientific method. Expelled from Eden, helpless in the face of an all-powerful, indifferent or hostile, and ever-threatening reality, mankind, victimized like Rotpeter, has to learn to observe its foe assiduously, to study nature, so as eventually to learn to outwit, utilize, and conquer her for its own advancement and salvation. If we substitute for man's natural Rotpeter's human environment, we can easily conclude that the course Rotpeter follows must be called Baconian. He observes and studies human beings continuously and makes discoveries about them that will lead to his liberation.

The most crucial observation he makes pertains to human freedom from assault by arbitrary force. He notes that humans go about "unmolested" ("unbehelligt"). With this observation, "an exalted goal dawned on [him]" ("Ein hohes Ziel dämmerte mir auf"). Human beings appear to be free. If he were to become like them, if he were to become human, he, too, would be free. The sociopolitical setting, the state of the human society that engenders in the ape such "seemingly impossible fulfillments" ("scheinbar unmögliche Erfüllungen") (Kafka 1994, 307) is of decisive importance to the ape's metamorphosis. It is a society that seems to guarantee its members freedom of movement.

Freedom on the human scale, to be sure, is quite different from "freedom on all sides." It is not absolute freedom. What signifies it is a privative syllable, "un,"—"*un*molested" ("*un*behelligt"). It is freedom from rather than freedom to, freedom from arbitrary assault, protection from the kind of aggressive power that had overturned Rotpeter's life. "Unmolested" points toward existence under the rule of law, a civil society with legal protection and constitutional guarantees of all individuals' rights—above all, the fundamental right of equal protection against aggression by superior might. It signifies a state in which the basic aspect of liberal government holds sway. The text makes the crucial role of the individual as the foundation of this human society quite apparent. It lies in a textual detail that, read out of context, seems rather puzzling and can be easily overlooked. Immediately prior to his observation that humans go about "unmolested," it seems to the ape "as if [these human beings] were only one" ("als wäre es nur einer"); and in the following sentence, in referring to human beings as "unmolested," he commingles singular and plural: "So *this* human being *or these* human beings were walking about unmolested" ("Dieser Mensch oder diese Menschen gingen also unbehelligt.") (Kafka 1994, 307; emphasis mine).

Every individual's freedom from "molestation" by superior power makes all human beings equal, and thus one, in the ape's sight. They are all like one insofar as each is equally free. Their equality gives them the appearance of uniform likeness: "forever the same faces, forever the same movements" ("immer die gleichen Gesichter, immer die gleichen Bewegungen") (Kafka 1994, 307). This notion of the individual is bound up not only with freedom, but also with equality to the point of likeness. The individual, in this context, does not express individuality, but equality of status and condition. While individuality betokens difference, uniqueness, each individual's inviolability under the law stresses a sameness of status that partakes of uniformity. Individual uniqueness is not what the individualism of modern capitalism and democracy envisage. They aim for the opposite—the uniform equality of all individuals as consumers and as citizens. It is not the fact that each individual is different from all others and unique that concerns the Declaration of Independence, but that all are presumed to be created equal. It is this equality of protectedness of all individuals that the ape espies as characterizing human life around him. When he resolves to join human beings in order to gain release from his cage, his "exalted goal" will not be freedom, but equality of treatment. He strives to become like human beings not because he likes them—"In themselves there was about those human beings nothing that especially appealed to me" ("Nun war an diesen Menschen an sich nichts, was mich sehr verlockte") (Kafka 1994, 307 f.), he avers—but because he aspires to share in their common security from aggression.

Rotpeter's aspiration to join the human species will entail a further extension, a heightening and intensification of the ego's Baconian reality principle—observation. It will compel him to advance from mere passive watching of his captors to active imitation. His attempts to mimick them decisively strengthen the interaction between him and them, resulting in his education in the ways of humanity and finally his liberation from the cage. Considering this sequence we realize that a purely Freudian approach, limiting itself to the psychology of the individual, will not suffice to do full justice to Kafka's text. Because of the essential part played, in Rotpeter's way out of the cage by the sociopolitical example of equal and protected freedom for the members of human society, consideration of the Freudian notion of the ego has to expand to include its social and political foundations and implications. The attraction freedom from assault exerts on the captured ape is essential to his project of assimilation to the human species, and it also leads to the broad sociohistorical context of Kafka's text.

The geographically closest social context pertains, to be sure, not to freedom, but to the colonial imperialism of Kafka's Europe. Hagenbeck, a famous concern in Wilhelminian Germany, has marauded in colonial Africa. Its result has been the ape's capture and brutal incarceration. A native of Africa has been enslaved and is being exported to Europe as a captive, subject to barbarously inhumane treatment. The face of mankind presented to the African is European imperialist capitalism in its most unmitigated, its German-Wilhelminian form. However, if the next element in the narrative plot is kept in mind—the attraction that the sight of freedom and equality among his captors exert on their exotic prisoner—a very different frame of reference emerges. It is the context of the liberal-bourgeois democracy of Western society in general and the United States in particular. Thus "A Report" demonstrates the extreme two-sidedness that modern Western humanity presented to its victims in the rest of the world. Hated and resented as the source of unspeakable misery, dislocation, deracination, and heartbreak, on one side, it showed, on the other, the beacon of individual rights, equal security from aggression, and limitless opportunity for the future of an individual capable of gaining admission into it.

All countries of the West showed that dual face to the world of the twentieth century, but none more so than the United States of America, scene of Kafka's novel, *Der Verschollene* (*Amerika*). Some aspects of the intertextual relationship between Kafka's novel and the ape's report I have tried to show elsewhere (Sokel 1964, chap. 20). Here I want to single out analogies between the historical myth of "the land of unlimited opportunity," as America was called in Kafka's Europe, and the "exalted goal" of assimilation to humanity that the discovery of "unmolested" freedom among human beings inspired in Rotpeter. His liberation from the cage can come about only through successful mimicking of those fortunate beings who already own the riches of liberty and equality. Those are, of course, not granted to all creatures; they are restricted to the individuals of a single group. The society of the "unmolested" excludes outsiders. However, in Rotpeter's view, the privileged group will extend its privilege to outsiders on condition of their successful assimilation to those who already enjoy the insiders' enviable status. This severely restricted nature of freedom is part of the brutal and forbidding face that the West, in its Imperialist aspect, shows to the rest of creation. It relegates those with the wrong, the victims', identity to the "box wall" of prison. However, in both stories—Kafka's "Report" and Western history—Western humanity also offers another face, at least potentially, to its victims: the prospect of equal freedom extended to those who, shedding their identity, are able to assimilate to the victors. On first sight, such a reading bears close resemblance to one that sees Kafka's text as an allegory of Jewish assimilationism and conversion. In such a reading, Rotpeter's renunciation of his species identity appears as morally shabby opportunism and ultimately futile self-betrayal. However, what speaks against a Jewish-assimilationist reading of Rotpeter's "Report" is not only the obvious discrepancy between Jews as "the people of the Book" and a transcendent God's chosen people being fundamentally set aside from nature with which simian existence is associated in "A Report." Even more importantly, a Jewish-assimilationist reading of Kafka's story ignores an essential dimension of its sociopolitical aspect—the pull of attraction that the promise of the equality of freedom has for its hero. After all, equal freedom and security of all individuals from arbitrary power were not prime characteristics of European cultures that sought to exclude Jews from their midst. Rather, the vision of "undisturbed" freedom of the individual shone forth from liberal societies, above all the American, instilling hope in the downtrodden, but aspiring immigrants on the ships that were taking them to a new world. It was the hope of an unprecedented experiment, which a leap across the space between species certainly suggests, with which the news of a life of equal and protected freedom of all individuals inspired the immigrant as it does the ape in Kafka's story.

At the core of Rotpeter's vision of his freed future, as at the core of the poor immigrant's hope of a liberated life in the New World,

lies the absence of predestinating essentialism, the racist's conviction that an individual's past and descent might forever bar him or
her from entering the charmed circle of the privileged. The lack of
preordained, unalterable exclusion connects Rotpeter's with the
American immigrant's dream. If capable of acquiring the language
and behavior of the dominant group, any individual can become
free and prosper. Any immigrant can become an American even as,
in the ape's assumption subsequently verified by events, any creature can become human provided the necessary "effort" (Kafka
1994, 312) and ability are marshaled and tenaciously applied. It
never occurs to the ape that the human community might deny him
acceptance merely because of his descent and origin.

The human response to Rotpeter's learning effort will prove him
correct. His past and species, his "essence," his race, will not be
held against him. On the contrary, the "civilized world" (Kafka
1994, 301) will shower him with admiration and affection, and not
only after he has mastered his mutation of species being. From the
very beginning, his captors evince an interest in him. They gather
around his cage, seek to stimulate him, are curious about his re-
sponses (Kafka 1994, 306). Very soon they evolve from jailers into
teachers. His "racial" heredity is not an obstacle, but quite the opposite. It is precisely because he is an ape, member of an alien
species, showing an eager willingness to become human, that humans appreciate, encourage, and love him—a love he feels "like a
kiss on my entire sweat-dripping body" ("wie einen Kuss auf
meinem ganzen schweisstriefenden Körper") (Kafka 1994, 311).
What counts is not his biologically inherited native identity, his
past, but his effort at and achievement of change. In the attitude
human beings adopt toward him, effort and achievement take the
place of nature, species or "race," as determining identity.

Effort and achievement are bound to the individual, and it is
solely as an individual that humans value and cherish Rotpeter.
What distinguishes him from other apes and makes him an individual—his ambition unique among apes, his "exalted goal," and his
extraordinary effort to actualize it—is the standard by which human beings judge, enthusiastically accept, and richly reward him.
What liberates and catapults him to eminence in human society is
his demonstration of the colossal range of individual capability, his
role as the initiator and performer of a bold and unique experiment,
"hitherto unrepeated on earth" ("sich bisher auf der Erde nicht
wiederholt hat") (Kafka 1994, 312).

Yet, his old apish identity plays a vital role in his success. For
Rotpeter is celebrated and beloved not only because he has aspired
to and succeeded in ceasing to be an ape and becoming human,
but also because he has done so as the ape he has remained in his

bodily appearance and biological makeup, a fact borne out by his sexual behavior "in the manner of apes" ("nach Affenart") (Kafka 1994, 313). His entire phenomenal success would not have been possible if he had not been an ape to begin with and continued to be one all the time. It is precisely because he is an ape succeeding so well in *aping* humans that he is the beneficiary of applause and "scarcely surpassable successes" ("kaum mehr zu steigernde Erfolge") (Kafka 1994, 313). Thus his apish identity constitutes a crucial element in the human reception of his project. It bears testimony to the liberal openness of human society and its unprejudiced appreciation of achievement by the Other. Rotpeter's success depends on his dual identity—as an ape and as a human being. If he were only human and had never been an ape, there would, of course, have been no special achievement in his acquiring "the average education of a European" ("die Durchschnittsbildung eines Europäers") (Kafka 1994, 312), and he would be an ordinary and obscure person, and certainly not the celebrity he has become as an ape. However, if he had remained nothing but an ape, he would, had he survived at all, be an animal in a cage. His identity as a world-famous individual lies in the union of ape and human being, in the simultaneity of two identities—one original and one acquired.

However, this duality is not a static coexistence of identities, but a process, a continuous, dynamic interaction, and the performance that is its result. His identity is a work in progress as well as a finished product. It is creating and creation in one. Rotpeter has, at the time of writing his report, created himself by an enormous and unprecedented "effort" ("Anstrengung") (Kafka 1994, 312). This work, however, is never really completed. In every performance on stage of the variety shows, and indeed in every act of his social life among human beings, he recreates himself, reiterating and varying his original self-creation of an ape attempting to be human. For Rotpeter, identity is performance. It is not a static essence, a given, but a constantly reenacted self-representation.

Rotpeter is literally a self-made man. Insofar as he is a man, a human being, he has made himself, with the help of humans, to be sure, but still basically on his own, "at bottom alone" ("im Grunde allein") (Kafka 1994, 299). As a self-made man he corresponds, as an enacted metaphor, to the classical American myth. The myth implies the triumph of the individual over his circumstances, or the victory of present and future over the past. No inherited nature, no anterior group membership, prevents the individual from making himself, given sufficient daring and ingenuity.

The self-made man bears a very close relationship to the Freudian notion of the ego, according to which the ego succeeds, not only by adapting the organism to its surrounding reality, but likewise by changing reality, making it conform to the advantage of the individual. Rotpeter not only changes himself, but in the process influences his surroundings, inducing human society to accept him as a free and honored member. The story of the ego, as exemplified by Rotpeter, is like the myth of the self-made man: a triumph of the individual over his inherited collective identity and thus over the past in which the latter is rooted. In terms of the "ecstasies of time," to use Heidegger's term, or the tenses of existence, Rotpeter's biography begins, exactly as the myth of the self-made man, in a terrifyingly underprivileged past. An overwhelmingly strong will, coupled with extraordinary cleverness and ironclad concentration on the goal, enables the individual to free himself from this past, and accomplish a dizzying ascent into a present totally unlike it. What is the self of the self-made man? It is the achievement that transformed a wretched past into a glorious present. It is the work itself of fashioning a new self.

This has a close bearing on the genre, the generic form, of "A Report." Rotpeter's report is not an autobiography in the traditional sense. It does not narrate a life. Instead it describes the making of a self, the educational process that has resulted in Rotpeter's finding himself as what and where he is now. It dwells on his overcoming of his original identity that had kept him in the cage, and his finding a way out by remaking himself into a new being. His report is "to show the guiding line on which a former ape invaded the human world and established himself there" ("es soll die Richtlinie zeigen, auf welcher ein gewesener Affe in die Menschenwelt eingedrungen ist und sich dort festgesetzt hat") (Kafka 1994, 300). His report is an immigrant's story, describing an outsider's maneuvering in wresting for himself a firm place in the insiders' society.

His livelihood and standing as an entertainer, however, depend, as mentioned, on his forever repeating the process of his formation. Each time the "former ape" steps onto the stage, he has to prove himself there. His act has to be a confirmation of his ability to maintain his human status. What his public pays to see is his sliding from the apish creature his physical appearance presents to them into the manners and behavior of "a European with an average education." In each performance he repeats the metamorphosis from ape to human being. It is this ever-renewed transformation taking place in their sight that thrills each of his audiences anew. Put in temporal terms, each of his stage performances shows the past changing into the present, or, putting it perhaps more accurately, it shows the present, as the presence of an ape's body, ascending into a future in which the physical ape will meet his public as a socialized human being.

Rotpeter's "being" can perhaps best be defined, in Jean-Paul Sartre's terms, as a lack of being. Rotpeter is what he is not and is not what he is. He is not the human being his mimetic behavior pretends to be, since he performs it in and with the body of an ape. Neither, however, is he identical with his ape's body, since his behavior is that of a human being. Thus his "being" is lack of being. No unitary, positively definable identity defines him. His "identity" is not a condition or a substance. It resides in his achievement.

His achievement, however, is founded on the ejection of his past to a point at which he lost the inner continuity of his being. "This achievement," he confesses, "would have been impossible if I had wished to hold on stubbornly to my origin, to the memories of my youth" ("Diese Leistung wäre unmöglich gewesen, wenn ich eigensinnig hätte an meinem Ursprung, an den Erinnerungen der Jugend festhalten wollen."). The Academy requests a report on his "äffisches Vorleben," his existence as an ape prior to his capture (Kafka 1994, 299). Rotpeter, however, cannot meet this request. In order to enter and succeed in the new, the human world, he had to forget his memories of the old one.

A significant gap between the assumptions of the Academy and the reality of Rotpeter's life becomes starkly evident at this initial point of Rotpeter's text. The "Exalted Gentlemen of the Academy" ("Hohe Herren von der Akademie") (Kafka 1994, 299), whose request for a report Rotpeter answers, view life with assumptions contradicted by Rotpeter's experience. The traumatic violation and overturning of his existence, caused by the rapacity and aggressive incursion of Western imperialist society, has wrought a radical discontinuity in his life. As we have seen, it forced him to abandon the continuity of his inner life, since it allowed him to save his physical life only by radically altering it. The "Exalted Gentlemen of the Academy," however, ignore the brutal side of their culture, entertaining a scientific and profoundly liberal interest in all life no matter how alien to their own. The ethos of objective science, of knowledge for its own sake, the open-minded, liberal curiosity of the Enlightenment combines in them with a belief in the permanent continuity of the self. They overlook the fundamental dislocations brought about by the colonial imperialism that is the other face of the liberal civilization that has founded and sponsored learned societies like their own.

The "Exalted Gentlemen of the Academy" represent the classical modernism of the nineteenth and early twentieth century also on account of what might be termed their historicism. Their desire to learn about Rotpeter's "prior life as an ape" expresses an interest in the past for its own sake. They wish to understand the past historically, i.e., from the past's own perspective, and, from pure thirst for knowledge, seek to share in it. Their desire presupposes a faith in the unfractured continuity and persistence of memory, and, with it, the unbroken identity of the self. That faith too makes the exalted academicians typical representatives of classical modernity.

Rotpeter's inability to meet their request shows that the assumptions of classical modernity no longer hold. His experience reflects a world-historical change from classical modernism to what might be described as postmodernism. The expansive capitalism and colonial imperialism of the West—the hunting expedition that captured our hero has been sent to Africa by the "firm" of Hagenbeck, a business enterprise—have produced a world in which the past has become irrelevant, and holding on to it tenaciously has grown incompatible with a tolerable life. In its capitalist-colonialist aspect, modernity has brought about a radical rupture, a total discontinuity in the life of its individual victims as in the general course of history. The same modernity that is represented by the Academy's search for pure knowledge has brought forth the world-penetrating and -subjugating social order that subjects all regions and all creatures to its sway. To it Kafka's simian hero owes his enslavement, but also his subsequent "whipped-on evolution" ("vorwärts gepeitschte Entwicklung") (Kafka 1994, 299) to a humanoid being. Rotpeter's "whipped-on evolution" forms a part of the "whipped-on development" (the German word "Entwicklung," used by Kafka, denotes both "evolution" and "development") of economy and technology whipped forward by capitalism as it spread across the globe. "Simian nature raced, somersaulting, out of me and away" ("Die Affennatur raste, sich überkugelnd, aus mir hinaus und weg") (Kafka 1994, 311 f.), the ape recounts, and adds that, springing over into his teacher, it turned him insane. But this "furiously somersaulting"—the German word "rasen" signifies both "to race" and "to rave"—expulsion of apish nature reflects, in terms of the historical context, the breathlessly advancing expulsion of nature as a whole by the onslaught of a ravingly forward-racing humanity. Both expulsions of nature, on the individual as well as on the global scale, aim for the utterly new, the unparalleled, the hitherto unimaginable, for efforts, achievements, and sensations that, like the humanization of an ape, have never yet been seen on earth.

In such a world, holding on to the past and one's inherited identity has, as we have seen, become a form of the death instinct. In close analogy to the ape's death-threatening longing to return to his origin, the death instinct in Freud's *Beyond the Pleasure Principle* is life's striving to return to its distant past in inorganic nature. Similarly, in *The Dialectic of Enlightenment*, Horkheimer and Adorno interpret the deathly temptation that the sirens' songs hold for Odysseus and his sailors as the pull of the past, life according to in-

stinct, the dreamed-of unconscious unity of the organism with surrounding nature. Like Odysseus, the caged ape has to resist the
sirens' call of his past in order to save his life by finding a way out
of his deadly cage. Instrumental reason, which thinks in terms of
the future, of possible harm and advantage, has to take the place of
instinct that, according to Freud, is embedded in a past transmitted
from the collective life of preceding generations. Rotpeter's initially
disastrous encounter with the colonialist-capitalist West necessi-
tates his concentration of all his psychic energies upon his liberation from the cage in a way that would save his physical being.
Compelled by this strenuous concentration, his "memories more
and more shut themselves to me" ("verschlossen sich mir die Erinnerungen immer mehr" (Kafka 1994, 299). Thus he can no longer
be what the Academy wants him to be—a historian of his whole
life. His life has been torn apart and fallen into two absolutely separate halves. It has lost all inner coherence. Rotpeter has become
irredeemably alienated from his own past existence. His utterly
vanished memory shows that the violent incursion by the modern
West has irrevocably destroyed the inner unity of its victims' lives.

This fragmentariness of Rotpeter's existence bears a close connection to the contingency of his victimization. That it had been
only Rotpeter who had been hit by the shots of the hunting expedition and torn away forever from his group had been due to pure
chance. There was no inner necessity, no special predestined meaning, no fate involved. This enormous revolution in an existence had
been nothing but a fluke, a mere contingent accident.

Richard Rorty, frequently considered the voice of postmodernism
in American philosophy, sees in contingency the most practicable
key to the description and understanding of the world. What Rorty
calls "contingency" comes close to that lack of "grand narratives"
viewed by Jean-Francois Lyotard as most characteristic of the age
he calls "the postmodern condition." Postmodern society, according
to Lyotard, no longer has "grands récits" (Lyotard 1979, 63), grand
narratives that pretend to give unity and meaningful coherence to a
culture. Rotpeter's life that can no longer be recounted as a whole,
as a unity, constitutes, in terms of an individual's biography, an analogue to the disappearance of a "grand narrative" in society as a
whole.

Connecting Rorty with Lyotard, we might say that history as a series of chance occurrences, without a causally determined, linear
coherence and unitary direction, has ceased to be a narratable
story, a "history" in the original sense with which the French word
"histoire" and the German word "Geschichte" still indicate the intimate link of history to narrative. Seen from a postmodern perspective, history lacks a mythos in the Aristotelian sense of a causally

transparent and, therefore, explicable and interpretable sequence of events that makes any entity—whether a culture, a society, or an individual life—representable in narrative terms. It is this nondetectability of any connection between events and their antecedent "reasons" that establishes the analogy between postmodern "history" and Rotpeter's life. Rotpeter's fateful capture took place without any reason that had to do with him. He finds no understandable cause of a fate that has torn him away from his fellow apes. "Why that?" ("Warum das?") he asks himself and, by implication, his readers, and finds no reason. "Tear open the flesh between your toes, you will not find the reason. Press your back against the bar of your cage until it almost cuts you in two, you will not find the reason" ("Kratz dir das Fleisch zwischen den Fusszehen auf, du wirst den Grund nicht finden. Drück dich hinten gegen die Gitterstange, bis sie dich fast zweiteilt, du wirst den Grund nicht finden.") (Kafka 1994, 304). Even as the bar of his cage would cut him in two, if he were to persist in his search for a reason of his punishment, so his violation and capture have actually cut the course of his life into two parts. The German word "Grund" signifies both explanatory cause or reason and the ground on which something or someone is enabled to stand and rest. Thus the text alludes both to the lack of a meaningful rational explanation of Rotpeter's fate and to the absence of a ground that would support his existence on a bedrock of meaning. This groundlessness of his fate makes his past and the experiences in it literally meaningless, lacking any interpretable sense. His past is inapplicable, and a stubborn clinging to it fatal. Since his past that has formed him now condemns him to death, only the future can perhaps save him. His past's desertion of him forces him to create himself anew.

Rotpeter's self-staged metamorphosis corresponds to the second fundamental principle of Rorty's postmodern anthropology, the "self-fashioning" of the individual that issues from the contingency of his/her existence. Rotpeter cannot tell the story of his past life, but he is able to report on a specific strategy pursued by him in response to a special situation in his life. He can deliver the description, not of a whole life, but of a unique "achievement," an experiment performed by him as an "artist" ("Künstler") (Kafka 1994, 310) whose creation is himself.

However, what enables the individual's self-creation is a society that permits and even encourages it. According to Rorty, the enabling of self-creation is the distinguishing mark of a society ruled by the principles of liberal democracy. Rotpeter's achievement likewise depends on the society around him. As we have already seen, the very thought of recreating himself as a human being would have never occurred to him without his witnessing the undisturbed freedom of movement human beings seemed to enjoy, and the success of his experiment would not have been possible without the constant energetic encouragement and assistance by the same humanity that had originally taken his freedom from him. Rotpeter relates that it was the emotional attitude he learned from human beings that formed the precondition of his way out from the cage. "Today I see clearly: without the greatest inner calm I would have never been able to escape. . . . That calm, however, I surely owed to the people on board ship" ("Heute sehe ich klar: ohne grösste innere Ruhe hätte ich nie entkommen können. . . . Die Ruhe wiederum aber verdankte ich wohl den Leuten vom Schiff.") (Kafka 1994, 305). The individual does not fashion himself alone; society is his co-creator. Rotpeter's jailers become his teachers. Without their good will, their active aid, their solidarity with *his* will, his project could never have been begun, and it certainly could not have been carried out to its triumphal conclusion. By the essential role society plays in it, the idea of individual self-creation in postmodern thinking and in Kafka's story differs from its precursors in Nietzsche and existentialist thought. Although at bottom a lonely road, self-creation also requires the collaboration of many individuals. In Rotpeter's words, it was "accompanied in stretches by excellent people, advice, applause and orchestral music" ("streckenweise begleitet von vortrefflichen Menschen, Ratschlägen, Beifall und Orchestralmusik"), even though "at bottom alone" ("aber im Grunde allein") (Kafka 1994, 299). It is an "achievement" that somehow always takes place on stage, in a public space, as interaction between the individual and a society that meets his effort halfway. Rotpeter benefits from and utilizes the liberalism that represents the other, the—in a double sense—"human" face of Western society. It is a society that shows its solidarity with the struggling alien who seeks to refashion himself in its image.

"Solidarity" is the third noun in the programmatic title of Richard Rorty's key text of postmodern philosophy, *Contingency, Irony, and Solidarity*. For Rorty, solidarity is the opposite of cruelty. Solidarity defines cultural—and not merely political—liberalism. Human solidarity with it is essential also to Rotpeter's project. About the sailor who was his first, untiringly helping teacher, Rotpeter says that "he was not angry with me, he understood that we fought on the same side against apish nature" ("er war mir nicht böse, er sah ein, dass wir auf der gleichen Seite gegen die Affennatur kämpften") (Kafka 1994, 310)—an example of liberal solidarity building bridges over the chasm separating not merely races, but species.

However, a profound irony underlies the idea of the individual's self-creation, and, in this context, let us recall that "irony" is the middle member of Rorty's liberal-postmodern triad. The freedom to create oneself offered by modern Western society has narrow limits. It is by no means "freedom on all sides," but merely a "way out," freedom profoundly relativized and restricted. Self-creation remains limited to a single model that it has to imitate—Western mankind's way of life. The former ape acquires something specific, in geographic-cultural terms, and rather narrowly defined—an "average *European* education" ("die Durchschnittsbildung eines Europäers"). The new self that he has created for himself is his ability to master "average European" behavior and conventions. There was no other choice if he wished to escape his cage and *live*. He was forced to assume "that freedom was not a choice" ("dass nicht die Freiheit zu wählen war") (Kafka 1994, 312; italics mine). Rotpeter could not recreate himself as just anything, but only as something desired and appreciated by the society that had imprisoned him. Thus self-creation can have no other goal but conformity with a prevailing form of life. The ape is free to create himself in its image, but not free to conceive and project a self according to his own deepest wish. He does not even possess the liberty of postmodern architecture of choosing one of many models of the past at the disposal of the present. He can, and must, adapt himself to one single model—Western society of the twentieth century.

In that sense, Kafka's little text helps to uncover fallacies and boundaries of contemporary, postmodern thinking. Dissenting from Lyotard, "A Report" shows that, in a global frame, there can indeed be found one "grand narrative," one single overarching historical tendency—the Westernization of the world that also means its final subjection to the dominion of man. Against Rorty's idea of free self-creation, Kafka's text makes clear that the individual's "freedom" to create himself is nothing other than successful adaptation to the world-dominating culture that has uprooted one. It is not true freedom, "freedom on all sides," which it would be if it offered the possibility of forming the self according to an infinite variety of norms and patterns. However, it is a "way out," infinitely preferable to existence in the cage of colonial imperialism that preceded it.

Through this doubleness of the evaluating perspective that is built into Kafka's text, it makes us see, in the world it depicts, conformity and liberation as interchangeable. With that "A Report to an Academy" exhibits an astounding, paradigmatic relevance to a century that has advanced from the colonialist imperialism of its beginning via the liberal "capitalism with a human face" of its middle to the global uniformity at its end.

Bibliography

Kafka, Franz. 1967. *Briefe an Felice und andere Korrespondenz aus der Verlobungszeit.* Ed. Erich Heller and Jürgen Born, with an Introduction by Erich Heller. Frankfurt am Main: S. Fischer Lizenzausgabe von Schocken Books, New York.

———. 1994. *Drucke zu Lebzeiten.* Ed. Wolf Kittler, Hans Gerd Koch, and Gerhard Neumann. Frankfurt am Main: S. Fischer Lizenzausgabe von Schocken Books, New York. Translations from the German text are my own.

Freud, Sigmund. 1955. *Beyond the Pleasure Principle,* in *The Standard Edition of the Complete Psychological Works of Sigmund Freud.* Translated from the German under the general editorship of James Strachey in collaboration with Anna Freud. Assisted by Alix Strachey and Alan Tyson. Vol. 17 (1920–1922): *Beyond the Pleasure Principle: Group Psychology and Other Works,* 7–64. London: Hogarth Press and the Institute of Psychoanalysis.

———. 1957. "On Narcissism: An Introduction," in *The Standard Edition of the Complete Psychological Works of Sigmund Freud.* Translated from the German under the general editorship of James Strachey in collaboration with Anna Freud. Assisted by Alix Strachey and Alan Tyson. Vol. 14 (1914–1916): *On the History of the Psychoanalytic Movement: Papers on Metapsychology and Other Works,* 73–102. London: Hogarth Press and the Institute of Psychoanalysis.

———. 1961. *The Ego and the Id,* in *The Standard Edition of the Complete Psychological Works of Sigmund Freud.* Translated from the German under the general editorship of James Strachey in collaboration with Anna Freud. Assisted by Alix Strachey and Alan Tyson. Vol. 19 (1923–1925): *The Ego and the Id and Other Works,* 12–66. London: Hogarth Press and the Institute of Psychoanalysis.

———. 1966. "Project for a Scientific Psychology," in *The Standard Edition of the Complete Psychological Works of Sigmund Freud.* Translated from the German under the general editorship of James Strachey in collaboration with Anna Freud. Assisted by Alix Strachey and Alan Tyson. Vol. 1 (1886–1899): *Pre-Psycho-Analytic Publications and Unpublished Drafts,* 295–397. London: Hogarth Press and the Institute of Psychoanalysis.

———. 1991. "Abriss der Psychoanalyse." In *Gesammelte Werke: chronologisch geordnet,* ed. Anna Freud in collaboration with Marie Bonaparte. Vol. 17, 63–183. Frankfurt am Main: S. Fischer, 1991–1998.

Horkheimer, Max, and Theodor W. Adorno. 1947. *The Dialectic of Enlightenment.* Trans. by John Cumming. New York: Herder and Herder, 1972. (Original version Amsterdam: Querido, 1947; (c) 1944).

Lyotard, Jean-Francois. 1979. *La condition postmoderne: rapport sur le savoir.* Paris: Éditions de Minuit. (English version: *The Postmodern Condition: A Report on Knowledge.* Translated from the French by Geoff Bennington and Brian Massumi. Foreword by Frederic Jameson. Theory and History of Literature. Vol. 10. Minneapolis: University of Minnesota Press, 1984. The reference here is on p. 37).

Neumann, Gerhard. 1975. " 'Ein Bericht für eine Akademie.' Erwägungen zum 'Mimesis'-Charakter Kafkascher Texte." *Deutsche Vierteljahrsschrift für Literaturwissenschaft und Geistesgeschichte* 49 (1975): 66–83.

Rorty, Richard. 1989. *Contingency, Irony, and Solidarity.* Cambridge: Cambridge University Press.

Sokel, Walter H. 1964. *Franz Kafka: Tragik und Ironie: Zur Struktur seiner Kunst.* Munich-Vienna: Albert Langen, Georg Müller, 1964.

NICOLA GESS

The Politics of Listening: The Power of Song in Kafka's "Josefine, the Singer"†

"Solving the riddle of its huge effects"—this is the task that the narrator of Kafka's story sets for himself and every reader in regard

---

† This essay appears for the first time in this Norton Critical Edition. Printed by permission of the author. Page numbers to this Norton Critical Edition appear in brackets.

to Josefine's song. Many of these effects are owed to a critical assimilation of a certain tradition of thought about music prevalent in Kafka's lifetime: the belief in the power of music to create and represent a people.

In the nineteenth and early twentieth century, the effects of music on its listeners were widely discussed, a discussion of which Kafka was aware. Even though he was by his own account deeply, profoundly "unmusical,"[1] he was, like the narrator of Josefine, fascinated by the riddle of music—in the narrator's words, "what this music is really all about" [p. 95]. In a famous diary entry, Kafka literally made the price of writing a necessary *resistance* to the lure of thinking about music and in this way testified to the power of music over him. He wrote:

> It is easy to recognize in myself a concentration on writing. When it had become clear in my organism that writing was the most productive direction of my being, everything rushed in that direction and left empty all those abilities that were directed first and foremost toward the joys of sex, eating, drinking, philosophical reflection on music (des philosophischen Nachdenkens der Musik). I starved in all these directions. [p. 196]

The discussion about music shortly before and during Kafka's lifetime focused less on the so-called "autonomous," individual, listening subject of the late eighteenth and early nineteenth centuries than the crowd. A key contribution was made by Nietzsche's[2] treatise *The Birth of Tragedy out of the Spirit of Music* (1871), which, on the evidence of certain remarkable echoes, Kafka appears to have read. Here, Nietzsche addresses the impact of Wagner's[3] music, describing the transformative effect of the music of Greek tragedies and Wagner's music dramas on the crowd of listeners. As persons they are transported, possessed; they lose their individuality and become part of a larger entity, the mass.[4] This mass is then deemed to be itself creative: in a deep sense, it has brought forth the very music it is hearing; it is at once the result and the creative origin of this music.[5] Nietzsche illuminates this paradox by inter-

1. "Do you realize that I am completely unmusical, with a completeness that in my experience does not exist anywhere else at all?" *Briefe an Milena* (Frankfurt a.M.: Fischer, 1986), 65.
2. Friedrich Nietzsche (1844–1900), the most influential of modern German philosophers, creator of the concepts of the "genealogy of morals," "will to power," and " 'super'-man" [*Editor*].
3. Richard Wagner (1813–1883), great German opera composer of *Tristan and Isolde*, *The Ring of the Nibelungen*, *Parsifal*, and others [*Editor*].
4. In *Franz Kafka—Tragik und Ironie. Zur Struktur seiner Kunst* (Munich/Wien: Albert Langen, Georg Müller, 1964), Walter Sokel likens the role of song in Kafka's story to the role of the "Dionysian spirit of music" in Nietzsche (514f).
5. See Friedrich Nietzsche, "The Birth of Tragedy out of the Spirit of Music," in *Basic Writings of Nietzsche*, trans. and ed. Walter Kaufmann (New York: Random House, 1968), esp. 44–67.

preting the individual composer as the mouthpiece of the collective. The composer's song is always already a "song of the people," even though this people will be truly realized as a unity only through listening to his song.[6]

Over the years Nietzsche decisively distanced himself from Wagner as an artist who betrayed his art by seeking to impose his own individual will through it. This is the Wagner whom the devotees of Wagner were nonetheless ready to adore: for them, Wagner was a spiritual leader who impressed his will on his listeners, a "higher" will that gave form to the mass created by his music; and it is this form that is said to realize, for the first time, the true essence of the mass as a *German* people, a Volk. We may postulate a fundamental aversion on Kafka's part to this ideology from the fact that not one of his copious diaries or letters contains even a single mention of Wagner—and yet this musical discussion was "in the air."

In the perspective of the early Nietzsche and the Wagnerians, music thus produces two sorts of effects. The first was a familiar element of an earlier, Romantic music ideology: music destroys the autonomy of the subject by dissolving it into an amorphous substance moved by primordial sensations, emotions, and fantasies. But in the newer perspective, the result is not a dangerous chaos. For the shapeless mass is given form by a musical leader (Führer) who voices its true being and thus functions as its creator, exemplar, and mouthpiece. In this perspective, the effects of music are no longer anxious ones. Instead of being seen as destructive violence, music is lent a constructive, yet authoritative power, aiding in the formation of a Volk (unified people). Particularly in times of war, this formation is linked to military aims. It was, after all, at the time of the Franco-Prussian War of 1870/71 that Nietzsche wrote his *Birth of Tragedy*, which declared that Germany needed Wagner's music in order to prepare itself for the war and "console" itself after the war as a victorious German people.[7] Nietzsche's claim was to exercise a prophetic power: at the time of the First World War, German soldiers carried Beethoven's symphonies to the front, using Beethoven's "brazen sound" as a device to strengthen discipline;[8] and in the 1920s reactionary musicologists declared Beethoven the leader of the German people, hearing his music as a call for a military regime of law and order, as a bulwark against an inferior Anglo-French "civilization."[9]

6. See ibid. 48–52.
7. See ibid. 123, 138–39; also, Friedrich Nietzsche, "Richard Wagner in Bayreuth," in *Unfashionable Observations*, trans. Richard T. Gray (Stanford: Stanford UP, 1995), 259–331, esp. 278.
8. Hermann Abert, "Zu Beethovens Persönlichkeit und Kunst," in Rudolf Swartz, ed. *Jahrbuch der Musikbibliothek Peters für 1925*, 32 (Leipzig: Peters, 1926), 10.
9. Adolf Sandberger, "Das Erbe Beethovens und unsere Zeit," in Adolf Sandberger, ed. *Neues Beethoven Jahrbuch* 3 (1927) (Augsburg: Benno Filser), 18–29.

The ideal of the Volk, surfacing in these concepts, was central to the Völkische Bewegung (popular or "folkish" movement) that became increasingly strident in the years around the First World War. A slogan of this movement was "Volk statt Masse" (a people instead of the masses). It promulgated the nationalist and often racist idea of unifying the modern masses into a Volk in which individual differences would no longer exist. It was also directed against everything this movement connected with modernity—e.g., industrialization, capitalism, socialism, women's liberation, and the metropolis: the Volk was to be a pre-modern collective. And it entailed the idea of a leader figure, thought to represent the Volk and its interests while at the same time giving it form and direction.[1]

In his 1921 essay "Massenpsychologie und Ich-Analyse" (group psychology and the analysis of the ego), Freud[2] famously analyzed the dynamics between the masses and their leader, revealing the psychological mechanisms at work in the ideal of unification—the mechanisms he called idealization and identification.[3] The single individual projects his own Ich-Ideal (ego ideal) onto the leader. He then starts to worship the leader as his ideal, seeing himself represented in the leader and shaping himself on this model. Since all individuals in the mass idealize the same leader in an act of collective self-projection, they can now identify with each other. The leader becomes the representation and model of a new Massen-Ich (group ego). Interestingly, Freud's example for these mechanisms is a concert situation.[4] He describes how a mass of women and girls, who are all madly in love with the performer, throng around the singer or pianist after his performance. All of them idealize the same person and are therefore able to identify with each other, instead of getting jealous, which would be the case in a mere crowd of individuals. Adorno,[5] in his reading of Freud, picks up on this observation when he notes that the power of the leader over the masses seems to be based on his "orality," his powers of verbal sound and verbal gesture.[6] While the ideals of the Völkische Bewegung were influential for nationalist politics, they were also structurally similar to the ideals of the Zionist philosophy of Herzl[7] that

1. See Jost Hermand, *Der alte Traum vom neuen Reich* (Frankfurt: Athenaeum, 1988) and Jost Hermand and Frank Trommler, *Die Kultur der Weimarer Republik* (Frankfurt: Fischer Taschenbuch, 1988).
2. Sigmund Freud (1856–1939), Viennese creator of psychoanalysis.
3. Sigmund Freud, "Massenpsychologie und Ich-Analyse," in *Studienausgabe* (Frankfurt: Fischer, 1974), 10: 61–135.
4. Ibid. 112.
5. Theodor W. Adorno (1903–1969), German philosopher, leading member of "The Frankfurt School," studied with dialectical precision the interconnections of modern society and culture.
6. Theodor W. Adorno, "Freudian Theory and the Pattern of Fascist Propaganda," in *Soziologische Schriften I* (Frankfurt: Suhrkamp, 1997), 408–34, esp. 427.
7. Theodor Herzl (1860–1904), founder of Zionism [*Editor*].

engaged Kafka in the last years of his life.[8] Herzl's idea was to re-
unify the Jewish people by creating a political structure like an art-
form, with the political leader functioning as an artist dealing with
human material. For Herzl, as for many in his generation, Wagner
and his music dramas were the main inspiration behind this concept; Herzl meant his Zionism, like Wagner's operas, to be a kind of
Gesamtkunstwerk (total work of art).[9] He wrote: "Moses' exodus
would compare * * * [to the Zionist movement] like a Shrove Tuesday *Singspiel* of Hans Sachs to a Wagnerian opera."[1]

Kafka's "Josefine, the Singer" takes up the myth according to
which the musician has the power to represent and create a Volk by
way of music. As the title and the first sentence announce, the
story will concern a singer and a people, with the second sentence
adding the missing link between the two, namely, the "power of
song" [p. 94]. When Josefine is not singing, the mice are divided
into at least three different groups—the "followers," the "opposition," and the rest of the "crowd" [pp. 105, 96, 98], who quarrel
with each other about Josefine's song. There are also a few isolated,
single individuals, such as those prone to "enthusiasm" [p. 104],
and the narrator, who distance themselves from any kind of group
through their peculiar behavior.[2] However, at Josefine's performances, all differences disappear. As the narrator observes: "Opposition can be offered only at a distance; when you sit before her,
you understand: what she is squeaking here is no squeaking"
[p. 96]; that is, all doubts about the quality of her song vanish. The
song "carrie[s]" the listeners "away" [p. 94] from themselves. They
are "plunged into the sensation of the crowd" [p. 98]; "feeling" here
means both the feeling of melting into a mass and some specific
emotion—like warmth—that this mass might be feeling [pp. 95,
98]. The listeners establish physical contact with each other, "as
body press[es] * * * on body" [p. 98], as they "huddle up against
one another" [p. 100]. Consequently, the listening crowd seems to

8. See Christoph Stölzl, "Kafka: Jew, Anti-Semite, Zionist," in Mark Anderson, ed., *Reading
   Kafka. Prague, Politics, and the Fin de siècle* (New York: Schocken Books, 1989). For interpretations of the mouse people as Jews, see Mark Anderson, *Kafka's Clothes: Ornament and Aestheticism in the Habsburg Fin de siècle* (Oxford: Oxford UP, 1992),
   194–216, and Karl Erich Grözinger, *Kafka und die Kabbala. Das Jüdische im Werk und
   Denken von Franz Kafka* (Frankfurt: Eichborn Verlag, 1992). For more on Herzl and
   Kafka's allusions to him, see Benno Wagner's essay in this volume [p. 302].
9. See Carl E. Schorske, *Fin-de-Siècle Vienna: Politics and Culture* (London: Weidenfeld,
   1979), 146–80.
1. "Moses Auszug verhält sich dazu wie ein Fastnachtsingspiel von Hans Sachs zu einer
   Wagnerschen Oper." Theodor Herzl, *Tagebücher* (Berlin, 1922), 1:44; quoted by
   Schorske, *Fin-de-Siècle Vienna*, 163. "Shrove Tuesday": a Catholic holiday, the Tuesday
   immediately before Ash Wednesday—also called Pancake Day. "*Singspiel*": an old-
   fashioned musical comedy featuring folk songs interspersed with banter [*Editor*].
2. See Wolf Kittler, *Der Turmbau zu Babel und das Schweigen der Sirenen. Über das Reden,
   das Schweigen, die Stimme und die Schrift in vier Texten von Franz Kafka* (Erlangen:
   Palm und Enke, 1985), 190.

be one great body, breathing, listening, and feeling warm [p. 98], turning into a "big warm communal bed" in which everyone may "[relax] his limbs, * * * indulg[ing] * * * his desire to unwind and stretch out" [p. 102]. Unlike mice in everyday life who, according to the narrator, never stop chattering, this great body does not talk. It fills the space between the narrator and Josefine with a ceremonious stillness, thereby absorbing Josefine's song. Filling the silence and supplementing the chatter, this song is experienced not so much as a single individual's but rather as the utterance of the listening people. The narrator observes: "This squeaking that arises where silence is imposed on everyone else comes almost as a message from the people to the individual" [p. 100]. Josefine appears as a mouthpiece giving voice to the people. Experiencing Josefine's song as their own, the listening crowd turns creative, dreaming dreams about its past and its present, all of which are contained in its song. These dreams, just as the whole concert situation and the song, also serve military goals. The narrator admits that "precisely in times of trouble * * * we listen to Josefine's voice with even greater intensity. * * * It is as if we were drinking hastily * * * a communal goblet of peace before the battle" [p. 100]. He also calls Josefine's performances "scant pauses between battles" [p. 102].

Thus, Kafka's story is about a crowd and a singer, and whenever the singer calls, the crowd obeys and gets together to listen to her song. This song has the power to unify the crowd into a Volk ready for battle, experiencing the song as its own utterance. But, then again, other aspects of the story seem to call this narrative into question. Keeping the above-mentioned tradition in mind, one wonders: why are we presented with a performer and not with a composer? Why a female and not a male performer? Why only vocal and not also instrumental music? Why coloraturas and not proper melodies? Why such a spectacle of making gestures and pulling faces and not simple, authentic expression? In all of these aspects, Josefine and her song are radically unlike the early twentieth-century's ideals of German heroes and their music, such as Beethoven, Wagner, or Bruckner, giving voice to a German essence and mirroring and creating the Volk. Indeed, all of these aspects serve only one goal, that of calling the song's aesthetic and ethical quality as well as its supposed power into doubt. For they are taken out of yet another repertoire of ideological suppositions about music circulating in German-speaking countries in the nineteenth and early twentieth centuries.[3] At least since the early

---

3. Anderson describes another set of "ideological assumptions about music" (*Kafka's Clothes*, 196) at the turn of the century, partly overlapping with the one I am going to sketch: the racist stereotype of "Jewish music," famously formulated by Wagner, and the assumption that women, just like Jews, were unable to compose music of any quality,

nineteenth century, German music critics had been eying musical performance with suspicion since it threatened not only to distort the musical essence laid down in the score but also to invite mere sensual pleasure—and not the spiritual elation or the "essential refinement" of the listener. This was thought to be true in particular of female performers, especially female singers, and even more so if they sang songs rich in musical flourishes.[4] For the coloraturas written for the female voice were considered the epitome of mere sensual stimulation in music, lacking any kind of higher quality and purpose.[5] German critics never tired of degrading this kind of music in aesthetic and ethical terms. And by so doing, they served nationalist agendas, because they attributed this kind of "poor" music to France, Italy, or the Jews, while proclaiming the German-speaking lands as the home of "good," i.e. spiritually rich, "essential" music. One of the strategies to degrade this music was to accuse it of being fake, inauthentic, and theatrical. Wagner, for example, reproached the German-Jewish Jakob (Giacomo) Meyerbeer,[6] who worked mainly in France, with striving for mere "effects" in his music, famously defining "effect" as "effects without a cause."[7] Wagner portrays him as a manipulative hypocrite, tricking the listener into beliefs and feelings that have no reality or reason behind them and rarely reach beyond a superficial level.

It is precisely this suspicion that the narrator entertains in Kafka's story. He suspects that there might be no "cause" behind Josefine's "effects," that far from being of the greatest "beauty" [p. 95] her song is in truth something even less than ordinary, indeed a mere "nothing[ness]" [p. 100]. He produces numerous arguments to support his claim, concentrating above all on Josefine's theatricality. For example, she is said to feign injuries, fatigue, bad temper, and weakness at her performances in order to move the audience. The narrator concludes: "In addition to a concert, we have drama" [p. 107], involving weeping, limbs that hang lifelessly, and collapsing—all of them being empty effects since in truth Josefine experiences nothing of the sort. According to the narrator, this kind of empty spectacle is so important to Josefine's art that "to under-

covering up their "metaphysical 'lack' or 'nothingness' with an artificial, seductive, 'theatrical' appearance" (209). Thus, for Anderson, the narrator gives a "guileful portrayal of Josefine as both Jew and woman" (210).

4. For Kafka's allusions to the negative assumptions about female performers in nineteenth- and twentieth-century Germany, see Elisabeth Boa, *Kafka. Gender, Class and Race in the Letters and Fictions* (Oxford: Clarendon Press, 1996), 175–80.

5. For another account of the musical "paradigm of femininity" and its influence on Kafka, see Christine Lubkoll, "Dies ist kein Pfeifen. Musik und Negation in Franz Kafka's Erzählung 'Josefine, die Sängerin oder Das Volk der Mäuse,' " in *Deutsche Vierteljahresschrift für Literaturwissenschaft und Geistesgeschichte* 4 (1992), 748–64, esp. 751–56.

6. Giacomo Meyerbeer (1791–1864), German composer, mainly active in Paris [*Editor*].

7. Richard Wagner, *Oper und Drama*, in *Dichtungen und Schriften* (Frankfurt: Insel, 1983), 7: 98.

stand her art, you must not only hear but also see her" [p. 96]. This point demonstrates, on the one hand, her dependency on effects and, on the other, the "nothing(ness)" of her song because it needs the visual spectacle as a cover-up. The narrator expends great effort on convincing the reader of this "nothing(ness)" by repeating again and again that Josefine is not singing but really "just squeaking" [p. 95 ff.] like every other ordinary mouse or indeed even less competently than they. But the narrator not only calls into question Josefine's art, he also portrays Josefine's persona as a nerve-wracking diva, hysterical and childish in her behavior and thus not to be taken (and indeed not taken) seriously.

How do these two different traditions of thought about music fit together? How can Josefine's song fulfill a task considered so deeply important and serious as uniting a people in times of war and at the same time be denied any kind of aesthetic and ethical value and declared a ridiculous fake? Joining these two traditions turns out to be an intricate rhetorical trick of the narrator. For while he is all too ready to question the quality of Josefine's song, he is not at all ready to question the quality of the mouse people. Rather, questioning the former serves as a means of strengthening the latter. Contradicting his own previous remarks, the narrator presents the mouse people as a unity existing eternally and independently of any external events, describing them, for example, as an "immovable body" unswervingly "continu[ing] on its way" [p. 107], even though it only becomes this body for the duration of Josefine's concerts. He talks about the mouse people as if it were one single individual, for example when he notes that "the people take care of Josefine the way a father looks after a child [p. 99]" or that "our people * * * draw different conclusions and calmly reject [Josefine's] claim" or that "the people hear her out and pay no attention [to her argument]" [p. 104]. The narrator talks about the mouse people in this way even though, in several instances, he notes that the people is indeed split into different groups, even into various individuals. Thus, the individual is not at all necessarily integrated into the people, and the narrator's fear of being "cut * * * off so inscrutably" from the people [p. 105] shows that he knows about this. But he holds on to his wishful idea of the people as a unity in which every single mouse is always already integrated; which looks after every "comrade with * * * more than fatherly, with humble * * * concern" [p. 105]; and which exists independent of the vicissitudes of the day, simply being one big, unshakable whole. This is why he cannot allow the people to be in need of Josefine and why he has to claim that after her disappearance, "we will not miss very much at all" [p. 108]. While Josefine's performances are necessary to establish the people, the narrator has to suppress this fact in order to truly establish a belief in the people's existence. Thus, he mentions Josefine's power to unite the people but only to doubt the power of her song afterwards. Instead, he now tries to attribute the power to the people itself—for example, by calling the song a message of the people or by claiming that Josefine's concerts are "not so much a song recital as a popular assembly" [p. 100] or by suggesting that it is "rather the ceremonious quiet" of the audience and not her singing "that enchants us" [p. 96]. Hence, once the people is established, the narrator takes pains to claim that the power has come from the people in the first place, that not the song but the people "moved" itself, that for this people the song is not really necessary at all.[8] Here, then, Kafka adverts to the second tradition of thought about music in order to suppress the musical "origination" of the people and to establish the people itself at the origin.

"Josefine" joins the two traditions of thought about music only in order to subvert both of them. Kafka's story demonstrates that, despite the first tradition, music does not simply have a mysterious power to move listeners outside their rational selves; rather, this power is attributed to it. But while the narrator develops this insight, he suppresses another insight necessarily accompanying the first and as a result constructs a contradictory and self-subverting narrative. For, contrary to his intentions, not only the power of music but also the mouse people *itself* is shown to be the result of a performative process, existing only as a fantasy and only for the duration of the performance. Josefine's singing functions as a space of projection for the audience onto which they project an idealized version of themselves as a unified people. Then, listening to the song, they hear the voice of this people speaking to them, identifying with this voice and thence melting into the very unity they envisioned. So while, according to the narrator, there is nothing special about Josefine's song, there might just as well be nothing special about the mice. As Josefine's song only seems to have a certain power, the mice only seem to be a unified people—and then for only as long as the music lasts. In yet another way, Kafka's story subverts the second musicological tradition. It shows that "poor" music in fact does what "good" music was supposed to do: it creates, however evanescently, a people. So either it is not "poor" after all or, on the other hand, the opposition between "poor" and "good" music collapses. It turns out that theatricality and make-believe stand at the heart of the power at work in the performance situation. So what was "poor" about the "poor" music is actually what makes the whole process work.

8. In *Music in the Works of Broch, Mann, and Kafka,* John A. Hargraves interprets "the narrator's attempt * * * to tell Josefine's story," "criticizing" and finally "killing her," as an attempt to "control and censor the emotions set loose by music," which Kafka appears to have been frightened of as well [p. 329].

Meanwhile the question remains, reaching beyond Kafka's story and the scope of this text: why music? For the narrator is wrong to claim that music is not necessary for the mouse people. It may not have a mysterious power, but it is necessary as a space of projection. But why use music as a space of projection and not, say, any other of the fine arts? The answer is a traditional one: ever since the late eighteenth century, music had been labeled, at first critically and later positively, as the art most difficult to decipher. It means something to the listener, but it seems impossible to pinpoint this meaning. This indefinability makes music into a playground of the fantasies and wishes of its audience, chief among them the desire for an immediate kind of language with privileged access to deeper truths, such as the realm of the divine, of the will, or of the essence of a people. Similarly, in Kafka's story, Josefine's song is first emptied of meaning and then filled with a new one. The narrator claims that Josefine's singing is really just a squeaking, squeaking being the language of the mouse people. However, in Josefine's song, this "squeaking is freed from the bonds of daily life" [p. 103]; that is, as a language, it is deprived of its signifying function. Uttered for its own sake, it points to language as a play of sounds without definitive meaning.[9] It is this very absence of reference that invites the listeners to make music a space of projection. In this respect, Josefine's song is at first filled with the contents of dreams. Listening to Josefine's song, "the true body of her audience * * * has withdrawn into itself" [p. 102], dreaming dreams about their identity. Then, the contents of these dreams are declared to be the contents of the song: "into these dreams comes the sound of Josefine's squeaking * * *. Something of our poor, brief childhood is in it; something of lost, irretrievable happiness; but something of the active present-day life is in it as well" [pp. 102–03]. However, these contents are still very vague and incomplete; "something" of everything seems to be in the song, thereby transferring the indistinctness of musical meaning into an indistinctness of verbal meaning. In other instances, however, the meaning becomes more concrete, when the song becomes a "message from the people" [p. 100]. Yet there is no content to this message; or rather, the supposed origin of the song, the people, becomes its only message: the song is treated as evidence of the existence of a people. Hence, in Kafka's story music is used as a space of projection because of its openness of meaning; and precisely in line with this openness, *the story itself* becomes a space of projection for musical tradition. As we have seen from Nietzsche's early writings and the Wagner reception of the early twentieth century, the dominant tradition available to

9. See Kittler, *Turmbau zu Babel*, 226–228.

Kafka was one in which music was "instrumentalized" as a medium for the political fantasy of becoming and being a unified people.

A final set of concerns: is Kafka's story truly about music? For, as was pointed out above, the theatricality of the performance seems to be just as important for its effects. Furthermore, as the narrator claims, the mouse people is not only "totally unmusical," it also has nothing more than "an inkling of what song is" [p. 95]. This makes their judgment altogether dubious: how can they know whether Josefine's song is song at all; and their mistrust is further enhanced by the narrator's own doubts about the nature of Josefine's squeaking. This, now, is one of several indications that this story may not be specifically about music. Is it about art in general? What we do know for sure is that some kind of art is being consumed here: an audience is watching some kind of performance, be it a song recital, a play, or a monologue. But quite a peculiar performance it is, because there seems to be nothing special about it. In no way do Josefine's actions differ from those of everyday life, except that an audience has gathered to watch her after she has called for them. So—doubts multiply: is this story really about art, or does this gathering together and watching point to a specific behavior of the mouse people? And is it not rather that this behavior makes up the actual art performance, since the behavior (and not Josefine's song) constitutes the difference from everyday life? The narrator strongly suggests that it is really the "ceremonious quiet" produced by the listening audience that "enchants" this audience [p. 96]. In "The Silence of the Sirens" Kafka represents the Sirens as having "an even more terrible weapon than their song—namely their silence" [p. 128]. In "Josefine," too, silence appears to be more powerful than the song; indeed, for the narrator, silence is the sole source of the power experienced during the performance. But note that here the silence does not originate from the singer;[1] rather, the audience enchants *itself* by being silent. In their silence, they listen to themselves as a unified people, to the sounds of their communal listening, their "breathing with awe" [p. 98].[2] The unusual silence produces the situation of ceremony, elevating the performance situation above everyday life and creating a "stage" for Josefine's song. The short episode about the child's interrupting the performance and being immediately shushed by the audience proves how active

1. Admittedly, one could claim with the narrator that Josefine is not really singing at all—and Josefine's later refusal to sing goes hand in hand with her total disappearance, which does not seem to bother the audience very much.

2. As Gerhard Kurz notes with regard to *The Burrow* (paraphrasing the work of Martin Seel), "silence is not simply acoustic emptiness. (In silence, we can already hear our own circulation rustling.) If we immerse ourselves in silence like the animal 'I' ('deepest submersion'), it begins to 'rustle.' It is experienced as an intensity, as the being of emptiness become fullness. Experiencing this, the animal 'I' would experience 'rapture' " [p. 344].

the audience is in providing Josefine with her special status. It is altogether aggressive in the way it prohibits this one individual, the child, from disturbing the communal silence so as to protect another individual, Josefine, whose voice it wants to be heard.[3] In this way, Josefine's distinction, her song, and the power of her song, appear to be the creations of the audience.

The same is true for Josefine's power to gather the crowd. In order to do so she takes up a theatrical pose, "her little head tilted back, mouth half-open, eyes turned toward the heights" [p. 98]. This posture "indicates that she intends to sing," that is, it functions as a sign that is read and obeyed by the mice. But Josefine's sign does not reach far enough. The mice need to send out messengers gathering the listeners and to post sentinels on the roads waving to the newcomers. Hence, Josefine's initial sign initiates a chain of signs spreading the meaning of her posture everywhere. However, the fact that Josefine's initial sign needs messengers and sentinels in order to be effective is kept a secret and never told to Josefine. As a result, the illusion is preserved that Josefine has the power to gather her people by using signs immediately understood by everyone, not needing the help of any mediators, while in truth it is once again the mice who attribute this power to her.[4]

Hence it is the audience that makes Josefine's song into song. It is the audience that establishes the work of art it is watching and listening to.[5] This fact not only makes reception the most important component of art, it also brings the whole performance situation into close proximity with ritual. But what is this ritual about? Why are the mouse people so interested in it, imbuing Josefine and her song with their power? The performance situation establishes an (albeit temporary and illusory) identity of the mouse people. This is its primary function. And since Josefine and her song are to be used as a projection space for the identity of the mouse people, she has to emblematize the features ascribed to the mouse people by the narrator. According to him, the life of mice is defined by a continuous "struggle for existence" [p. 101], "shirking [being] utterly unknown" [p. 104] among mice. So he argues that Josefine, despite her demands to be relieved of work, "does not actually aspire to what she literally demands. She is reasonable, she is not work shy; * * * even if her demands were granted, she would surely not change her way of life, her work would never get in the way of her song" [p. 104]. Similarly, her negative character traits are described as also typical of the mouse people in general. Her ability to stand her ground against the opposition, as "insolent," "arrogant"

3. See Kittler, *Turmbau zu Babel*, 192.
4. See ibid. 196–97.
5. See Menke, *Prosopopoiia*, 749–56.

[p. 96] and "unworthy" [p. 103] as her reactions may seem, only mirrors the ability of her people to survive in an antagonistic environment. "Josefine asserts herself, this nothing of a voice, this nothing of an achievement asserts itself and makes its way to us," writes the narrator, noting at the same time that her "thin squeak in the midst of grave decisions is almost like the wretched existence of our people amid the tumult of a hostile world" [p. 100]. Finally, the art-less quality of Josefine's song also fits into the cultural decline of the mouse people. As the narrator writes, "we are too old for music, its excitement, its uplift does not suit our gravity: wearily we shoo it away; we have fallen back on our squeaking; some squeaking here and there, that is what suits us" [p. 102]. All throughout, Josefine's persona and her song are portrayed in a way to agree with the qualities of the mouse people. She remains the ordinary mouse, her song remains an ordinary squeaking, and this assures that the mice can identify with her. This is quite in line with the point that Adorno stressed about Freud's theory: the ordinariness of the leader is necessary for the mechanisms at work binding the masses and their leader. This fact is complemented by the idealization of the leader figure. In Kafka's story this idealization occurs through the attribution of a special position and power to Josefine and her song, achieved, for example, through the self-imposed gathering on her command and through the self-imposed silence of the audience.

If Josefine's performances are necessary for the founding of an identity of the mouse people, what then will happen after her disappearance? Is this the end of a mouse people capable of identifying itself as such? On the one hand, one could claim that her disappearance serves the narrator's desire to downplay her importance in order to stress the independence and timelessness of the people. On the other hand, he suggests that the memory of her squeaking will be just as loud and lively as her squeaking was when she was still present. Noting that "even during her lifetime" her squeaking might never have been "more than a mere memory" [p. 108], the narrator emphasizes the audience's participation in the creation of Josefine's song. And so, after her disappearance, the audience might still participate in her song by keeping her memory alive. Josefine's song might become a myth, building the foundation of the people's identity, being celebrated in ritualistic performances and itself functioning as the space of projection. And yet, on the other hand, the narrator also seems to doubt that such gatherings will still be possible after Josefine's disappearance. And this, in turn, raises the question of whether the mouse people would still be able to identify itself as a mouse people should the gatherings stop and the memory of Josefine's song no longer be kept alive. But Kafka's story provides no answer to this; it only confronts us with these questions. In this way, "Josefine" at once foreshadows and at the same time subverts a new kind of political ideology gaining ground among Kafka's contemporaries, such as the Conservative Revolution and Zionism and one ultimately practiced, in the worst case, by National Socialism[6]—this is the construction of a folkish identity by way of artistic performances and by way of a leader who fancies himself a great artist and his state one gigantic "total work of art." In this matter, Kafka specifically contributes an analysis of how actual or fictive listening behaviors in the late nineteenth and early twentieth centuries could become models for nationalist politics and be concretely "instrumentalized" for political agendas.

VIVIAN LISKA

Positions: On Franz Kafka's "Poseidon"†

Abstract

In addition to the traditional, allegorical interpretations, Franz Kafka's "Poseidon" can also be read a parable of the hermeneutic[1] situation itself. The various positions of the God of the Seas who has never really seen the seas correspond to the hopelessness of any attempt to achieve a definitive reading. The fruitless search for neutral intellectual understanding is contrasted with the positive alternative of experience through involvement.

Kafka's allegorical figure of thought (*Denkbild*) entitled "Poseidon" is a demythologizing play on traditional cultural material, transforming the energetic, earthshaking Greek God of the Seas into the tragicomic figure of a stressed-out administrator. In the guise of a grotesque mythological contrafact,[2] a parable arises about the limits of knowledge, the presumptions of rationality, and the unreadability of the world. The present essay begins by sketching possible biographical, psychological, socially-critical, religious, and philosophical readings and provides a brief overview of existing interpretations. Then it attempts to make clear the hermeneutic

---

6. See Peter Reichel, *Der schöne Schein des dritten Reiches. Faszination und Gewalt des Faschismus* (Munich: Hanser, 1991).
† Originally published as "Stellungen: zu Franz Kafkas 'Poseidon,' " *Zeitschrift für deutsche Philologie*, 115 (1996), 226–238. Translated by Eric Patton. Page numbers in brackets refer to this Norton Critical Edition.
1. Interpretive, as referring to hermeneutics, the study of the principles of interpretation and explanation [*Editor*].
2. In music, an entirely new composition produced by using the chord structure of a given, established composition [*Editor*].

dimension of the text from the connection between the reader's difficulties in understanding and the implicit epistemological[3] problems in the text.

From a narrative perspective that is at first unclear, the parable tells of Poseidon's conscientiousness and thoroughness in his administrative work, which is imposed upon him by some higher impersonal and nameless authority, and of his dissatisfaction with this office and his desire for "more cheerful work." A change in these conditions, however, does not seem possible. Several alternatives are suggested and then taken back at the same time in opaque arguments. The reasons for this "case [having] * * * absolutely no prospects of success" lead to the central paradox of the parable, which takes this absence of any "prospects" literally: This is a god of the seas who has hardly seen the oceans, his empire and the domain of his life, and probably never will, as we may well conclude from the end.

The bizarre play between the mythical realm of the Greek god and modern bureaucracy first evokes the parodic figure of a grim, mistrustful, continually dissatisfied administrator entangled in an inscrutable hierarchy, who has missed his true life owing to the pressure to master his realm, the need to look after his daily business, and the impenetrable restrictions imposed on him from above.

A number of allegorical interpretations suggest themselves. The text can first be read in connection with Kafka's own unhappy official work or as a parody of the paternal work ethic. There are also parallels between Kafka's description of his own literary activity and Poseidon's tasks: the continual need to make corrections ("he did the accounts over again"), the awareness of doing work that was "imposed on him"—the sense of which he doubts again and again, although "nothing really appealed to him so much as his present office." Above all, there are resonances with Kafka's recurrent feeling of being outside of real life, of glimpsing it only from afar—or further, from the depths of a lonely observation post—and, like Poseidon, never having really seen the seas. This would also be the sense in which to understand the rare "trip," the forays into real life; and the "quick little tour" at the end would perhaps represent the dream of a final experience of real life before death (Kafka was already aware of his tuberculosis at this point in time).

From a socially-critical standpoint, we can read the text as a general parody of administrative activity: the boredom, the deceitful superiors ("one must try to seem to accommodate him"), the au-

3. Having to do with knowing, more precisely, with epistemology, the study of the method, grounds, limits, and validity of knowledge [*Editor*].

thoritarian conservatism ("that was how it had to be"), and the use of the anonymous pronoun "one" (German: *man*) echoing the language of the civil service, in which the individual evades his responsibility by appealing to anonymous higher authorities. A psychological interpretation might recognize in the grotesque playing-down of the mythological Poseidon figure an impotent rebellion in the face of an omnipresent but inaccessible authority or father figure, who stands as a super-ego behind the omnipresent authority of the "one." From a religious point of view, this authority has the characteristics of an angry, calculating god; the requirement that "that was how it had to be" would refer in this context to a monotheistic imperative, a transcendent and unexplained commandment.

But the epistemological implications and possible interpretations extend beyond this. From this perspective, a number of questions present themselves right away. Why is there no "more cheerful work" for Poseidon? Why is his situation hopeless? Why has he barely seen the seas? These questions open up a perspective that makes Kafka's text a figure of thought (*Denkbild*) for the problem of modernity that Max Horkheimer and Theodor W. Adorno later characterized as the "Dialectic of Enlightenment."[4] "Poseidon" stages a confrontation between mythical and rational interpretations of the world. The master of the seas has shrunk down from a reigning to a regulating god. The mythical explanation of the powers of nature has given way to calculating, scientific analysis. The German word for calculating (doing the accounts)—*rechnen*—is etymologically related to "ratio" (reason). No longer trapped in a tradition or supra-personal system of thought, the calculating rational thinker no longer depends on "assistants" (or "auxiliary powers") but relies on his own reason in his search for meaning. In his enlightenment-based presumptuousness, he wants to administer and master "*all* the waters," or totality, to see appearances in the "depths of the world's ocean" from the bottom as a unity ("world's ocean" as opposed to the previous plural "waters"), yet he clearly never reaches a conclusive result. The new god of Enlightenment is weary of his office and has found no final truth. His work proves never-ending in this late phase of the modern age. The essence of things is not accessible through reason. Like the man from the country in Kafka's parable "Before the Law," who must be satisfied with "the fleas in [the doorkeeper's] fur collar" [p. 68], Poseidon

4. The title of a groundbreaking critique of the assumptions of Enlightenment thought, written in California in 1942–44 by Theodor W. Adorno (1903–1969) and Max Horkheimer (1895–1973), both eminent German professors of philosophy exiled from their homeland [*Editor*].

has hardly glimpsed the object of his search for knowledge.[5] His will to power, his claim to a "superior [or 'masterful'] position," and his desire for totality obstruct his view of any real alternatives. He cannot jump over his own shadow, cannot escape from his own-most element—calculating thought—as he cannot imagine a position "unrelated to [or 'outside'] the waters" without torment. His rebellious intent remains caught within his own limitations.

Poseidon's epistemological distress is countered by the authority of mythologizing law-giving in the words "no one really thought of removing Poseidon from his office * * * and that was how it had to be." The impersonal authorities confirm the hopelessness of his situation, even if from another vantage point: Now it is not Poseidon's limitations that stand in the way of a redemptive alternative but rather the maintenance of the status quo and cosmic order in the name of tradition. So both myth and rationality, though opposed to one another, equally hinder the fulfillment of Poseidon's dream of "more cheerful work";[6] he struggles in vain against the authority and claim to eternity of the mythical world order. The apparently powerful Poseidon, chained to his reason, is powerless, because like the man from the country he cannot seize the freedom to overstep the law and *act* otherwise.[7] The fatiguing of the thirst for positivistic knowledge and the (religious or generally traditional) continuance of conservative authority are both factors of little weight: Poseidon's work remains unsatisfied and dissatisfying, and the opposing voice of mythic authority remains without legitimation. The mythic idea has become a worn-out cliché: From the standpoint of the modern Poseidon, the mythic image of the God of the Seas "dashing (or, literally, 'riding in a carriage') over the waves" has a tired and ridiculous effect—as we can see from the ironic combination of traditional poetic language and the humorous slang of the time. For its part, mythic thinking does not take Poseidon's complaints seriously: The expectation of some change in the situation seems just as ridiculous from this perspective as does myth for

5. The parable "Before the Law" shares other similarities with "Poseidon." Like the God of the Seas, the man from the country has a position that is both unsatisfactory and "intended only for [him]" [p. 69], and he waits in vain for "admittance" as Poseidon waits to travel the seas. The man from the country spies a light behind the door, while Poseidon catches a fleeting glimpse of the seas; both visions remain inaccessible. Like the man from the country, Poseidon cherishes false hopes, whose respective fulfillment—being let in through the door, having a change in position—is awaited from an obscure and deceptive external authority. Both parables illustrate the futility of the thirst for knowledge, the insufficiency of reason before the law, and the misrecognition of one's own freedom.

6. A more audacious translation would be "gayer" (*fröhlicher*) work. For the writer-philosopher Nietzsche is very likely on Kafka's mind, and one of Nietzsche's early masterpieces is entitled *Die fröhliche Wissenschaft* ("*la gaya scienza*"). Nietzsche's best translator, Walter Kaufmann, titled Nietzsche's treatise *The Gay Science* [*Editor*].

7. An allusion to the hero of "Before the Law" [p. 68] [*Editor*].

the man of reason. The Enlightenment rejects myth as explanation; the belief in the possibility of rational knowledge itself becomes a myth.

The calculating Poseidon appears as a failing, Enlightenment-oriented god of the thirst for objective knowledge who, although he has repressed the old, mythic ruler of nature as a fictional explanation of natural forces, now seeks in vain as the governor of the exact sciences to exercise his will to power, to a "superior position," from the distance of the observer within the subject/object distinction. This term of Nietzsche's—"will to power"—is not a chance reference; Poseidon has often applied for "what he called more cheerful work." He observes the world from the bottom of the sea, and in this he resembles those thorough calculators in Nietzsche's *The Gay Science* who have a reason for everything, the "mechanists who like to pass as philosophers * * * [who are seeking] the doctrine of the first and last laws on which all existence must be based as on a ground floor."[8] Nietzsche explains earlier:

> That the only justifiable interpretation of the world should be one in which *you* are justified because one can continue to work and do research scientifically in *your* sense [you really mean mechanistically]—an interpretation that permits counting, calculating, weighing, seeing, and touching, and nothing more—that is a crudity and naiveté * * *. Would it not be rather probable that, conversely, precisely the most superficial and external aspect of existence—what is most apparent, its skin and sensualization—would be grasped first * * *.[9]

Nietzsche's alternative to senseless, never-ending calculating and weighing "from the bottom up" resembles Poseidon's dream of a "quiet moment" of existential revelation: just "a quick little tour" on the surface of the sea, if not the sensual perception of the sea in general.

Hardly having seen or really traveled the seas equates to missing real life and is to be understood in an existential philosophical sense as well. Only the "quick little tour" that Poseidon dreams of before the end would equal giving up the epistemological relationship to the world and experiencing authentic existence. In contrast to calculation and theoretically isolated consciousness, or the purely expedient, rational viewpoint, the entire physical/mental/spiritual person participates in the "tour," or the sublation of the subject/object distinction. In his continuous postponement of an authentic mode of existence, the calculating Poseidon misses the fully "engaged fulfillment of life"

8. Friedrich Nietzsche, *The Gay Science*, trans. Walter Kaufmann (New York: Random House, 1974), 335.
9. Ibid.

that Kafka evoked with equal longing and hopelessness.[1] This life fulfillment is realized by Poseidon only when he is thinking about temporality, facing death—the "end of the world."

We can also find implications for the philosophy of language in
the comparison between Poseidon, who desires another position,
and the decree of the supra-personal authority who determines that
Poseidon must remain God of the Seas. Language and the concepts
with which the poet plays have always already been "taken," used
by others. "Poseidon" must remain God of the Seas because this
linguistic concept is common property and cannot therefore be
changed at will. Instead of an omnipotent, immediately masterful
creative power, there is—as in the difference between the reigning
and the regulating god—only a functional ordering of pre-existing
material. Poseidon must remain God of the Seas because the poet
can speak only as the regulator or administrator of an already ex-
tant reserve of ideas. Like the narrator, he also speaks only as a
"mouthpiece," not as a creator; he is not an authoritative voice but
rather part of a collective authority [the "one" encountered in the
German word *man* in this text]. In the extreme case, myth as supra-
personal conceptual material loses its original explanatory function
over the generations and has a worn-out effect, like the cliché of
Poseidon dashing over the waves. His "office," however, as an example of the linguistic and conceptual archive of the collective,
cannot be changed. Poseidon, it is said, is dissatisfied with his "office"; the alternatives are characterized as "positions." These syn-
onyms "office" and "position" only seem to be interchangeable:
"office" refers to a long-term public post and "position" to a provisional, personal position. As a contrafact of the myth, "Poseidon"
puts into question even the relationship addressed here between
common conceptual property and poetic mythopoesis.[2] The demythologizing impetus expresses its own creative failure in "that
was how it had to be," but at the same time, with this "new" "Poseidon"—this text itself—it brings about a refutation of the decree
pronounced in it. The law-giving authority of tradition is thereby
given the lie by the text itself: Kafka's short and amusing mytho-
poetic story is itself the redemption of the utopia of Poseidon's
being relieved of his eternal, monotonous post.

Like these briefly sketched suggestions, most interpretations by
earlier critics have tried to conceive of this figure allegorically and to
fit it into a respective interpretive framework, whether biographical,
psychological, socially-critical, religious, or philosophical. Several examples will be given here primarily to indicate aspects of the text that

1. Hartmut Binder, *Kafka-Handbuch* (Stuttgart 1979), 1:135.
2. The making of myths [*Editor*].

were either misunderstood, not understood, not interpreted, or perhaps not clearly interpretable, the blank spots and difficulties in understanding that were overlooked or incorrectly resolved in the
various interpretations. For example, the reading of the Poseidon figure as "the distorted modern image of the powerful, very busy administrator" (Norbert Kassel)[3] is all too simplifying: The "power" of
Poseidon is by no means clear and is actually one of the problematic
aspects of the text, for if Poseidon is a "powerful" figure, he is also
one whose work is imposed upon him, who apparently cannot change
his own position, who does not know that he is being deceived; in
short, a figure who is subordinate to the opinions and directions of
others. Another view, that the text embodies the "combination of two
totalitarian areas of mythic dependency: humans' dependence on the
unknown masters of nature and the masters' dependence on unknown, mastered nature" (Karin Keller) overlooks in its symmetrical
arrangement the complex reciprocity of the interdependencies, claims
to power, and Poseidon's position in this constellation.

Another difficulty in understanding this text can be demon-
strated by means of a further simplifying interpretation, which sees
"the driving out of despair by hope in the view of the end of the
world" (Hans Reiss). Isn't it rather a case of the "driving out of
hope" on Poseidon's side, who remains in his hopeless situation for
reasons that defy all logic?[4] And in addition, isn't this hope taken
back in the same breath? The passage reads: "He *used to* say that
* * * he could still do (*would still be able to make*) a quick little
tour" (emphasis added). From what standpoint in time can this
statement formulated in the past tense be made?[5] Either Poseidon
has given up his hope in the course of the years, or someone is
speaking here who has "outlived" Poseidon and knows what really
happened, namely, that he never took his little trip. Who is speaking here anyway, and from what position in space and time?

It is not so easy to figure out the perspective from which the
words are being spoken here. Though the text begins from an au-
thorial, apparently neutral perspective, the first use of the pronoun

3. All further quotes from the Kafka criticism are taken from Binder, 2:364–384.
4. The arguments that are apparently supposed to prove the necessity of the status quo are
quite illogical: the "great Poseidon" must have a "superior position" (tautology); the administration of "one particular ocean" would be "not less" than that of all the oceans
(disregard for mathematical proportionality); the proposals made to Poseidon regarding
his wish for "more cheerful work" (being in charge of "one particular ocean," having a
position "unrelated to the waters") do not actually address that wish at all. All are false
arguments.
5. Could it be, as Käte Hamburger has postulated about the narrative past tense, that here
the "past" nature of this tense has been suspended, so that hope still exists within the
narrated world? Against this possibility we must first note the striking phrase "he used to
say," which is usually used to refer to something said by someone who is now dead, i.e.,
something definitely past and gone. More importantly, the present tense is used twice in
the text [in the German subjunctive], in contrast to the past form "he used to say."

"one" ("It cannot be said that" [One cannot say that]) signals the appearance of a personal voice. In the phrase shortly after, "what he called more cheerful work," an implicit distinction is made between the expression of the narrative voice and that of Poseidon. The neutrally descriptive tone of the first sentence shifts in a barely perceptible manner. A first-person narrator appears ever more clearly behind the mask of the use of "one" (in the German), the confusing passive voice, and indirect forms such as "whenever various proposals were made to him," "it turned out that," and "it was also very difficult to find something else." It is not always clear from what perspective one could assign "the great Poseidon" "*only*" a superior position and "*not possibly*" "one particular ocean" (emphasis added). Are these Poseidon's opinions? Or are these illusory justifications made by the supra-personal authority for Poseidon, who hopes all unawares for change? The decree of the supra-personal authority—"Furthermore, his complaints were not really taken seriously; * * * he had been fated to be the God of the Seas from the beginning of time, and that was how it had to be"—departs from Poseidon's position. If this last sentence of the first paragraph is obviously outside of Poseidon's perspective, then the following paragraph apparently begins from Poseidon's own perspective, for after the decree from elsewhere we now read: "Meanwhile, he was seated [*here*] in the depths of the world's ocean" [emphasis added]. We are here transferred into Poseidon's position again. With the introductory words ("He used to say") and the complex temporal construction of the last sentence, the text ends again outside of Poseidon's viewpoint. This disorientation of location that oscillates between external commentary and an interior viewpoint distorts an objective, general overview—even the commentary betrays an individualized voice and is thus only a subjective point of view—and manifests the interplay between an apparently neutral perspective of observation and an involved perspective of experience, which, as I will go on to argue, also becomes the central content of the story.

In the allegorical interpretations previously mentioned, the uncertainty in perspective and the disorientation of place and time are not taken into account. But the question cannot be avoided: From what perspective, from what position does this narrative proceed? And isn't the text concerned precisely with "positions," with Poseidon's powerless-powerful position, and above all his position with regard to the sea and the possible—or rather impossible—alternatives to this position? The problem of perspective presented on the level of the narrative form is encountered again as the content of the text, and it reflects the problems of the reader and his or her hermeneutical situation vis-à-vis the text. The result is a threefold connection of the perspective problem: as narrative form, as the main theme of the text, and as an implicit hermeneutical challenge to the reader to consider his or her own position.

The text begins with the description of a location: "Poseidon sat at his desk." We learn about his mode of activity—he does the accounts (calculates)—but next to nothing about its content. Rather, Poseidon is concerned with his own position (*Stellung*) which does not satisfy him (*ihn nicht zufriedenstellt*). He applies for another, we read; he can only ever receive a "superior *position*"; he is offered alternative "positions"—note: only apparently—that don't appeal to him, however. The very idea (*Vor-Stellung*) as a mental location as well as the ideas (*Vor-stellungen*) that others have of him fill him with rage. The fact that Poseidon is concerned less with the content of his work than with the assumptions and conditions of his position regarding the sea, his reflective perspective, establishes an analogy to the reader's activity of understanding and to his or her own hermeneutic situation. Like Poseidon's consciousness of never coming to a final conclusion, the reader's expectation of a clear, final truth, as promised by traditional myths and (traditionally enlightenment-oriented) parables, is instead steered toward his or her own process of reflection. What emerges from the parable is not a meaning beyond the text that can be objectified but rather one's own position vis-à-vis the text. Hence, the position of the reader toward the text can be seen as analogous to Poseidon's position toward the sea: Like Poseidon before his endless task of occupying a position intended for "mastery (superiority)," the reader tries in vain to manage "all the waters," to "master" them in an orderly fashion, and to put the totality of that which is to be understood here into a system of rational meaning that creates unity.

The narrator speaks of Poseidon's hopeless situation. The central paradox of the God of the Seas who has "hardly seen the oceans" results from the inadequate positions or perspectives that Poseidon occupies. We find him "at his desk, doing the accounts (calculating)," "in the depths" of the world's ocean, and on visits "to the heights" of Olympus: each of these three positions corresponds to a perspective from which his view of the sea remains obstructed. In parallel to this, we can develop three hermeneutical positions. The first "position" is the theoretical distance of the "desk" at which Poseidon carries out his endless calculations. As a position of observational distance, it stands in contrast to immediate experience, and even hinders it, for we read explicitly that *only after the "final reckoning"* could the "quick little tour" take place [emphasis added]. This provides an illustration of the core statement of Wilhelm Dilthey's[6] hermeneutics:

6. Wilhelm Dilthey (1833–1911), for many years professor of philosophy at the University of Berlin, was the chief German post-Romantic thinker of hermeneutics. He sought to

"Observation * * * destroys experience."[7] Dilthey connects this idea to the problem of temporality and the ungraspableness of the present moment: "It is never the present * * *. [One tries in vain] through any kind of effort to experience the flow of life oneself"—just as Poseidon tries in vain to calculate the flowing waters—"for the moment is fixed by the attention that now holds fast *that which itself is flowing*" (emphasis added).[8] With the exception of the end, the story "Poseidon" floats in a temporality of timelessness; the occurrences seem endlessly repeatable: "endless," "continually," "from the beginning of time," "that was how it had to be." When, at the end, it is a question of actually seeing the sea, the register of time changes: "fleetingly," "hasty," "moment," "just before the end," "still * * * quick." Theoretical observation aimed at timeless truths destroys the moment experienced as presence through its very contemplation. The complex layers of time in the last sentence reveal this connection: the sentence begins in the past-tense form of narrative perspective and ends with the future imperfect. The only present-tense form in the sentence is a subjunctive ("he was waiting" [*er warte*]) and thus only an idea (*Vor-Stellung*). This can only be experienced, not observed, and thus escapes the calculating Poseidon like the seas, whose symbolism refers to temporality.[9] For hermeneutic activity, this means that meaning changes with time, historically, and cannot be finally grasped, because we are also carried along by history, as in the image of the tour.

Poseidon's second "position"—on the bottom of the sea—also has its hermeneutic counterpart. Poseidon does not travel through the seas, does not go "dashing over the waves," as the myth would have it. The cheerful, careless naturalness of this ironic image contrasts with the tedious work of calculation "*in the depths of the world's ocean*" and opposes the surface to the depths. Taking Poseidon's implicit bottom-up "thoroughness" (*Gründlichkeit*) literally, the text now situates his position in the depths (*Grund* = "bottom" [*Editor*]); he is at the bottom of the sea and sees it "from below." Objectivizing observation thus sees things from the viewpoint of their ground (*Grund*), the foundations (*Grundlagen*) of the reasons for them. However, the experience of the sea, the "more cheerful work," lies, according to this conclusion, not in the fixed position

---

give a rigorous foundation to humanistic study; at the center of his thinking is the concept of "experienced life," which is a matter of historical contingency and changeableness [*Editor*].

7. Quoted in Hans Georg Gadamer and Gottfried Boehm, eds. *Philosophische Hermeneutik* (Frankfurt a.M.: Suhrkamp, 1976), 193.

8. Ibid.

9. Cf. Hans Blumenberg: "The rules of time seem to be what remain of the cosmos for the sea." Hans Blumenberg, *Shipwreck with Spectator: Paradigm of a Metaphor for Existence*, trans. Steven Rendall (Cambridge, Mass.: MIT Press, 1997), 9.

at the bottom but in the bold movement of traveling the seas themselves, not in the—impossible—knowledge of their absolute essence but in their "function" for the person experiencing them. The seas cannot be known in their essence as an independent object but can only be experienced (*er-fahren* [*fahren* = "travel"— *Editor*]) in involved experience (*Erlebnis*). Relating this to the hermeneutic position, we may say that in his or her efforts to objectify and recognize the foundations or ground of the text, the reader misses its function as experience, as journey, as a process that involves his or her historical and individual person.

Similar principles apply to Poseidon's third "position," the destination of his journeys, the heights of Olympus. Olympus itself, the highest place and location of all-seeing "Jupiter" (why not "Zeus"? "irregular breathing"? temporal disorientation? whim?) conveys, after the distance of theory and the ground, the distance of the heights, the overview, the overall perspective. As with his view from the depths, Poseidon cannot see the seas from this position either. The journey from the depths of the sea to the heights of Olympus leads from one standpoint to another—from the analytical bottom-up perspective to the synthetic overview. Only in the moment of changing over, in the process itself, are the seas to be seen "hast[il]y," "fleetingly." This epiphanic, momentary character sticks with the last image as well: The "quick little tour," finally free of destination and purpose, remains a utopia—literally, "without a location." It is the utopia of u-topia, the abandonment of every position, even the abandonment of the mastering thirst for knowledge itself.

Alternatives are suggested to the three positions "actually" taken by Poseidon: (1) administering a particular sea; or (2) a position outside the water. Of course, they are immediately found to be inappropriate or intolerable and are thus rejected. We read: "[H]e could not possibly be put in charge of, let us say, one particular ocean" because, as the wholly incomprehensible argument goes, administering a particular sea would amount to "not less but only more small-minded" work. In addition, such a reduction would not do justice to Poseidon's claim to a "superior position." These suggestions prove also to be only apparent, only false hopes meant to calm the tormented Poseidon. But even before they are presented, they are already negated by reasons presented in the tone of false self-evidence ("not possibly, * * * let us say * * *," "the great Poseidon could only be given," "by the way"). This sequence—wish, possibility, reasons for impossibility—is a form of that "marking time in place" emphasized again and again by Kafka and in the literature on Kafka, an apparently logical movement that actually never goes anywhere, because each step, each movement of thought, is taken back in the same moment. Poseidon's endless calculation that never moves forward is illustrated as such in the text itself: For every possibility there is a counterargument, every suggestion proves to be impossible to execute from the start, and the logical causality that the reader expects to have a starting and finishing point is frustrated. The goal, which is a change in Poseidon's office and the end of his accounting work, remains unattainable even after the end of the text, eternally always the same distance away. In addition, the last words of the first paragraph ("that was how it had to be") indicate that the entire discussion of alternatives to Poseidon's position is a deception, that the reasons are only apparently based on logical causality, and that behind them there are only existentially or ideologically motivated justifications (such as the conservative attitude of myth here). As was already concluded from the narrative form, no statement or argument is purely based on reason and thus neutral; every standpoint has its position already inscribed in it.

Why is the administration of "one particular ocean" not a smaller but rather a "more small-minded task"? Why, with this alternative, would Poseidon lose his "superior position"? The relationship between the "particular ocean" and "all the waters" corresponds to that between the particular and the general, or between the part and the whole. What lies behind the apparent contradiction that the calculation of the part is not less infinite than that of the whole? Perhaps the insight that the calculability of the part, as in the hermeneutic circle,[1] is bound up with knowledge of the whole, and thus the administration of the "particular" remains endless. The masterful position of distant observation would thus be undermined: Upon entry into the circle—the "little tour"—linear causality is abandoned, according to which the whole consists of the sum of particular and ascertainable parts that simply need to be added together. Now, if the calculation of the particular or part is not less infinite than that of the general or whole, this insight destroys something like the goal of traditional allegory, which is to reach some ungraspable and general ideal through a graspable, finally ascertainable particular. If that which is particular, concrete, and ascertainable according to expectation—such as traditional parables are—itself remains unascertainable and incalculable, this leads us to Kafka's statement * * * that "truth is indivisible" and that the endlessness of the search for truth is experienced as endless in every particle.[2] The logical expectation that part of the waters, a particular sea, would mean less work, is negated. This "error in cal-

---

1. The notion that one cannot understand the meaning of a part of a work until one understands the whole, even though an understanding of the whole depends on an understanding of the various parts. Interpretation is therefore a temporal process involving continual adjustments of an initial hypothesis [*Editor*].

2. Franz Kafka, *Nachgelassene Schriften und Fragmente II*, ed. Jost Schillemeit (Frankfurt a.M.: Fischer, 1992), 62.

culation" remains irresolvable for Poseidon and for pure logic—and would thus also be a danger to his "superior position."

The second alternative that proves to be insupportable for Poseidon is a position "unrelated to the waters." Seen metaphorically, this refers to renouncing the seas and the search for knowledge itself. The very thought is unimaginable for Poseidon. In the suggestion of a position "unrelated to the waters" there lies— literally—another paradox: It would mean that Poseidon is for the present time *in* the water and nevertheless has hardly seen the seas. This apparent violation of logic also actually causes Poseidon's divine breath—the logos—to become "irregular," and his entire autocratic, statuesque breast, the source of this breath, begins to heave. Like the forest one cannot see for the trees, the waters that surround Poseidon do not let him see the seas.

This contradiction thus leads to a further hermeneutic dead-end: In contrast to the distance of the previously mentioned positions, it is now the excessive nearness that hinders knowledge. This concealing closeness is the hermeneutic starting point, related to the "hiddenness of the self-evident," in the words of Hans-Georg Gadamer.[3] But as mentioned, the contradiction is only apparent: It confirms the implications of the entire text, namely, that the seas are not a positivistically calculable sum of water but an invitation to a journey. Poseidon neglects this invitation, pushing it back to the end of time, but is aware of its possibility. As long as the reader remains fixated like Poseidon on the position of administration, of mastering the text with an absolute, objectifiable, generalizing meaning, his or her work is also endless and finally "hopeless." In the face of the contradictions and paradoxes, the disorientation and oscillations in perspective, the reader attempts—as Kafka scholarship proves—new calculations again and again. But the coherently allegorical, objectifying interpretation distorts the view of the rationally ungraspable nature of the seas. "The sea," writes Hans Blumenberg in his reflections on the metaphor of ship travel, "is the sphere of the unreckonable and lawless, in which it is difficult to find one's bearings."[4] To see and "really travel" the seas means not only to recognize the qualities just mentioned but also to recognize that this sphere cannot be calculated but only personally experienced in the aporias[5] of calculation and the various epistemological perspectives—in the process of reflecting upon one's own position vis-à-vis the text. In contrast to the fixed positions of Poseidon, the

3. Hans-Georg Gadamer (1900–2002), a major twentieth-century historian and theoretician of hermeneutics. His magnum opus is *Wahrheit und Methode* (Truth and method), 1960 [*Editor*].
4. Blumenberg, 8.
5. Logical dilemmas [*Editor*].

"little tour" indicates an insight into the fruitlessness of object-oriented thought and the renunciation of an autocratic claim to totality, a secured observation post, the goal-oriented thirst for knowledge aimed at mastery. "The move from land to sea," writes Blumenberg, is for the man or woman of reason "a mis*step* into the inappropriate and the immoderate."[6] The renunciation of the measurable would be, like ocean travel in Blumenberg's words, a "crossing of boundaries," the "hasty and audacious" entry of the man or woman of reason into the sphere of incalculability.[7] And perhaps after calculating in vain, the reader will encounter the wishful notion of a "quiet moment," in which his or her serious, fixed position can be given up along with the calculating search for meaning and thirst for knowledge, and—after the final reckoning, of course—the reader can smile about "Poseidon" and about him or herself.

But perhaps—after all, we are reading Kafka—this final "reckoning," the renunciation of calculation and the reckoning with its compulsions, is only apparently final: For why does Poseidon push his hope for the end of the tiresome calculations back to the extreme end of time? Why does he prefer no other position to his own? How seriously can we take Poseidon's complaints and his hopes for salvation, as the text itself says? Is there not a completely different reason why he remains at his post behind all the apparent reasons for the impossibility of changing his situation? Is his calculating work, despite all its hopelessness, not the work that "appealed to him" the most? In Kafka's story *The Burrow*, the creature says: "[A]ll these are very laborious calculations, and the delight that the sharp-witted mind takes in itself is sometimes the sole reason why it continues its calculations" [p. 163]. Perhaps Poseidon also secretly gets pleasure from the endless, senseless calculation of the seas, as does the reader in the search for meaning and an interpretation of the text. And what if, after a renunciation of a position of mastery—of the mandate of one's own understanding, of a fixed epistemological perspective—what if the endless calculation as the experience of reflection upon the text were itself the more cheerful work, the little tour * * * ?

6. Blumenberg, 9.
7. Ibid.

BENNO WAGNER

"No one indicates the direction": The Question of Leadership in Kafka's Later Stories†

"And so, disciple Kafka," runs an imaginary conversation between the playwright Bertolt Brecht and Kafka that Brecht himself composed: "You find that the legal and economic organization of your society has become quite uncanny?" "Yes." "You no longer feel at home in it." "No." "You think a bureaucrat's file is an uncanny thing?" "Yes." "And now you are clamoring for a leader (ein Führer) whom you can follow, disciple Kafka?"[1]

Brecht's didactic fable rightly intuits a keen political awareness in Kafka's work. Unfortunately, Brecht misunderstands its function. Kafka addresses the topic of leadership as a political issue requiring clarification and at the same time as a poetic opportunity; this is something different from saying that he is "clamoring for a leader." On this question, as with many other issues of political power, Kafka's contribution is original—and subtle. Yet it is precisely his political consciousness, whether explicitly grasped by Kafka's readers or not, that propelled his "irresistible rise" as a modern classic after World War II. What Brecht and other blatantly politically minded authors called Kafka's "manifold uselessness" (to the Communist program) is a source of the fascination he exerts: it is the resistance of an oeuvre that cannot be colonized by any of the dominant political ideologies of the twentieth century.

Some of this blindness in Kafka's critics is based on plain ignorance of the facts. Today we know that Kafka was a leading representative of the largest workmen's insurance institute in the Hapsburg Empire in the years 1908–1922.[2] As a result, he knew a lot more about the legal and economic organization of his time than any of the experts of political economy so much in evidence after World War I. Kafka was not in the least indifferent toward real, daily, empirical politics; and his viewpoint far exceeded that of the anxious petty bourgeois suffering passively from the hiddenness and impersonality of modern life and longing for reassuring leadership. Kafka's writings are intricately connected to the vibrancy of political issues and events of his day. And, furthermore, it is exactly

---

† This essay appears for the first time in this Norton Critical Edition. Printed by permission of the author. Page numbers in brackets are to this Norton Critical Edition.

1. Walter Benjamin, "Gespräche mit Brecht," in *Benjamin über Kafka*, ed. Hermann Schweppenhäuser (Frankfurt: Suhrkamp, 1981), 151. Translated by the editor of this Norton Critical Edition.

2. For a comprehensive understanding of Kafka's professional profile, see *Franz Kafka, Amtliche Schriften*, eds. Klaus Hermsdorf and Benno Wagner (Frankfurt: Fischer, 2004).

the web of what Brecht called Kafka's "mystifications"—the complexity and detail of Kafka's prose—that contains the rules and strategy of Kafka's leadership game. This serious game is played out through fictional reflections on leadership that illuminate the issue of leadership from many different angles; and these reflections embed the voices and positions of real persons of a certain cultural notoriety.[3]

To explore some of the rules and stakes of this game, we can take our lead from a "Marxist" intuition somewhat more penetrating than Brecht's. Four decades later, the French critics Deleuze and Guattari write,

> Kafka is an author who laughs with a profound joy * * *. And from one end to the other, he is a political author, prophet of the future world, because he has two poles that he will know how to unify in a completely new assemblage: * * * that of the bureaucrat with a great future ahead of him, plugged into real assemblages that are in the process of coming into shape, and that of a nomad who is involved in fleeing things in the most contemporary way and who plugs into socialism, anarchism, social movements.[4]

The last part of these remarks is cogent for its image of the nomad; it also represents an improvement to Brecht's account, too, by assigning to Kafka the opposite political impulse—an affinity with "socialism." But this is also a tendentious claim that needs to be adjusted. It is rather these critics' first observation—that Kafka laughs—that leads us immediately to our reading of "disciple Kafka's" conversation on political leadership.

It happened at a formal meeting at his insurance institute. Kafka, along with two of his colleagues, had been promoted, and now they were expected to express their gratitude to the president; but Kafka could not restrain his laughter. As he described this occasion afterwards to his fiancée Felice Bauer:

> I can also laugh, Felice, have no doubt about this * * *. It even happened to me once, at a solemn meeting with our president * * * that I started to laugh, and how! It would be too involved to describe to you this man's importance; but believe me, it is very great: an ordinary employee thinks of this man as not on this earth but in the clouds. And as we usually have little op-

3. The intention of such texts is not to establish firm hierarchies of superior authority or right/wrong distinctions between them. Unlike statements of political theory, platforms, and propaganda that claim the sole superiority of a single point of view, Kafka's texts generate new combinations of ideas that in turn create a space in which readers can discuss and negotiate positions anew—a space that readers may enter and share according to their alertness and knowledge.

4. Gilles Deleuze/Félix Guattari, *Kafka. Toward a Minor Literature* (Minnesota: University of Minnesota Press, 1986), 41.

portunity of talking to the Emperor, contact with this man is for the average clerk—a situation common of course to all large organizations—tantamount to meeting the Emperor. Needless to say, like anyone exposed to clear and general scrutiny whose position does not quite correspond to his achievements, this man invites ridicule; but to allow oneself to be carried away by laughter at something so commonplace and, what's more, in the presence of the great man himself, one must be out of one's mind * * *.[5]

The ensuing scene of carnivalesque derision is one of many such moments in which Kafka reveals himself as a "laughing author." And this laughter is not itself politically neutral: for one thing, observe its presence in the related political reflections of Kafka's Chinese narrator in "Building the Great Wall of China" as he meditates on the distinction between the Emperor's two bodies, one physical and one imaginary,[6] and the craving of the individual subject to communicate with the Emperor. These situations can, under certain circumstances, be a laughing matter:

This, then, is how the people deal with past emperors, although they mingle the current ones with the dead ones. If once, once in a lifetime, an imperial official touring the provinces accidentally comes into our village, makes certain demands in the name of the ruler, examines the tax rolls, visits schools, questions the priest about our doings and then, before climbing back into his sedan chair, summarizes everything in long admonitions to the assembled community, a smile flickers across all our faces, each man looks furtively to the next and bends down to the children so as not to be observed by the official. [p. 121]

A key variation on the "laughing" anecdote appears in one of the short stories that Kafka wrote four years later, in 1917, in his sister's little hut in the Alchimistengasse, next to the Hřadschin, Prague's medieval castle. In "The New Lawyer" an anonymous member of the bar reflects on the difficulties of integrating into his profession a certain Dr. Bucephalus who had formerly served as the warhorse of Alexander the Great (!). As the narrator admits,

Nowadays * * * there is no great Alexander. To be sure, many know how to commit murder; nor is there any absence of skill in striking one's friend with a lance across the banquet table;

---

5. Franz Kafka, *Letters to Felice*, eds. Erich Heller and Jürgen Born, trans. James Stern and Elisabeth Duckworth (New York: Schocken, 1973), 146.

6. "The emperor as such, to be sure, is, for his part great through all the hierarchies of the world. But the living emperor, a man like us, rests as we do on a couch that, while generously proportioned, is still comparatively narrow and short" [p. 119].

and many feel that Macedonia is too narrow, so that they curse Philip the father—but no one, no one, can lead the way to India. Even in those days India's gates were beyond reach, but their direction was indicated by the royal sword. Today the gates have been carried off to another place entirely, farther away and higher up; no one shows the way; many carry swords but only wave them in the air; and the gaze that tries to follow them grows confused. [p. 60]

The interplay between the two scenarios is revealing. While in both instances the narrator, in the case of Kafka's anecdote, and the protagonist in "The New Lawyer" are lawyers, we deal here with two different (although complementary) perspectives on the nexus between power and knowledge.

Consider the first mode, the "laughing" one. It depicts a peacetime scenario, focusing on the representational—the display—aspect of sovereign power in the midst of the corporate culture of a highly industrialized society. The president of Kafka's insurance institute, like the leading staff in "all large organizations," has his share in the imaginary body of the Emperor: he is a representative of the Emperor, himself the arch-representative of imperial power. But while the Emperor, as a real person, has no other duty than that of representing the totality of power, the industrial or bureaucratic leader, on the other hand, is "exposed to clear and general scrutiny"; he is inevitably judged for his professional competence and achievement.

Now this president of the insurance institute—a former judge and legal adviser to Bohemia's leading engineering firm, who had been installed in office in 1897 by a powerful lobby of railway, engineering, and mining interests—is obviously no role model of professional authority in the first place. But his imperial posture and his "usual * * *, totally meaningless and unnecessary speech"[7] overstretch the gap between his assumed power and his actual knowledge to the point of driving Kafka "out of [his] mind."

Kafka's laughter is also the symptom of an unresolved question at the root of imperial power. In Kafka's view, "President" Dr. Otto Přibram conveyed in his person, so to speak, two crucial "imperial messages." As the chairman of the Workmen's Insurance Institute of Bohemia, he was responsible for fulfilling the promise of physical and social security for Austrian workmen, a promise the Emperor made in the "Thronrede"[8] that for the first time introduced

7. *Letters to Felice*, 147.
8. A "Thronrede" ("speech from the throne") is a programmatic speech held by the Emperor at the opening of each new legislative period. These speeches were commonly full of great plans and promises for the Emperor's subjects.

Austrian accident insurance legislation. Furthermore, as the father of Ewald Přibram, a former classmate of Kafka's at high school, he had, in one way, lived up to the Emperor Franz Joseph's promise to protect the Jewish subjects of his empire. "[F]or a special reason, I owed the president special gratitude," Kafka notes in his letter to Felice, a reason that is explained only in another letter: "The Institute is closed to Jews. * * * There is no explaining how two Jews * * * got in, and it won't happen again."[9] And it is evident from the reports and commentaries Kafka had written for his institute by the time of this scene in early 1911 that the same atmosphere of insecurity as regards legal protection prevailed all throughout the field of workmen's accident insurance. If Kafka's knees also shook with fear while he went on laughing louder and louder, we have here a symptom not only of the employee's respect for his superior but also of the horror latent even in so literally ridiculous a political organization.

This horror had been realized by the time of the second scenario, at the climax of World War I. This second scenario, that of "The New Lawyer," is a wartime scenario. People are now not so much concerned with security and insurance but with expansion, with crossing and transgressing borders: their place, their way of life ("Macedonia") is "too narrow," and so they are looking for new, dynamic leadership beyond their boundaries [p. 60]. Here we deal with the idea of leadership in the modern sense. The dominant dimension of the problem is no longer vertical and static, a question of hierarchy, but horizontal and dynamic, a question of the movement of populations; the problem is not the stability of an immobile organization but collective movement in a new direction. It turns out, however, that since the days of Alexander the Great, the map of political (and military) movement has changed: in modern times, the promised land for any leader and for any people has moved "farther away and higher up" [p. 60]; it cannot be reached by movement across a horizontal plane marked by the (social) likeness or equality of its elements. This reintroduction of the vertical axis of transcendental power into the dynamic concept of the political creates what political scientists have called "the movement-state" (*Bewegungsstaat*)—as, for example, the Nazi regime that would seize power in Germany in 1933. As opposed to the static, the "laughing" scenario, the consequences of this inevitable failure of "vertical," hierarchical leadership are anything but ridiculous; in fact, they will consist of arbitrary murder.

9. Franz Kafka, *Letters to Friends, Family, and Editors*, trans. Richard and Clara Winston (New York: Schocken, 1977), 165.

In 1922 the much-discussed German political philosopher Carl Schmitt wrote, "The normal proves nothing, the exception proves everything."[1] This aperçu is part of the context of Schmitt's reflections on the moment of "exceptionalism" that refers to the sovereign's invocation of a state of emergency to warrant decisions taken outside the law and which are then regarded as irrevocable. Kafka's two scenarios of leadership both anticipate and refute this axiom of political philosophy. In modern times, as we know from the "disciple Kafka," the Archimedean point of true knowledge is no longer available.[2] The normal proves nothing, and neither does the exception. The exception, however, can be murderous.

At the same time, "leadership" remains a problem to be tackled; it is obviously more than a merely backward-looking desire. Kafka makes this very clear in a parable written in December 1917, when the Hapsburg Empire is in fact already doomed: "They were given the choice of becoming kings or the kings' messengers. As is the way with children, they all wanted to be messengers. That is why there are only messengers, they charge through the world and, since there are no kings, call out their now meaningless messages to one another. Gladly would they put an end to their miserable life, but they dare not do so because of their oath of allegiance."[3]

In the "Revolutionswinter" of 1918/19, Germany, for one, was flooded with messengers and murderers; between the founding of the Weimar Republic and the killing of Walter Rathenau,[4] 376 political murders have been counted. The famous lecture given by the sociologist and political thinker Max Weber entitled "Politics as Vo-

1. Carl Schmitt, *Political Theology. Four Chapters on the Concept of Sovereignty*, trans. George Schwab (originally published 1922) (Cambridge: MIT Press, 1985), 22. Schmitt (1888–1985), German expert on legal theory and the law of states, was a leading figure in the right-wing intellectual movement called the "conservative revolution." His 1932-treatise on "The Concept of the Political" was regarded by the Nazi government as a theoretical legitimation of its so-called *Führerstaat* (state governed by a single leader). Schmitt also wrote in favor of Hitler—*Der Führer*—after Hitler had party dissidents killed in the infamous "Röhm Putsch" of 1934. According to Schmitt, "Der Führer schützt das Recht" (*Der Führer*—Adolf Hitler—protects the law). After the Second World War, Schmitt was sentenced by the Allies to five years in prison and banned from teaching at German universities.

2. When the Greek mathematician Archimedes (285–212 BC) first formulated the law of leverage, he said, in order to illustrate the technological impact of his discovery: "Give me a place to stand and rest my lever on, and I can move the Earth." Ever since, the "Archimedean point" has served as a metaphor for the paradoxical claim of acting inside a system as if one were acting outside of it (as for example in the claim to possess in this world a kind of knowledge independent of and superior to mere worldly knowledge).

3. *Franz Kafka. The Great Wall of China and Other Short Works*, aphorism #47, ed. and trans. Malcolm Pasley (Harmondsworth: Penguin Books, 1991), 86.

4. Walter Rathenau (1867–1922), Jewish industrialist and influential political essayist ("The Mechanics of the Spirit"). Rathenau was Minister of Reconstruction (1921) and Foreign Minister (1922) of the Weimar Republic. He was assassinated by members of one of the proto-fascist "Freikorps," a network of former officers and soldiers of the Wilhelminian army that served as a basis for the rise of Hitler.

cation" adds another critical dimension to these questions of leadership and political organization.[5] Weber expresses his contempt for the "sterile excitation" of the new class of sword-waving political dilettantes trying to occupy the vacant center of political power.[6] At the same time, he seems to re-assert Kafka's diagnosis of the leadership dilemma when he describes the only choice available for modern political organization: either "leadership democracy" with a party machine blindly following a charismatic leader or "leaderless democracy"—namely, the rule of professional politicians without a calling, without the inner charismatic qualities that make a leader, what the party insurgents in this situation call "the rule of the clique."[7]

Evidently, Kafka's "Denkbilder" (his poetic images that give rise to thought [*Editor*]), have close connections to even the most advanced levels of the political thought of his times. But it is in the allusive "depth" of his images, by virtue of what Brecht dismissed as Kafka's "mystifications," that his leadership game becomes most fully involved in the roots of practical political issues of his day, of the political platforms, projects and events in the period that historians have termed "the end of Old Europe."[8] To understand better the motives and meaning of Kafka's political intervention, we will look briefly at the constellation of discourses at which his in(ter)ventions were aiming.

The period in question decidedly calls for a *theoretical* study of political leadership. The phenomenon on which Brecht's criticism of Kafka is based—namely, the typical modern mass leader (*der Führer*), himself a man from the crowd—only became predominant in the decades following World War I. Whoever had wanted to claim top-level political leadership in Central Europe before World War I had to compete with, confront, and challenge the traditional system of leadership—namely, the monarchic principle. In the same period, we witness in the field of philosophy what the German sociologist Arnold Gehlen called the loss of a "grand key attitude,"[9] the intellectual stance that claims to penetrate all departments of life. But, as a function of the ever-increasing complexity of modern societies, this attitude, which aims at a comprehensive worldview, was clung to by many even as an empty model. And so it would seem that be-

---

5. Max Weber (1864–1920), German political scientist, economist and sociologist, is a towering figure in twentieth-century social thought. Among his most influential writings are *The Protestant Ethic and the Spirit of Capitalism* and *Economy and Society*.

6. Max Weber, "Politics as a Vocation," in *Essays in Sociology*, ed. H. H. Gerth and C. Wright Mills (New York: Oxford University Press, 1946), 115.

7. Ibid., 113.

8. For an example, cf. Josh Brooman, *The End of Old Europe: the Causes of the First World War, 1914–1918* (Harrow: Longman, 1985).

9. Arnold Gehlen, "Über kulturelle Kristallisation," in *Studien zur Soziologie und Anthropologie* (Neuwied/Berlin: Luchterhand, 1961), 315. Gehlen (1904–1976), along with Carl Schmitt, was a conservative thinker fascinated by the rising Nazi State; but, though

tween the philosophical death of the grand key attitude in the middle of the nineteenth century and the political death of "the age of discussion" proclaimed by Carl Schmitt immediately after World War I,[1] we witness the transfer of the pathos of the grand key attitude from philosophy to politics; the strongest challenge to traditional leadership becomes the mass longing for the leader's gesture that, so to speak, "points the way to India."

This all-comprehending gesture of modern political leadership is, in fact, a complex structure that can be analyzed into the following four elements: (1) a social or ethnic group defined by a vital problem (a so-called "question," as the German language has it, viz. "the worker's question" ["Arbeiterfrage"], the women's question ["Frauenfrage"], the Czech question ["tschechische Frage"], the Jewish question ["Judenfrage"]); (2) an individual with a biography that establishes his membership in the group "in question"; (3) a significant experience or event that befalls this individual and opens up to him a new view of that problem and a vision of its solution; (4) and, as a result of this exceptional event, the possibility of his "explaining everything," i.e., of subsequently developing an interpretation of that social or ethnic group, an interpretation in the sense of understanding the group's desires and concerns and of guiding it to its fulfillment.

Two of the "questions" cited above were of immediate concern for Kafka—the "Czech question" and the "Jewish question"—and the respective leadership gestures that arose in their midst. These political questions provide much of the deep-rooted content of the leadership game that Kafka transcribed into his literary work.

II

The foremost interpreter of the so-called "Czech question" was Thomas Garrigue Masaryk (1850–1937), the first president of the Czechoslovakian Republic after the collapse of the Hapsburg Empire. Masaryk was well-known to Kafka from his student days, when this brilliant Czech intellectual was just beginning to emerge as a leading player in Czech national politics. Masaryk's first gesture of leadership, though, aimed at society at large rather than the nation.

In his 1881-treatise *Der Selbstmord als sociale Massenerscheinung* (Suicide as a phenomenon of mass society), a book that Kafka not only bought in its Czech translation of 1904 but read very closely, Masaryk merged the discourses of social statistics, medi-

---

his most deplorable statements (as, for example, on the topic of racial supremacy) were comparable with those of Carl Schmitt, he was successfully "de-Nazified" after World War II.

1. Cf. Carl Schmitt, *The Crisis of Parliamentary Democracy*, trans. Ellen Kennedy (Cambridge: The MIT Press, 1988), Preface.

cine, and religion, thus combining the absolutely modern stance of the sociologist with the pre-modern gesture of the doctor-priest. According to Masaryk, modern half-education and its physiological symptom, nervousness, had a common root in the rapidly spreading network of the modern communications media and of accelerating vehicular traffic. Dr. Masaryk's remedy is a humanistic education that would form the basis of a modern religion, a re-*ligio* (re-connecting) of information with a deeper knowledge. As his thought develops, he offers this prescription for journalism, the "modern form of brain-work" (*Geistesarbeit*):

> We think in a telegraphic and stenographic mode: that is, we are asking for compact, precise, and manifold information. The journalist must and may therefore be laconic as long as he can rely on the deep and comprehensive basic education of his reader. But most of all, the journalist must himself have this education; otherwise he is just a "journalier," literally, a "day laborer," even less, an "hour man," a "minute apparatus."[2]

When Masaryk split with the Young Czech party in 1893, it was exactly because, in his view, their political program consisted of nothing more than a slew of political slogans and nationalistic archaisms,[3] an early chaotic form of the very "media-politics" our civilization has brought to electronic and professional perfection. He was searching for a different path. In 1893 he founded *Nase Doba* (Our times), a review for "science, arts, and social life" and in 1896 was appointed to the chair of Ethics at Charles University in Prague. It was only in 1899 that he began—involuntarily, but also irrevocably—to turn into a political leader. In the fall of that year a Jewish day laborer, Leopold Hilsner, was brought before a criminal court in the southern Bohemian village of Polna for allegedly killing the young tailor's apprentice Agnes Hruza. For several months, the Czech and German nationalist papers united in claiming the case as one of Jewish ritual murder[4] and spreading anti-Semitic hysteria throughout the country. Although, during the entire trial, ritual murder was never explicitly mentioned as a motive for the crime, evidence against Hilsner

---

2. Cf. Jean d'Armes, *Masaryk. Proletariersohn—Professor—Präsident* (Berlin: C.A. Schwetschke & Sohn, 1924), 15.

3. The "Young Czechs" split off as a radical nationalist party from the "Old Czechs" in the constitutional crisis of 1863. They were struggling for a Bohemian State Law—that is, for constitutional independence from Vienna.

4. According to the "libel," Jews are supposed to be bent on drawing the blood of a murdered Christian victim—Christian blood being a necessary ingredient in the baking of the matzoth or unleavened bread that Jews consume during the Passover holidays. While the origins of this grotesque idea reach back as far as the 12th century, it gained major impact in the second half of the 19th century when this "religious" narrative was connected to the new discourse of race and to the yellow press, a powerful medium of distribution. The "blood libel" actually circulates in anti-Semitic quarters of the Middle East today.

was collected as if it were: prosecutors tried to give an account of the facts adapted to the medieval blood libel "narrative." After Hilsner was found guilty and sentenced to death, Masaryk made a stand and publicly called for a revision of the trial. He wrote:

> In my analysis of the Polna trial, I will try to make up for the shame of our national journalism that by its slanderous and hate-mongering coverage of the Hilsner affair has created a Bohemian and Austrian Dreyfusiade for us.[5] * * * So much lack of judgment and consideration, so much inhumanity on the verge of cruelty, * * * such a phenomenon can only be explained by the nervous overexcitement and the abnormal situation of our Bohemian and Austrian life in general.[6]

In a word, nationalism, for Masaryk, was not the answer to any national question, such as the "Czech question." If it were to be resolved, the national question had to be translated first into a social question, which, in turn, was not amenable to materialistic solutions but only to the cultural and ethical program of "giving the spirit predominance over matter, of illuminating the hearts and minds of the people."[7] For a small (Czech) nation in a modern world on the way to "universal," cosmopolitan society, the only possible way of understanding nationhood was as the peaceful coexistence of different nations on the same territory. "Humanity," as a crucial passage in the program of his new "Realist" Party runs, "is our highest goal, but there is no humanity, after all, outside of the nations that form humanity."[8]

This formula also bears on our second case involving leadership—the so-called "Jewish Question"—and helps us to see why the issue of leadership resounds across Kafka's writings in and after the First World War. Masaryk's analysis points up the fact that the "Jewish question" was conceived in the way in which modern national questions were being posed and answered. If Masaryk, in his neo-archaic

5. An allusion to the "Dreyfus Case": Captain Alfred Dreyfus, a Jewish-French officer in the French Army, was sentenced to lifelong deportation to Devil's Island for allegedly passing secrets to Germany. He was subsequently pardoned and then, in the weeks before the first Hilsner trial in the fall of 1899, convicted again in a frenzy of anti-Semitic hatred, stirred up by organs of propaganda. Unlike Hilsner, Dreyfus was eventually completely rehabilitated (in 1906).
6. Thomas G. Masaryk, "Die Nothwendigkeit der Revision des Polnaer Processes," offprint from the weekly paper *Die Zeit* (Vienna), 1899, 1. While Masaryk succeeded in having the first sentence against Hilsner quashed by the Supreme Court in Vienna, Hilsner was again found guilty and sentenced to death in a second trial (in 1901), this time on charges of sexual murder. Under diplomatic pressure from Berlin and Paris, the Emperor changed his second death sentence to life; thereafter, in 1918, a few months before the end of the Empire, Hilsner was pardoned and set free.
7. Thomas G. Masaryk, *The Czech Question*, quoted in Roland J. Hoffmann, *T.G. Masaryk und die tschechische Frage*, vol. 1, *Nationale Ideologie und politische Tätigkeit bis zum Scheitern des deutsch-tschechischen Ausgleichsversuchs vom Februar 1909* (Munich: Oldenbourg, 1988), 150f.
8. Quoted in Hoffmann, *Masaryk*, 49.

idiom of the doctor-politician (cf. Kafka's "A Country Doctor"! [p. 60]), was lamenting the "abnormal" situation of the Czech people in the Hapsburg monarchy, he was at the same time offering a set of disquieting choices to the Jews of Europe: they could either completely assimilate to their host nations and hence disappear as a distinct ethnic and cultural group; or else they could claim to be considered as a nation. But if they chose the latter alternative, then, compared even to the "abnormal" nations in the "ethnic prison house" (Völkerkerker) of Europe, they would be a completely abnormal one, without a territory, a national language, a state, or political leadership.[9] On the other hand, if they "preferred not to" either assimilate or to nationalize, they would inevitably be excluded, according to Masaryk's formula, from the order of humanity.

When Masaryk's book on suicide was first published in Vienna, Theodor Herzl (1806–1904)—the father of Zionism, of the idea of a Jewish nation-state in Palestine—was still a law student at the same university. A member of the German students' corporation "Albia," Herzl was sufficiently aware of, and oppressed by, the new order of racial nationalism to leave the corporation on his own accord. He became a journalist, and it may be more than a coincidence that he became a "good journalist" in the strict sense of Masaryk's definition: his first feuilletons for the *Wiener Allgemeine Zeitung* and the *Neue Freie Presse* were widely appreciated for their elegant style and their deep feeling. Like Masaryk, his call to leadership did not sound early. And like Masaryk, it was again an anti-Semitic trial—the infamous Dreyfus affair of 1894/1895—that triggered his emergence as a leader.[1]

Herzl and Masaryk make a most instructive case for the comparative study of political leadership in Kafka's time. While Masaryk was anxious to calm down the overheated nationalism in Bohemia, Herzl's achievement ran in the opposite direction: he appealed to the hidden usurpatory energy of his people that arose from their very exclusion from the universe of nations.[2] In a striking anticipation of the rhetoric of the Old Commandant in Kafka's "In the Penal Colony" of 1914, Herzl's introduction to his 1896 political platform entitled "The Jewish State" compares the oppressed situation of the Jews to a boiling teakettle:

> Now I believe that this power, if rightly employed, is powerful enough to propel a large engine and to despatch passengers

9. Most Jews living in Bohemia and Moravia at this time spoke German, read German books, and sent their children to German-speaking schools.
1. The Dreyfus affair was soon acknowledged as an historical analogy for the Hilsner affair.
2. Cf. Josef Fraenkl, *Theodor Herzl. A Biography* (London: Ararat 1946), 37; and Adolf Böhm, Die *zionistische Bewegung, eine kurze Darstellung ihrer Entwicklung* (Berlin: Welt-verlag, 1920–21), 152f.

and goods: the engine having whatever form men may choose to give it * * *. In consideration of my own inadequacy, I shall content myself with indicating the cogs and wheels of the machine to be constructed, and I shall rely on more skilled mechanicians than myself to put them together.[3]

While—at least until 1909—Masaryk's ideal leader is a doctor or a priest, Herzl's is an engineer of human energy.[4] Hence, the opposing views of the role of imagination and poetry in the two concepts of leadership. Masaryk conceives of poetry as enriching the receptive powers of the leader: "Poetry enhances our imagination, and we need it in politics to see the future and the others' soul. Imagination enables the politician to understand the people and the nations."[5] For Herzl, on the other hand, imagination, or "the idea," is the formative agency of political change: "Only what is fantastic is able to move the masses," Herzl wrote to Baron Hirsch after their conversation in spring 1895 about the project of a Jewish state, meaning to "move" his people not only in a figurative but also in a literal sense.

III

Kafka, the contemporary and colleague of the narrator of "The New Lawyer," not only reads the "old books" but also the new ones; and he is more than a passive reader: he is a writer. His fictitious worlds might seem to exist far from the tumult of the battles surrounding him, but in fact they register their reverberations, and more: his allusive images displace and rearrange the conflicting voices of his day and offer the reader new angles of observation and evaluation. Kafka is well aware of the views on leadership posited, for example, by Masaryk and Herzl, and he analyzes them in the strict sense: he splits them into their component parts and then restructures them in new combinations.

This means, in the first place, that he inverts the relation between politics and poetry postulated by Masaryk. For Kafka, the facts and the images of leadership are subordinate to poetry; leadership serves writing as a model of organization, not the other way around: "Great, tall commander-in-chief, leader of multitudes," writes Kafka to himself in his diary in the winter of 1922 in Spindelmühle in the Riesengebirge (Giant Mountains): "lead the despairing through the mountain passes that no one else can find

3. Theodor Herzl, *The Jewish State* (New York: Scopus Publishing Company, 1943), 14.
4. A glance at Anson Rabinbach's important study *The Human Motor. Energy, Fatigue, and the Origins of Modernity* (New York: Basic Books, 1990) reveals to what extent Herzl had in fact relied on the discursive energies of the discourse of his day as the "territory" of his political maneuvers.
5. Quoted in d'Armes, *Masaryk*, 49.

beneath the snow. And who is it that gives you the strength? He who gives you the clear vision."[6] In his famous inaugural lecture on "The Problem of Small Nations in the European Crisis," Masaryk had written: "it would help us greatly if I could show you a good map of the European nations; but no such map exists. * * * You will find political maps, maps of railroads, etc., but no ethnographical ones."[7] As a leader whose base is his own mastery of the materials of study, reflection, and writing, Kafka will discover and survey territories (and the risks and chances inherent in them) that are invisible to others, supply maps of imaginary lands and peoples who do not factually exist.

In the spring of 1917, when the "timeless" Hapsburg Monarchy was drawing nigh its end and the birth or rebirth of its nations appeared as a shining promise to many, Kafka stages the modern drama of leadership in a seemingly fantastic but in fact stenographic and telegraphic China—a country and people, that is to say, whose "questions" can be read as a shorthand encryption of the manifold social and political "questions" haunting Kafka's own time. In the narrative fragment "Building the Great Wall of China," the highly cultivated Chinese, threatened by uncivilized nomads from the north, rely on the Great Wall as a safeguard against attacks. But the reflections of the narrator, who is himself engaged in the building project as a "[leader] of the middle rank" [p. 114], soon make it clear that the Great Wall is only an affair of fragments, consisting, in fact, more of gaps than wall; and so his reflections move inexorably to the intentions or purposes of the high command behind the system of piecemeal construction and hence to the question of leadership.[8] The story is organized by this question, and among the various dialogues it entertains with contemporary voices on the issue, we can trace very clearly those of Masaryk and Herzl and the "solutions" they offer; their presence is immediately signaled by the figure of the first-person narrator in Kafka's story whose autobiography alludes to Kafka's as well as to the writings of Masaryk and Herzl. He is one of those semi-educated professionals who fit precisely into Masaryk's cultural criticism insofar as he is capable of only fragmentary and erratic reflections. On the

6. Franz Kafka, *Diaries 1910–1923*, ed. Max Brod (New York: Schocken Books, 1976), 412.

7. Thomas G. Masaryk, "The Problem of Small Nations in the European Crisis. Inaugural Lecture at the University of London, King's College, London" (London: Council for the Study of International Relations, 1917), 11.

8. While the question of leadership is not the story's only concern, it is its central concern. Like all Kafka's narratives, "Building the Great Wall of China," is a highly condensed protocol of a complex fusion of many different issues. These range from poetic production via the birth of culture from the tension of Apollinian and Dionysian powers to Austrian accident insurance to the threat of anti-Semitism to the question of the political destiny of Europe during and after the Great War.

other hand, his manner of introducing himself literally copies the opening scene of Herzl's utopian novel *Old-New Land*.[9] This Chinese narrator is thus a compact stenograph of Kafka, the accident insurer; Kafka, the writer; and Herzl's fictitious hero Friedrich Loewenberg. The Chinese narrator writes:

> I had the good fortune, when I passed the highest test of the lowest school at the age of twenty, that the Wall was about to be built. I say good fortune because many who had previously reached the apex of the education that was available to them were unable to apply their knowledge to anything for years, knocked around uselessly with the grandest blueprints in their heads, and wasted their lives in droves. [p. 114]

What follows—the narrator's seemingly bizarre description of the relation between the Chinese people and its leaders—is at once an exact protocol and a grandiose parody of the leadership discourse of nation-building. In an attempt to put an end to his ponderings on the system of piecemeal construction, the narrator confesses:

> We * * * have really only come to know ourselves as a result of poring over the decrees of the highest leadership; and here we have discovered that without the leadership neither our book learning nor our human understanding would have sufficed for even the small tasks we perform within the great whole. In the leadership office—where it was located and who occupied it no one I have ever asked knows or knew—in this office there surely revolved all human thoughts and desires and, in countercircles, all human goals and fulfillments; but through the window the reflection of the divine worlds fell on the hands of the leaders as they drew their plans. [pp. 116–17]

This perspective is consistent with the point of view of a "leader of middle rank," someone like Kafka in his professional capacity, who was responsible for safety measures against the irrational rule of government supervision throughout the entire bureaucracy in the Hapsburg Empire—that empire, which according to its mythical self-description, served as Europe's "bulwark" against the barbarous Slavs. But note here the probably fatal conceptual inheritance coming down to the new nations from the ruins of the Monarchy: they cannot escape that blind spot in human knowledge so deeply embedded in the absolutist model of divine legitimation. Traces of this "Chinese" confession are stunningly present in Masaryk's foreword to *The Czech Question*:

9. Cf. Theodor Herzl, *Old-New Land* (Tel Aviv: Haifa Publishing Company, 1960), 6f. The first (German) edition appeared in 1902, and Kafka read it in the summer 1910 when he became increasingly interested in the "Jewish question" and Zionism.

I believe * * * that the history of the peoples is not accidental, but that it is the fulfillment of a determined plan of providence. Therefore, it is the task of historians and philosophers, it is the task of every people to understand this plan and to know its place in it. * * * But I also believe that even the most penetrating spirit would not be able to reveal these plans of providence.[1]

Meanwhile, it is striking how closely Kafka's Chinese subordinate architect and supervisor describes the position that Herzl assigns to his readers; for Herzl, too, imagines his new Jewish state as a bulwark of culture, namely as "a portion of a rampart of Europe against Asia, an outpost of civilization as opposed to barbarism."[2] And his "Outline" of *The Jewish State* literally follows the principle of piecemeal construction—"short aphoristic chapters will therefore best answer the purpose"[3]—so as not to tax the intellectual capacities of his readers. Finally, in a resumé article on the first Zionist Congress in Basel, Herzl assigns the job of legitimizing the leaders of the Zionist movement against any suspicion of profit-making to the scrutiny of the philosophers and poets: "They must be able to read the inside of our words and to vouch for our opinions."[4] But as in Kafka's China, despite all the scrutiny and all the reverence paid to the state's organization of labor and planned development, the ultimate purposes of the high command—the so-called New Society of *The Jewish State* and *Old-New Land*—inevitably remain beyond the grasp of the masses. Every state, Herzl argues, in establishing the legitimacy of his high command, the New Society of Jews, represents "a mixture of human and superhuman." There remains in it an element of inscrutable, incontrovertible authority. In the case of the Jewish state, this mixture springs from the role of the Zionist movement, which Herzl defines in reference to the ancient Roman legal institution of "negotiorum gestio" as follows: "When the property of an oppressed person is in danger, any man may step forward to save it. This man is the gestor, the director of affairs not strictly his own. He has received no warrant—that is, no human warrant; higher obligations authorize him to act."[5] Herzl's definition of the New Society plainly anticipates the exceptionalist gesture of Carl Schmitt's political theology [as discussed on p. 307], which Kafka foregrounds in his Chinese story by looking at it from the perspective of the people whom it affects. Through the popular parable of the river and the flood, his Chinese

1. Quoted in Hoffmann, *Masaryk*, 138.
2. Herzl, *Jewish State*, 45.
3. Ibid., 30.
4. Theodor Herzl, *Der Baseler Congress* (Vienna: Verlag der "Welt," 1897), 22.
5. Herzl, *Jewish State*, 90.

narrator reflects on the restraints ordained by certain select interpreters of "nature," who impose limits on any rational understanding of leadership by the people [cf. p. 117]. This parable alludes to
Herzl's imposed distinction between the human subject and the
"superhuman" leader.

Meanwhile, Kafka's literary stenographs are much more than re-
productions or parodies of things he read. Situated beyond real
maps and populations, his lands and peoples serve as a laboratory
for a series of experimental variations on the major cultural risks of
his turbulent times. Masaryk's ideal of brotherhood through common labor on the project of human civilization—an ideal that
David Littwak, the hero of *Old-New Land*, will carry to the civil-
isatory outpost of Neudorf, Palestine—reverberates in Kafka's
China as a dream:

> every fellow countryman was a brother for whom they were
> building a protective wall and who was thankful all his life,
> thankful with everything that he had and was: unity! unity!
> breast on breast, a round dance of the people, blood no longer
> confined in the meager circulatory system of the body but
> rolling sweetly and yet returning to its source through the in-
> finity of China. [p. 115]

The solution to Kafka's "Chinese question," though, is not "unity of
blood" but diversity of imagination. When Kafka's Chinese architect and supervisor wearies of his metaphysical reflections on the
invisible high command "whose minds are roiled with enormous
worries, know about us, know our unimportant work, see us sitting
together in the low huts" [p. 118], he produces a surprising change
of perspective. To understand the nature of the empire, he suggests, one must not address the teachers of political law and history
whose few precepts are hidden under a fog of confusion generated
in the very process of teaching them. Instead "people should be
asked about * * * this question concerning the empire * * * since
in the end the empire is supported by the people" [p. 119]. Here
the process of interpretation as between the leaders and the led is
inverted: the masses are now the subject and the leaders the object
of understanding. But what follows is, alas, neither a practical
carrying-out of the centralized and standardized public opinion
research which Kafka, professionally charged with the safety ques-
tionnaires for Bohemian factories, was one of the first to employ in
an expert way;[6] nor does it resemble the technical fantasy of data
collection Herzl so vividly described in *Old-New Land*. Kafka's
China is depicted as the very opposite of the progressive Old-New

---

6. Cf. Franz Kafka, *Amtliche Schriften*, 123ff. and 819ff. For Herzl's informatic utopia, cf.
　Old-New Land, 151f.

Land: space and time still rule over politics, communication is organized via slow, contingent, and even hopeless forms of human transmission—such as messengers or traveling inspectors, the latter the direct opposite of the motorized and ubiquitous traveling offices in Old-New Land. We recall one of the wonderful "laughing" passages from "Building the Great Wall of China":

> If once, once in a lifetime, an imperial official touring the provinces accidentally comes into our village, makes certain demands in the name of the ruler, examines the tax rolls, visits schools, questions the priest about our doings, and then, before climbing back into his sedan chair, summarizes everything in long admonitions to the assembled community, a smile flickers across all our faces. [p. 121]

And why? Because though every village is loyal to the Emperor—who is invisible, in far away Peking and above the clouds—from village to village this loyalty refers to a different emperor: "In our villages, long-dead emperors are set up on thrones, and one who lives on only in song has recently issued a decree that the priest reads aloud in front of the altar" [p. 120]. But the marvelous paradox, for Kafka, is that this apparent dysfunction is functional. It is precisely the twofold weakness of empire—(1) the failure of the government to develop the institution of the empire with sufficient precision; and (2) the "weakness of imagination or conviction among the people" [p. 122]—that allows the Chinese architect and supervisor to conclude that "weakness appears to be one of the most important means of unifying our people; indeed, if one may be so forward as to employ such an expression, it is the very ground on which we live" [p. 123].

But this praise of a weak organization of political power and a weak imagination of the leader is not Kafka's last word on the Chinese issue. A few days after leaving his Chinese architect behind, Kafka seems to retract his conclusion in a codicil to his endless reflections on political authority. In "A Page from an Old Document" [p. 66], we find a scenario of nomad invasion which, in the world of the architect, had only existed in "the books of our elders" [p. 117]. This time the narrative voice belongs to a man from the crowd, a shoemaker dwelling at the gates of the Imperial Palace. The nomads have invaded the capital and are camping in front of the palace, taking a daily toll of raw oxen they are devouring dead or alive in bloody feasts. In the shoemaker's account, "blood" no longer signifies unity but violent conflict and slaughter; and the cause of the ordeal is precisely the weakness in leadership which, in the architect's report, is the foundation of Chinese political organization: "The Imperial Palace has attracted the nomads but does not know how to drive them away again" [p. 67]. Here, again, Kafka's narrative entertains complex allusions to the medial-political narratives of his day. In the ritual murder trial against Hilsner, the shoemaker of Polna was among the witnesses confirming Jewish blood rites going on in and around the village, while Hilsner was a shoemaker's apprentice. The bloodthirsty nomads, then, can be read either as related to the fantasy of ritually-murdering Jews or to the creators of that fantasy, the newspapers invading Polna with their daily increasingly bloodthirsty journalism ("Blutjournalismus"). Like the nomads in "A Page from an Old Document," both the fantasy and its malicious instigators appear to multiply and spread independent of space and time, and of both it could be said that "it seems that every morning there are more of them" [p. 66].

IV

What, finally, is the "lesson" to be learned from "disciple Kafka"? Although we have been dealing with only a selection of the voices involved in his leadership game—and this leadership game in turn is only one of the many allusive dialogues entertained by his Chinese narratives—this lesson is clearly bound up with his powers as a writer, as a poet. You will not find, nor are you meant to find, a single lesson provided in the form of an argument, a position, one dominant train of thought. Among the various pleasures that Kafka claimed he had to sacrifice at an early age in order to fulfill his being as a writer was, along with food, sex, and music, the pleasure of "philosophy."[7] While Kafka's narratives scarcely lack reflections (however contradictory or circular they may turn out to be), the allusive richness of his imagery stimulates the reader to move outside the text toward one or more among the multitude of voices these texts evoke. Reading from the other side of the divide, we discover how many of the contemporary discourses on leadership came to inhabit Kafka's narratives. But they do not reside innocently there, they are not mere citations: by dint of context, these voices and positions are commented on, tested by the narrative as a whole. The voices "audible" to any given reader enter into dialogue with each other, while Kafka's "scriptures," the narratives that have triggered these crypto-conferences, remain "unalterable" and, so to speak, withdraw.[8]

Kafka's stories create a fundamentally new cognitive or intellec-

7. Franz Kafka, *The Diaries of Franz Kafka 1910–1913*, ed. Max Brod, trans. Joseph Kresh (New York: Schocken, 1948), [p. 196].
8. Cf. the commentary of the priest on the parable "Before the Law" in *The Trial*: "The text is immutable, and the opinions are often only an expression of despair over it." Franz Kafka, *The Trial*, trans. Breon Mitchell (New York: Schocken, 1998), 220.

tual attitude to the issues of his day. As a "Schriftführer" (literally, someone in an office who is responsible for the "script" of a protocol or a record or minutes; in the figurative sense, someone who leads others through his writing), Kafka follows the model of leadership posed by the Chinese architect: his words elicit in his readers the desire for a message to his readers, but this message—a reliable meaning, a clear-cut argument—never arrives. Instead, like the Chinese, we have to look for leadership "in the people," i.e., in the readership that Kafka's writing addresses. And here, just as each of the Chinese villages possesses its own version of the person of the leader and the history of the dynasty, any social or academically specific group of readers will possess its own view on the hierarchy and history of meanings in a Kafkan text. This poetic "leadership game," which is at the same time a "readership game," creates the very kind of unity by weak and contingent association that Kafka's Chinese narrator described as the foundation of Chinese culture.

Hence, Kafka is neither the anxious petty bourgeois secretly longing for leadership (as suggested by Brecht), nor does he fit the image of an anarchic, subversive, rebellious writer (as suggested by Deleuze/Guattari). In a time of mass slaughter based on accredited "truths"—especially in Germany and Austria, it was the intellectuals who provided propagandistic justifications for the First World War—Kafka's poetic sensitivity and political responsibility led him to look for a new way of connecting aesthetics and politics. This method, as we have suggested, involves his listening carefully to the political harangues of his day with the aim of re-poeticizing (or even: re-enchanting) this "Lumpensprache," the rowdy language of "media-politics." Unlike Friedrich Nietzsche, who bemoaned and fled this clamor and whose literary-philosophical "first language" was in fact conceived in absolute discontinuity with the *Lumpensprache* surrounding him, Kafka first copies (or mocks) this language and then inverts its function in new combinations. And so apart from the manifold political messages that may be read into his texts, their final political impact lies in his use of language to restore the medial qualities of detachment and calm reflection. We could call this restoration "literature." And the outcome? Instead of directing his readers to this or that country on the ideological map (the sword-waving business entertained by most of his contemporary writers), Kafka offers them another attitude toward the complexity of modern knowledge, a new economy of knowing, based on a way of reading his stories: like the Chinese architect, readers are invited to travel through them, across new provinces of knowledge, feeling the risk of the journey and noting the importance of small differences and, occasionally, of laughter, against the backdrop of an age of violent uniformity. Then as now, his thought-pieces offer an alternative to the fruitless choice between beating some sort of single reliable meaning out of them or incessantly discovering the structural impossibility of any such meaning. There is a stance toward the world at large in this. It is best articulated through the detailed study of his submerged European culture and, following the twofold reference to politics and poetics in Kafka's leadership game, through the procedures and strategies of literature itself.

JOHN A. HARGRAVES

Kafka and Silence: An Alternate View of Music†

In all of Kafka's narratives, there is scarcely a mention of music: * * * Kafka's characters are in near-complete ignorance of this art * * * [and] Kafka's spare Prague German is in a way the very antithesis of a musical style.

Kafka himself was unmusical, of this there is no doubt. Though enthusiastic about the theater, Kafka in his diaries reveals little interest in concerts, operas, or the public musical life of Prague. He writes to Milena Jesenska, "Do you realize that I'm completely unmusical, of a completeness which in my experience simply doesn't exist elsewhere?"[1] In a letter of 25 August 1920 he allows that being unmusical isn't necessarily a misfortune, and that "to understand musical people you need to be almost unmusical," a typically enigmatic statement which reveals his antipathy for things musical in general. He seems to have been fascinated by Grillparzer's story *Der arme Spielmann* (The Poor Musician, 1848); though he at first denies this interest, and in sending Milena a copy of the story warns her that he finds the work curiously repellent and pathetic. In his [possibly apocryphal—*Editor*] conversations with Gustav Janouch, Kafka does discuss music and his mistrust of it * * *.

> Music creates new, subtle, more complicated, and therefore more dangerous pleasures . . . but poetry (*Dichtung*) aims at clarifying the confusion of pleasures, at raising them to consciousness, purifying them and therefore humanizing them. Music is the multiplication of sensuous life; poetry . . . disciplines and elevates it.[2]

† From *Music in the Works of Broch, Mann, and Kafka* (Rochester, NY: Camden House, 2002), p. 161, 166–77. Reprinted by permission of the publisher. Page numbers in brackets refer to this Norton Critical Edition.
1. Franz Kafka, *Letters to Milena* (London: Secker & Warburg, 1953), 62.
2. Gustav Janouch, *Gespräche mit Kafka* (Frankfurt: S. Fischer Verlag, 1951), 86. trans. JAH.

However, the very absence of musicality and music as a theme in his prose does not prevent the reader from noticing that Kafka does indeed present, however tentatively, the potential power of music, not so much as a form of art, but as a metaphor for a latent metaphysical force at work behind the foreground of human existence. * * *

In "Investigations of a Dog,"[3] music becomes a metaphor for supraverbal perception. A dog looks back at his long life, and remembers a crucial formative incident from his youth: while walking through the woods, he comes suddenly upon a "troupe" of seven dogs, who act like no other dogs he has ever seen. Most striking of all, they refuse to greet him, a major transgression of a universal dog law. Instead of acknowledging his presence, they proceed to perform a kind of circus act: they line up in formations, walk around on their hind legs, and do gymnastic stunts. The whole is accompanied by music, a music which the narrator simply cannot comprehend, even while acknowledging its great power over him. He mistakenly thinks that the dogs themselves are making the music, instead of merely performing in time to music. It is some kind of band music and it exerts a powerful force on him: just as he is on the point of asking them to explain what is happening, the music takes hold of him, spinning him around, and throwing him this way and that in a frenzied tarantella, finally releasing him from its power and depositing him in the middle of a confused jumble of wooden stakes. From this refuge he observes the performing dogs closely, and sees that they perform not willingly, but under some compulsion: "it was not so much coolness as the most extreme tension that characterized their performance; . . . why were they afraid? Who forced them to do what they were doing? [p. 136].[4] Once again, he asks them to clarify, and he is ignored. The dogs continue to perform their unnatural acts, transgressing without shame or guilt against canine moral codes, finally disappearing with their music into the darkness from which they had come. Music, the blaring of brass, signals a missed epiphanic moment for the dog. Who forced them? He cannot say. In the story's opening lines, he senses something incomplete, not right, with his perception of the world about him [p. 132].[5] When he comes closest to breaking

---

3. "Forschungen eines Hundes" (1922), first published in *Beim Bau der chinesischen Mauer, Ungedruckte Erzählungen und Prosa aus dem Nachlaß*, eds. Max Brod and Hans Joachim Schoeps (Berlin: Gustav Kiepenhauer Verlag, 1931).
4. Franz Kafka. *The Complete Stories*, ed. Nahum Glatzer (New York: Schocken, 1983), 283. (Henceforth "Stories" and page reference.) Translation by Willa and Edwin Muir.
5. Stories, 278, ". . . I find on closer examination that from the very beginning I sensed some little maladjustment, causing a slight feeling of discomfort. . . . "

through, to seeing through the *Bruchstelle* (fracture), music, perversely, throws him off the track. The critic Wilhelm Emrich uses the word "musikalisches Gesetz"[6] to express the noncommunicability of the message which the dog is so near to, yet so far from. The narrator cannot decide finally whether this is music or noise; music in the sense that it contains some truth he wants to know but cannot, and noise in the sense that it is the summation of many truths, each interfering with and canceling out the other. This seems clear in the text: "a clear, piercing, continuous note which came without variation literally from the remotest distance—perhaps the real melody in the midst of the music."[7] This "beguiling music" may well contain the answer the dog is looking for, but he cannot filter out the truth from the music ("konnte die Antwort von der Musik nicht sondern"). Emrich compares this musical message to the telephone's humming in *The Castle*: the conversations of all the officials represent the sum of all knowable truths, and thus are incomprehensible.[8]

This crucial experience of his youth sets the future course of the young dog's life: he cannot leave off from his efforts to explain it. This need to understand what happened, he says, robbed him of his childhood and started him on the course of scientific investigations which eventually become his life. These investigations concern the dog's system of procuring food. Thus, this is another example of the theme of *Nahrung* (nourishment) in Kafka (cf. *The Metamorphosis* and *A Hunger Artist*). Here, the investigation concerns the central matter of dog-life, that is, the source of food.

Ritchie Robertson[9] takes an allegorical view of this enigmatic story which yields useful insights. In this allegory, dogs are below the level of cognition which would enable them to see the existence of human beings in the world. The first dogs are a circus act. The narrator dog has wandered into the tent of a travelling circus; thus the overly bright day (spotlights), and the haze (smoke) within the tent. The thicket of sticks into which the dog is driven would be the chair legs of the gallery. Alongside this allegory, music is used as a signal of confusion and blindness; music appears to overwhelm the narrator three times: in his confusion, he thinks the animals make the music, rather than just dance to it. The human masters who are forcing the trained dogs to do their routines are invisible to the narrator. This cognitive blindness is evident when the narrator dog, a

---

6. "musical law." Wilhelm Emrich, *Franz Kafka* (Bonn: Athenaeum, 1958), 153.
7. Stories, 284; [p. 137].
8. Wilhelm Emrich, *Franz Kafka* (Bonn: Athenaeum, 1958), 154.
9. Ritchie Robertson, *Kafka: Judaism, Politics and Literature* (Oxford: Clarendon Press, 1985).

pariah who seems to live apart from men, says: "For what is there actually except our own species? To whom but it can one appeal in the wide and empty world?"[1]

The dogs know that their sustenance comes partly from the earth, and partly from above; in terms of this allegory, then, from that which has been left there for them (or perhaps carrion), and partly from the hand of man. The hand of man is also behind the confusion attending the "soaring dogs," *Lufthunde*, an allusion to German *Luftmensch*, a person who can live on seemingly nothing. For these *Lufthunde* are pets, lapdogs, who are mostly carried around in the arms of their owners. The narrator regards them with envy and contempt; contempt for their idleness, and envy of their leisurely, luxurious existences, which they can devote to "artistic" endeavors.

During his musings on his life, the narrator dog describes the original dogs, his distant ancestors, as somehow having more "authentic" language ("The true Word could still have intervened . . . and that Word was there, was very near at least, on the tip of everybody's tongue, anyone might have hit upon it."[2]) But now that truth, that word is gone, even if one could look inside oneself it would not be there. What is it, this truth that dogs will not consciously know or impart to one another? Is it knowledge of the compact dogs have with man? This would explain the lost authenticity of the race, the greater submissive (*hündisch*) quality of dogs today. The narrator tries to explain the difference between his generation and his ancestors': back then, dogs had not yet become as *hündisch* (this means "beastly" as well as "submissive"). All dogs pathetically assume that *Nahrung* (nourishment) comes from the earth or the sky at least partly as a result of their efforts at watering the earth (the chief dog law: "Make everything wet, as much as you can"). The narrator even sees in the dogs' "water" the chief source of food found on earth. However, he is mistaken, not only about the role their peculiar *Bodenbearbeitung* (soil preparation) plays in the food chain, but also about the importance of sayings, dance, and song in procuring food. He says, in his investigations, "The people in all their ceremonies gaze upwards."[3] In terms of the allegory, the rituals which the dogs perform with words, dance, and song can be seen as tricks, begging routines performed by animals to procure food from the humans but for whom cognitively there is no category; phrases like "in die Höhe" [upward], and "von oben herab" [downward] are evasions, repressing the cognition that dogs are not alone.

1. Stories, 289; [p. 141].
2. Stories, 300; [p. 148].
3. Stories, 304; [p. 151].

In the final section of the story, the narrator dog tells of his attempt to understand the nature of nourishment by starving himself, a dog equivalent of mortification of the flesh. Alone, forsaken by all other dogs, he is half dead with hunger and exhaustion; he is seeking the insight of the hermit in ecstasy, to escape "this world of lies," to escape even himself, "a citizen of falsehood."[4] He is awakened by a large hunting dog. This dog tries to make the narrator leave; he must leave, for this dog must hunt. Neither understands the reason for this compulsion (as before with the circus dogs), but it is clear that this dog is accompanied by hunters, human beings, and as they are discussing this compulsion, music again enters the narrative. As before, the narrator dog thinks he hears the hunting dog start to sing: the hunter denies this, but admits that he will be singing soon. The narrator resists the insight that the music might come from another, noncanine source, just as before with the circus dogs. This melody which he hears hovers in the air "according to its own law."[5] This music has an extracanine origin which the narrator dog can only perceive in his ecstatic, starved state, his "Außer-sich-sein" (the word ecstasy, ek-stasis, means "being outside of oneself")—it can only be the music of the hunting horns, deafening and sublime.[6] The melody strains the capacity of the dog's perception; he wants to relate what he has heard and seen, but "later it seemed to me that such things could not be told."[7] At the same time that it delivers the unheard message, music obliterates the insight that they are not alone in the world.

The central function of music as the bearer of an unheard and unhearable message is consistent with the general tenor of this enigmatic story and with other interpretations of the existential situation of the narrator and the dogs. The narrator's presentiments of another world, of a higher order, take him only to ecstasy, not insight. He still imagines music to emanate from other dogs, and he expands his scientific investigations to include this "music of the dogs." Just as he imagines that food production really is the result of dogs' pawing the ground, marking their territory, and producing food from "above" via ritual and song, he likewise thinks that music is the product of dog culture. In one respect, his observations are correct: he says it is possible to investigate music production more "dispassionately" than food production, since the results don't particularly matter to dogs. For them, the practical consequences of food procurement are highly important; they remain, indeed, too "doggish" to be objective in carrying out food-deprivation experi-

4. Stories, 312; [p. 157].
5. Stories, 314; [p. 159].
6. Ibid. [p. 159].
7. Ibid. [p. 160].

ments; they just gobble it down when their hunger is too much. There is an even more negative association here: the dogs are un-knowing, and afraid of knowing more than they do. The conspiracy of silence which the dogs mutely agree to allows them to keep their illusions intact, that they are the only creatures who matter.[8] It is the not knowing which allows them to maintain their "freedom"—the dog admits, he does not want to trade half knowledge for complete knowledge; why not? "Easy to answer: Because I am a dog."[9] And, true to his dog nature, when he expands his researches to dog music, nothing much comes of it; "It is regarded as very esoteric and politely excludes the crowd."[1] Also true to his nature, the "border area" of study—which examines that music which does in fact successfully conjure up food—is the area of music which interests him the most. But even here he has no success at musical research. He suspects a more deep-seated reason for his scientific incompetence: an "instinct," and "by no means a bad one." This instinct turns out to be the wish to preserve freedom: this instinct, for the sake of knowledge (*Wissenschaft*), not the *Wissenschaft* that he has been discussing, but one of a higher order, has caused him to value freedom. He senses that the freedom that he now possesses is a miserable thing, but still it is freedom. This sarcastic final line[2] points clearly to the dog's need to preserve his state of innocent ignorance of the real state of things in the world. To investigate too closely the musical phenomenon *per se* would bring him too dangerously close to the knowledge which he fears. The whole can be interpreted narrowly as *Wissenschaftskritik* (critique of science) or more broadly as a satire on the biased nature of humankind's epistemological explorations, in whatever area.

Music is in a sense the reverse of silence, as it is the opposite physically and morally of Hermann Broch's *Stummheit* (mute-ness),[3] and silence (*Schweigen*) is a constant theme in Kafka. In the novels as well as the shorter narratives, silence has meaning, of-ten it seems to have the force of action. Here the narrator dog is clearly upset by the silence of his fellows, which is a defensive act, even though rooted in higher cognition. The feeling this conveys to the narrator and reader is often that of an aggressive act. Kafka turns the myth of Odysseus and the sirens upside down in "The Silence of the Sirens," in which their silence is a more "fearsome weapon" than their song. In *The Castle*, [the protagonist] K. is constantly met only with silence from the inhabitants of the Castle,

8. Stories, 290; [p. 141].
9. Stories, 291; [p. 142].
1. Stories, 315; [p. 160].
2. "But nevertheless freedom, nevertheless a possession" (Stories, 316).
3. Cf. Broch's essay "Geist and Zeitgeist," in *Geist and Zeitgeist* (New York: Counterpoint, 2002).

whose knowledge is infinite, and the boundlessness of whose knowledge is concentrated in the wordless humming of the telephone line. Kafka's use of music in his writing is related to this theme of silence. It is clear that silence is to be preferred to music. In *Description of a Struggle*, Kafka writes: "Stummheit gehört zu den Attributen der Vollkommenheit" (Muteness is one of the attributes of perfection).

This theme of silence versus music is also important in Kafka's last work, *Josefine*. The metaphor of music has often been read to mean art as a whole, and the story is read as Kafka's final critique of art, especially writing. For the interpretation of this story it is important to know that for Kafka music was a problematic area which came for him to symbolize his loneliness and isolation. The diaries repeatedly mention the emotion, or perhaps gap in emotion, which music brought about. On December 13, 1911, he attends a concert of Brahms's choral music in Prague, and writes: "the essence of my unmusicalness consists in my inability to enjoy music connectedly . . . the natural effect of music on me is to circumscribe me with a wall."[4] His love of literature, rather than music, isolates him: "There is, among the public, no such reverence for literature as there is for music." On December 16 he writes that he despises (and envies) Franz Werfel (whose book *Verdi* was Kafka's deathbed reading), in part because he is "gifted with a sense of music," as well as young, healthy, and rich. "I am entirely shut off from music."[5] Writing has channeled all his talents away from the rest of life: "[Writing] . . . left empty all those abilities which were directed toward the joys of sex, eating, drinking, philosophical reflection and above all music."[6]

With Kafka's ambivalent stance toward music in his own experience, his choice of a singing mouse for his archetypal artist is freighted with irony. (This irony is tempered by Kafka's awareness of his imminent death; the reference in the story's opening paragraph to Josefine's "Hingang" (departure) must be read in this light.) This ambivalence is even reflected in the title, which although "not pretty" (nicht hübsch), as Kafka put it, is extraordinarily apt, being, as he said, "something like a scale," in that it balances off two alternative titles, "Josefine, the Singer or the Mouse-Folk." The inability to decide (on a title, on anything) is a theme in the narrative: Is the predominant figure the artist, or the society for which she creates? Is Josefine an artist, or a charlatan? This tentativeness pervades the entire narrative: the narrator cannot state anything unequivocally, no sooner is a statement made,

4. *The Diaries of Franz Kafka*, trans. Joseph Kresh (New York: Schocken Books, 1948), 176.
5. *Diaries*, 182.
6. *Diaries*, 211. [A problematic translation; see p. 196.]

than it is denied or at least put in doubt. Josefine is presented as "our singer," and to hear her is to know "the power of song." But the narrator cannot even say for certain that she can sing, and if so, then perhaps no better than anyone else in the mouse-folk; perhaps her singing is just "piping," after all, an activity unconsciously performed by all mice. The hidden meaning of music, however admired as an art it may be, is subject to the doubts and reversals of Kafka's narrative perspective: music's inexpressible meaning can require faith not always available to the "unmusical":

> I have often wondered what this music of hers truly means—after all, we are entirely unmusical, so how is it that we understand Josefine's singing or, since Josefine denies that, at least believe we understand it? . . . is it really singing? Isn't it perhaps merely piping? (Ist es vielleicht doch nur ein Pfeifen?)[7]

Pfeifen can mean "to whistle a tune," or "to blow a whistle," or "to play on a pipe or flute." But its most common German usage, "to whistle at," means "don't give a damn" about something. So Josefine's artistry is at least partly humorous, even ridiculous. Moreover, whistling is the European equivalent of booing; but since *pfeifen* (piping) is an unconscious habit of mice, the narrator concedes there might be the occasional *pfeifen* (whistling? booing?) from Josefine's audiences while she is performing. So what initially the narrator sees as a high art form of piping, is soon undermined by piping with overtones of a nervous habit (whistling) and a kind of booing. Indeed, some foolish youngster once started to pipe along in one of Josefine's performances, but was promptly shushed by her mouse-peers, employing yet another form of the verb *pfeifen* (niedergepfiffen), she was "piped down." In any case, the nature of Josefine's art is placed in suspicious light by Kafka's choice of the word *pfeifen*.

The highly ambivalent attitude of the mouse people toward Josefine's singing is a reflection of Kafka's own attitude toward music, and of Kafka's family's attitude toward him and his writing.[8] Kafka's distrust of music in part derives from an acute acoustic sensitivity[9] which he makes clear in conversation with Janouch, himself a composer: "with music we can achieve deep resonances in our emotions . . .";[1] but it is precisely the uncontrolled nature of the

7. Franz Kafka, *The Metamorphosis and Other Stories*. Trans. Donna Freed (New York: Barnes and Noble, 1996), 191; [p. 95].
8. Ursula Mahlendorf examines the story's latent psychic drama using a Freudian schema: Kafka's personality is split among the characters, the Mousefolk are the superego, and Josefine is the id, while the narrator represents Kafka's ego. But the Mousefolk can also be seen as a projection of Kafka's feelings about his parents, particularly his father. "Kafka's *Josefine the Singer or the Mousefolk*: Art at the Edge of Nothingness," in *Modern Austrian Literature* 11, no 3/4 (1978), 199–242.
9. Mahlendorf 222.
1. Janouch 111–12, quoted by Mahlendorf.

emotions loosed by music which threatened Kafka: according to Mahlendorf, "Kafka lacked the means of controlling and regulating the emotions aroused by his receptivity." Writing, on the other hand, he could use precisely for defensively controlling sensory stimulation, she continues. The narrator's attempt (ego) to tell Josefine's story, to do it in his language, is an attempt to control and censor the emotions set loose by music; he does this by narrating her story, criticising her, and finally, reporting her disappearance, that is, killing her. Josefine is the artist (the id) whose creation, music, is too threatening to the narrator to be allowed to continue.

Writing is used as a defense mechanism against unwelcome insight: the narrator keeps the reader off balance by using a dizzying technique of statement and negation, statement and retraction. The narrator's inability to determine whether Josefine's singing is really art is also a sublimation of the writer's doubts about his own writing. The second statement of the story: "Anyone who has not heard her does not know the power of song"[2] can be read to mean the narrator himself has not really heard Josefine's music: the "unmusicality" of the other mouse-folk, after all, is shared by their fellow-mouse narrator. The irony and humor in many of the narrator's descriptions of Josefine,[3] or her art, supports this view of the narrator: For example, the third sentence of the story, "There is not one among us who is not swept away by her singing" (German: Es gibt niemanden, den ihr Gesang nicht fortreißt) is ambivalent, since *fortreißen* could mean "sweep away" or "transport," but possibly also "tear away," or "drive away." The narrator admits that the mouse-folk really prefer "peace and quiet," prefer silence to music, for life is hard, and its many problems occupy their attention at the expense of an art form which seems remote from their daily lives, as it seemed "esoteric" to the dogs, and even "dangerous" and undisciplined to Kafka in his conversations with Janouch.

But the narrator's ambivalence (toward writing as well as music) produces conflicting statements: music may be "remote" from the mouse-folk's concerns, but musical occasions still play a role in their society: as art, it is a figuration of their pitiful existence as a people ("Josefine's thin piping amid grave decisions is almost like our meager existence amid the tumult of a hostile world"[4]), it has a social and political function, for her concerts are more a *Volksversammlung*, in which the people share a kind of communion together before an imminent battle. And it is a comfort in times of trouble: It gives the mice the strength to bear their misfortunes, even if it cannot stave them off. But the predominant attitude of

2. Freed 191; [p. 94]
3. Josefine is sometimes made to seem a caricature of the diva personality.
4. Freed 200; [p. 100]

the narrator, while conceding in some instances the efficacy of Josefine and her singing, is disapproval, discredit, and disavowal. This attitude toward the artist as charlatan, as seen also in *A Hunger Artist*, complicates the interpretation of this last work of Kafka: if the artist is a charlatan, how do we appropriately evaluate this artist's writing?

Perhaps the most remarkable thing about this story is Kafka's using his own musical blind spot convincingly to portray an attitude toward (an) art, an attitude which was reflected in his own personal family history.[5] The zigzagging statements and inability of the narrator to make final judgments on Josefine's art reflect Kafka's own concerns, but they reflect real societal attitudes toward art: here and in *A Hunger Artist* Kafka has anticipated today's performance art, and the debate as to whether it is genuine art. Art is a negotiation: Josefine is an artist because society, at least sometimes, agrees that she is. The narrator alludes to this in his comparison of her singing to cracking a nut: "Here is someone creating a solemn spectacle of the everyday."[6] Like performance art, her physical presence is required: you must see her as well as hear her to understand (or believe you understand) her art. But this agreement is tentative, and ultimately dissolves into indifference. Kafka uses the lens of his own unmusicality to focus on the hostility of a public toward an art form; the constantly reversing, negating style of the narration, like a switchback road on a mountainside, consumes much time and verbiage to proceed what in reality is a very short distance. In fact, the story really does not "progress" at all; the entire story is contained in essence in the first paragraph. Under the magnifying glass of Kafka's narrative style, we examine closely and get more detail about the relationship of the mouse people to Josefine, but the narrator does not move from any of the statements made at the outset.

One commentator has noted that the opening paragraph is like an overture containing all the themes of the work to come.[7] (The only important fact missing from this exposition is Josefine's demands and their rejection.) We learn the singer's name: Josefine; she is uniquely female among Kafka's protagonists (though only a mouse, she borrows her name from Josef K. of *The Trial*, who did end up "like a dog"). Here are the other facts presented in this first paragraph: her song has power; there is no one not moved by her song; the people are unmusical in general, preferring quiet; their

5. The hostile indifference of his father towards Kafka's writing is documented in the *Brief an den Vater* (*Letter to His Father*), among other places.

6. Freed 193; [p. 96].

7. Ruth V. Gross, "Of Mice and Women: Reflections on a Discourse in Kafka's 'Josefine, die Sängerin oder Das Volk der Mäuse,'" in: *Franz Kafka: A Study of the Short Fiction*, ed. Allen Thiher (Boston: Twayne Publishers, 1990), 130.

lives are hard, music is remote from their concerns; the mouse folk
are cunning and practical, which is their greatest asset; they take
comfort from this asset, more than they would from any possible
"happiness" which music might provide. Josefine is the sole exception to this: she loves music and knows how to communicate with
it; with her departure music will disappear from the lives of the
mouse folk, for an unknown period.

Do the mice actually hear music? Although the narrative continues with what appear to be contradictions, some of them are resolved if one reads the second statement literally; whoever has not
heard her cannot appreciate the power of song. But the narrator
does not say anyone actually does hear her. That there is "no one
who is not overwhelmed" by her song is not quite the direct admission that "all the people are thrilled by her song" would be. And one
looks in vain through the story for a direct statement that the mice
people actually hear her music: what they hear is "piping," and, although for various social reasons they agree to call it art (at times),
they do not hear it as music. Even Josefine concedes this: she sings
to "tauben Ohren" (deaf ears) and does not think her people understand what they hear. In a typical "switch" the narrator says it is not
just piping which she produces: no, if you sat far away and listened,
you would hear—what? Only a kind of soft and tender . . . piping!
not different from that of everyone else. It is not the sound but the
sight of Josefine which makes her performance special; Josefine has
a suspicion (Ahnung) that all this is so; the narrator says the fact
that they listen to her at all is proof that what she creates is not
music: why else would she deny so passionately that her audience
hears her?

The mouse people are so unmusical that they would suppress or
ignore a real singer; Josefine is laughable but the folk would never
laugh at her, even though laughter is always close to the surface for
the troubled mouse folk; the reason for this is that they see Josefine
as their protégé, as someone they must protect; she maintains the
opposite: she doesn't care a fig for their protection (Ich pfeife auf
eueren Schutz) to which the mouse people respond, Ja, ja, du
pfeifst. This (intentionally?) humorous response reemphasizes the
disconnect between singer and people: either they do not hear, or
she only pipes, and does not sing.

The mouse people stand in a parental role in relationship to Josefine, a situation which enrages Josefine, but which she is powerless
to change. She has repeatedly demanded that the mouse people re-
lieve her of the burden of earning her living; although they could
easily do this, they refuse. Josefine wants this indulgence as explicit
recognition of her art and it is precisely this that the mouse society
will deny her. She threatens, like a child, to withhold her music, to

shorten her performances, to cut out the coloratura arias in her concerts, if her demand is not met. But the mouse people simply ignore these threats, as a parent would; they ignore her words as much as they ignore her music, even while at concerts. They are impervious to these threats, neither they nor the narrator even notice the changes that she makes to her programs. Like Kafka's own parents, their response is distant, uncomprehending, "grundsätzlich wohlwollend, aber unerreichbar."[8] This describes closely Kafka's own lack of comprehension of music, and his reason for making Josefine a musician.

Josefine insists on gathering an audience about her, even in times of severe hardship and danger; the mouse folk, even under duress, grant her this, but when they do gather around to listen, the comfort she provides is a subliminal, dreamlike kind of plea-sure, of which the adult mice are barely conscious. This, too, may be a veiled reflection of Kafka's reaction to music in concert; his inability to enjoy it in a "connected" way, as mentioned in the diary entry above.

The mice have some stereotypically Jewish traits: the narrator remarks that they have no youth (Jews are said to be "born old"), though they have a certain weariness and hopelessness, they are tough and confident, they possess a practicality that gets them through their difficulties, they are threatened, they live in scattered communities, they have a particular kind of humor and backbiting gossipiness, and they are "unmusical," a stereotype repeated by Richard Wagner and Otto Weininger, which gained currency against the backdrop of politically and culturally "correct" anti-Semitism of Vienna. But this stereotype, like that of the Jews being the "people of the Book" (and Germans the people of music) is a subtext in the story and in Kafka's narrative stance.

One can see this story in a historical continuum: Josefine's situation is not constant: as in *Investigations of a Dog*, there was an earlier time of authentic music, the knowledge of which is traditional among the mice. Both singer and public have an intuition (Ahnung) of this lost past authenticity.[9] However, this is not the end of the story: the narrator says with her departure music will disappear from their lives altogether—who knows for how long? By the story's end this predicted event has already happened: Josefine has disappeared. (Again using silence as an act, the narrator has either withheld information or has learned something in the course of the narration.) With Josefine's passage from the scene, the connection to the authentic music of the past is permanently severed; the mice have no historical record, and will forget her. The ironic last state-

8. "Well disposed at heart, but unmoved," Freed 208.
9. Freed, 192: "We have some idea about what singing is, and Josefine's art does not correspond to these ideas"; [p. 95].

ment is a striking exponentiation of the silence that her "departure" really is; for her *Erlösung*, her redemption, intensified by the adjective "gesteigert," is not only to be silenced, but to be forgotten, "like all her brothers." It is hard to conceive of a more negative statement on her art than this.

GERHARD KURZ

The Rustling of Stillness: Approaches to Kafka's *The Burrow*†

I

A characteristic quality of Kafka's work is the recurrence of certain images, motifs, and figures: for example, animals, children, businessmen, artists, officials, soldiers, students, women; the hunt, the struggle, the trial, the game, the theater, silence, music, the trip or the journey (the quest!), fatigue, distraction, sickness, fasting, eating and drinking, filth, purity, the woods, snow, the city, the village, noise, riding, staggering, rocking, calculating, washing; the colors: black, white, red, yellow, and brown.[1]

One striking motif is that of the building or burrow. It occurs, for example, in *The Castle*, "A Report to an Academy," "A Visit to the Mine," "The City Coat-of-Arms"; in story fragments and reflections, such as the reflections on the construction of the Tower of Babel; and in Kafka's studies of Kierkegaard, in which he speaks of "the constructive destruction of the world."[2] A letter from Kafka to Max Brod on July 12, 1922, begins with the words: "Dearest Max, Right now I'm either running around or sitting there stonily, as a desperate animal in its burrow must do * * * ."[3] A story fragment probably dating from the spring of 1917 contains this motif right in its title: "Building the Great Wall of China." And Max Brod gave

† From "Das Rauschen der Stille. Annäherungen an Kafkas 'Der Bau,'" in: *Franz Kafka. Zur ethischen und ästhetischen Rechtfertigung*, ed. Beatrice Sandberg and Jakob Lothe (Freiburg i. Br.: Rombach Verlag, 2002), pp. 151–174. Translated by Eric Patton. Reprinted by permission of the publisher. Page numbers in brackets refer to this Norton Critical Edition.

1. Additional examples in Barbara Beutner, *Die Bildsprache Franz Kafkas* (Munich: Fink, 1973).
2. "His argument is accompanied by a bewitchment. One can escape from an argument into the world of magic, from a bewitchment into logic, but both simultaneously are crushing, especially when they are a third thing, living magic or a non-destructive but rather constructive destruction of the world." Franz Kafka, *Nachgelassene Schriften und Fragmente II*, ed. Jost Schillemeit (Frankfurt a.M.: Fischer, 1992), 105. All citations have been translated by the editor of the Norton Critical Edition from the *Kritische Ausgabe der Werke Kafka*, ed. Jürgen Born, et al. (Frankfurt a.M.: Fischer, 1982ff).
3. Franz Kafka, *Briefe 1902–1924*, ed. Max Brod (Frankfurt a.M.: Fischer, 1966), 390.

the title *The Burrow* to another fragmentary story that Kafka wrote in the winter of 1923/24 in Berlin during the last year of his life. The title corresponds well to Kafka's plan. Dora Diamant, with whom Kafka lived in Berlin during that winter, remembered: "One of his last stories, *The Burrow*, was written in a single night. It was winter; he began early in the evening and was finished around morning; then he worked on it again."[4]

The story fragment "Building the Great Wall of China," with its description of a wall consisting of parts with many gaps between them, reflects on the genesis and structure of a text in general and particularly on the meaning and validity of the Holy Word. The form of the Wall evokes the form of the Word. The entire "system of partial constructions" contains gaps, some of which are larger than the parts themselves. "Legends" have grown up around the "construction" [p. 113]: this alludes allegorically to the different parts, textual forms, and messages out of which, in a process lasting centuries, the Torah, the Five Books of Moses, and the Bible were created. Traditions, stories, commentaries, and interpretations—the "legends," so to speak—arose around these texts. Kafka's story involves the attempt to protect the Empire, the "most obscure [of] * * * institutions," from external attacks and internal dissolution through the construction of the Wall. The allegorical "construction" of the story invites an understanding of the "institution" of the Empire as the institution of religion, which must be protected by the written Word. The Chinese people, all of whose "thoughts went to the Emperor," allegorically represent the Jewish people [pp. 118–19]. (This connection is strengthened by the assignment of colors, among other things. The Jews were described with the color yellow in the Middle Ages, and in Kafka's epoch, yellow is the stereotypical color for the Chinese.) But the elements of Jewish religiosity are also connected to elements of Christian religiosity.[5] In his youth, the narrator of this story discovers the construction of the Wall "thirty years" after its "annunciation" (see *Luke* 3:23 and 2:10).

II

The story fragment *The Burrow* is also about the "institution" or "construction" of religion and art. The first sentence reads, "I have established my burrow, and it seems to be a success" [p. 162]. The

4. *"Als Kafka mir entgegenkam . . ." Erinnerungen an Franz Kafka*, ed. Hans-Gerd Koch (Berlin: Wagenbach, 1995), 179. [A delightful volume of reminiscences of Kafka by those who knew him in his lifetime—*Editor*].

5. Cf. Giuliano Baioni, *Kafka, Literatur und Judentum* (Stuttgart: Metzler, 1994) esp. 38ff; Ritchie Robertson, "*Die Erneuerung des Judentums aus dem Geist der Assimilation, 1900 bis 1922*," in Wolfgang Braunart, et. al., editors, *Ästhetische und religiöse Erfahrungen der Jahrhundertwenden. II: um 1900* (Paderborn: Schöningh, 1998), 184ff.;—, "Kafka und das Christentum," *Deutschunterricht* 5 (1998), 60–69.

narrative form of the fragment is not easy to describe.[6] In a precise sense, it is not a story told by a narrator from a certain distance. *The Burrow* is written in the first-person perspective; the reader learns only whatever the narrative "I" thinks, experiences, and perceives. Rather than a direct first-person narrative, however, we encounter trains of thought, considerations, and "calculations"—an interior monologue, in other words, that often becomes an internal conversation describing almost exclusively the immediate present of the narrative "I." Past events, since they repeat themselves, are transferred into the iterative present ("After such moments, I am in the habit of * * *" [p. 167]).[7] Reflection and experience go hand-in-hand; they may converge, but they also diverge in a barely perceptible manner. Indeed, it is often barely possible to decide whether reflection and experience are converging or whether an experience is only being "played through" or whether one-time or repetitive events are being described.

This structure changes at the end of the text with the perception of a deadly threat. Now, past and present, experience and reflection become clearly separate, and we may speak more readily of a first-person narrative.

The narrative "I" seems to be locked into its train of reflections and shrewd calculations. Formulations such as "as will perhaps be granted me" and "[b]ut you do not know me if you think," however, seem to indicate an awareness of some authority that is announced and before which the "I" justifies itself; and the comment about the "the nervous anxiety of the moment" hints at the epoch of the author, in which nervousness was a key psychological concept.

The narrative "I" is an animal. It remains uncertain what kind of animal it is that has dug its burrow here. Fur, claws, and scrabbling paws are mentioned. It calls itself an "old master builder" and thinks of its nearing old age; its memory is already becoming dim. The underground burrow it has dug is supposed to protect it from enemies outside and inside. The burrow has huge dimensions, countless tunnels, more than fifty rooms, and a central "castle court." Different phases of action can be distinguished in the course of the narrator's reflections: first, the description or presentation of the burrow; then, an exit from the burrow; a return; and, finally, the ultimate struggle against an imagined opponent. The an-

6. For a precise analysis of the narrative form and its function, see Kurt Druckenthaner's essay " 'Der Bau'—Ermittlungen hinsichtlich einer dunklen Erzählsituation," in Gerd-Dieter Stein, editor, *Kafka-Nachlese* (Stuttgart: H.D. Heinz, 1988), 153–79; as well as Heinrich Henel, "Das Ende von Kafkas 'Der Bau'," *Germanisch-Romanische Monatsschrift*, 22 (1972), 3–23.

7. Lengthy retrospective passages have been crossed out in the manuscript; consult the supplementary volume to volume II of the posthumous writings (*Nachgelassene Schriften*) in the Frankfurt critical edition, esp. 429f, 436f.

imal "I" began the burrow in its youth: "Between that time and now lie the years of my manhood" [p. 188]. The burrow is its life, house, home, cavern or hollow, hole, nest, and above all its castle, with which it protects itself against the "world's hostility" [p. 170]. The burrow is not an aboveground construction like the Great Wall of China or the Tower of Babel but rather a kind of inverted construction, an underground hollowing-out although made, of course, according to a "total plan." Depending upon its moods and hopes, the animal "I" images the burrow as a house that it has established as its owner, a castle that it defends, a cavern into which it retreats as into the body of a mother, and a nest into and out of which it slips. The description of the entry as a "hole" is charged with sexual significance. In the "dreams" of the animal "I," "a lascivious snout sniffs incessantly around it" [p. 163]. Its imagination of an intruder with its "filthy craving" ends in a fantasy of sexual violence. The animal "I" would "leap onto" him from behind in a "frenzy" and "bite into his flesh, tear him limb from limb, rip him to pieces, and drink his blood" [p. 172]. Enemies are excited with "desire" to follow the creature, because, when it goes down into the burrow, it openly exposes its "dearest possession" to all those around.

The animal "I" organizes the relationship of the burrow to the surrounding world through a series of oppositions. With the burrow, the entire world is divided into an inside and an outside; the "hole" of the entry is the bridge between the two. The inside is the burrow with its passages and rooms, and outside are the "open woods," the "highways," the enemies, the "wanderers, without a home" [p. 164]. Opposed categories are homeland/foreign land; below/above; inside/outside; house/world; quiet/noise; peace/danger. The opposition is unstated but implicit when the outer world is referred to as "the world above," as "life," or as "outside." The burrow is then thought of implicitly as the "underworld," as "death," or as "prison."

In a series of considerations, descriptions, assumptions, explanations, corrections, reservations, and retractions, the animal "I" tries to assure himself that his burrow is secure against "intruders" or "enemies" and more generally the risks of life. The creature calls these continuous thoughts "calculations" or "considerations" and does not conceal the fact that what is behind them is fear. But it also does not deny that they even give it pleasure: "All these are very laborious calculations, and the delight that the sharp-witted mind takes in itself is sometimes the sole reason why it continues its calculations" [p. 163]. To be sure, these calculations do not provide any security. In spite of all its cleverly devised habits and construction measures, the animal "I" is never rid of the awareness of being defenselessly exposed to possible attacks; it even fears that precisely the cleverness of its own construction measures have increased their endangerment, for "trickiness of so fine a weave can be suicidal" [p. 162]. The obsessive calculation of complete security is itself a symptom of existential anxiety about the "security" of life. Thus, the voice that speaks of security is also the mouthpiece of another voice that denies security. The inner monologue exposes an ambivalent, conflicted consciousness. This ambivalence shows up in the sequences of relativizations and retractions, such as "not even my exit will save me from them, as indeed it probably will not save me at all" or "[a]nd so I can enjoy my time here to the fullest and spend it without a care—or I could and yet I cannot" [p. 169]. The ambivalence also shows itself in immanent contradictions, such as "I lie here in a little chamber secured on all sides—there are more than fifty like it in my burrow—and between dozing and unconscious sleep, for which I choose the hours as my moods dictate, time passes" [p. 164]. If the place were really secured on all sides, then more than fifty like them would not be necessary!

What most disturb the animal "I" are the entrance and exit to the burrow. This is secured by a "labyrinth." Later, the creature judges this labyrinth to be only "overly fussy puttering" [p. 167]. At that place "on the dark moss," the animal "I" is, surprisingly, "mortal." These formulations also have an erotic connotation. In order to secure itself against danger at the entrance, in order to be able to monitor everything, the animal "I" wishes to be simultaneously outside and inside the burrow, to be in the state of "sleeping deeply and at the same time of being able to keep a close watch on myself" [p. 170]—put more generally, both to exist and to know itself as existing, to exist and to be in possession of itself, in such a way that it could still monitor its own mortality. Its wish is thus aimed at omnipotence and omniscience—put in philosophical terms, at absolute consciousness. But the wish remains only a wish.

III

Interpreters of this text have already determined[8] that it can be read as a "semi-private game" (Malcolm Pasley), as an allegory of Kafka's literary creation, which includes autobiographical readings,

---

8. Cf. e.g. Heinz Politzer, *Franz Kafka. Der Künstler* (Frankfurt a.M.: Fischer, 1965), 489ff; English version: *Franz Kafka: Parable and Paradox* (Ithaca: Cornell UP, 1962); Walter H. Sokel, *Franz Kafka. Tragik und Ironie* (Frankfurt a.M.: Fischer, 1976) (1st ed. 1964), 416 ff; Jost Schillemeit, "Welt im Werk Franz Kafka," *Deutsche Vierteljahrsschrift für Literaturwissenschaft und Geistesgeschichte* 38 (1964), 174ff; Walter Biemel, *Philosophische Analysen zur Kunst der Gegenwart* (Den Haag: Martinus Nijhoff, 1968), 96ff; Karl-Heinz Fingerhut, *Die Funktion der Tierfiguren im Werke Franz Kafkas* (Bonn: Bouvier, 1969), 189ff; Henel (see note 6 [p. 335]); Hartmut Binder, *Kafka Kommentar zu sämtlichen Erzählungen* (Munich: Kröner, 1975), 301ff; Malcolm Pasley, "The Burrow," in Angel Flores, editor, *The Kafka Debate* (New York: Gordian, 1977), 418–25;—"*Die Schrift ist unveränderlich. . . .*": *Essays zu Kafka* (Frankfurt a.M.: Fischer Taschenbuch,

and that it thematizes itself in a reflexive turn. It is almost a requirement that we read the discovery of the "hissing in my walls" and the problems with "air flow" as an allusion to Kafka's tuberculosis, which was diagnosed in the autumn of 1917.

Kafka often compared himself and his life as a writer to the life of an animal. For example, he wrote to Felice Bauer on May 13, 1913, that he "curled up on the forest floor as animals do" and on February 11, 1915, that he tried to "burrow into" his apartment in order to be able to write. A year later, on January 18, 1916, in another letter to Felice, he described his task as being "to crawl away somewhere in a hole and secretly listen to myself." A diary entry reads, "Now all protected and crawled into my work."[9] I have already cited the comparison to a "desperate animal in its burrow" in the letter to Max Brod in 1922. In letters to Milena in 1920 he compares himself to an old "mole"[1] that digs "tunnels,"[2] then with a "forest animal" that lies in a "dirty pit," an "animal" that belongs in the forest and not, as the letter suggests, to Milena or to human society.[3] In an early, well-known passage from a letter, Kafka calls for "books that affect us like a misfortune, that cause us a lot of pain, like the death of someone whom we loved better than ourselves, as if we were cast out in the forests, cut off from all human beings * * *" [p. 193].

In such passages the forest is imagined as a place of (also sexual) wildness, of distance from society and civilization, of loneliness, of being disowned, of a "spiritual struggle." In the letter to Milena in which he calls himself a "forest animal," the "forest" becomes a metaphor for literature (perhaps through the idea of the letters [as sticks], the forest as an image of writing?):

1995), 75ff; Henry Sussman, *Franz Kafka: Geometrician of Metaphor* (Madison: Coda Press, 1979), 147ff.; Beatrice Wehrli, "Monologische Kunst als Ausdruck moderner Welterfahrung. Zu Kafkas Erzählung 'Der Bau,' " in *Jahrbuch der deutschen Schillergesellschaft* 25 (1981), 435–45; Andrea Reiter, "Franz Kafkas autobiographische Erzählungen 'Der Bau' und 'Die Forschungen eines Hundes': Selbstanalyse oder Gleichnis?" in *Sprachkunst* 18 (1987), 21–38; Manfred Schmeling, *Der labyrinthische Diskurs. Vom Mythos zum Erzählmodell* (Frankfurt a.M: Athenäum, 1987), 99ff; Ewald Rösch, "Franz Kafka ein Dichter der Angst? Zur Deutung seiner späten Erzählung 'Der Bau,' " in Günter Birtsch/Meinhard Schröder, editors, *Angst—ein individuales und soziales Phänomen*, in *Trier Beiträge* 21 (1991), 46–56; Günter Samuel, "Vom Abschreiben des Körpers in der Schrift. Kafkas Literatur der Schreiberfahrung," in Hans Joachim Piechotta et al., editors, *Die literarische Moderne in Europa I* (Opladen: Westdeutscher Verlag), 352–473, esp. 468ff; Seiji Hattori, "Der Blick und das Rauschen. Phänomenologie und Physiologie der Selbstbeobachtung in 'Der Bau' von Kafka," in *Studien zur deutschen Literatur und Sprache* 29 (Tokio, 1997), 153–67; II: in—, 1999, 149–63.

9. *Tagebücher in der Fassung der Handschrift*, ed. Michael Müller (Frankfurt a.M.: Fischer, 1990), 548.
1. Franz Kafka, *Briefe an Milena* (Frankfurt a.M.: Fischer, 1986), 185.
2. Baioni, 176f, calls attention to a passage from a letter of Flaubert's, in which Flaubert compares his work as a writer with the work of a mole: "One must bury oneself in one's work and labor on with head bowed like a mole." Gustave Flaubert, *Correspondence*, Troisième Serie (1852–53) (Paris: Louis Conard, 1927), 349.
3. *Briefe an Milena*, 262.

* * * then I saw you outside in the open, the most wonderful thing I had ever seen, I forgot everything, forgot myself completely, stood up, came nearer, although anxious in this new and yet homey freedom, still I came nearer * * *. but basically I was just the animal, belonged just in the forest, lived here in the open just through your favor * * *. You would have to, even if you stroked me with the most kindly hand, recognize strange things that pointed to the forest, to this origin and real homeland * * *.[4]

The figure of a building is itself an old and antique metaphor for the crafted, constructed aspect of an aesthetic formation. Pindar,[5] for example, conceived of the poet as a master builder (Pythian Odes, III, 113–115). The notion of the poet as master builder or poeta faber[6] has a mythic archetype in the master builder Daedalus,[7] who created the labyrinth on Crete. In a deleted section of Kafka's manuscript, the animal "I" says that there was something "of a master builder" in his blood, that "even as a child I drew zigzag and labyrinth diagrams in the sand." With the construction of the entrance labyrinth, the creature seeks to prevent intrusion into the burrow. Daedalus created artificial wings for himself and his son in order for them to flee Crete; Icarus,[8] his son, fell from the skies (see Ovid, *Metamorphoses*, VIII). The conspicuous emphasis and ironic retraction of the creature's desire to improve the burrow "in a flash" (literally, "on wings") alludes to the myth of Daedalus through more than a figure of speech:

> When I return, when peace has been restored, I will put the final touch on everything, and everything will be done in a flash. Yes, in fairy tales everything is done in a flash, and this consolation also belongs to the world of fairy tales. [p. 183]

Kafka's use of the labyrinth motif is probably also inspired by Virgil's *Aeneid*, VI. Aeneas begins his trip to the Underworld at

4. Ibid.
5. Pindar (or Pindarus) (522 BC–443 BC) is regarded as the greatest if also the most difficult and obscure lyric poet of ancient Greece. His poems celebrate the athletic victories of the nobility in intricate meters [*Editor*].
6. Cf. Gerhard Goebel, *Poeta Faber. Erdichtete Architektur in der italienischen, spanischen und französichen Literatur der Renaissance und des Barock* (Heidelberg: Winter, 1971).
7. In Greek mythology, a master builder of Athens, who was exiled to Crete and placed in the service of King Minos; here he built the labyrinth and fathered a son, Icarus. Cf. Schmeling (note 8 [p. 337]). Schmeling's shrewd observations have the disadvantage that he, like the more than few readers of Kafka who have been taken with the labyrinth model, grasps the entire burrow as a labyrinth. Cf. too Heinz Ladendorf, "Kafka and Art History II," in *Wallraf-Richartz-Jahrbuch* 25 (1963), 242ff; on the poetological reception of the Daedalus myth, see Felix Phillip Ingold, *Der Autor am Werk. Versuche über literarische Kreativität* (Munich: Hanser, 1992), 11ff.
8. With his son Icarus, Daedalus sought to escape from the labyrinth with wings he constructed from feathers and wax; although Icarus was warned not to fly too close to the sun, for the wax would melt, he disobeyed his father and fell into the sea and drowned [*Editor*].

Cumae, where Daedalus had built a temple on whose gate the labyrinth of Crete was depicted.

The figure of a building is also an old metaphor for religious order.[9] One goal of Christian piety is "edification." In the Jewish tradition, the Law or religion is presented as a "house" (as in *Exodus* 38:21, for example). With its "zig-zag structure of passages," its "beautifully vaulted and rounded" castle court that lies purposely not in the middle of the burrow, its "quiet" and "peace," the burrow also recalls a sacral structure, a church or Solomonic temple. The "most holy" place of the latter is also not in the middle of the structure (*I Kings* 6:16). In religious tradition, such as in Teresa of Avila ("the interior castle") and Luther ("A Mighty Fortress is Our God"), God or belief is imagined as a castle.

We may also read the description of the burrow as a "work" in a literary way. The animal "I" is anxious because it has only one "specimen" [German: "Exemplar," normally meaning a copy of a book] of the castle court [p. 166]. It calls the entrance labyrinth the "work of a beginner" and a "construction" and self-critically refers to it as "overly fussy puttering, not really worthy of the burrow as a whole" [pp. 167–68]. According to Malcolm Pasley, the phrase "work of a beginner" may refer allegorically to Kafka's early *Description of a Struggle*, a truly labyrinthine work. Pasley sees in the central "castle court" another allegorical reference to Kafka's *The Castle*, on which Kafka worked from February to September in 1922.[1] But this attractive conjecture gives rise to the question of which place Kafka's other two novels have in Kafka's literary edifice.

The creation of the "work" of the burrow required "hands" and "forehead," calculation, and "almost dreamlike" labor at night [p. 166]. The burrow is said to be complete, yet its flaws are only too apparent to the animal "I." But "revisions" are no longer possible. The notion of revision characterizes the movement of thought not only here and in other texts by Kafka, such as in the passages: "But the best thing about my burrow is its silence; of course this is deceptive, at any time the silence can suddenly be shattered, and then everything is at an end"; or "No, I'm not the one, though I thought I was, who watches me sleeping; rather, I am the one who sleeps, while the one who wants to deprave me watches"; or "I find nothing, or, rather, I find too much" [pp. 164, 171, 178]. "Revision" also characterizes Kafka's relationship to literary, mythological, biblical, and historical tradition, which he subjects to subversive revisions.[2]

9. Cf. Article "Bauen," in *Reallexikon für Antike und Christentum* (Stuttgart: 1950), 1: 1265–78.
1. Malcolm Pasley, "The Burrow," 419 f.
2. Cf. e.g. Marthe Robert, *Das Alte im Neuen. Von Don Quichotte zu Franz Kafka* (Munich: Hanser, 1968); English version, *The Old and the New: from Don Quixote to Kafka*, trans. Carol Cosman (Berkeley: University of California Press, 1977); Rolf J. Goebel, *Kritik*

And it applies to his work on the text itself. In quiet hours the animal "I" busies itself with working on the burrow, with "improvements," the "work of embellishment," "the final pressing and smoothing down," in order to give the walls "sweep and verve." The animal "I" says of its work: "It is certainly not mere self-praise, it is simply the truth—I am able to do [it] with unsurpassed skill" [p. 182]. The remark that the burrow "cannot tolerate a neighbor who can be heard" may be read as an expression of an artistic sensibility that was not unknown to Kafka [p. 189]. The "entirely unobstructed" exit or point of departure could refer to work on this text itself [p. 163].

The burrow consists of the main chamber, the "castle court," many smaller chambers for provisions, many connecting and criss-crossing passages, and an entrance/exit. The animal "I" sometimes gathers all its provisions in the main chamber. Such formulations may be read as a metaphorical description of a textual structure. Seen as a textual model, the "construction" of the text represents a—rhetorical—arrangement of places (passages) and passageways[3] that includes the various connections, criss-crossing textual movements, and concentration on a center.

It is not difficult to connect the relationship between the animal "I" and its burrow to the author Kafka's relationship to his work. On the one hand, there are references to the identity of the "I" and the burrow—the castle court, it says, "is so much mine that here in the end I can even calmly accept the fatal wound from my enemy, for here my blood seeps into my own soil and will not be lost" [p. 175]; when the creature watches over its burrow, it is "not as if I were standing outside my house, but outside myself" [p. 170]. On the other hand, the burrow contains something threateningly foreign. The creature inspects its walls in "research" and makes discoveries. The "I" who calls itself so emphatically "master, sole master" of the burrow is yet not its master. The author is not master of the meaning of his work; the burrow "appears" to be a success. Kafka's journal entry of February 11, 1913 regarding *The Judgment* is well known; in it, he notes "connections" that "dawned on me" in the story [p. 198].[4]

The outside world, from which the animal "I" protects itself with the burrow, is also the site of its hunting expeditions. It hunts prey[5] both inside and outside the burrow and stores it, carrying

---

und Revision. Kafkas Rezeption mythologischer, biblischer und historischer Tradition (Frankfurt a.M./Bern/New York: Peter Lang, 1986).

3. In rhetoric "places" (topoi, loci) function as "textual building blocks"; cf. e.g. the essays in Thomas Schirven/Gert Ueding, eds. *Topik und Rhetorik* (Tübingen: Niemeyer, 2000).

4. On the hermeneutic relation of the author Kafka to his work, cf. Gerhard Kurz, *Traum-Schrecken. Kafkas literarische Existenzanalyse* (Stuttgart: Metzler, 1980), 85ff.

5. Cf. the identification of writing with hunting: "And the real prey is first found hidden in the depth of the night in the second, third, fourth hour" (*Briefe an Milena*, 229).

"these goods between [its] teeth," as provisions in strategically located places. It enjoys their odor, sometimes throwing itself on them in a crazed fashion and devouring them in ecstasy, and "on awakening find[s] still hanging from [its] teeth a rat, perhaps, as incontrovertible proof of night work that already seems almost dreamlike" [p. 166]. Through this Eucharistic act of feeding and drinking it defends itself against the crush of the provisions—in an allegorical sense, the crush of poetic inspiration.

One figure of the outer world is evoked with particular detail and affect. It is a figure who is both feared and desired. It is "someone of my own kind, an expert, a connoisseur of burrows, a fellow member of a woodland order, a peace lover, but a depraved thug who wants to dwell where he has not built" [p. 172]. It is not difficult to recognize this figure as a literary critic, an interpreter. It is a "woodland brother" of the animal "I" in that it is also a settler. "Waldbruder" (woodland brother) is an old German word for "hermit." In the affect-laden description of the killing of this enemy, the wish for him to intrude becomes apparent:

> If he were actually to appear now, if his filthy craving were actually to lead him to discover the entrance, if he were actually to set to work lifting up the moss, if he were actually to succeed, if he were actually to adroitly force himself in * * * so that finally, in a frenzy of pursuit, free of all scruples, I could leap on him, bite into his flesh, tear him limb from limb, rip him to pieces, and drink his blood, cram his corpse down to the rest of my catch * * *. But no one arrives, and I remain entirely dependent on myself. [p. 172]

Just as the animal "I" 's relationship to his woodland brother is ambivalent, so is its relationship to the outside world. It wants to be completely alone, yet at the same time to be seen, "to create a sensation." At least, the way the "procedure" (from the Latin *procedure*, "to come out," "step out," "appear") of the creature's descent is described and the word-playing juxtaposition of the words "sensation" (German: "*Auf*sehen," also meaning "to look up") and "descent" ("Hin*ab*steigen") suggest this interpretation:

> But now, spoiled from having watched all the goings-on at the entrance for so long, it is a huge torment for me to start the descent, which in itself positively creates a sensation, not knowing what will happen all around me behind my back and then behind the trapdoor once it has been put back in place. [p. 171]

IV

Toward the end, the animal "I" describes one of its favorite plans, which, however, it has not yet carried out. The plan consisted of separating the castle court except for a "small foundation that, unfortunately, could not be detached from the ground," creating a hollow space around the castle court, in which it can play "literally on the body of the castle court" while leaving the true chamber empty:

> I had always imagined this hollow space, probably not without some justice, as the most wonderful abode I could ever have. To hang from this dome, to pull yourself up, to slide down, to turn a somersault, and once again to feel the ground under your feet, and to play all these games literally on the body of the castle court and yet not in its own true chamber. * * * [pp. 179–80]

By realizing this favorite scheme, the animal "I" hoped to hold the castle court, "literally hold it tight between [its] claws," and to protect it. The joy of actually seeing it would be postponed until later. This situation would be a fulfillment of its desires:

> Then there would be no noises in the walls, no insolent excavations right up to the court itself; then peace would have been guaranteed there, and I would be its guardian, I would have to listen, not with revulsion to the excavations of the little creatures but with delight to something that fully eludes me now: the rustle[6] of silence in the castle court. But all this beauty is exactly what does not exist, and I must get to work. * * * [p. 180]

Emptiness, peace, rustling, stillness—these concepts have a religious and aesthetic history around 1920. Peace, stillness, and emptiness are key words in the entire text. "But the best thing about my burrow is its silence," we read at the beginning [p. 164]. In the small, round chambers, the animal "I" sleeps "the sweet sleep of peace" [p. 164]. It loves to tell of the muteness and emptiness of the burrow: "everything, everything quiet and empty" [p. 175].

As the opposition of "noises in the walls" and the "rustle of the silence" makes clear, rustling as opposed to noise represents an undetermined, indeterminable, purposeless sound, which is, however, perceptible as a regular, continuous acoustic fullness. Rustling is an aesthetic phenomenon. A "noise," perceived aesthetically, becomes rustling. The creature would perceive the rustling of stillness with "delight."

6. The German verb "rauschen" (noun-form "Rauschen") has many layers of meaning, including "to rustle," "to roar," "to sough," "to whir," "to produce the sound of rushing water" [Editor].

In his phenomenology of rustling, Martin Seel[7] characterizes the quality of rustling as a "formless shape"[8] resulting from an "over-abundance of shapes"[9] and as an

> occurrence without something occurring. * * * The rustle of the trees in a wood is a sound, or actually a multitude of sounds, whose source cannot be detected by listeners. They are surrounded by sounds that, to them, do not follow from individual tones or tone-sequences that through listening could be traced back to a specific sequence of events.[1]

Using the example of the calm, smooth sea, Seel notes that the phenomenon of rustling results not only from the experience of fullness but also of emptiness when perceived in an aesthetic attitude. Emptiness is the absence of beings, of forms, but *as* emptiness it exists and has intensity. Silence is not simply acoustic emptiness. (In silence, we can already hear our own circulation rustling.) If we immerse ourselves in silence like the animal "I" ("deepest submersion"), it begins to "rustle." It is experienced as an intensity, as the being of emptiness become fullness. Experiencing this, the animal "I" would experience "rapture." In this state, one is "beside oneself" for joy, taken away, "transported." (Luther translates the Greek word "ekstasis" with "Entzückung" [trance]; see *Acts* 10:10). Without this pleasure of self-abandonment, in rapture, the silence would be experienced as something terrifying. In Georg Büchner's *Lenz*, Lenz Oberlin asks: "Don't you hear anything, then? Don't you hear the horrible voice screaming all across the horizon, the voice people usually call silence?"[2]

In the context of an allegorical self-interpretation, this passage can be read as the formulation of an aesthetic program. The "games" that the animal "I" would "literally" play on the empty "body of the castle court" are games with an aesthetic intention,[3] both acrobatic and childlike: hanging on the round surface, pulling yourself up, sliding down, going head over heels. More than a few characters in Kafka's works are silent artists of the body, artistes (e.g., in "Up in the Gallery," "A Starvation Artist," "First Distress," "A Report to an Academy"). In this passage, the acrobatic art is

---

7. Martin Seel, *Ästhetik des Erscheinens* (Munich: Hanser, 2000), 223–53. Citations from 229ff. English version: *The Aesthetics of Appearing*, trans. John Farrell (Stanford: Stanford UP, 2005). Citations from 143f.
8. Seel, *Ästhetik*, 233; *Aesthetics of Appearing*, 145.
9. Seel, *Ästhetik*, 231; *Aesthetics of Appearing*, 144.
1. Seel, *Ästhetik*, 229–230; *Aesthetics of Appearing*, 143.
2. Georg Büchner, *Werke und Briefe*, ed. Werner R. Lehmann (Darmstadt: 1984), 88. Büchner, (1813–1837), a brilliant medical student and playwright, is considered the forerunner of both naturalism and expressionism in German literature. His unfinished masterpiece, which provides the text to Alban Berg's opera, is *Woyzeck* [*Editor*].
3. According to Kant's aesthetics, art is a sincere "Spiel mit Gestalten" (play with forms); cf. *Critique of Judgment*, par. 14 and 53.

practiced outside the "true" sphere. Its forms (*förmlich*) on a geometric structure remain this side of the "true chamber." In that space there are no forms, only the rustling of silence. Art, as it is understood here, aims at a self-transcendence beyond forms and meanings to an emptiness that is experienced as full. An art of forms (*förmlich*) would be a kind of "foreplay," a kind of play that takes place in a "hollow space" but not yet in the actual space of emptiness. Here it can only be completed "formally" (*förmlich*) as well. Emptiness as the "true space" of art requires the auto-sublation of art. Since the animal "I" wants to postpone the joy of seeing the actual space to a "later" time, this art also means a postponement of real action.

This aesthetic program would have to apply to this text itself. Its art as well would remain outside "the true space" and would work toward its own sublation. But one could understand the contradictory, opaque aspects of the text as a sign of rustling.[4]

In a letter to Felice Bauer, written in the night of January 22/23, 1913, this rustling that dissolves forms and meanings appears as part of a poetological primal scene, according to the critic Gerhard Neumann's ingenious interpretation. Kafka writes about a dream:

> As yesterday, for example, when in a dream I ran to a bridge or a quay railing, grabbed two telephone receivers that lay by chance on the balustrade, held them to my ears, and desired now nothing more than to hear news from "Pontus"; but I heard nothing from the telephone, nothing but a sad, powerful song without words and the rustling of the sea. I well understood that it was impossible for human voices to push their way through these tones, but I didn't give up and didn't go away.[5]

This passage alludes to Ovid's exile and his *Epistulae ex Ponto*. What the dreaming Kafka hears in the two "telephone receivers" is not an identifiable human voice, not words, but rather wordless song from an uncertain source, and the rustling of the sea. The song and the rustling are more powerful than "human voices," but in contrast to the paradoxical sharpness of the *Burrow*-passage, they are still perceptible as "tones."

In Kafka's work there is a striking group of motifs involving rustling or related acoustic phenomena that are vague and unarticulated compared to words. In the fifth chapter of his novel *The*

---

4. Cf. Seel, *Ästhetik*, 242ff; *Aesthetics of Appearing*, 151ff., on rushing/rustling as "limit phenomena" in art.
5. Gerhard Neumann, "Nachrichten vom 'Pontus.' Das Problem der Kunst im Werk Franz Kafkas," in Wolf Kittler/Gerhard Neumann, eds. *Franz Kafka. Schriftverkehr* (Freiburg i. Br.: Rombach, 1990), 164–98.

Castle, rustling is again connected to the modern medium of the telephone:

> In the Castle the telephone evidently functions extremely well; as it was explained to me, there the telephones are constantly in use, which of course greatly accelerates the work. We hear this uninterrupted telephoning in the local telephones as rustling and song. * * * Now, however, this rustling and this song is the only correct and trustworthy thing communicated to us by the local telephones; everything else is deceptive.[6]

In his first telephone contact to the Castle, K. hears from the receiver

> a humming, like one K. had never before heard on the telephone. It was as though from the humming of the voices of innumerable children—but this humming wasn't humming either but rather the song of the most distant, the very most distant voices—as though from these voices in some downright impossible way a single high-pitched but strong voice were forming that struck the ear as if it demanded to penetrate more deeply than only into one's paltry hearing.[7]

This group of motifs also includes the droning of the court in "Advocates," the rustling in the fragmentary story "The Tormenting Demon" and the fragmentary drama "The Warden of the Tomb," the squeaking of Josefine in "Josefine, the Singer or the Mouse People," the rustling in "The Worry of the Father of the Family" [p. 72], the screech of the jackdaws in "A Page from an Old Document" [p. 66], and the peeping of Gregor's voice in *The Metamorphosis*.

The motif of aesthetic rustling dates back at least to Hölderlin's[8] poetry (e.g., "Bread and Wine") and Romanticism. In Romantic poetry, the rustling of the forest, spring, or fountain represents an experience of the breaking down of boundaries. Adorno interpreted the motif of rustling in Eichendorff's poems as an expression of a "self-extinguishing of the subject."[9] (This is, of course, under the reservation of the "as if"!) A history of the motif of rustling would also have to examine the aesthetics of early Nietzsche in depth.

6. *Das Schloß, Roman*, ed. Malcolm Pasley (Frankfurt a.M.: Fischer, 1982), 116.
7. Ibid. 36.
8. Friederich Hölderlin (1770–1843), one of the greatest of German poets and theorists of poetry. He longed for the ideals conveyed to him by the literature of classical Greece; he died mad [*Editor*].
9. Freiherr Joseph von Eichendorff (1788–1857), German poet and novelist, a major figure among German Romantic writers, termed "the last champion of romanticism." His most famous novel is *Memoirs of a Good-for Nothing*. Theodor W. Adorno, "Zum Gedächtnis Eichendorffs," in *Noten zur Literatur I* (Frankfurt a.M.: Suhrkamp, 1965), 127. English version: *Notes to Literature*, trans. Shierry Weber Nicholsen (New York: Columbia UP, 1991), 68–69 [*Editor*].

Inspired by Schopenhauer, Nietzsche differentiates in his *The Birth of Tragedy from the Spirit of Music* between two "artistic energies which burst forth from nature herself," the "image world of dreams" and the "intoxicated [rauschvolle, 'rush of'] reality," which does not "heed the single unit but even seeks to destroy the individual and redeem him by a mystical feeling of oneness."[1]

In *The Burrow* the animal "I" experiences not simply rustling noises but also silence as rustling. "But the best thing about my burrow," it says at the beginning, "is its silence" [p. 164]. One can understand this statement in the context of the modern tradition of an aesthetics of silence, of stillness, of emptiness. Mallarmé, for example, drew up the program of a "poëme tu, aux blancs" (a silent poem made entirely of white).[2] The language of the poem is intended to carry over into silence not only at its white borders but in its own immanent movement.

This aesthetic program has a religious pre-history. In religious tradition, silence, stillness, and emptiness are distinguished as forms of an intense submersion in God. From St. Augustine to Kierkegaard to Heidegger,[3] silence is conceived as the ground of language. The mystic Meister Eckhart,[4] whose writings the young Kafka probably read in the edition by Hermann Büttner (Jena, 1903; see the letter to Oskar Pollak on September 11, 1903), understands emptiness ("void of all creatures") as a prerequisite for receiving God's fullness (see his tract *"Von der Abgeschiedenheit* [On Retirement from the World]"). Whoever is empty of all, will become full of God; emptiness becomes fullness.[5]

1. Friedrich Nietzsche, *Werke* in drei Bänden, ed. Karl Schlechta (Munich: Hanser: 1966), I:25. *Basic Writings of Nietzsche*, trans. and ed. Walter Kaufmann (New York: Random House, 1966), 38. On the difference between "Rausch" ("rush," ecstasy) and "Rauschen" (rushing, rustling) see Seel, *Ästhetik*, 227ff; *Aesthetics of Appearing*, 142ff.
2. Stéphane Mallarmé, *Oeuvres complètes*, ed. Henri Mondor/G. Jean-Aubry (Paris: Gallimard, 1951), 367. For this tradition, to which Richard Wagner, Maeterlinck, Rilke, et al. belong, see Hugo Friedrich, *Die Struktur der modernen Lyrik* (Hamburg: Rowohlt, 1967), 116ff; Christian L. Hart Nibbrig, *Rhetorik des Schweigens* (Frankfurt a.M.: Suhrkamp, 1981). Modern examples after Beckett are discussed by Hans-Thies Lehmann, "Fülle, Leere," in *Merkur* 49 (1995), 431–38.
3. Søren Kierkegaard (1813–1855), Danish philosopher, whom Kafka read with special interest given the similarities in their life-situation: both were feverishly-inspired writers and thinkers unable to bring their engagements to a conclusion in marriage and family. Martin Heidegger (1889–1976), influential German philosopher concerned with the meaning of Being and only secondarily of human existence. His major work is *Being and Time* (1927) [*Editor*].
4. Meister Eckhart (c. 1260–1327/8) German mystic and theologian; his writings are marked by a vivid concrete imagery alluding to the mysteries of the soul [*Editor*]. Cf. the article "Leere" and "Schweigen, Stille," in *Historisches Wörterbuch der Philosophie*, ed. Joachim Ritter, et al. 5:157–159; 8: 1483–1495.
5. Cf. the notes from Kafka's Octavo Notebook (October 1917–late January 1918): "Muteness belongs among the attributes of perfection" (*Nachgelassene Schriften*, 50); "Heaven is mute, only the echo to him who is mute" (Ibid. 58). "Before setting foot in the Holiest of Holies, you must take off your shoes, but not only your shoes but everything, traveling clothes and luggage, and under that, your nakedness and everything that is under the nakedness and everything that hides beneath that, and then the core and the core of

The paradoxical connection of rustling and stillness occurs in variations in two other texts by Kafka. In *Researches of a Dog* it is said of the seven music-dogs who appear to the dog-protagonist that they "produc[e] a terrible clamor the likes of which [he] had never heard before. * * * They did not speak, they did not sing, in general they held their tongue with almost a certain doggedness, but they conjured forth music out of that empty space" [p. 134]. In "Josefine, the Singer" the narrator asks himself whether Josefine's singing is not actually a "squeaking" * * *, (in words found in the manuscript) a "soft, somewhat hissing, squeaking sound." He wonders what it is that delights him about it: "Is it her singing that enchants us, or is it rather the ceremonious quiet that surrounds her weak little voice?" [p. 96] The silence of the sirens in "The Silence of the Sirens" is even more irresistible than their song.

In a journal entry at the end of 1913, Kafka reflects on dying and the "incomprehensibility" of death. He sees dying as "nothing other than surrendering a nothing to a nothing" and death as a "roaring nothing." These formulations retract themselves before the "incomprehensibility" of [one's own] death. One cannot represent one's own death, cannot even think it, since it is the end of one's own consciousness: "For how could you, even as a nothing, consciously surrender yourself to the nothing, and not only to an empty nothing but rather to a roaring nothing, whose nothingness consists only in its incomprehensibility" [p. 200].

The passage from *The Burrow* cited above contains a further point. It reveals, as do the reflections of the animal "I" otherwise, an ambivalence in the creature's (conceived) attitude to the "true chamber." On the one hand, we read that it postpones the "joy" of seeing it till "later." This assumes that it wants to see the room and enter it. On the other hand, we then read that if one had to choose between the hollow space and the castle court, one would choose the hollow space "for all the days of [one's] life." What would the animal "I" actually guard as guardian of the castle court if it no longer listens to the "insolent excavations" of the intruders? The word "peace" hints at what causes this ambivalence: it is its own death that the animal "I" desires and continually postpones till "later." It seeks postponement.

V.

As a place in the underworld, the burrow is already a grave that the creature digs for itself. The entry hole has a "trap door." This

---

the core, then the remainder and then the residue and then even the gleam (*Schein*) of the imperishable fire. Only the fire itself is absorbed by the Holiest of Holies and lets itself be absorbed by it; neither can resist the other" [p. 213].

meaning of death is suggested as well by expressions such as "bliss-ful falling asleep," "sweet sleep of peace," "salvation," and "fading out"; it longs "to take leave of everything here"; it says, "I drop everything." The phrase "whenever I go out" also has a double meaning. When the animal "I" is tired of life "here," then someone will "summon [it] to him," whose "invitation" it cannot resist. It expresses its intention to leave the burrow behind in good order. It seeks stillness and "peace" and considers that it ruins these it-self through its mere existence, as one must conclude. The Eu-charistic eating and drinking intends the transformation of the prey into emptiness. At the entry hole, the animal "I" is "mortal," speaking revealingly of "risking its life." In view of the expecta-tion of a "decision" for death (compare the "decision" at the end of *The Trial*), the play in the hollow area represents delay, "post-ponement" of the "true" action. The animal "I" asks itself why it hesitates "to do at once what is necessary" when after all "the meaning of the lovely hours" in the burrow consists in the fact that "here in the end I can even calmly accept the fatal wound from my enemy, for here my blood seeps into my own soil and will not be lost" [p. 175]. The enemy—that is the creature itself, its own death wish.

This ambivalence also characterizes the behavior of the animal "I" toward a noise that wakes it from a deep sleep and which it per-ceives as deadly aggression. It surmises that the noise is caused by the digging of "some sort of trivial" creatures. It hears a "slight hiss-ing, audible only after long pauses, a nothing" [p. 181]. The hissing is audible everywhere. That means that it also hears "nothing" as a hissing. The creature's anxiety is a reaction to this nothingness, or more precisely, as one can put it with Kierkegaard's *The Concept of Anxiety*, anxiety is a shock and thereby the experience of a tran-scendence of the self, of a nothing, negatively understood. (Kafka studied Kierkegaard intensively beginning October 1917.)[6] The an-imal "I" first suspects the cause of the hissing to be a horde of smaller creatures and then a single, large creature, which it calls "hisser," "digger," its "enemy" and "attacker."[7] It attempts to deci-pher the plans of this attacker and interprets the hissing as a "hiss-ing or squealing," then as a "rustling or rushing sound" of ground water, and then finally as "a hissing sound [that] cannot be re-interpreted as a rushing one" [p. 185]. This also describes a possi-ble reaction by the public—a "hissing and booing" that cannot be

6. Cf. here the reflections of Peter Pfaff, "Die Erfindung des Prozesses," in Frank Schirrmacher, ed. *Verteidigung der Schrift. Kafkas "Prozeß"* (Frankfurt a.M.: Suhrkamp, 1987), 17ff.
7. Cf. the analogous movement in *Das Schloß*, where out of the "humming" of voices like children's a single voice evolves. *Das Schloß*, 36.

re-interpreted as the rushing sound of applause. Hissing is an animalistic, aggressive articulation of displeasure, of driving something away. In *The Metamorphosis* the father shoos Gregor into his room: "Pitilessly his father came on, hissing like a wild man."[8] Hissing, one could say, lies underneath or this side of human articulation, while rustling lies beyond. That which the animal "I" experiences as a threat from without actually comes from his burrow, and since it and the burrow belong together, from itself as well. It is "preoccupied with the hissing in [its] walls" [p. 184]. "As long as I knew nothing about [the creature]," it says, "it cannot have heard me at all, for I was quiet then." This peculiar sentence equates being heard with knowledge or knowing. It indicates that the enemy is a figure of its own knowledge, of its own consciousness.

It has known the noise of this other creature since the "early days of the burrow." In the meantime, the noise disappeared, stopped completely, was forgotten. Now the other creature is returning and believes that he "has given me sufficient time to prepare to receive him" [p. 188]. Understood in light of this passage, the first sentence of the story acquires an additional meaning: "I have established my burrow, and it seems to be a success" [p. 162]. The entire text develops a play of meanings around the words "establishment" (Einrichtung), "to put in order" (einrichten), "to settle into" (sich einrichten), and "direction" (Richtung).[9] "Einrichten" means "to make ready," "to aim," "to build," "to plan," "to furnish," "to put in order," and "to prepare." Read from the end, the burrow is set up (eingerichtet) against this other creature and for his "reception." The "organization (Einrichtung) for a defense," it says, is "on a scale of relative importance, way below the arrangements (Einrichtung) for a peaceful life" [p. 184].

Since the animal "I" is so "preoccupied" by this noise, its strength declines toward the end, and we read more frequently about its distractions and tiredness. The damage piles up; it begins to destroy the burrow itself. It scrapes holes in the walls, makes piles of earth in the tunnels: "ugly humps, disturbing cracks" are made and no longer repaired. The strength that it has left fails

8. *Franz Kafka, The Metamorphosis*, trans. and ed. Stanley Corngold, Norton Critical Edition (New York: Norton, 1996), 15 [*Editor*].

9. Cf. the (eschatological) significance of the word "direction" (*Richtung*) in "The New Lawyer" [p. 59] and "A Report to an Academy" [p. 76ff.] and the autobiographical diary entry: "It is easy to recognize in myself a concentration on writing. When it had become clear in my organism that writing was the most productive direction of my being, everything rushed in that direction and left empty all those abilities that were directed first and foremost toward the joys of sex, eating, drinking, philosophical reflection on music" [p. 196]; "my way of life is set up, established (*eingerichtet*) solely for writing" (*Briefe an Felice*, 66); "my entire being is directed (*gerichtet*) toward literature; I have rigorously held to this direction up until my thirtieth year" (Ibid. 456).

"when it comes to making a decision" [p. 188]. This sentence, too, is ambivalent: strength always fails even before the decision that actually needs to be made.

VI

A religious struggle is nested within this struggle of the animal "I" for self-assertion and self-abandonment. Or, put another way: This struggle is furnished with religious meanings that invite a reading of it as an allegory of (Jewish) religion. Or yet again: It is not possible (for me) to decide whether this religious dimension is to be understood as something staged by a narcissistic artist who desires to be like God, or whether this text (or this staging) also treats of the "establishment" (Einrichtung) and the end of the (Jewish) religion. This dimension of meaning (as far as I understand it) is created not through continuous allusions but through periodic, esoteric allusions, the use of key words and phrases from the Biblical pre-text. Because of these "weak" indications, the following thoughts represent no more than an attempt. And they are also subject to the reservation that the text we have is, after all, a fragment.

Along with the architectonic clues of the burrow already mentioned, its "criss-cross passages," this dimension of meaning is evoked by words such as "act of mercy," "providence," "prudence," "salvation," "heavens," "believe," "sacrifice (as a verb)," "sacrifice (as a noun)," "guilt," "hope," "joy," "peace," "master," and "feeding and drinking" as Eucharistic acts, "solemnity of the place," "desire to follow me" (cf. *Deuteronomy* 13:5, "to thrust thee out of the way which the LORD thy God commanded thee to walk in"), "submersion." The animal "I" is given the traits of God of the Old Testament: it is "sole master" of the burrow, "entirely dependent on itself," trusts no one; its burrow can stand no "neighbors" (cf. *Exodus* 20:2). The darkness of the burrow could be an allusion to I. Kings 8:12–13: "The LORD said that he would dwell in the thick darkness. I have surely built thee an house to dwell in, a settled place for thee to abide in for ever." The "little folk" who "feed on earth" alludes to the cursing of the snakes in *Genesis* 3:14: "And the LORD God said unto the serpent, Because thou hast done this, * * * dust shalt thou eat all the days of thy life"; the cursing of the burrow alludes more generally to the curses of God (see, for example, *Genesis* 8:21; *Deuteronomy* 11:26, 28ff, 28:25; *Isaiah* 24:6). The expeditions of the animal "I" to the world above allude to the appearance of God (cf. *Exodus* 3:19). The formulation "procedure of the descent" casts this descent as a ritual and a legal procedure.

(The Jewish religion is a "legal" religion. God is the law-giver of Israel, who has given himself to be known through the covenant with Israel; see *Exodus* 34). "Revision" also has a legal meaning. In the description of the work on the castle court, the sentence "But for this kind of work I have only my forehead" [p. 165] could be an allusion to the figure of speech "to have the nerve" and to the intellectuality of Jewish religious practices and the stubbornness of the Jewish people (*Ezekiel* 3:7–9), the "ground water" and the sand indicating the Sinai desert (see *Numbers* 1:1). The mention of the "journey" or "journeys" evokes a traditional (pre-Zionist) Jewish self-conception (see, for example, *Deuteronomy* 2:7 and Joseph Roth's essay *Wandering Jews* [1927]).

In the Jewish-Christian tradition, God is also represented as a master builder.[1] The rational "distribution" of the burrow and its provisions could allude to the process of the Creation as well. In *Genesis* 1, the world is "divided" in the course of creation into light and darkness, sky and earth, earth and water, heights and depths, evening and morning, days and years, creatures and humans, man and woman, work and rest. The castle court could perhaps allude to the temple of Solomon in Jerusalem, of which there is really only one in Jewry; the many small rooms, in which the creature "rests" (cf. the commandment to rest on the Sabbath; *Genesis* 2:2ff; *Exodus* 20:11) might indicate synagogues (the "temple"; cf. young Kafka's visit to the synagogue with his father in "Letter to His Father"). Since the labyrinthine "first work of a beginner" is so emphasized in the text, it suggests a religious meaning here as well. Perhaps the labyrinthine "all too fussy" and "far too flimsy" work of a beginner can be understood as an allusion to the oldest story of creation—according to the theological knowledge of Kafka's epoch—the creation story of the so-called Jawist, recorded in the 10th century B.C.[2] When he speaks of God, he always uses the tetragram JHWH (Jahwe). His representation of God is anthropomorphic. God makes human beings like a potter, meets them in the evenings in Paradise like the owner of an estate, and banishes them, not without having first made them clothes from hides (cf. *Genesis* 2:4–25; 3:1–24).

Here, the fall into sin leads to knowledge of good and evil ("as

---

1. Cf. the article "Bauen" (note 9 [p. 340]); Donat de Chapeaurouge, *Einführung in die Geschichte der christlichen Symbole* (Darmstadt: Wissenschaftliche Buchgesellschaft, 1985), 11f; Friedrich Ohly, "Deus Geometra. Skizzen zur Geschichte einer Vorstellung von Gott," in Norbert Kamp/Joachim Wollasch, eds. *Tradition als historische Kraft* (Berlin: de Gruyter, 1982), 1–42.

2. This early dating is nowadays contested. See the instructive survey of the various standpoints represented in the scholarly discussion in Erich Zenger et al., *Einleitung in das Alte Testament* (Stuttgart: Kohlhammer, 1995), 88ff.

gods," *Genesis* 3:5; "the man is become as one of us," *Genesis* 3:22) and to mortality (the animal "I" is "mortal" at the entry/exit).

The sentence "but I wriggle my way though the labyrinth" may be an allusion to the snake in this remarkable narrative work (*Genesis* 3); the mention of the "torments of this labyrinth" an allusion to the curse and promise of torments (*Genesis* 3: 16–19); the "trap door" at the entrance, to the fall into sin; the "thorn bush" into which the animal "I" throws itself to punish itself for its "guilt," to the fall into sin and its consequences (*Genesis* 3:18). Perhaps this is also an allusion to the burning bush in which God appears to Moses (*Exodus* 3:2). In comparison to the later creation story of the so-called Elohist, in which God figures as the almighty god of creation who creates the world according to a clear "plan" (*Genesis* 1), this anthropomorphic story can appear as "all too fussy" and the "wall" between God and human beings "thin," labyrinthine in its order and significance.[3]

Both stories of creation do not speak of a creatio ex nihilo.[4] There is actually the idea of creation from the earth (*Genesis* 1:24). This may explain the choice of words around building and establishing or putting things in order (einrichten). The remark about the "war of annihilation raging until now," out of which the "might of the burrow" is to arise, could be explained as an allusion to the theomachies out of which the God of Israel emerges as sole lord (cf. *Exodus* 20:3; *Psalms* 74:13–17; 89; *Isaiah* 51:9ff; *Job* 26:7–13).[5] An earlier, nomadic mode of existence of God is hinted at ("the old desolate life"). The formulation describing the smells "each one of which delights me in its own way" quotes the story of creation directly (*Genesis* 1:12, 21, 24, 25). The ten corridors that lead out of the castle court (cf. the "one-tenth-hearted" attempts) probably refer to the ten commandments.[6]

A further allusion to the tabernacle or tabernacle tent should be considered, the precursory construction to the Solomonic temple for the "home" (*Exodus* 26:1) of God during Israel's wanderings through the desert. The tabernacle tent was transportable, its construction "weak-walled" and a complicated "fussy puttering" (cf. *Exodus* 26, 27, 35–40). The interior of the burrow with its tun-

3. Thanks to Tilman Kurz for this insight.
4. Cf. the article "Creatio ex nihilo" in *Religion in Geschichte und Gegenwart*, vol. 2 (Tübingen: Mohr-Siebeck, 1999), columns 485–89.
5. Cf. Otto Kaiser, *Der Gott des Alten Testaments*, "Theologie des Alten Testaments," part 2 (Göttingen: Vandenhoek, 1993), 90ff.
6. Cf. too the cabalistic doctrine of the ten Sefiroth, the "potencies, in which the active God is constituted, in which—spoken in the language of the cabalists—it acquires a visage." Gerschom Scholem, *Von der mystischen Gestalt der Gottheit* (Frankfurt a.M.: Suhrkamp, 1977), 32. In *The Trial* this number plays an important role. At the close K. splays out all (ten) fingers.

nels and rooms would then relate to the Solomonic temple, interpreting the burrow as a Jewish religious symbol. A collage of these biblical narrative components should also be considered.

If one assumes the possibility of these allusions, then the master builder, unlike God (cf. *Genesis* 1:31), is not satisfied with his creation/burrow. He continually undertakes revisions, dreams of a total reconstruction of the "exit" (cf. the decision of God to create a new heaven and earth, *Isaiah* 65:17), which would bring him "salvation." This god is no sovereign or loving god but mistrustful, calculating out of fear, reflecting, greedy, wild, and lonely. He suffers and doubts himself and his burrow, fights against the world, sees himself in a "war of annihilation," and is himself in need of salvation. He has become old. His end, which earlier was still in the "distance," is now near. He "basically" wants it himself. He interprets the "hissing or squealing" of the enemy, for whose reception the burrow is established, in a messianic and eschatological fashion with regard to the final "decision": "someone is coming at me" (cf. *Matthew* 3:11). This other figure's penetration into the burrow, during which it "bores its snout into the earth with a single mighty thrust," is imagined as a sexual act [p. 186].[7] It is both feared and longed for.

If this interpretation is accurate, then the text is also about the establishment of the Jewish religion. The animal "I" would then be a kind of travesty interpretation of Jewish history from "olden days" until the present in the form of a fictive persona. In one passage, this significance of the animal "I" becomes clear. In its memory, the animal "I" can no longer distinguish between its own deeds and general practice. It speaks of "[its] long march through the passages, but that is no trouble, it is a chat with friends, the way I used to chat with friends in the olden days or * * * the way I used to, or the way I heard that it used to be" [p. 176].

From the perspective of this text, the establishment of the Jewish religion is conceived of as a deeply ambivalent "work." It is to be a house and provide protection in the universal struggle. At the same time, this work itself demands its own sublation, a sublation into the "rustling of silence."

The expectation of a messianic figure of salvation is interpreted here as a delay and displacement of the "actual" action, in contrast to the Jewish and Christian messianic idea.[8] Compared to this real

---

7. On the religious significance of sexuality in Jewish mysticism, see Frank Möbus, *Sünden-Fälle: die Geschlechtlichkeit in Erzählungen Franz Kafkas* (Göttingen: Wallstein, 1994), 38ff.

8. Cf. the legal procedure termed "Verschleppung" (protraction) as explained to Josef K. by the painter Titorelli in *The Trial*. Jewish messianic expectation is explained in political terms by Gerschom Scholem as "life in postponement," the cost of which lay in the fact that the Jewish people "in exile were not ready to enter life at the historical level." Scholem, *Über einige Grundbegriffe des Judentums* (Frankfurt: Suhrkamp, 1970), 166f.

action, the establishment of the burrow appears as "only provisional," its "entrance" an "exit," a departure and entrance into the transcendence of silence.[9]

9. In light of this text, Kafka's remark "I had not been led into life by the admittedly already heavily sinking hand of Christianity, like Kierkegaard, and have not caught the last hem of the Jewish prayer mantle as it flies away, like the Zionists. I am end or beginning" acquires new kinds of meanings and emphases (*Nachgelassene Schriften*, 98).

Franz Kafka: A Chronology

1883	Born in Prague on July 3, son of Hermann Kafka, a fairly affluent tradesman, and his wife Julie (née Löwy). Hermann Kafka's father was a butcher; among Julie Löwy's forebears were several learned rabbis.
1885–87	Birth and death of his brother Georg.
1887–88	Birth and death of his brother Heinrich.
1889, 1890, 1892	Birth of his three sisters—Gabriele (Elli), Valerie (Valli), and Ottilie (Ottla), his favorite. All three were murdered by the Nazis.
1889–93	Attends elementary school (German Boy's School) at the Fleischmarkt in Prague.
1893–1901	Attends the Old Town *Gymnasium*, together with mostly middle-class Jewish boys. First attested reading of Nietzsche in the summer of 1900.
1901–06	Studies law at the German University in Prague along with occasional courses in German literature.
1902	Vacation with Uncle Siegfried Löwy, a country doctor. Meets his lifelong friend and future editor Max Brod and participates in discussions on empirical psychology at the [Café] Louvre Circle, a reading group.
1904–05	Writes "Description of a Struggle."
1905	Vacation in Zuckmantel and first love affair. Meets regularly with friends sharing literary and intellectual interests, including Oskar Baurn, Max Brod, and Felix Weltsch.
1906	Works in a Prague law office before graduating with a doctor's degree in law. Begins a year's internship in Prague, first at the penal court, then at the civil court.
1907	Writes "Wedding Preparations in the Country," part of a novel. Begins his first regular job, at the "Assicurazioni Generali," an Italian insurance company.
1908	Moves to the partly state-run Workers' Accident Insurance Institute for the Kingdom of Bohemia

in Prague, where he will rise to a position of considerable authority (*Obersekretär*) until being pensioned in 1922. His first publication: eight short pieces under the title *Meditation* in the journal *Hyperion*.

1909   Spends vacation with Max Brod in Riva on Lake Garda in Austrian Italy. Publishes "Airplanes in Brescia" in the daily newspaper *Bohemia*, one of the first descriptions of airplanes in a German newspaper. Further publication of two pieces from "Description of a Struggle."

1910   Begins keeping a diary. Sees a performance of a traveling Yiddish theater. Trips to Paris and Berlin.

1911   Repeatedly attends performances of another Yiddish theater troupe from Eastern Europe (Yitzak Löwy and his players). Studies Hasidic tales and parables. Becomes interested in "alternative medicine": vegetarianism, sunbathing, natural healing. Writes earliest drafts of the unfinished novel *The Boy Who Sank Out of Sight* (a.k.a. *Amerika*).

1912   Gives a public address in Prague, "On the Yiddish Language." On the evening of August 13, with Max Brod, puts together his first published book, *Meditation*, and meets his future fiancée, Felice Bauer, with whom he will correspond for five years. Writes *The Judgment* in a single night, September 22–23; in September and October, *The Stoker* and an early version of *The Boy Who Sank Out of Sight*; and from November 17 to December 7, *The Metamorphosis*. Reads parts of the unfinished story aloud to friends on November 24 and in December gives a public reading of *The Judgment*. *Meditation* published by Rowohlt.

1913   Reads the whole of *The Metamorphosis* aloud at Max Brod's. Meetings with Felice in Berlin. Publication of *The Stoker* (the first chapter of *The Boy Who Sank Out of Sight*). Publication of *The Judgment*. Kafka visits Eleventh Zionist Congress in Vienna.

1914   In June, formal engagement to Felice Bauer in Berlin, followed, in July, by its being broken off. Outbreak of World War I as he begins writing *The Trial*. In October, work on *The Trial* having come to a standstill, he writes *In the Penal Colony* as well as the last chapter of *The Boy Who Sank Out of Sight*.

1915	Wins the Fontane Prize for literary achievement for *The Stoker*. Reunion with Felice Bauer. In Prague lives for the first time in an apartment of his own. Publication of *The Metamorphosis* in *Die weissen Blätter* and then in book form in November.
1916	With Felice in Marienbad. Public reading of *In the Penal Colony*. Writes several of the stories collected in *A Country Doctor*.
1917	Lives in rooms in Alchemist's Lane, then in the Schönberg Palace. Further work on "A Country Doctor" and other stories. Second engagement to Felice Bauer shattered by the diagnosis of his tuberculosis in September. Takes leave from his office and joins his sister Ottla in Zürau. Writes a series of aphorisms. In December the engagement is dissolved.
1918–19	Studies Kierkegaard. Meeting with Julie Wohryzek. Appearance of *In the Penal Colony* and *A Country Doctor*. Engagement to Julie Wohryzek. Writes the never-mailed "Letter to His Father."
1920	Conversations with Kafka allegedly recorded by Gustav Janouch. Correspondence with the Czech literary personality Milena Jesenská. End of the engagement to Julie Wohryzek. Resumes literary work after a pause of more than three years.
1922	Beginnings of *The Castle*. Writes "A Starvation Artist" and *Investigations of a Dog*. Last conversations with Milena. Lives with his sister Ottla in Planá in the Czech provinces, where he continues work on *The Castle*.
1923	Meets Dora Diamant (Dymant), his last consort, and from September on lives with her in Berlin-Steglitz. Inflation and cold. Writes *The Burrow*. At Kafka's behest Dora Diamant burns several of his manuscripts. The collection *A Starvation Artist* goes to press.
1924	Very ill from tuberculosis of the larynx, writes "Josephine, the Singer" while attempting to recover in his parent's apartment in Prague. Visits various hospitals and sanatoria, finally Kierling near Vienna, where he is accompanied by Dora Diamant and his doctor, Robert Klopstock. On June 3, at the age of forty-one, Kafka dies, and on June 11 is buried in the New Jewish Cemetery in Prague. Milena writes in an obituary: "His stories reflect the irony and

prophetic vision of a man condemned to see the world with such blinding clarity that he found it unbearable and went to his death." Posthumous publication of *A Starvation Artist*.

1925   Posthumous publication of *The Trial*.

1926   Posthumous publication of *The Castle*.

1927   Posthumous publication of *The Boy Who Sank Out of Sight*.

Selected Bibliography

• indicates works included or excerpted in this Norton Critical Edition.

Adorno, Theodor W. "Notes on Kafka." *Prisms*. Trans. Samuel and Shierry Weber. London: Spearman, 1967. 245–72.
• Allen, Danielle, "Sounding Silence," *Modernism/modernity* 8.2 (2001): 325–34.
Anderson, Mark M. *Kafka's Clothes: Ornament and Aestheticism in the Habsburg Fin de Siècle*. Oxford, UK: Clarendon Press, 1992.
———, ed. *Reading Kafka: Prague, Politics, and the Fin de Siècle*. New York: Schocken, 1989.
Beck, Evelyn Torton. *Kafka and the Yiddish Theater: Its Impact on His Work*. Madison: U of Wisconsin P, 1971.
Benjamin, Walter. "Franz Kafka. On the Tenth Anniversary of His Death." *Illuminations*. Ed. Hannah Arendt, trans. Harry Zohn. New York: Harcourt Brace, 1968. 111–40.
Bernheimer, Charles. *Flaubert and Kafka: Studies in Psychopoetic Structure*. New Haven, CT: Yale UP, 1982.
Blanchot, Maurice. "The Diaries: The Exigency of the Work of Art." Trans. Lyall H. Powers. *Franz Kafka Today*. Eds. Angel Flores and Homer Swander. Madison: U of Wisconsin P, 1964.
Boa, Elizabeth. *Kafka: Gender, Class, and Race in the Letters and Fictions*. New York: Oxford UP, 1996.
Brod, Max. *Franz Kafka—A Biography*. Trans. G. Humphreys Roberts and Richard Winston. New York: Schocken, 1960.
Cambridge Companion to Kafka. Ed. Julian Preece. Cambridge, UK: Cambridge UP, 2002.
Citati, Pietro. *Kafka*. Trans. Raymond Rosenthal. New York: Knopf, 1990.
Coetzee, J. M. "Time, Tense and Aspect in Kafka's 'The Burrow.' " *Modern Language Notes* (96) 1981: 556–79.
Cohn, Dorrit Claire. *Transparent Minds: Narrative Modes for Presenting Consciousness in Fiction*. Princeton, NJ: Princeton UP, 1978.
Corngold, Stanley. *Franz Kafka: The Necessity of Form*. Ithaca, NY: Cornell UP, 1988.
• ———*Lambent Traces. Franz Kafka*. Princeton, NJ: Princeton UP, 2004.
Deleuze, Gilles/Guattari, Félix. *Kafka—Toward a Minor Literature*. Trans. Dana Polan. Minneapolis: Minnesota UP, 1986.
Gilman, Sander. *Franz Kafka: The Jewish Patient*. New York and London: Routledge, 1995.
A Companion to the Works of Franz Kafka. Ed. James Rolleston. Rochester, NY: Camden House, 2002.
Greenberg, Martin. *The Terror of Art: Kafka and Modern Literature*. New York: Basic Books, 1968.
Gross, Ruth, ed. *Critical Essays on Franz Kafka*. Boston: Hall, 1990.
• Hargraves, John A. *Music in the Works of Broch, Mann, and Kafka*. Rochester, NY: Camden House, 2002.
Heller, Erich. *Franz Kafka*. New York: Viking, 1974.
Kafka, Franz. *Amerika (The Man Who Disappeared)*. Trans. Michael Hofmann. New York: New Directions, 2002.
———*The Castle*. Trans. Mark Harman. New York: Schocken, 1998.
———*The Metamorphosis*. Norton Critical Edition. Ed. and trans. Stanley Corngold. New York: Norton, 1996.
———*The Trial*. Trans. Breon Mitchell. New York: Schocken, 1998.
Karl, Frederick R. *Franz Kafka: Representative Man*. New York: Ticknor and Fields, 1991.
Koelb, Clayton. *Kafka's Rhetoric: The Passion of Reading*. Ithaca, NY: Cornell UP, 1989.
Kurz, Gerhard. *Traum-Schrecken: Kafkas literarische Existenzanalyse*. Stuttgart: Metzler, 1980.
• ———"Das Rauschen der Stille. Annäherungen an Kafkas 'Der Bau.' " *Franz Kafka. Zur ethischen und ästhetischen Rechtfertigung*. Ed. Beatrice Sandberg and Jakob Lothe. Freiburg i. Br.: Rombach Verlag, 2002.

- Liska, Vivian. "Stellungen. Zu Franz Kafkas 'Poseidon." *Zeitschrift für deutsche Philologie* 115.2 (1996): 226–38.

Murray, Nicholas. *Kafka*. New Haven, CT: Yale UP, 2004.

Pascal, Roy. *Kafka's Narrators: A Study of His Stories and Sketches*. Cambridge, UK: Cambridge UP, 1982.

Politzer, Heinz. *Franz Kafka: Parable and Paradox*. Ithaca, NY: Cornell UP, 1962.

Robertson, Ritchie. *Kafka: Judaism, Politics, and Literature*. Oxford and New York: Oxford UP, 1987.

- Sokel, Walter H. *The Myth of Power and the Self: Essays on Franz Kafka*. Detroit, MI: Wayne State UP, 2002.

Stach, Reiner. *Kafka: The Decisive Years*. New York: Harcourt, 2005.

Thiher, Allen. *Franz Kafka: A Study of the Short Fiction*. Boston: Twayne, 1990.

Udoff, Alan, ed. *Kafka and the Contemporary Critical Performance: Centenary Readings*. Bloomington: Indiana UP, 1987.

Wagenbach, Klaus. *Kafka*. Cambridge: Harvard UP, 2003.

Wood, Michael G. *Franz Kafka*. London: Tavistock, 2004.

Zilcosky, John. *Kafka's Travels: Exoticism, Colonialism, and the Traffic of Writing*. New York: Macmillan Palgrave, 2003.